THE DEATH PIT

This book may be read as a standalone.

Whispers of Atlantis: BOOK V

by Jay Penner

In this anthology:

The Atlantis Papyrus

The Wrath of God

The Curse of Ammon*

Sinister Sands

The Death Pit*

(*) may be read as a standalone

https://jaypenner.com

To all those who lend a helping hand to those who need it.

JAY PENNER
HISTORY AND FANTASY

Choose your interest! A gritty and treacherous journey with Cleopatra in the Last Pharaoh trilogy, or thrilling stories full of intrigue and conflict in the Whispers of Atlantis anthology set in the ancient world.

THE LAST PHARAOH

WHISPERS OF ATLANTIS

https://jaypenner.com

ANACHRONISMS

---◇---

an act of attributing customs, events, or objects to a period to which they do not belong

This book is set at a time when almost no modern construct existed with respect to time, distance, size, directions, and other everyday things we take for granted. Therefore, I have taken certain liberties so that the reading is not burdened by linguistic gymnastics or forcing a reader to do mental math (what is a *kor*?). My usage is meant to convey the meaning behind the term, rather than striving for historical accuracy. I hope that you, reader, will come along for the ride, even as you notice that certain concepts may not have existed during the period of the book. For example:

Directions—North, South, East, West

Time—Years, Minutes, Hours...

Distance—Miles

Other concepts—Imperial, Stoic

DRAMATIS PERSONAE

Nemur–Scribe of the Royal Court of Urim

Ibbi-Sin–King of Urim and Lord of Sumer and Akkad

Emmu-Sin–Prince of Urim, son of Ibbi-Sin

Dumumi-Ningal, called Ningal–Princess, wife of Emmu-Sin

Nigir-Kagina - General of Urim

Geshtinanna-Kalame, called Geshtinanna–Chief Priestess of Urim, daughter of King Ibbi-Sin

Atturapi–Chief of the Martu (Amorites)

Kindattu–King of Elam

DIVINITIES

Gods were an integral part of life and permeated all aspects of social structure and decision-making.

Enlil - air god, father of gods

Nanna - moon god, patron god of Urim

Inana- goddess of love, war, and fertility (Ishtar of the Akkadians)

Enki - god of water, wisdom, creation

Ereshkigal - goddess of the netherworld

Etemenniguru - *é-temen-ní-gùru* - the great Ziggurat of Urim, "the house, foundation that bears splendor / aura" and shrine for the patron god Nanna

BEFORE YOU READ

Please take a few minutes to read this page–it will help ground you to a long bygone era and provide some information that will make reading the novel more enjoyable.

This book is set during the third dynasty of the Sumerian civilization, around 2000 B.C. Sumerians gave us the 60-second minute and 60-minute hour, made the first use of wheels, created the first known systematic writing (the cuneiform), defined the first codified laws (yes, even before Hammurabi), and advanced many developments in agriculture.

At the time of the events of this novel, the Great Pyramid of Giza is five hundred years old, the Code of Hammurabi is three hundred years away, iron has not yet been invented, and Cleopatra will not be born for nearly two thousand years! We do not know if the Sumerians had a term for themselves—they simply referred to themselves as "the black-headed people" and in this novel, we will use "Sumer/Sumeria" (a named used by Akkadians) sparingly to refer to their land and people. This civilization was completely lost to history until excavations in Iraq in the 19th century and the deciphering of ancient Akkadian cuneiform tablets that shed light on an even older civilization. The Akkadian cuneiform drew its origins from Sumerian, and over time, Sumerian died, leaving Akkadian as the dominant method.

People confuse the various civilizations in and around Mesopotamia. The Sumerians were different from

Akkadians, who were different from Elamites, who were different from Amorites, who were different from Hittites, who were different from Assyrians. All these fascinating civilizations rose and fell at different periods (sometimes overlapping) and in different regions (sometimes overlapping). At the time of this book, the Sumerians inhabited regions in southern Iraq, the Akkadians in middle/central Iraq, the Assyrians (a young civilization then) in modern Syria and northern Iraq, and the Elamites in modern south-western Iran. The Amorites were likely nomadic and may have arrived from what is modern Syria, though their origin is disputed. There is much we do not know about this ancient period.

In some cases, I have chosen to use names of the period for their locations. For example, Ur, as we know now, was called *Urim*. The Amorites mentioned in the bible were called *Martu* by the Sumerians. Similarly, the Babylon we know today was likely Babiliim, and it was a small town at the time of this novel.

As I always do in my books, you will find a section of notes at the end of the book shedding more light on known history, and you will find a link that takes you to a Google Earth "flyby" of all the locations in this book. I also describe the meanings of several names in the book, which you might find enjoyable to read.

Having said that, my dear readers, this is a novel and not a historical treatise, and I hope you will come along for a tumultuous ride!

Jay

MESOPOTAMIAN
CIVILIZATIONS

MESOPOTAMIA

NINEVEH

ASSYRIA

ZAGROS
MOUNTAINS

AKKAD

ELAM

BABYLON

NIPPUR

SUSA

ISIN

SUMER

EUPHRATES
RIVER

URUK

LAGASH

LARSA

URIM

ERIDU

SURIMMU

CHAPTER 1

URIM

FUNERAL SUPERVISOR

Fifty.

Forty-four women, from ages fourteen to fifty, and six queen's guards, men from nineteen to thirty.

That is the number of royal attendants, *travelers* they call them, that will walk the path to the netherworld with their deceased queen. They wait in a line, dressed in their patterned white knee-length gowns. They are all holding small baskets of bread to help them in the initial walk to the afterlife. Some are chatting with their neighbors, laughing. A few are weeping silently. Others are stoic and look ahead, with not a word to the person beside her or him.

He has seen such events before–not too many–but the *size* of this sacrifice has surprised him. After all, the practice of sending attendants to death had been put to an end by the forefather Ur-Nammu, the man who rebuilt this great city of Urim after the end of the Akkadians of the north. But the terrible situation now, with the barbarian invasions and failing crops, has made the current king resort to even greater appeasement of the gods. The king has determined that the gods are unhappy with the sacrifices that accompanied the dead royals, and thus he has sought their blessings by expanding this ritual to a grand scale.

The entrance to the tomb is right ahead. The narrow passageway, topped by a sharp triangular brick arch and reached through a series of descending limestone steps, hides a large rectangular subterranean chamber. The chamber is forty feet in length and twenty feet wide, cut into the sand and earth, and fortified by dull orange bricks. Beyond the chamber is the sacred inner sanctum where the queen's body has been placed, along with food and royal implements, after a daylong ritual.

The king, Ibbi-Sin, has left the location, and it is now up to him, the supervisor of the funeral ceremony, to complete the ritual. He must now prepare the travelers for the final journey to join their queen and provide her comforts in the netherworld.

He looks at his fire-burnt clay tablet with the list and reads off the names. Not that he remembers them all, but this is a checklist he is expected to follow.

"Fifty. No, wait." He furrows his brows and goes back to the top of the long tablet, and taps each name.

"Forty-six. Forty-seven. Forty-eight. Forty-nine. Fifty. Fifty-one?"

It was supposed to be fifty. He had been told fifty.

He calls the scribe standing nearby.

"Did you not say fifty?"

The man looks confused. "Yes?"

"There are fifty-one names here."

The man takes the tablet from the supervisor's hand and counts it. He scratches his chin. "I always thought it was fifty..."

Irritated at this carelessness, he dismisses the scribe. To be sure, he decides to count the lineup.

They are all standing with their backs to a mud wall on a coarse stone platform that leads to the descending stairs of the tomb. Some have flowers on their heads. Guards have given a heady concoction of the joy flower to a few who might have been resistant at the last minute. It makes them light-headed, soporific, and most importantly, cooperative.

He starts from the right. "One, two, three, …" and he goes on, and he counts the lineup twice.

There are forty-five women instead of forty-four.

Someone made a mistake in the initial count. Stupid scribes. They say the scribes are the most gifted of us all, but they can't even count!

He walks back to the beginning of the line and waits for the chief-priestess to begin the final prayers. She is a royal too, a daughter of the king: *Geshtinanna-Kalame*, named after the goddess of agriculture, now in service of the temple at the great Ziggurat of Urim, *Etemenniguru*.

Geshtinanna walks down the wide ramp to get to the platform, followed by her attendants and guards. She is a diminutive but imposing presence, with her lustrous black wig decorated with gold leaves, her neck adorned by carnelian beads, and her eyes surrounded by thick blue eyeliner. Her bronzed skin shines because of the oil.

Two naked priestesses follow her, playing a sad yet melodious tune as they hold one-foot-long lyres made of Syrian wood. A man walks behind them, beating a drum. The travelers kneel as she passes them, except one woman who stares on defiantly.

Geshtinanna walks down the steep thirty steps to the entrance of the subterranean tomb. And there she makes prayers to Enlil, Inana, and Ereshkigal, seeking their blessings for those that will walk to the netherworld, and for those left behind in these difficult times.

The chief-priestess' attendants throw flowers on the floor and light two oil lamps. They set the lamps on bronze pedestals placed by the side of the tomb entrance.

The chief-priestess looks at the supervisor. Her bright eyes shine with purpose. She nods to him.

He takes a deep breath.

The ceremony is now complete.

The supervisor turns to his men and nods. They hold small thumb-sized clay pots on bronze trays.

Poison.

It takes between five to eight minutes for the potent concoction to act, and those who have survived it say that the joy flower reduces the cramps and burning.

A man walks to the assembled line of travelers and starts at one end, serving the clay pots to each traveler. He watches as each woman picks up a pot gingerly and drinks from it. Some blink away their tears, some sniffle, and some have to be helped as their hands shake. The laments of their husbands, sons, daughters, and mothers can be heard. This is a send-off, one that brings joy to the families, for they know that their loved ones will accompany the queen to the netherworld where, in service of the queen, they can live a better life than what they have experienced here.

He gets bored of watching them, and his attention drifts briefly to the affairs at home. There is a shortage of grain, and his wife never forgets to remind him that–

Commotion.

One of the women, the same one who would not kneel before the chief-priestess, is protesting and refusing to drink from the clay cup.

How dare she interrupt this sacred, holy ritual?

He walks toward her. She looks familiar, but then in this city of thirty-five thousand, many look familiar.

"What is happening?" he asks the guard.

"She refuses to drink, sir," he says, keeping his voice low. The chief-priestess is watching this from afar, and his ability will be called Into question if there is a disturbance.

The woman is swaying where she stands. It is clear she has consumed the heady drink from the joy flower, and yet she has the resolve to obstruct this proceeding.

"What is your name?" he asks her.

She looks at him. Her eyes are tearful. She is beautiful, and she has features of the Eastern lands. She struggles to speak as drool spills from the corner of her red lips. Red not because of the alluring pastes the women put on their lips, but because she has bitten them until they bled.

"Dumumi-Ninshubur," she slurs. "Ninshubur. I am not supposed to be here."

Her voice is weak.

She is not supposed to be here?

He has never encountered this before. He pulls out the tablet from his bag and once again scans through it–and finally, at the bottom, he finds her name.

It is the last name.

It's clear.

Ninshubur.

"Your name is here," he hisses at her. She shakes her head and tries to free herself from the guards who hold her firmly.

The supervisor's cheeks grow hot. All eyes are on him. The other travelers'. The chief-priestess'. The guards'.

"Your name is here, Ninshubur. *Here!*" he says, pointing to her name.

She shakes her head weakly and sways like a drunk dancer. Tears flow down her cheeks.

"I heard. She, she, she," she says. Copious amounts of drool spill from the corner of her mouth.

What is she mumbling?

He feels trapped. But then he snaps out of it. Enlil, the father of his gods, will be watching. Ereshkigal, the goddess of the netherworld, will be livid! Such disrespect will not be tolerated. Perhaps she's changed her mind and thinks that offending the gods of Urim has no consequences, for she is probably not from here.

He nods at the guard. They hold her firmly. And as people watch with morbid curiosity, he grips her nose and pinches her nostrils so she can no longer breathe.

She struggles. She lets go of her legs, so the guards are forced to hoist her. The murmurs from the crowd grow louder.

Her mouth finally opens for air.

He makes sure to pour not one, but two little clay cups of the drink into her mouth.

He then shuts her lips, forcing her to gulp down the poison.

She sputters and gasps when he lets go of her lips. Then, she whispers something.

"What?"

"Pregnant. I'm pregnant," she says, her voice barely a whisper. "Husband. My dear husband. Where…"

What?

He pulls the gown opening below her armpit and peers inside to see her belly.

A clear bulge.

Not the bulge of a woman who has been fed well, but one who carries a child. He is flabbergasted. Pregnant women and children were never listed for the tombs, and he was unaware of any change in the rules.

Frightened, he hopes this whole episode ends as quickly as possible. He pretends he did not hear what she said.

Her eyes are beginning to roll, but she is fighting harder now. Her words are incomprehensible—she is babbling. "Husband. My husband did not…"

He has had enough. Another nod. A third guard walks closer.

He lifts the small, heavy club in his hand and strikes her head behind her ears. It makes a dull thud.

There are gasps and shouts from the crowd.

Her eyes grow wide, and then she slumps. The guards know how to strike the women so that they do not bleed from their noses or mouths.

The supervisor orders everyone to file into a line and walk toward the entrance. The mood is somber.

The women wave to their families, standing on higher ground, looking down. And in one line, some holding each other's hands, they begin to walk down the stairs. A great noise of ululation rises from the crowd. Guards are on either side, sometimes leaning to help those that are wobbling or struggling to walk. The six male guards meant to join the queen's journey enter the tomb last—they will be given their poison after the supervisor confirms the death of the women. Three guards carry Ninshubur inside.

Once they have all entered, he walks down. The high-priestess is standing by the door side. She glares at him as he walks by. He withers under those eyes and hurries along to complete the procedures.

The dark chamber inside is musky. Fine dust pervades the space, and lamps flicker at all corners. The room is bare.

He addresses those before him. "Enlil blesses you. The queen awaits you. The king wishes you a joyful afterlife in service of the queen in the netherworld. Ereshkigal welcomes you. Inana will protect you. You may pray now."

Two priestesses shake small bronze bells and begin to pray. Their hymns and the tinkle of the bells echo in the dark, empty chamber. The travelers split and half line up by the northern wall, the remaining half by the southern.

Guards stand by his side, ready to club and give a merciful end to any that do not expire. The poison is beginning to act on the travelers. Many salivate uncontrollably. Some are beginning to swoon. Guards help many sit with their backs to the wall. Some lie down and curl into fetal positions. Some hug those next to them, perhaps acquaintances, and some others hold hands. He seeks Ninshubur to make sure she is creating no more trouble—but she has not arisen from the strike to her head. The guards have placed her at the tail of the line on the northern wall, closer to the entrance. He checks her breathing—there is no sign of life.

The supervisor waits.

The chatter dies down.

The hymns and the bells stop.

Some are now struggling, choking, writhing on the floor. These unfortunate wretches have not been afforded a simple death—the guards club them with enough force to kill them.

The dull *thwacks* continue.

He makes sure that Ninshubur earns another blow—for he does not want a pregnant woman to wake up in darkness and die in terror. *Mercy comes in strange ways*, he thinks. He makes a small prayer for her unborn child.

The ritual is now complete.

And there is now nothing but deathly silence.

No tortured breaths.

No weeping.

No clawing the floor.

The travelers have all departed this world to walk behind the queen.

The male guards accept their poison, double the dose, and take their positions. Their families will be compensated.

He waits until they have expired. Thankfully, no more clubbing is required.

He orders the foreman to seal the entrance.

And finally, as he walks out into the hot and burning sun, he wonders if he will ever be picked for this sacred mission, so that he may leave his struggles behind and walk to the netherworld in service of a king or a queen, like the fifty-one travelers who departed—including Ninshubur, who, he does not know how, had ended up in the line without the desire to do so.

He hopes Ereshkigal, goddess of the netherworld, will be kind to Dumumi-Ninshubur.

CHAPTER 2

NEAR URIM

NEMUR

I squint under the glare of the afternoon sun. The land beneath my feet is dry—the few brushes of green long dead in the drought that has plagued my land for two years. The Euphrates has shriveled, forcing us to walk even greater distances to plant the crops and dig canals. Boats get stuck in the mud near the harbor. The river is to my right, a little distance away, with the shrinking marshlands on both sides. The musky smell of water weeds and reeds is strong even here, but I like it. I am happiest when near the river.

In the far distance, on the other side of the river, I can barely make out the hazy outline of the great Ziggurat, the Etemenniguru, that reaches for the heavens. It is located in my city of Urim. Every time I travel somewhere and return, the bulk of this enormous sacred temple is what I first see, and it gives me great comfort. It beckons me to its shadows; it tells me I am home. Our kings have built one in every city—Urim, Eridu, Uruk, and many more—but the one in my city is the most impressive.

The return home is supposed to be a joyous occasion with good tidings. But my heart is heavy. The king had entrusted me on a mission to deliver a request for help, but I return empty-handed. The message from king Ibbi-Sin to the governor of Larsa has fallen on deaf ears. The bastard refuses to raise a hand to help, for he believes there is no risk to him.

The walk is boring. I sometimes wish the king would grant me a mountain donkey, the one the people of Elam call the 'horse', but that beast is the privilege of few. The ass that walks with me is stubborn, and riding him is a risk. No sooner than my behind is planted on his back, he will kick and jump and make sure I go flying, much to the amusement of those around.

He has a lustrous deep-brown coat compared to the other gray donkeys, and he thinks he is king.

My two guards are far behind me, and considering their behavior, they would happily abandon me at the first sign of danger. As usual, they entertain each other with lewd humor or salacious gossip about the many women they know, but I am in no mood to be part of crassness today. I remove the king's missive from my bag and read the tablet again as I trudge.

Speak to Nawirtum, governor of Larsa, saying the words of Ibbi-Sin, your king!

The enemy, let loose by the monkey on the east, threatens the doors of Urim. Do not think that Enlil is no more by the side of his son Ibbi-Sin! He tests us. It is now your turn to show your loyalty by dispatching five hundred of your best men and one thousand bags of grain.

If the Martu lays waste to the city of your king Ibbi-Sin, do not think he will spare yours! May you see the wisdom in these words and act accordingly. May you send your response through Nemur, the loyal messenger of the king and his son.

The safety of Urim and the great lands of Ur-Nammu is not just the king's responsibility, but yours as well. May you think of this as urgent!

How could the governor not see the danger? Ensconced in his fortress and happy with his queens, he seeks to make no changes or raise his hand in help. No doubt the man is emboldened by the independence of other powerful governors who no longer believe they must submit to the king. Such is the sad state of affairs of our land.

His response is that of a coward, but I dared not say that to his fat face.

Speak to Ibbi-Sin, my king, saying the words of Nawirtum, your servant:

With a heavy heart, I beg the king's forgiveness. Enlil and Enki have shown their displeasure to my lands, for the barley barely grows, the wells are dry, and the shepherds lament the death of their sheep. The clouds that form make no shape of comfort and the crows fly over the palace thrice every morning, a sign of the gods' displeasure. I have managed to maintain my small fortress and army so that I may protect my king's frontier. If I send my best men, then may the king know that the invaders will ruin the city and expose the king further. I will send words to other chieftains to gather their men, so I may be service to you. May the king stand strong, for no mischief will survive the anger of Enlil!

I dread having to give this message to the temperamental king. No one dares say it, but he is like a beast whose limbs are losing their sensation one by one. When he orders a hand to raise, the hand stays where it is. The king is aging, but his two able sons are dead, the alliance of his three married daughters has proved to be worthless, and the remaining prince is wracked by illnesses. Many people are questioning if Enlil, father of the gods, and Nanna, our patron god, still grace king Ibbi-Sin. Why else would the barbaric Martu invade us with confidence? Why does the sun burn so bright that our crops are dying? Why does the river Euphrates move further away from us, like an angry maiden shying away from a curious man?

The only comfort I have is that there is great value in my service as a scribe. There are not many of us left in Urim; some have resigned their posts and gone to other cities, some have died, and most lack the mettle to join the school of royal scribes.

We take dictations from the king and other royals.

We walk to other governors and give them the king's messages, and we return with requests and answers.

It is we who speak the glory of Urim and our king to all lands belonging to our lord, king Ibbi-Sin.

It takes us years to be qualified. We are afforded special protection by the king, and we are answerable to him.

We cannot be arrested and tried before anyone but the king. And for that, I am thankful, for my privilege affords me a certain arrogance, even if not riches yet—a scribe in service for six years is a junior. I pride myself in having greater knowledge than the many ignorant around me, for our years in school—sitting cross-legged, getting beaten with a stick, etching words on tablets and reading from them—have taught us a great many things.

I can count and add numbers.

I understand the movement of the stars as the gods drag them with their fingers.

I know seasons.

We are even taught of the many lands that are far away.

How many know that to the far west of us is a land ruled by men called Pharaohs, and that they have built gigantic pyramids, like our glorious Ziggurats but not as beautiful?

Or to the far east, beyond Elam, is the land of Meluhha with its carnelian and spices?

How many know about building irrigation systems, maintaining trade records, keeping a budget of the treasury, assigning value to crops, smelting copper, draining pus from a tooth—we learn all that. My tales widen the eyes of listeners, and our skills are valued by all kingdoms and provincial administrators. The gods have made some men superior, and I will proudly say that I am one. Not that all that means much, for my pay is that of a junior scribe. Barely sufficient, but better than those who toil in the burning sun selling vegetables or butchering sheep.

My head itches. The confounding lice have infested my hair again—the cleansing oil has become expensive, and I have had to use it sparingly. Nawirtum is a cockroach, and his fortress is full of bugs. I will have to shave my head and wear a wig once I return to Urim, though my beloved wife hates it. I will have to ask her if she prefers a bald head, or one with hair full of lice.

I wince as something sharp pricks my sole. This path is worn and dusty. The fine grains get under my sandals and irritate my feet. My back aches from all the walking, but it keeps me fit, unlike the other scribes in the employ of the royal house. All they do is sit and eat and write. Well, it is not just my back that aches...my loins too. I have been away for thirty-four days now, away from my beautiful wife, on this wretched journey.

I long to be with her. My dear wife, who now bears my child, and I long for the day I will hold the baby.

My first wife died in childbirth, but the gods have blessed me with another wife. My mother named me Nemur, *leopard*, though my wife laughs at the name, saying I am gentle like a sheep, sweet like honey, and hard-working like an ass.

I break into a smile thinking of her. She makes the best hot mutton in the entire city, a skill she has learned from her mother. She cooks at home always and does not bring food from outside. She chatters incessantly, and it is her voice that brings life to our home, for I am a man of limited words. She argues with me, and the boldness is due to the fact that I do not strike her, as is within my rights as a husband. That restraint has infused greater joy in our life.

She gossips about the palace, about the affairs of the many maids, about the insolence of the royals, and other topics in which I show little interest. Her latest favorite subject is whether my pay will increase and if we can build a better house within Urim's prosperous sections.

I look forward to holding her in my arms.

My Dumumi-Ninshubur, Ninshu.

CHAPTER 3

URIM

NEMUR

A scribe's duty is to his king.

And as a junior scribe who has not yet spent six years in His Majesty's service, I am expected to report to the royal house as my first act upon entering the city. My wife will have to wait. The fourteen-foot tall outer mud-wall protecting Urim has recently been completed, its northern gate now manned by sentries who question anyone who enters or leaves. Unfettered movement is now a thing of the past, for every man is under the glare of suspicion, as if he cavorts with the enemy if he steps out of the city. But many must travel—for trade, for managing their pastoral businesses, for seeing their families in other towns. I know that there is frustration in the city about these impositions.

The royal seal I carry gets me a respectful nod, and I am waved in, along with my guards. The smell of the city is strong here. It is like a hot blanket that smothers me. I hurry along the narrow path that takes me through the dense mud houses hugging each other, desperately fighting for space.

I dodge the sheep, dogs, cows, naked children, and people as I make haste toward the palace complex, which is near the *Etemenniguru*, the great Ziggurat that towers over Urim. City ordinances prohibit families from letting their sheep loose in the streets, but a *shekel* here and a beer cup there to officials has made many rules useless. The palace complex and the *Etemenniguru* are protected by a larger, sturdier inner wall. It is the order of the divine that should there be an invasion, normal people may die, but the greater men and women shall be protected. That is what they all say, but I do not like it. What gods would let a farmer or a metalworker die as if they do not matter, but let a greedy official live because he hides behind a wall? Not all my fellow scribes like what comes out of my mouth, but that is not my concern.

Exiting a vast expanse of nothingness and entering a dense, noisy, smelly, and sweaty city can be uncomfortable, and is now exacerbated by the fact that the response of cockroach Nawirtum is about to earn me an earful. If Enlil's benevolence is upon me, I will leave the king's presence with my head on my neck.

Ardumu is carrying a bale of hay—he lives near my house, a dour man with six children. He is like a boatsman who sails on an ocean of sorrow. I greet him. "Ardumu, may the—"

He avoids my eyes and hurries away without a word. The man needs a good puff from the smoke of the joy flower. I gently kick a dog out of the way and make my way toward the entrance of the inner wall.

I notice many hastily built mud prayer mounds and enquire of a shopkeeper if something tragic happened recently.

He tells me that the queen died eight days ago. I am surprised, for she seemed healthy. The king does not have any more wives.

She took fifty travelers with her, he says.

The king has re-introduced the practice, and the *travelers* are voluntary. It is a foolish man or woman who would accept being a traveler, for they had a better than normal life in service of the royals. I think of them as both stupid and greedy, for they forego the life the gods have bestowed upon them, ending it before their time, and seek comfort in the netherworld in service of their masters as if they are unsatisfied with what they have. *They should not call them travelers—they should call them fools,* I do not say loudly, for that would be sacrilegious.

I finally arrive at the inner wall. It is a different world once one crosses these gates. The wide stone-paved paths, beautiful homes, gardens, palaces, the great Ziggurat—*Etemenniguru,* everything is nothing like the rest of Urim. Even as a well-regarded junior scribe, I have not yet earned quarter in the homes behind the wall. The guards wave me through after checking my seal. They have seen me before, and yet they act high and mighty when they must let me in. *You are guards!*

I chuckle to myself, remembering when one of my fellow scribes received a tongue-lashing from the king. He had mistranslated phrases (called a regional chief a dog instead of blessed one). Will I be a recipient of the king's colorful invectives? Only Father Enlil knows. The reason I chuckle is that the king is now weak, and he needs all the scribes he has, for there are not too many of us. Even if he is displeased, I reckon I can walk away with not more than a stern scolding. I am a scribe, a smart one, but I am not a negotiator between kings and governors.

The orange-and-blue painted palace is ahead, guarded by a few sentries. It has many rooms, most empty, and one has to wonder why one needs a house with empty rooms. But no one has sought my opinion on this matter.

A captain ushers me to the royal chambers, which are deep in the palace toward the north-eastern corner. I pass meeting rooms, granaries, two small prayer rooms, several courtyards, and even a sacred chamber of the dead where they bury priestesses. Which fool designed the throne room so far away? This is not my first time before the king—though more of my missions have been in service of the prince, chief-priestess, chief-scribe, and other high officials.

The royal chamber is large, but it is surprisingly sparse. The blue-colored walls have paintings of kings hunting or fighting enemies, rows of dancers and singers, lions and other animals. Tall bronze lamp holders are scattered around the room. The standard of Urim, a bull with a golden crown, hangs on the wall behind the king. The throne is on a large stone platform, and His Majesty is there receiving information and conducting his daily business. I am asked to wait on the side as he speaks to others. Someone is receiving an earful about the delays in constructing barges, which are critical to moving grain and cattle on the river. I fidget where I stand, and my heart beats faster—I wish whoever is before me has something nice for the king to lift his foul mood, because what I am about to convey will cause him to throw a tantrum. The man in front of the king is now on his knees, shaking his head so vigorously that I worry it will detach itself from the neck and fly off to the Elamite kingdom. *Heh heh.*

Who is next–

"Nemur!" the court usher yells. My heart jumps up to my neck and punches my jaws. Many eyes turn toward me. I scramble to the front of the room and kneel before the king. I touch my head to the floor before facing him. Ibbi-Sin is a slight man, but his eyes are sharp, and his greying hair cascades down to his shoulders. I must admit that the king looks majestic in his shepherd's hat with curled lambswool.

King Ibbi-Sin looks stern. "You were sent to Nawirtum?"

"Yes, Your Majesty."

"What does he say?"

I remove the response clay tablet and hand it to an attendant, who takes it to the king.

"The cockroach refuses to help, Your Majesty."

The court is suddenly quiet. I can hear the king breathing. I have realized over the years that even kings, divine beings themselves, feel fear and worry. *What is His Majesty thinking?*

I look up furtively. He is reading the tablet. His eyebrows are furrowed, and his face is tight with anger. Finally, the king hands the tablet back to the attendant.

"Rise. Did you impress upon him the urgency?"

I stand and address him. "I did, Your Majesty. I conveyed Your Majesty's words as written. And then I spoke to him at length—I impressed upon him that a weakened Urim would also threaten his governorate."

His Majesty nods but says little.

"I told him that the wound on a lion's head causes its legs to lose strength."

"He is the anus," says prince Emmu-Sin, sitting on a royal chair beside the king. "And all that comes out of him is shit."

I may have a few choice sentences to add, but I keep that to myself. I have eluded the king's wrath. Or, if I may guess, the king is facing similar resistance elsewhere, so he is not surprised.

His Majesty takes a deep breath.

I muster courage. "Your Majesty. I subtly threatened him that Urim will prevail, and that his divine Majesty will not forget the governor's cowardice."

King Ibbi-Sin smiles. "But he did not reconsider his position, for he believes we will fall, and that he will magically prevail with the blessings of Enlil."

"He could be building alliances that we are unaware of. Or the treasonous bastard is conspiring with the Martu," says Prince Emmu-Sin. He has a soft voice, he speaks well, and he is known to be intelligent. He is a kind man who prefers to listen to poems rather than cries of mercy from men headed to execution. But his ailments keep him from supporting his father. Next to the prince sits his wife, Ningal. She has been a great source of comfort to the prince. Without her, he would have been dead long ago. She is an exceptionally beautiful woman with kind eyes, but it is not her place to comment on the king's strategy. She is here in support of the prince and his needs, a remarkable act of affection when one might use maids and slaves.

The king scoffs. "Nawirtum is a tactless fool. He thinks the Martu or the men of Elam will keep him in power. They will parade him on their dirty streets and hang him for the town's enjoyment."

May I go home, Your Majesty, and leave the great men to argue?

I did not say that, because then my legless body would have to crawl home.

They bicker amongst themselves—the king, the prince, two senior officials of the court—and then they decide to call on chief-priestess Geshtinanna to hear what her divine senses say. She is a radiant beauty herself, but not a pleasant woman, and I fear she might turn on me for the failure. She is the king's unmarried daughter and a princess. Her words are treated as law, and her importance is next to the king, who is fond of her. I hope to vanish from here before she arrives.

Finally, King Ibbi-Sin realizes I am standing there. "What is the health of his fortifications?"

"They appear adequate, Your Majesty. The city is fed and guarded."

The king looks frustrated. He knows, as I guessed, that Nawirtum has men and supplies to spare but has deliberately chosen not to help the king. And we do not have enough manpower to launch an attack on him. A lion attacking its brother while a pack of hyenas circles at its rear is not the best strategy. The king would do well to have me as an advisor, but he has never sought–

"What is your assessment, Nemur?" the prince asks suddenly. "You are aware of our strength. You have seen his."

It is as if Inana's hands reach out to my tongue and pull it out, even as my mind is unwilling, and forces me to spew my lion and hyena thought.

Then, I stand mortified. Were my words insolent?

But the king nods. The prince and his wife look on without anger. Finally, Prince Emmu-Sin smiles. "You are wise for a scribe. And you are willing to say what you think when others shirk."

The king rubs his chins. "You are correct, scribe. Now is not the time to teach Nawirtum a lesson he will never forget. There will be time."

I am thrilled. Relieved. One day, this will lead to an increase in my salary and an allotment of a piece of land within the inner wall. Enlil smiles upon me. All this if the king remembers my name and the chief-scribe is not jealous of my presence. He is a vile man.

Now may I leave?

As if he read my mind, the king finally flicks his fingers and makes a *dismissed* gesture. My heart feels like a bird set free from a cage. It is time for someone else to enjoy the king's company. A guard escorts me out of the palace. It is a beautiful building, with all its paintings, ornaments, wall hangings, gorgeous maids, priestesses, many princesses, stuck-up big-mouthed generals, and captains in their fancy skirts and leather belts. The open space and air invigorate me. Let kings do what kings do. I have to get to my wife, explain the danger the city faces, and decide whether we must abandon the city we love, or stay and defend it in any way we can. It is a frightening prospect and a seditious idea, but one that must be contemplated if we are to bring a child to the world.

My house is far from the palace complex. It is closer to the south-eastern section of the city. It is a modest house—one that I have built myself, with the aid of workers, and it is sufficient for now. There is no central quadrangle, and we have three rooms, of which two have no windows. My wife, Ninshubur, is not entirely happy with it, but I have convinced her that with my rising stature in the court, it will not be long before we walk among the gardens of the inner city. It is a prayer and a hope, and she has believed me thus far. She is pious and believes all my words.

I am not pious.

I lie sometimes.

I sneak and eat purchased food from the stalls sometimes.

I think one of our neighbors is pretty, though I tell my wife that the woman is dull and boring.

I feign excitement at her work, sometimes.

I even lie that her lentils and bean cake is delicious—it's quite terrible.

Such is our marriage.

I am tired by the time I arrive near my house. My neighbors are nearby, and I raise my hand in greeting.

They look at me with concern or sadness.

It is all strange.

Where are the boisterous shouts? Where are the generous yet friendly insults?

When you were away, thirteen men visited your house, and they all came out looking happy! as one of my fine neighbors would always say.

But he scurries inside his house. I shrug this away and arrive at my door. The front of the house looks dusty and dirty—why has she not swept the area? She is particular about matters of cleanliness. The houses here are not densely packed. There is space around each structure. I am about to knock when I notice that the door is ajar.

Does she not know to keep it closed?

I open the door and enter, and the fine dust floating in the air assaults me. *What?* She keeps the house swept, preventing dust from continuously accumulating on the floor. Where is she?

"Ninshubur? Ninshu?"

No response. I quickly cover all three rooms. They all feel uncared for. And she is nowhere to be found. I notice that some of our possessions—a bronze lamp, a copper idol of Enlil, a small silver chain we hung on an idol of Inana— all are missing. Has she put them away for a reason?

Where is she? Is she out to the market?

She is pregnant. She may have relaxed on her duties at home. And she had no idea I would be returning on this day. It would be presumptuous to assume she would be here waiting. It is late to go to the bazaar, but maybe something was needed urgently. I relax and sit on the bed. Then I lie down on it to rest and ease the pain in my back.

I wake up with a jerk. Had I dozed off? How long? It's evening, and gentle orange sunlight paints the floor. Silvery particles are floating in that beam through the window. My cheeks are coated with fine dust.

And Ninshu has not returned.

I begin to worry.

This is not normal.

Women do not venture out to buy vegetables at this time. And as her husband, I have forbidden her to do so. While Urim is safe compared to the lawlessness in Eridu, there are many instances of women being molested or robbed, and now with all the turmoil in the royal houses, the situation is deteriorating. I decide to speak to my neighbors. And then, when I am about to step out, a face peeks inside.

Mother.

No, she is not my mother. I call her mother. She is a kindly old widow who lives opposite my house and sees Ninshu as her daughter. I have much love for her, and for the treats she sometimes makes and brings to us.

"Nemur?" she says softly as she ambles inside. But missing is her toothless smile and good-natured inquiry after my health.

My pulse quickens. "Mother. I was about to come to you. Have you seen Ninshu?"

She walks up to me. Mother is a short woman, and the top of her head is near my chest. She looks up at my face, and her old, leathery palm caresses my cheek. *She has never done that.*

"I always knew you were a noble family, beloved of Enlil and Inana," she says.

I am irritated—I am not in the mood for a lecture or acknowledgment of our piety. "Yes, Mother. Do you know where Ninshu is?"

She looks at me, puzzled. Her eyes widen somewhat—and her face changes from motherly affection to concern. "Do you not know?"

"Know what, Mother?" I ask, alarmed.

Where is Ninshu?

She jerks back. "You wait here," she says, her voice shaking. "Wait. I will be back."

My legs feel weak. I am tempted to follow her but decide to wait. Had Ninshu decided to leave me and not return home?

The time passes slowly. I hear shuffling outside. Mother returns with her son, Engar-Dug, a handsome youth who has been of help to my house when I have been away. He helped me when I built my house, lending his strong shoulders and skilled hands.

"Sit down," she says. Engar-Dug greets me, but he looks serious.

"What is going on, Mother?" I ask, now alarmed. My voice barely squeaks from the throat.

"You sit. You say you do not know where Ninshu is. We thought you knew. We were preparing a feast in your honor."

"Knew what?" I shout this time. Enough of these foolish vague sentences. What is it they know that I do not? Is she having an affair? What feast?

Her crinkly eyes soften as she looks into me.

Her voice shakes when she says, "She has traveled. Ninshu has traveled."

She went to her father's home?

"Where has she traveled? She is not supposed to leave alone!" I yell. My cheek feels hot.

Mother holds my wrists, and her son stands by her protectively, as if I would strike at the woman. What is wrong with them?

"No, Nemur. Listen. Your wife has traveled with the queen!"

It takes me a moment—like when a bolt of lightning flashes, the thunder takes time to make itself heard—to understand what she is saying.

A great roar of horror engulfs my being like a violent river bursting through a dam.

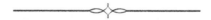

It is dark outside.

My body is frozen.

I am unable to move.

My mind is unable to think.

I do not know my emotions. Rage, sorrow, fear—they are all mixed within me like a swirling storm.

I do not remember what Mother said, and I nodded along, barely comprehending the words. They have asked me to rest and said that they will tell me more tomorrow. But they cautioned that I must not act in haste and fall afoul of our gods.

Why?

Why did she travel?

How could she travel without me knowing?

How?

Many questions and no answers. How *could she* travel without my knowledge?

How?

Why?

I have seen those who walk the path to the afterlife willingly, with their families' blessings. I have seen those that have died of ailments. Even those that have broken laws and been executed, as they must be. There are those that take their lives willingly, desiring to join the netherworld, tired of their life on earth and hoping for better judgment. Others die in war, in invasions, in floods. There are many reasons. But the walk with the queen is a sacred act. Those who *travel* prepare for it. Tell their loved ones. They are sent off with feasts and prayers. Their loved ones watch as they take the final steps.

And then there is my wife.

One who I loved, cared for, fed, clothed, protected, walked hundreds of miles in service of the king to earn a salary for. And she had decided to go away, with not a message, not a consideration. She *knew* my opinions on the matter. She *knew* I disapproved of this ritual, introduced by the king after two hundred years of pause. She was happy with me! We were awaiting a child who would carry the glory of my family. She threw it all away without telling me!

Anger bubbles up from my belly.

Anger borne out of deception and lies.

My tongue feels bitter. I blink away tears of rage and frustration. *Bitch!* I should go to her house near the eastern borders of the kingdom, where Elam meets our land, and spit on her father and mother for giving birth to a woman who would take away all my dreams with not a dust grain of thought. *Greed*—greed that my house is not big enough, my salary not high enough, my stature not important enough, my valuables not shiny enough. Like walking behind a dead queen would give her everything in a place we know *nothing* about. Why even bother to live and be married? Why not kill oneself when they reach the age of adult responsibility? Why have Enlil and Inana and Enki given us birth on this land and long lives and rivers and mountains and flowers and sex, if they wish for us to die with the hopes of getting something better? Did our forefathers not say that we are all here in the service of gods? *Here.* On this land. We offer food to Enlil. We celebrate Nanna. We do it *here.* Not by dying!

Ninshu worked as an attendant and maid in the palace. She did not even like the queen and barely did any work for her. Why would she walk to the afterlife seeking to serve her? This is like a girl who hates snakes but decides to become a snake keeper. What had gone through her stupid, womanly mind?

We all have heard of what happens after death.

We go to the netherworld ruled by Ereshkigal.

We are judged.

People say many things about the netherworld, but our priests have been telling us that good deeds on this earth will lead to a better life there, where we will not eat clay and dust, and that offerings made by the living reaches us. And that instead of living in dreadful dark caves, we will walk the gardens of Enlil. People choose to go as travelers in service of queens and kings, because those of exalted positions live with comfort in the netherworld. That is *greed!* We are on this world to do the best we can and live the best life, not look forward to a greater life in the netherworld. *Stupid! Stupid!* If the gods judge her harshly for her greed, she will walk desolate forests and dark rivers as a demon. Oh, Ninshu, you stupid woman!

I clench my fist and pace around. I can barely breathe. The anger and sorrow ebb and flow, each emotion overtaking the other in turns, twisting me, punching me. Finally, seeking but finding no answers, I collapse on the reed mattress. It is unmanly to cry, but with no one to watch or judge, I sob in frustration and sadness. *Why, Ninshu, why?*

The gentle howl of the wind tells me nothing.

I stay that way, my mind blank, for a long time.

I cannot sleep.

I reach for a jug of water, stale now, and take a few gulps.

My mind is tired, but now I can think.

Something is bothering me, but I cannot place it.

My father used to say that when a man cannot help but feel the sensation that something is not what he thinks it is, it is a god whispering in his ears that he must ask himself more questions and seek answers.

I first try to understand *why*. This is a thought that schools have taught us. To always question and ask *why*, and from that comes answers.

Why did Ninshubur choose to travel with the queen?

My pride that I could think at a level beyond the illiterates in this city is soon deflated. I cannot find one reason.

Ninshubur had never, not once, indicated that she was unhappy. She had her complaints and nags like all wives, but nothing in her demeanor suggested that she would seek to serve the queen in the afterlife, or that she even entertained the idea of being a willing traveler. I had no reason to believe she wished to leave me. And I had no reason to believe she was so devoted to the queen that she would follow her.

She was even looking forward to her baby–

Baby.

Ninshu was pregnant.

I am jolted.

When King Ibbi-Sin re-introduced the sacrifice of royal attendants, he established a few rules.

No boys before the age of twelve.

No girls before the age of ten.

No blind man or woman.

No man or woman accused of adultery.

No man who has been accused of fornication with a cow or sheep.

No man or woman suffering from ailments of skin or stomach.

No man or woman for whom Enlil was not the god of the house.

No man who reared more than fifty sheep or twenty cows.

And no pregnant women.

Not only that, but no wife could be sent without her husband's permission, and no daughter without her father's. And no one had sought mine!

That was the rule. No pregnant women could be sent to the death pits. How did she end up as a traveler?

My mind begins to race.

One did not walk to the tombs on the day of the ceremony and give themselves. The queen had hundreds in her service, and a traveler was always voluntary. Their families were interviewed by the priests. The chief-priestess herself vetted many. When a name was finalized, a scribe wrote it on a sacred tablet. *The traveler list.*

The list was then blessed by the chief-priestess and verified by the chief scribe. The list was checked off against the attendants during the ceremony. With safeguards in place, how did my wife slip through even when pregnant?

It is tempting to get up and run to the palace to find the chief-scribe. That would be the easiest way to get to the truth, but I know that no such thing is possible. The inner wall gates are shut at dusk, and even high officials are not allowed inside, let alone a junior scribe. Besides, the chief-scribe is no admirer of mine, and he might have me thrown out for questioning the sacred process.

What should I do?

On my knees, I pray to the lord of my gods, Enlil, and to the great patron of my city, Nanna.

I will ask Mother.

In the morning.

No.

Now.

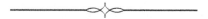

Mother nods in understanding when I tell her I must ask her questions, now that I am back to my senses. She looks at me with pity, and I hate it. Does she think I am to blame for my wife deciding to leave this world?

I can barely see her in the darkness. The single oil lamp flickers in a corner. Her son is somewhere in the shadows, choosing to keep his silence.

"I gave her no cause, Mother," I say and explain that there was nothing that suggested she was even contemplating volunteering to travel.

She asks me more questions.

Then, she reaches out and caresses my cheek with her wrinkly palms. "I believe you. I believe you."

That gives me some relief.

"Ask me, son," she says, firmly clasping my palms, "and I will answer what I can."

"Did you see her on the day she left? Did you talk to her?"

She shakes her head. "No. I was away in the fields with my son. We then made our way to the tomb to watch the ceremony."

"And you saw her there? You are certain?"

"Very much," she says, sadly. "I was able to peek through the crowd. They are rude to old women! But I saw her in the lineup. I shouted her name, asking where you were, but she did not hear me or pretended not to. She was wearing that shimmering blue gown you said you gave her."

The tiniest glimmer of hope that she could be wrong, dies. "And you are certain she is... gone. She went into the tomb. To the *death pit?*

I suppress my chokes. A man must not weep before a woman, even if she is one he calls Mother.

"Well, they carried her," she says haltingly.

"Carried?"

And then she explains how something seemed to have happened, she couldn't see, but that they physically carried Ninshubur inside.

"What do you mean, they carried her inside?"

"I do not know, son. Looked like she was tired, or the poison—"

I hang my head, controlling myself. She reaches and holds my hand again. There is something comforting in her gesture. I have questions.

"Mother, you know that pregnant women are not allowed by law to be taken as travelers."

Her eyes open wide, and her hands shoot to her mouth. "I remember now! Oh, Enlil, Nanna!"

She makes many gestures to ward off evil.

"You have worked in the palace and know many, Mother. You were there. Who was the supervisor on the day?"

CHAPTER 4

URIM

NEMUR

It is early in the morning when the sun is still waiting to be ascendant. I stay on the main path to the inner city, waiting for him. I have his description. He walks quietly and purposefully. As he nears me, I cross the path and stand in front of him. He looks up, surprised. He does not know me, nor I, him.

"Sir."

His eyebrows raise. "Yes?"

"I must speak to you about the travelers who accompanied the queen."

He looks irritated. "What business do you have? I have nothing to tell you. I need to get to work, get out of the way."

"Dumumi-Ninshubur."

Now he looks surprised. His eyes open wide. I *know*, without even having to force him, that he recognizes her name.

He stammers. "I know of no—"

"You know. Please. She was my wife."

The man looks like he wants to run. But he is much older than me, and frail. I can catch him. I hope he realizes from my stance and the urgency in my voice that I will not let this go.

"Ah, yes. Yes. I remember. What about her?"

"Was she on the list?"

He looks annoyed. "Of course she was on the list, you fool! We do not send anyone on a whim."

"Did you know she was pregnant?"

Again, the way he jerks makes me realize he *knew*. "No! We do not send pregnant women. You are out of your mind. I must go now."

I know that to persevere will cause violence. I am no soldier, and it is quite likely that this man was. I have no intention of getting a knife in my gut and dying like a dog.

"I wish to do you no harm, sir. All I must know is the scribe who gave you the list. I was her husband. Please!"

He appraises me. Something changes in his demeanor. A relaxing. Suddenly, his shoulders slump. It looks as if he is about to unburden himself. "Iddin," he says. "Iddin of the royal court."

Iddin! I know Iddin! He studied with me. He is a junior scribe who joined the courts when he was twenty-two years old, as I was, and we both have been six years in service. I barely know him, for he is a reticent man who keeps to himself. My face feels hot. What in the glorious name of god had transpired? It was getting more confusing by the hour.

The supervisor continues as if to unburden himself. "I do not know anything, young man, but I do know that your woman's name was the last," he says haltingly, his eyes darting in every direction.

He is hiding something more, but he has given me enough.

"She asked for you in the end," he says, again haltingly.

I grab his hand with gratitude. "May Enlil bestow riches upon you," I say, and he lowers his eyes with guilt. Someday I hope to return to him to find out what happened in his presence.

It's now time to find Iddin. I know that he gets to work later in the day. He will be home at this time. Besides, confronting him in the palace may not be the most advisable action.

Iddin lives in a small house. I have learned that his wife left him some time ago, taking with her two young sons. Even in my sorrow, I have a sense of relief that I will get the answer when I speak to him. I am tired, not having slept all night, and without much food since yesterday. Urim is waking up, and people are out to begin their daily work—metalworkers, traders, herdsmen, slaves, bakers, meat sellers, vegetable vendors, and so on, all scurrying about. It all feels normal, and yet the gods know what is within us.

His house is a long walk to the western corner, through a large noisy *bazaar* and several clusters of dense, crumbling mud huts of the poorest and the slaves. And unlike many other parts of Urim, open sewers run parallel to the homes, and ditches for the dead are in random empty spots by the houses. I rarely come to this foul area. The men look angrier and desperate, and it is difficult to walk the narrow mud paths without rubbing shoulders or bumping into others. I hurry along, ignoring vendor boys chasing me with stone bead necklaces. My stomach grumbles, but I will eat once I settle this matter.

Even as I am about these activities, my mind is asking the questions: *why*. But the *why* now has a companion in *how*.

The crowd is dense here. Someone is arguing something ahead— someone is always arguing in these backward places. A man rushes through the crowd, his face hidden beneath a veil, and someone yells at him. I barely dodge this rushing maniac as he shoves people out of the way and vanishes into the multitude. And then, the raised voices settle down, and the path returns to its normal hum of activities. I gingerly step over a dead dog carcass, pass a ditch with barely concealed rotting corpses, and narrowly avoid a vegetable cart hurtling towards me, pushed by a frantic vendor late for his position in the bazaar. The sheer cacophony momentarily dulls the turmoil in my head in a strangely comforting way. Iddin's house is not far ahead, for I know that it is by the side of a rare two-storied house of a local official, who has proudly carved his name on the door and the wall.

I am finally here.

Iddin's little house is nestled between the wall of the official's and a small bakery. His door is partially open, as it is in most houses in the morning. I slap my palms on the door.

"Iddin! Iddin!"

I hear no sound from inside. What is he doing? I lose my patience after a short while. I push my way through inside.

And before my eyes adjust to the darkness of the little windowless room, something feels sticky beneath my feet.

I look down in disgust. Has the sewer entered his quarters?

No.

It takes a moment to register what it is.

Blood. And copious amounts of it.

CHAPTER 5

BORDERS OF SUMER

The man from Elam stretches his back and looks at the land before him.

The hands of his gods have guided him to march on the land of *Sumer*, the black-headed people, those who dwell in their cities by the two great rivers. They are blessed by Enlil and Enki, and he must be careful before he leads his brave men to break their fortresses, loot their temples, carry away their men and women in fetters, and lay waste to their shrines, for those are what his gods have demanded, as they have told him in his dreams.

Had not his forefather given a daughter in hand to the king of Sumer? Had that alliance bore fruit? No. The black-headed people grew greedier and expanded their reigns, looked down upon others in supreme arrogance, and raised their weapons, and brought great storms upon the farmers of the east and even the shepherds that lived under the protection of the men of Elam. All that would end.

He adjusts his cap and walks out of his bare tent. His hardy men, those with their warrior manes and powerful shoulders, stand in a line. There, beyond them, behind a low mountain, is the small, fortified town of Luash—not one that the man from Elam cares for, but one that he would take as a warning to the rulers of Sumer. He knows his men thirst for this attack, for they seek to lay their hands on the silver and gold, on the slaves they may take home, the women they can ravish, and watch the blood flow on the streets. The town has a low wall around it, about twelve feet in height, made of sub-burnt brick, strengthened in places with pitch, and a shallow moat rings the wall. None of these impediments are such that he and his men cannot cross, scale, and destroy.

"Inshushinak looks upon us from the heavens, warriors of Elam, and he orders that we smite the black-headed dogs that dwell beyond the rivers! Urim, Eridu, Lagash, Uruk—those cities shall fall for the storm we unleash upon them, and may their laments be heard by our gods!"

The five hundred men, his advance party, all scream in chorus. "Glory be to Inshushinak. Glory to our king!"

He looks at them with pride. The women call them the naked man-gods with curled hair, for their luxurious manes cascade to their shoulders, and they fight naked, with an ox-hide belt on their waists and a protective bronze plate in front of their loins. But they wield their axes and swords like demons from the underworld, and for him, they will fight unto death.

"Like waves of a mighty sea, we shall wash over this town, like fishes we shall cross the moat, like monkeys we shall scale their walls, and we shall descend upon them like a raging fire!" he thunders to their cheers. And then he walks to the front of the army, organized in twenty loose groups of fifty men each. He raises his hand and then swings it toward the town, and the men begin to trot in that direction. He knows that they must not run, for that would tire the men before they are ready to engage the enemy. It is five thousand steps, and they are near the moat, a flimsy, hastily dug structure. His men have heavy hemp ropes with bronze claws that they can swing over and climb. The mud-wall is right ahead, and there, on its ramparts, are men with bows.

"Bring the ladders!" he shouts, and his men bring long bamboo ladders that they can place across the moat and run across. But he is impatient—the few ladders and the many men will cause delays and give an advantage to the enemy.

"You, you and you," he screams at three groups, "you hop across the ladder. And at the same time, you and you jump into the moat and climb up!"

His soldiers rapidly place the ladders across the moat and begin to run over them, hopping like dainty dancers. They hold their wicker shields in front to avoid any arrows. At the same time, several enthusiastic soldiers jump into the moat, which has reddish, dirty water in it, but is not deep enough for anyone to drown. He watches with excitement as men stream across the moat. But then, there are loud screams from the moat. He runs to the edge to look down—what happened?

Many of the men who have jumped are hunched in agony. What had—

Those bastards! The cunning black-headed people have implanted short, sharp stakes at the bottom of the water, invisible from above. He should have...

The arrows come flying from the ramparts like buzzing mosquitoes and begin to strike the men. Many are knocked off the ladders into the moat, injuring them, and the others scramble across and group together, protecting themselves with the shields. But the hardy warriors of Elam will not succumb to these fools and their little resistance.

"Charge! All across!" he screams. With a great roar, all his men push harder and faster across the ladders, protecting themselves.

He runs across, arriving on the other side.

The dull thuds of arrows have not ceased, occasionally striking someone, causing him to collapse near the feet of a fellow man. Some men are careless enough to lift and peek, only to have a bolt slam through their eyes and rupture the skull, causing a spray of blood to soak those around them. The king and his commanders know to remain hunched, like tense runners, waiting for the appropriate time when the archers have to pause to replenish. And that moment comes quickly. The whine in the air stops, and his men spring like gazelles and sprint toward the wall. It takes them minutes to reach the barrier, and his spearmen begin to launch their weapons with deadly accuracy at those on the wall. The melee, the screams, noises, arrows, grappling hooks, the gushing blood and breaking bones...all these excite him. It makes him whole. It makes him the king he is.

He runs ahead of his men, his long, powerful legs carrying him effortlessly. His faithful lieutenant knows what to do. As soon as they near the wall, two of his men place shields over his head to protect him from stones raining upon them, and then others drag the ladders and push them against the wall. And then, as a single lethal mass, they throw their spears to prevent anyone from congregating on the wall parapet, even as he clambers up the ladder followed by his men. He jumps from the ladder onto the narrow flat wall-top and evades a farm sickle that a man swings at his head. The tip of the flimsy sickle scratches his skin and draws blood.

He laughs at this pathetic attempt. He rushes the fool and grabs the man's neck, watching the whites of his eyes, relishing the fear. With the other hand, he raises his ax, a fearsome weapon of his choice, forged by the most skilled metalworkers, sharp as if made by the gods themselves. And then he hacks the man's shoulders.

He pushes him back and kicks him down, watching the screaming enemy as blood pumps out of his chopped limb. *Let him bleed to death.* By then, more of his men are streaming up, jumping onto the rampart and attacking the black-headed enemy where they can find. But surprisingly, there are not too many here. He makes a sign for his men to find a way to jump from the wall into the city ground. But as he runs, he is surprised by how much grass is on the rampart. These weak, soft vermin needed grass to provide succor to their feet, he thinks, before the acrid smell of burning pitch hits his nose. On either side, the grass is suddenly on fire, engulfing many of his men, and he barely escapes as the flames lick his calves.

His men scream and jump from the rampart to the outside, *the idiots!* "Jump! Jump to the town!" he screams, for the depth of the wall is no more than ten to twelve feet, and they can survive it. He leaps from where he is and makes a graceful fall, rolling on the thick mud and surviving without a broken bone. His men follow, and like monsters descending from the sky, they rain down on the ground, hundreds of them in unison. Some are on fire, and they are like flaming torches, flailing, shouting, and then rolling on the ground setting those nearby on fire. And amidst that melee, he hears the enemy charge at them–they were waiting below, knowing how all this would unfold.

I have underestimated them! he curses. But their numbers are small, he is sure, and they are untrained farmers and tradesmen and other pathetic denizens who know how to butcher sheep, but not face the fierce beasts from Elam. With a great roar, he leads his uninjured men on a blistering attack. It is a terrible mess—the smoke, fire, mud, dust—all exhilarating. His ax lops off a man's head, and then hacks the leg off another. He uses the backside of his ax, fashioned like a hammer, to smash another one's skull and let the brains splatter on the dull orange earth. His men are now hand-to-hand with the enemy, numerous, and once again, surprisingly capable. They are not running. They stand and fight, and their swords draw blood.

"Push forward!" he screams, and his commanders all shout in unison. They bunch closer like a giant wedge and begin to push, but again the demons of the town confound him. A band of archers is on the roofs of the homes, and they begin to shoot arrows, causing his men to drop like flies. Suddenly, the elation of crushing this little town vanishes. Would this venture end with his shameful demise, and would he be laughed at in his land? In the enthusiasm for the attack, his men have lost or thrown away their shields, and there is little to protect them. He uses his men as shields, ordering them to cover him, and they push hard forward—now no longer desiring to murder, but wishing to find a gate to escape.

"Find a gate!" he orders a lieutenant, and the order ripples through the troops, all in one great dense crowd pushing on another great dense crowd, in the narrow paths between crumbling homes. An arrow barely misses his head but strikes his toe. He grunts in pain and hunkers down.

There is a shrill whistle, one from his own men, and someone is pointing to an exit.

As if on cue, his men change direction.

He sits alone in his tent—angry, ashamed, frustrated.

How had he underestimated this little town?

The physician applies an ointment to his toe and wraps a linen bandage, tying the ripped muscle and stemming the blood. The bruises on his shoulder and back are turning purple.

He has lost several hundred men. In the moat, during the climb, others on the parapet, and more during the struggle in the town. He had finally led his men out by breaking open a gate and escaping slaughter. The enemy was cunning and prepared. No doubt that the rumors he had heard of this land—that their gods had abandoned them, that their quarrels had weakened them, that their men no longer had the will the fight—all had proven false. And this was not even a big, fortified town, let alone a great city like Urim, his ultimate prize.

He watches from a distance as the enemy throws the bodies of his soldiers off the parapet, letting them fall on the mud and rot with no one to retrieve them. He knows that he cannot push westward with his battered force, and that his strategy of bringing the advance party to test the defenses was a failure.

And then there is the matter of the Martu, those backward cattle-herders and shepherds who know no land, worship no good god, and who feast on raw flesh and sleep on mud, but had sought to ally with him in a quest to defeat the cities of Sumer and lay waste to their lands. He had rebuffed them, for how could his sacred hand be sullied in friendship with the filth that roamed the lands like wild beasts? But Inshushinak had sent him the unmistakable message today—that he must build alliances, and cannot seek to march a large army from the far Susa all by himself. He decides he must send an emissary to the chief of the Martu, the one they call the great herder, and announce to him that the king of Elam wishes to converse.

But there is something else.

The most egregious mistake was not any of what had transpired, but rather it was not listening to the words of the spy from Urim. The one who had warned of the town's defenses, of its deceptive moat, of its battle-hardy governor.

So, Kindattu, the king of Elam, the man from Susa, resolves to receive the messenger of the spy from Urim.

He had given no sufficient weight to those warnings, for they came from a woman.

He hopes no one has uncovered her betrayal, and that she is alive.

CHAPTER 6

URIM

NEMUR

Blood.

On the floor. On the wall. The sharp, distinctive smell of blood and feces is overpowering. And in the corner is Iddin, slumped against the wall. My eyes have adjusted to the dim light, and everything is clear. The ghastly gash on his neck is fresh, and he is drenched in blood from neck to feet.

I rush to him.

"Iddin, Iddin!"

But he is unresponsive. His eyes are glassy, and they look to the far void. His face is cold, but the blood is warm. The killer has cut Iddin so deep that bubbles form on the wound because of the air from his dying gasps. It is too late to stem the bleeding. I pin my hopes on Enlil's benevolence. "Iddin, who did this? How did Ninshubur get on your list?"

Iddin's eyes slowly roll up. His head slumps to one side, exposing his severed vessels. I recoil. I am no stranger to death, but I have not held a murder victim. I am no soldier. My mind flashes to the man who ran through the crowd as I arrived at Iddin's house. Was he the assailant? I curse myself for not getting a good look at the hooded figure.

I realize that my hand is wet with Iddin's life-fluid, having held him briefly. I wipe my hand on my kilt, smearing it in the process. I begin to panic—what if someone thinks I was the one who killed him? The laws are clear. To kill a man of the royal house is an offense punishable by death and confiscation of property. In a day, the gods have marched me down a frightening path—first with the confounding death of my wife, and now the man who would know how her name came to be on the list has been murdered. *What is happening? Help me, Father Enlil!*

Sounds.

Commotion outside. I jump up and get behind the partially open door. A girl peeks inside. I can see a few of her curls as she inspects the barren room, and then her head vanishes.

"Somebody killed him!" she screams.

That is it.

I cannot wait here and offer an explanation.

An outraged mob in Urim is worse than an enraged bull. There is little patience for offers of reason, and one can be beaten to death even before there is an intervention.

I dash out, surprising the girl right ahead. I slam into her, causing her to fly off the path, and before horrified onlookers can react, I run like a mad man, my kilt hitched to my waist and my legs hurling me past puzzled onlookers. Everything is a blur. The noises of pursuit recede as I run and run, past the homes and granaries, past the workshops and tanneries, past the dying gardens and bazaars. My house is far, and I am cautiously certain that no one knows where I live. But I find a new location, another dense cluster where traveling tradesmen and cattle-herders spend their nights in the company of prostitutes.

I pause to rest and find a dark corner between two buildings. I shoo away a curious dog that comes to inspect me. Does it smell my fear and desperation?

My body pulsates with energy. A realization. Would Enki and Enlil keep me alive, if they did not wish for me to uncover what was happening?

I am now certain that my beloved wife did not consent to be a traveler.

She was sent to her death. And I swear on the passion of Inana and the power of An that I will find out why and how.

CHAPTER 7

URIM

NEMUR

I sleep on the coarse, muddy ground between a whorehouse and a butcher shop, like a man without a home or a future.

All my energy has drained, and I realize I desperately need food. When the sky is suffused with light orange, I make haste to a local bazaar and buy wheat bread and soup. I stand behind a statue of Amar-Suen, one of our great kings, and keep my head low as I devour the meal. The warm barley and salt soup, and the coarse bread with slices of cucumber, bring back the fight in me. I decide to return to my house, feeling comfortable that no one near Iddin's home would have recognized me. I hurry as quickly as I can, avoiding the stares of people looking at the dried blood on my kilt, though it is not unusual with all the butchers in the city.

My home feels strange, as if it is not home, as if I have never dwelled there with my beloved Ninshubur. What had she gotten herself into? I know there will be no rest until I find out the truth. And if I learn that Ninshubur volunteered, then so be it, and I shall make peace with the gods—though I am now almost certain that she was not a willing traveler.

Sitting on a chair and staring at the empty wall, I begin to formulate my next steps. What can I do? Where do I go next to unravel this mystery?

The palace is where the hands of my gods guide me.

That is where the powers are, and that is where the answers are.

Iddin's master, my chief-scribe, a man of much influence and power himself who belongs to the line of influential officials in the royal court, is the one I must speak to. He has the ears of the king, the prince and princesses, the chief-priestess, and the generals, for he who is learned in words and poems is a man trusted with much wisdom. It is he who is approves the final list of travelers. A man on the street might ask, would the royals not finally read the names of those who willingly lay down their lives in their service? Alas, that is not to be. In most cases, the royals do not even look at the list, and the king's only order is a number and an announcement to all that they may volunteer to leave with their deceased master or mistress. It is then up to the chief-scribe and officials from the temples to put together the final list. And someone, somewhere in that bureaucracy of the death list, offered my wife as a sacrifice for reasons unknown.

But the chief-priest and I have an unpleasant history, for the man has no appreciation for candor. He sees my visibility among the royals as a threat, notwithstanding that he has been in his position for over twenty years, and I just six. Such is the nature of jealousy. Going to him will place me at risk, for it is an unspoken rule that the process and the list are blessed by the gods, and anyone questioning it risks serious penalty.

The house is filled with sadness. The clay pots and the oven weep for their mistress. They tell a story of someone who was by them and is no more. I feel her presence in the air, by the bed, near the utensils.

She is there but not.

This home will never hear the cry of a baby or the tinkling laughter of my wife, and someone, somewhere decided that it must be. I shall not dishonor the benevolent gods that it is their doing that an innocent, would-be mother was led to her death, so that her child may never sit on its father's lap.

We are taught from the days of our childhood that a house must be clean, and a clean house brings purity of thought and conduct.

I cannot leave the house the way it is.

The broom is leaning against a wall. I pick it and begin with one corner of the main room, sweeping the dust and small slivers of leaves and other detritus that floats inside when a house is uncared for. I make small piles in the corners, planning to throw them all out once it is dusk when no one can see me. I have no doubt that by now, rumors have spread in my neighborhood that something was not right with my wife's death. It will be a few more days before someone dares to bring it up to me. The death of a spouse is common—for our lives are uncertain, spouses remarry, and the life that gods have given us continues on.

My intention is to calm my mind as I immerse myself in a mundane activity. The *swish* and scraping of the broom are comforting. I put my head down and hunt every pesky little dirty corner and every–

Crack!

The noise of someone kicking open the door hits my ears. I am in a different room, and before I can react, three men explode into my room.

"Who–"

They land blows on me, on my back, my shoulders, my stomach. I collapse in agony. Someone puts a foot on my neck, and another growls, "Tie his hands back!"

"Who are you?" I shout, and the man presses his foot down, causing me to almost choke.

"Keep your mouth shut!" he hisses. I struggle futilely, but soon someone puts a blindfold on me. The knots on my wrists are tight and painful. *Who are these men? What do they want?*

Even in that frantic and frightening moment, I cannot help but guess that this has something to do with my visit to Iddin. And even as my belly pulsates with pain from the punch, I am relieved that if these men were here to kill me, I would be dead like a pig, like Iddin, with my neck sliced end-to-end and blood gushing out in torrents.

They are tying me up to take me somewhere.

It is almost comical how the divine test me—that for all my thinking on the fastest way to understand what was happening, getting kidnapped would be the best.

CHAPTER 8

URIM

NEMUR

When I am dragged out of the house, I hear Mother yelling from the side, *leave him; he has done nothing!* I shout back, asking her to care for my house.

They make me walk for a while, and as I stumble off the rough paths and hear the noises and the shouts, I know they are taking me to the inner city. The people must find it entertaining, for I hear shouts and murmurs, and someone even throws a pile of cow dung at me. These fools, do they know why I am being taken? I hear the loud clangs of the metalsmiths and the strong smell of drying fish. I know this route.

I can hear them talking to the guards of the inner-city gates, and then the air changes. It is more pleasant because of the orchards, more space and a lack of sweaty, dense humanity. It takes a while, and then I am dragged down somewhere, a dungeon or a cellar. I have heard of things called prisons, for at school, they taught that the kings of Akkad kept big ones where men and women were placed for punishment. We have no such thing in Urim, or at least not that I have been informed of. The kings keep condemned men in a small building before execution— otherwise, they are sent into slavery.

What is my fate? But before I worry about that, why are they dragging me? On the way, I try to induce them into a conversation, but they are clever. They keep their mouths shut, and once, one of them whips me on my buttocks when I ask a question. Bamboo canes can hurt. We eventually come to a halt. I hear a door open. The smell inside is rank and damp.

A man holds me firm while another removes my blindfold. It takes me a while to adjust to the darkness. It is an empty, bare room, with a hole in the ground on one side. They shove me inside. "Stay here until you are fetched, dog," he snarls. I decide not to respond. There is no value in enraging men driven by bloodlust and violence. The leader is a tall, hirsute, angry-looking giant. He gives me a deathly glare and they walk out, slamming the door. I ache all over.

What have you done, Ninshu? What have you gotten me into?

It is time for me to introspect the realities surrounding my wife.

Ninshubur is...*was* no ordinary woman. She was one of the palace maids, helping the royals and high officials—the prince, his wife, the queen, the chief-priestess, with various errands.

Her work revolved around conveying temple procedures to the palaces and ensuring that the various ceremonies followed protocol and were arranged to the priests' and priestesses' satisfaction. It was me who had recommended her to the temple committee, reasoning that the wife of a scribe was well-suited to palace duties.

There was something else that pleased the committee.

My wife was borne of a father of Urim and a mother of Elam, who my father married during his trade engagements when there was relative peace between the kingdoms. Her knowledge of the Elamite language had been helpful when emissaries or merchants were received in the palace for negotiations, or for supplying offerings to the temples in busy seasons when translators were short in number.

And the roving eyes of the men of the palace committee could not have ignored her beauty.

There are now many directions that my mind can venture into on what had caused her to be in danger, and yet I know nothing more than what I had imagined since yesterday.

My mind swirls through many other scenarios. Was she having an affair with someone high in the court? Was she pregnant with another man's child? Did she enrage the now-dead queen? Did she rebuff the chief-scribe's sexual advances? Did the king's frustrations with the Martu incursions lead to suspicion on anyone in the palace with foreign blood? Something else?

It is not only the many possibilities that haunt me, but also the question of why, if she was sent to death, had the perpetrator taken such a complicated route? Why not have her murdered at home, like Iddin? Or kidnapped and taken away to be sold somewhere? A woman known to the royals and murdered would garner much attention, but no one would question one sent away as a traveler through a divine procedure. It was a viciously clever way to not draw attention. But then, they had not factored the husband's unwillingness to accept that theory. And the more time I spend, the more I am convinced that she was sent to her death.

My back aches, and my shoulders hurt. I gingerly lean on the rough brick wall and contemplate my future. I have seen no omens in my favor—for the sky has remained cloudless, no birds have flown in threes, the dust cloud at home has displayed no cap of Enlil, and last night no dogs howled in unison. The gods tell me nothing, and yet they have kept me alive.

The light through the small aperture dies, leaving me in darkness. They have left no oil lamp for me to use.

Someone opens the door and rudely pushes a small clay plate with coarse bread, cucumber slices, barley sludge, and a pot of water. That is a good sign—my captors do not want me to die of hunger and thirst.

It gets cold at night. I shiver in the darkness and pray to my many gods. Enlil, Nanna, Inana, Enki, An, Utu, Ki, all of them, for surely they see the injustice heaped upon me. It is quiet here, and not even the howls of the dogs or the meows of cats roaming the streets penetrate the dungeon. My body finally succumbs to exhaustion.

I will wait to see what comes my way.

But I shall not leave without a fight.

CHAPTER 9

EASTERN BORDERS

KINDATTU

The king of Elam feels better today.

The festering wound on his toe, infected after the arrow punctured it, is finally healing. Every few hours, either he or his physician squeezed the pus and bandaged the toe, and he had clenched his jaws and hid the agony. He can now walk again without a pathetic limp.

The failed attack has made him rethink his approach. He needs alliances, at least until he is firmly in control and is victorious, after which he can discard them like rags and trample upon them. Kindattu has no desire to share his power, for he and he alone is the king of Elam, and will soon be the king of all Sumer and Akkad.

"The nomad chief is here, Great King," a lieutenant says. Kindattu grunts—the business of forging an alliance with barbarians is unpleasant but necessary. He has a loyal and well-respected interpreter. The Martu speak in a guttural tongue that sounds like dogs growling, another sign that these people must be eradicated like trash once he conquers these lands.

He walks out to a pleasant, cloudless sky. He has adorned his head with a jewel-laden tiara, and his crisp white gown is tied at the waist with a rich leather belt from which hangs a ceremonial scabbard. His thick beard is carefully coiffured and tied for this occasion. A king he shall speak as, and king he shall show as. He has given instructions not to bring the nomad chief and his band within the camp boundaries, lest those be seen as bad omens by his gods. It is a long walk on the hard, gravelly ground, and his feet throb by the time they near the cleared area where the visitor waits.

He is surprised when he sees the Martu chief.

The man is a head taller than Kindattu, who himself is no ordinary man. His shoulders are wider, his hair wilder, and his thighs look like that of a man that has never stopped walking since he was born. He wears a small loincloth that does nothing to hide his dangling penis. The man's lips are barely visible beneath a thick forest of gray-and-black beard and mustache. If his tribe is like animals, no wonder they have picked the biggest monkey as their leader, Kindattu thinks.

Surprisingly, the Martu chief kneels as Kindattu comes before him. The interpreter has been waiting, and he addresses Kindattu. "Great King, I introduce you to the leader of the Martu, by the name of Atturapi."

Kindattu nods at Atturapi and gestures for him to rise. No interpreter is necessary to follow the direction of a hand. Atturapi towers over Kindattu, who takes a few steps to sit on an elevated, hastily constructed reed-and-wood stool. Atturapi stands before him.

"My people have sent me to speak to the king of Elam," Atturapi says. His speech does not sound like dogs growling. He has a deep, soft tone. The interpreter conveys the words.

"And I am glad to speak to the chief of the Martu," he says. "Common matters bring us together."

"They say the king wishes to speak of an alliance," Atturapi says, and there is the slightest arrogant grin behind all the hair.

The presumptuous fool.

He nods. "The glory of Elam must spread to the land of Sumer, and our omens say that the mighty fist of Elam shall vanquish the enemy with the help of the strength of the Martu."

The chief's eyes shine with greed.

"And the arms of the Martu bring great power, derived by our glorious god Belu-Sadi," Atturapi says, raising his right arm and slapping his bicep.

Until I cut it off and let the dogs feast on it.

Kindattu gestures for the Martu chief to sit on another stool beside him. Atturapi makes himself comfortable.

"May we speak of our collaboration?" Kindattu asks.

Atturapi bows deeply. "For that, we are ready."

"How powerful are the defenses of Urim, Lagash, Eridu, and Uruk?"

"They are weaker than under their previous kings, but not weak enough for the king of Elam to take," he says.

The insolence of the man. I must cut out his tongue and force him to swallow it.

"But the Martu know the extent of their power and the weaknesses within," he says, smiling.

Atturapi grins. "We know where Shu-Sin's wall begins and ends. We know when the many fortresses are manned and not. We know when the cities are vulnerable during their ceremonies."

"What is Shu-Sin's wall?"

Atturapi takes a deep breath and thrusts out his chest. It is the sign of a man who feels a moment of self-importance when he is about to speak of a matter that the listener knows little of. Kindattu has seen this among all men before.

"The king before the current king of Sumer built a wall north of Urim. It takes a grown man fifty days of walking to come to its end. And he has built that to prevent us from foraging in their lands."

Kindattu is surprised.

A wall that long?

"Is it manned by sentries? How have you defeated this wall?"

Atturapi laughs. "We have found its end and walked by it. They do not have garrisons manning them anymore."

Kindattu cannot but help chuckle at the response. "As we advance south, we may bypass it?"

"No. They will man the eastern end, king of Elam, and it will be far for you to march your army across the entire wall. You can go down the Euphrates, but resistance will be much fiercer."

Kindattu contemplates the situation. Atturapi is knowledgeable and clever. He is not as much a barbarian as his men had painted these people to be.

"What do you suggest, chief of the Martu?" he says.

Atturapi swells with pride. He bows again. "The great king of Elam seeks my advice, and for that, I am honored."

Kindattu nods and raises his palms as if to approve of the chief's words.

"We are a clan of many tribes, king of Elam. I control some, while other chiefs control others. But we all seek unfettered access to the fertile lands along the rivers, a desire much hated by the kings of Sumer."

And what does he want in return?

Atturapi continues, "I can bring them together under a common goal that we shall soon roam these lands freely. But for that, great king of Elam, you must accept our presence as you seek to install your men in the cities. The land outside the city walls must be free for the men of Martu."

Kindattu considers the request. He knows from the messengers from this land that the kings of Sumer have a problem with the incessant incursion that displaced their own people. But then, there will never be large numbers of people of Elam in this region. Did it matter to him?

"What assurances does the chief of Martu give us that your uncontrolled access does not lead us to being held hostage for grain and pastoral lands for our cattle?"

Atturapi nods. "You have heard of stories that we are men who till no grain, and we know no home."

Kindattu is surprised. He nods.

"The tales of those who hate us must not be believed, king of Elam. We are shepherds and cattle-ranchers. We sow grain, and we reap our harvest. We trade with the kings of Sumer, and they seek our milk and cheese, but they give us no land to live. Should the king of Elam give us quarter, he will benefit from our skilled hands."

This man is surprisingly articulate, nothing at all like the wild beasts he'd imagined them to be.

"How much do you know to fight?"

Atturapi rubs his beard with his giant palms. He scratches his chin. "We are no army, and our men are no soldiers, king of Elam. But we fear nothing and no one, and if you give us blades, then we shall swing them until they are dead."

"How well do you know of the defenses of the large cities?" This is the part that is interesting to Kindattu.

"We are not spies and soldiers. We seek land to settle and eat. We can tell you the best paths for the soldiers, and we can tell you where the defensive walls are tallest. We can tell you which cities have more soldiers, and which have bigger granaries. But we do not sit on the Sumerian kings' councils or know the inner workings of the kings and their gods."

Kindattu is surprised once again at this honest assessment. He appraises the Martu chief. These nomads are not all as innocent and backward as he has been told.

"Tell me, Chief Atturapi, you say that all you seek is pastoral land and ground on which to live, and yet my men say you have run over several small towns near the town of Babiliim, and that your chiefs rule them as if they are kings. What nomads do that?"

Atturapi's eyes narrow. The shrewd chief of the Martu leans back and sighs. "That we are nomads is a fable concocted by the black-headed people and the Akkadians before them, king of Elam. It is true we were nomads, but there was a day in your forefather's time that even the great people of Elam were nomads. Not all men have sprung from the earth and built cities."

The clever bastard.

"That may be, for our gods determine the course of our peoples. And yet it does not explain why you have taken over someone else's towns and are running them as if they were your own."

The Martu chief laughs. He places his hands on his thighs and taps on them. "You are a king, great Kindattu. Do you think the men of Sumer would let the people of Martu build towns and live in them? They have attacked us for generations if we so much as break a single rule their kings bind us with. It is easier for us to take their towns when we can and live in them—but building empires is not what we seek, if the king of Elam worries about our ambitions."

Should there be even a spark, I will destroy you all.

"It appears, chief of Martu, that your people will be of great service to the army of Elam. You shall establish paths for us, provide us food, and scout weaknesses. And in return, I, king of Elam and servant of Inshushinak, shall provide ample land for your people to thrive and trade."

Atturapi bows.

"We shall destroy the arrogance of the kings of Sumer. Their women shall lament the death of their men, their men shall lament the ravishing of their women, their children shall lament the vanishing of their parents, and all this we shall do together."

"As the king of Elam wishes," says Atturapi.

Kindattu gestures to an attendant nearby. The man brings a small, ornate box. Kindattu opens it with flair and turns it toward Atturapi. "The king of Elam wishes to continue this cooperation. I offer you, chief of the Martu, enough shekels of silver to prove our intention."

Atturapi accepts the gift with a smile. This is enough money to keep his greed satiated for now.

"And I offer barley, dates, milk, and sheep meat for the king's army, all at the most favorable terms."

They come to an agreement for the Martu to wage a war of attrition against Urim, through small but enervating attacks, weakening the city and chipping away at its strength.

Kindattu bids good-bye to Atturapi, telling him that the Elamites would return to their city across the Zagros Mountains to regroup, plan, and return when the weather becomes warmer in eight months. Meanwhile, they agree to be in contact through messengers and share information on any changes. Kindattu plans to return with an invasion force.

But he is not done yet, for no king puts all his faith in an unknown people. Kindattu has learned that the governor of Isin, another large city of the people of Sumer, has declared himself king and has been a thorn in the side of the king of Urim, who sees himself as the king of all cities of Sumer. Ishbi-Erra is the governor's name, and Kindattu seeks to send an emissary to his court. If Ishbi-Erra does not cooperate, Kindattu will drag the man behind an ox-cart until his skin flays off, and will then impale him on a wooden stake for his men to see.

And there is the matter of the information that is trickling from the deepest recesses of the palace of Urim, the seat of the power of the Ibbi-Sin, king of Sumer. The woman who feeds him secrets has demands. Kindattu's man has established firm relations with her. As he limps back to his tent, the king of Elam decides that it is time to make final plans to bring Urim and the kingdom of Sumer below his heels—and for that, he will need to wage war with force and make deals with those who can weaken a kingdom from within.

CHAPTER 10

URIM

NEMUR

I stand shackled and manacled. Do they think that a man who has spent years hunched over a clay tablet, reading it or inscribing on it with a reed stylus, will suddenly grow mighty arms and slay all around him? I am certain Inana blesses me, but she has not given me the strength of otherworldly beasts.

This morning, the big scary man and his henchmen arrived at my dungeon and dragged me here, to the royal court, to stand before the king.

My initial fears that they were taking me to execution were somewhat allayed when I was taken into the palace. The king Ibbi-Sin; his son Emmu-Sin; the son's wife Ningal; the chief-priestess Geshtinanna; the chief-scribe Inim-Nanna; Nigir-Kagina, the general of the army; and the governor of Eridu are all present today. They are all not here to pass judgment on a minor scribe—there must be have been other important and weighty topics to discuss.

Behind the king are the fearsome members of the royal guard. They rotate their positions, and I know some by face and their postures. They do not speak in these gatherings— their purpose is to watch and protect the king. The man who threw me in the dungeon is here.

I am at once intimidated and proud that a lowly scribe would invite such a luminous gathering.

As is declared by laws that protect scribes, I am being given an opportunity to present my defense and answer questions before the king. Even in these depths of hopelessness, that privilege of audience before a considerate king is my hope.

I do not know yet what I am being accused of, but I will find out soon when my name is called. It feels as if the throne room is embraced by a dark, unmerciful fate, for there is not a worry-less face. The light from outside is insufficient due to a cloudy sky, and the lamps inside fail to bring brightness to the proceedings.

When my name is finally called, I am led before the king. Just days ago, I stood here as a messenger of His Majesty, conveying his words and bringing back those of a governor. And today, I am a prisoner. I kneel with difficulty, flinching as the manacle cuts into the back of my ankle. Unlike the barbarians elsewhere, the kings of Sumer have instituted a system of laws that govern our behavior. There are punishments for certain crimes—ranging from stealing sheep to murder. Those accused of crimes have a chance to present themselves before a magistrate and plead their case.

Commoners never come before the king, for their cases are disposed of by governors and magistrates.

But when the cases involve members of the palace or senior officials of the kingdom, they are brought before the king and his senior members for justice. All parties are heard, and then the king confers with the priests before dispensing justice. During the case, if either side is caught in an egregious lie before the king, then the penalties can be severe, including death. I know that the system is rife with corruption outside the palace, for there, those with money or who can offer other enticements like women or cattle find the favor of justice leaning toward them.

But one hopes to receive fairness in the throne room.

King Ibbi-Sin looks small and tired on his throne. Much weighs on those frail shoulders. A court official whispers something in the king's ears. Then, a priest brings a plate of incense and pours animal fat on it. He lights it and watches the fragrant smoke waft into the air, dancing with the flow, dissipating and vanishing. He whispers something to the court official, who conveys it is to the king. The smoke, they say, foretells many things, and the priests and priestesses interpret those signs.

Did the smoke declare my death warrant? I would know soon.

The court official declares loudly, "Nemur, junior scribe of the royal court, His Majesty's messenger, His Highness the Prince's messenger, Her Holiness the Chief-Priestess's messenger, now stands before the king for judgment."

A minister of the court who officiates judicial proceedings—from murder to property disputes—stands and bows to the king. "And I, magistrate of the royal house, representing the accuser, will question the accused."

Accused of what, you bald-headed big-belly?

The priest picks up a small bronze bell from his plate and rings it. The proceedings are now in motion. My face feels flushed, and my heart beats wildly. If they declare death, I prefer a swift execution, but not before I protest my innocence.

I ask Enlil to spare me from torture.

I had once seen a man, a Martu peasant accused of thievery, tied to a pole and whipped to death with a scourge, and his cries and the images of the chunks of flesh that tore off his back have never left me. What gods sanction such brutality?

I might find a way to kill myself if they announce torture.

Surely the gods that have kept a distressed, innocent man alive do not intend to further have him tortured?

"Do you know what you are accused of, scribe Nemur?" he asks. Two guards lift me by my armpits to let me stand. I shuffle awkwardly.

"No, honorable magistrate."

He looks offended. He puffs up his chest dramatically. "Well, well, may we all see a man so bereft of conscience that he perpetrates a crime, and yet recognizes no criminality in his act!"

I hold my tongue. *If I do not know what it is, how can I admit to it, idiot?*

The king looks at me. "Accused scribe Nemur. You have been brought before me for judgment. You have permission to defend yourself and to respond to the magistrate's remarks. You are offered this benefit, for you have been in service of the royal house."

I bow. "I thank His Majesty and all the high men and women of the royal house. I seek the guidance of Enlil and Inana. And I beg your forgiveness if my words to the magistrate cross the boundaries of royal conduct."

The chief-scribe narrows his eyes. He speaks up. "This is not the school, or a bazaar to run your mouth, scribe Nemur. May you—"

But the king raises a hand and shuts him up. "The man faces death. He has served me well. I shall warn him, but let him speak his mind."

No one understands the confusion in my mind. Is the king on *my* side? The gods want me alive. The omens from the rising incense must have told the king that his grace must be upon me.

I kneel and then, with difficulty, prostrate before the king. "I am eternally grateful for His Majesty's permission," I say in the most pathetic voice I can muster, though a rage burns in my body. *Why must I seek forgiveness and permission for things I have not done?*

"Rise, and may the proceedings begin," the king says.

The magistrate speaks to me again. "You say before this divine court that you do not know what you are accused of?"

This time the energy of An is in me. The power of a crackling lightning bolt courses through my veins.

If I must die, I will go fighting.

"I do not, honorable magistrate. I am a man grieving for his wife, and I have no understanding of the past few days and what it is that I am being accused of."

The magistrate shakes his head theatrically. His kohl-lined eyes open wide like a dancer's. "Ah! He says he does not know. Then let us tell us him!"

He gestures to an announcer nearby. The loud-voiced man announces, "Nemur, scribe of the royal house, you are accused of killing a man of the school of scribes, driven by jealousy or other madness."

I almost swoon hearing that.

What?

Blood roars into my ears, and I can barely breathe. I am no fool—I had guessed my charges, and I believed that someone had seen me flee from Iddin's house. But it was a different sensation hearing it aloud and knowing the implications of the accusation if I did not convince the king otherwise.

Guide me, Enlil. Guide me from the dark forests of deception and false accusations into the light of justice!

I take a deep breath. "And these charges I categorically reject as false. The gods know that I have committed no crimes, and I stand before His Majesty as falsely accused. That I have conspired to kill Iddin–"

"Aha! You know it is Iddin!" the magistrate yells as if he has caught me in an enormous trap. I look at him like he is a greater idiot than the Martu in the bazaars.

"I know it is Iddin," I retort. There is strength in my voice. "You and everyone here know that I am here before the king because you think I killed him. And I say that is as true as you accepting that Ishbi-Erra is the king of our land!"

The magistrate looks horrified—he knows that to even bring up Ishbi-Erra's name is to risk entering dangerous territory.

"You scoundrel! How dare you accuse me of even imagining that the rat Ishbi-Erra is king? How dare you link the two!"

Excellent. Push him over the edge and take his dramatics away.

"Because the charges you have leveled at me are as preposterous! What man can stand behind the words that I did those heinous acts? I am despondent by the loss of my wife, and the reason I went to Iddin was to find out why my wife traveled!"

Suddenly there is much confusion. This magisterial fool does not know it all—and I am about to make this a miserable experience for him.

"You lie!" the magistrate yells. "You make a story about your wife. No one told us–"

"No one told you my wife traveled, because you never bothered to find out!" I shout at him. Now that this has attracted much attention, I turn to the king. "Your Majesty, my wife was coerced into traveling against her wishes, and Iddin had a hand in placing her name on the list. My wife was pregnant!"

A womanly voice cuts through. The prince's wife, Her Highness Ningal, one who may have been served by my wife, is leaning forward in surprise. "Pregnant? How can–"

I take advantage of the situation. I shout with anguish, "The king's order has been desecrated! Enlil would be dishonored!"

The magistrate is dumb-struck. He tries to plow on. "It does not condone the fact that you killed—"

"I did not kill Iddin, and yet Iddin had a hand in my wife's death."

The chief-scribe, Inim-Nanna, finally opens his mouth. "What proof do you have that your wife did not travel on her own accord? Or that she was not pregnant by an affair with Iddin that you found out?"

As foul as this man's words are, I know that this is what I must use to get myself out. The king has remained silent—and that is a good sign that he is listening.

"May I describe my sequence of events, Your Majesty?" I ask, and my words cause the murmurs to stop. This is now a spectacle, just as I wanted.

The king raises his hand to silence any opposition. "Speak, Nemur," he says. I am elated he remembers my name. I have not known King Ibbi-Sin to be a cruel man, and his consideration of my position reinforces my loyalty to him.

"I bow to His Majesty. And to this council, I say this. I did not kill Iddin. I swear on Enlil, Inana, Nanna, and all gods of Sumer. I swear on the memories of my father and mother, on my forefathers who have served this land and prayed to the gods. I am certain my wife did not go willingly. And my events will take me from being a man condemned, to a man who must receive justice."

No one speaks a word.

"I ask this. How can my wife have traveled without my permission? Can the chief-scribe show my signed approval? How did the list preparers not know she was pregnant? Why was the man who gave that list to the tomb supervisor murdered before I could speak to him?" I say, deflecting the suspicion from me to someone else.

The king turns to the chief-scribe Inim-Nanna, who shrinks under the glare. Whoever had me arrested must be cursing themselves now, and my hunch is, it was the chief-scribe. But then, if he arranged my arrest, it would be stupid of him to have me dragged before a council where her death could be surfaced. As much as I hate the man, I doubt he had anything to do with Ninshubur's death—or if he did, he was not aware of the implications of his actions.

"Inim-Nanna, if what this man says is true, how did his wife's name go on the list?"

Inim-Nanna stutters and hems and haws. "I do not know who his wife is, Your Majesty. I would not know!"

"Dumumi-Ninshubur," I say, as loudly as possible. "Ninshubur, servant of the royals, messenger for temple processes, the one who spoke the language of Elam."

Several eyebrows shoot up. Many knew her—or at least who she was. His Highness the Prince Emmu-Sin jerks back, his eyes open wide in recognition. The chief-priestess, Geshtinanna, subtly grips the arm of her chair, and even Her Highness Ningal closes her mouth with her palm. I have no illusions on how much the royals care about servants in their house, for they are many, they live and die, but the fact that they at least recognize her will make it more compelling to argue my case. I am quietly surprised and proud of how my wife was known in the highest levels of the kingdom. The chief-scribe, Inim-Nanna, stays affixed to the ground, unsure how to react. He knows my wife. He has spoken to her several times.

I am about to make *his* life miserable.

"Honorable Inim-Nanna wishes to condemn me for a crime I did not commit, and he had no shame when he propositioned my wife several times in my absence!"

The invisible finger of guilt is now pointing toward this craven man. All eyes turn to him.

"What do you say, Inim-Nanna? Is this man's word true? And where is the list?" the king asks. To be caught in a lie to His Majesty would mean death, and not a pleasant one. Would Inim-Nanna like to be buried in the sand and left to die?

The chief-scribe sinks to his knees. "Your Majesty! As any man, I must attest that sometimes my carnal desires have led to distasteful behavior, and as ashamed as I am of my proposition, it was not only his wife! And besides, I have forced no woman to sleep with me."

I might have laughed at this pathetic admission if my life were not at risk and my wife was not dead.

"That is convenient for you to say, chief-scribe, and yet every man here can see that you could have had her killed for refusing your advances—and then have me executed, cleaning up the entire mess!" I yell, now disregarding any risk due to my words. What do I have to lose?

This horny old man probably pressed every woman around him for sex, but he has not left a trail of dead bodies and no known example of having someone travel, which is an insidious way to murder. But at this point, I will do anything I can to gain my freedom and hunt down the bastard who caused this in the first place.

Geshtinanna, a princess herself and the exalted chief-priestess, speaks up for the first time. "Inim-Nanna's proclivities are well known, and yet I have known no instances of women dying because they said no to him. Besides, every woman in the palace has said no to him at one time or another, and they are all alive," she says, the slightest of smiles curling up on her lips.

This was supposed to be a murder trial, but suddenly the throne room is filled with sniggers. Inim-Nanna is mortified but somewhat relieved, thinking no one here believes he engineered a murder.

Princess Ningal says with a smile, "Every time he speaks to me, his eyes are anywhere but looking at mine."

Her husband, the prince, glares at Inim-Nanna.

Someone laughs. Even the king is smiling. I do know that even if this smarmy man was involved, not much would happen to him, for Inim-Nanna is a relative of the king. It is extraordinarily rare for someone outside the family to have the powerful position of a chief scribe. But the king has, in the past, executed members of his family—which is why Inim-Nanna looks worried.

Then King Ibbi-Sin turns to me. "You have seeded doubts in our mind, young scribe. There are two subjects before me. Did you conspire to kill your wife? I think not. And that a pregnant woman, a woman who has served this court, was sent to her death is a preposterous claim, but one that must be investigated further. That is your responsibility. But we have not yet settled the question of the death of a royal scribe."

"Your Majesty, whoever had me arrested can first explain why."

The king turns to the magistrate. "Let our feet remain firm on the topic of the scribe's death. And then we shall return to what happened to his wife."

Relief courses over me. Support, any support from the king, is good news. Even if the support is mere words, considering the precarious situation the king himself is in.

The magistrate, who a while ago was pumped with bloodlust, has lost his appetite somewhat. He clears his throat and turns to me. At this point, it is clear that I have interested the entire court, and I will do whatever I can to throw darts of doubt in every direction. Who said Enlil is not with me?

"I have witnesses that place the scribe, Nemur, in the house of Iddin, the man who was slain, and he was seen fleeing the scene when men sought to stop and question him," he says, pushing up his voice as if finding me running was proof of murder. I know why the magistrate is struggling, or is at least worried. He has never tried a scribe before. He is afraid of learned men. Most who stand accused tend to be tradesmen and farmers, so terrified that they accept any accusation with hopes of the king's mercy. Some can barely understand the formal language of the court, and others cannot understand it at all. I am an unfamiliar, tricky beast to him, and that I shall take full advantage of.

I have nothing more to lose except my life, having lost my wife and child.

It is my turn to speak. "That I was there does not mean I killed him. That I was found fleeing does not mean I committed the crime. Iddin's neck had been slit ear-to-ear when I arrived at his house. I ran because, magistrate, you know as well as I that crowds with passion will hear to no pleas of reason if they set their minds on immediate justice. And I could not risk a crowd that is partial to the dead man, which is why I ran. Did they see a knife in my hands? Did they find a knife in Iddin's house?"

The king turns to the magistrate.

"No, we did not, Your Majesty, and that is because the accused ran with it!"

Very convenient.

"I had no knife in my hands, and there are witnesses who can attest to the fact that a hooded man ran through the crowd before me. I wager that he was the killer, and the magistrate intends to frame me for something I did not do!" This time I make the invisible finger of guilt point to the magistrate. Will he refute my bluff that I have witnesses to speak about the other man?

Realizing his precarious position, he backtracks. "I have heard there was another runner, but we have no reason to believe he had anything to do with this Iddin's death."

"But you do not know that. Have you found him?" I ask.

The magistrate has no answer, but he is staring at the chief-scribe, who is avoiding meeting the magistrate's eyes the way a student in school avoids the school-father's eyes.

"We have not," he says sheepishly.

"So, you do not have the knife. You do not have the other runner in possession. But you bring me before the king, putting to risk my life, saying I killed him? I think you had him killed!" I say, pointing to the magistrate this time.

He almost launches at me. "How dare you! You preposterous scum, I will–"

"Magistrate!" the king shouts, causing the man to freeze.

The room is silent. I am certain that no recent judgment was such a spectacle.

The king points his finger at the magistrate. "The young scribe's protests have merit. You brought him before the council without much thought, and now you act as if you are furious at his indignation!"

The magistrate looks like he would rather turn to dust and fly away in the wind. He wrings his hands and looks at the ground. And then he looks up and stares at the chief-scribe. I know, and I am sure everyone there knows, that I must have been hauled in on the behest of the chief-scribe, not giving the magistrate the time to do his due diligence.

It is as if the king has read my mind. "Did you do it on demand by Inim-Nanna?"

The magistrate nods sheepishly, and it is the turn of chief-scribe Inim-Nanna to display his red face.

The chief-scribe speaks. "Your Majesty, as everyone here can attest, we have a severe shortage of scribes to serve the needs of the kingdom. It takes years for them to gain the abilities needed to read and write, and the violent death of one requires investigation and trial before the king, by law. I know that Nemur and Iddin did not have a warm relation, and he was seen fleeing the scene, which gives the magistrate the authority to detain and present him."

"That may be the case, dear Inim, but he has failed to prove that Nemur committed the murder," Geshtinanna says. The chief-priestess has a powerful presence, and her words are rarely dismissed. "Besides, the scribe has fervently sworn on the gods, which he would not do if he were telling lies. The judgment in the netherworld will be harsh if he is being deceitful."

Princess Ningal's soft voice floats. "And grief causes men to react in different ways, including an unwillingness to accept what is true," she says as she gently holds the ailing prince's hand. There are rumors that the prince deludes himself to be a powerful warrior when he can barely walk, and Ningal, his wife, has been a steady and calming presence in his life. I know what she says is toward me, but below that is the sad acknowledgment of her own life.

King Ibbi-Sin questions the magistrate and me. Finally, he leans back and says, "I have decided."

I take a deep breath.

"The scribe Nemur cannot be found guilty of the murder. The magistrate must continue his investigation without hindering Nemur's freedom," he says solemnly.

Yes!

I kneel and place my head on the floor in gratitude until I am told to rise. This order means the magistrate cannot hold me in a cell and try to beat out a confession.

I must now convince the king to launch an investigation into my wife's death. But the king is not yet finished.

"Now, to the strange case of your wife," he says and snaps his fingers at someone waiting in the shadows. The man comes forward and whispers in the king's ears. The king then asks Inim-Nanna to join them, and as the court watches silently, they all confer. There are raised voices, but I cannot make out what is being said or what is going on. Finally, King Ibbi-Sin dismisses them.

He turns to me. "Young scribe. My officers tell me that Iddin has destroyed the clay tablet with the names, and that it is customary for the junior scribe to break the tablets at the completion of the ceremony. The supervisor at the site says he found nothing that warranted investigation. Without evidence that the final tablet has been tampered with, I am of the opinion that it is all speculation."

No, Your Majesty!

"It is true that I have decreed no woman with a child in her womb shall be sent traveling in service of their masters or mistresses, but then it is true that your wife being pregnant is hearsay. My daughter-in-law said the words of wisdom, young scribe, that your heart is injured by your wife's deception, and there are reasons within your marriage that did she not wish for you to know. What is between a man and his woman are not for this council to debate, and for that reason, it is upon your shoulders to do what you wish to. But beware not to sully the names of the royal house."

A snake is squeezing my throat. I control my anger. I want to shout and scream, *No, there is no hearsay. There is a conspiracy, and you refuse to see it.* It is as if the king can *sense* something greater, but he wishes for lowly men like me to stay away from uncovering it. I let out a small gasp—one that they make take for relief, but it is one of anguish.

The king is not finished. "But a scribe's duty is to the throne, young Nemur. And to defeat the anguish in your heart, you must apply yourself to service again and not let the mind wander the fields of distrust and doubt."

I say nothing. What can I say? If there is one person against whom I will not, and cannot, raise my voice, it is the king. I have to bide my time.

"You will return to your home and await orders for your next mission. Make no mischief, or I will have you flogged."

CHAPTER 11

URIM

NEMUR

Now a free man and back to my previous status as a scribe, I am escorted out of the palace respectfully by the guards. How much of a difference a king's action makes!

But my heart is heavy, and my wrists feel shackled even without them present. I sit beneath a palm tree to rest my aching hands and feet. I do not remember how long I sat there, my mind an empty vessel and without direction.

The cool wind brings energy back into me.

I idly stare at the massive *Etemenniguru* in the background. It will be dusk in a few hours, and then a long line of priests and temple servants will begin to ascend the steps, holding lamps and food offerings to Nanna and Enlil in the glorious temple at the top.

I have been there a few times—it is a magnificent place. They say Enlil himself arrives at midnight, with Nanna, to eat the offerings. What do the gods have in store for me? What should I–

"Honorable scribe Nemur," a voice calls out. I turn to see a man in the distinctive uniform of the prince's guard. *What now?*

"Yes, lieutenant," I ask meekly. I am tired.

"His Highness the Prince and Her Highness the Prince's devoted wife order your presence."

It is my turn to be surprised. Do they know something? Do they wish to help me?

I accompany the man to the prince's quarters, which is in one corner of the massive complex. I have never been here. An odd fear grips me—what if this is a ruse to have me vanish? I dismiss those worries as I walk past groups of people, servants, and slaves, all wandering about doing their duties near the prince's quarters. When I am finally ushered into their presence, the prince is on the bed, and his wife is sitting by his side.

I bow to both of them.

"You might be wondering why you have been ordered here, Nemur," says the prince in his raspy voice. He is a frail man, and now, without the gown covering his chest, I can see his ribs beneath his sickly-looking skin. I have served the prince a few times for his missives and dictations to governors.

"Yes, Your Highness."

"My wife and I were aware of your wife's presence in our service. She was a good worker, and her knowledge of the language of Elam was sometimes helpful when I received messengers."

"Yes, Your Highness. She spoke with reverence of her service to you."

The princess picks up a cup and places it at His Highness's lips. She turns to me. "She was a loyal servant. My husband and I agree that we cannot lose a man of your mettle for grief, for many enemies are at our doorstep, and we need every scribe to send our messages and convey our orders."

"Yes, Your Highness."

The prince speaks. "We do not know what is between a man and his wife, Nemur, but for your loss, here is silver that I hope alleviates the pain and helps you find a new wife."

How foolish are they?

He reaches for a box near him, and his wife picks it up on his behalf. She extends her hand and drops it in my palms, and I receive it from her with a bowed head. I pretend to choke with gratitude, though my head pulsates with anger. The king, his brood, no one understands the anguish of a common man. None. They care more about their name and their reputation than lifting a finger for someone who has served them for years. The prince begins to cough, and the princess wipes his mouth. In a strange way, I pity the king. Hostile enemies surround him, his own governors defy him, and his son is ill. The aging king bears all the burden himself, and yet he had the kindness to listen to me and let me go. Or he is desperate not to lose any more scribes, for we are too few and in great demand.

"May you live well," the prince says with difficulty.

"Rest, my husband," Princess Ningal says, gently holding the prince's head and laying it on the pillow. I watch her care with envy. If I were sick, I would die alone like a dog.

As I bow and begin to trace my steps, the princess walks up to me. I am startled to be standing so near royalty. She speaks to me softly, the tone of someone used to caring for so long that their voice changes. She is breathtakingly beautiful. "Ninshubur was who I commanded for all my temple duties," she says. "I heard a palace maid say she spoke of traveling for the queen, for her devotion to the palace had consumed her."

I am speechless. But the princess does not stop. Her eyes are moist. "My husband. He is dying. And he is burdened by the guilt that drove your wife to make her decision."

I am shocked. What does she mean? I want to scream, but I control my emotion. "What do you mean, divine princess? What guilt burdens him?"

"Ask no more of it," she says in the softest voice. "Find yourself a new wife, scribe Nemur, and never have her work for the men of the palace."

CHAPTER 12

URIM

NEMUR

They say that the gods infuse every man with a level of tolerance.

Some are unable to put a cat to death when it is of old age, and others find no qualm in torturing a helpless woman to death or throwing a child in a fire.

Some accept what is told to them, for the words of those imparting knowledge are held sacred—and others question all that is said, for people, by nature inflicted upon them by gods, may be deceitful.

Some discard their fathers, mothers, sons, wives, and daughters like they are refuse, and others find happiness in love, care, and service.

Some forget injustices heaped upon them by the powers above, and others seek revenge and do not rest until a price is extracted.

And as I walk home after an astonishing day, I do not know what my tolerance is.

Do I seek revenge for something I do not even understand? Or do I let these days dissolve into the air and find myself a new wife who will serve me to my end?

Do I protest to the king and put to question the prince's dignity, or do I accept that a man of royalty, by his status and divine blessing, is allowed to take pleasure in any manner he seeks, even if it is in the form of violation of another man's wife?

Has my wife traveled willingly, or was she driven by sadness that she did not wish to share with me...or was she murdered? The day began with the ascension of Utu, the god of sun, and I had questions. But as the sun prepares to rest in the distant lands, I have more questions. All I know is that I am now free, but everything is shrouded in dark clouds.

I know that my rage will resurface later, once I have had the chance to think. But now, I do not know what is right or wrong, what is true or false, what is sincerity or deceit. Enlil laughs at me from his abode, and Utu winks with his orange-gold rays.

The neighbors are curious once I return home, for now I am a spectacle, a strange being around whom there are swirls of doubt and gossip. I know they cannot decide what I am—a man scorned by his wife or the one who murdered her. A murderer of his wife's lover, or an innocent man in the middle of a sordid affair. They will want to know, and the inquiries will come soon. But for now, I have no desire to engage anyone. Many forget their wives and find younger ones, but some do not. I am that kind.

My body finally gives up soon after I come home. For all their faults, my neighbors have ensured no one has ransacked my house. It is as I left it days ago, only with more dust. I will seek solace in cleaning it, but not today.

I fall into a deep, dreamless slumber.

Someone is banging on my frail wooden door. "Scribe Nemur, the king has an order! Scribe Nemur!"

I have slept through the night and woken invigorated, even with the grief that burdens me. Such is the power of one's own bed. I open the door to find a burly guard standing outside, looking irritated. "The king demands your presence, sir," he says. "Now."

Considering no one is tying my wrists or beating me to the ground, I assume this is a regular mission. I was a man condemned yesterday, and today I am expected to carry on as if nothing has happened. I serve the king when there are doubts in my mind about his sick son.

"Wait here," I tell the guard, and slam the door on his face. I quickly complete my morning rituals and stuff my mouth with coarse bread, and wash it down with old beer. When I finally step out in the sun, now attired in a way that befits my title and role, the guard suppresses his unhappy grunts and sullenly follows me as I make my way back to the palace. I keep an eye out for anyone to confront me, but the world moves on, and I am another government official in their midst on his way to work. The people are more anxious these days with increasing reports of Martu incursions and news of Elam's propaganda against Sumer. One can see the tension on their faces over what the future holds for them. And their safety is all on king Ibbi-Sin's shoulders.

The king looks worried as I am ushered to his presence. "Are you of the sound mind and strong legs needed to deliver my message, young Scribe?" he asks me.

I bow to the king and vigorously claim my readiness. Pretenses are necessary to keep one's grace.

"I was pleased to see your fighting spirit yesterday, and you are a man that does not accept things readily," he says. "I need you to convey pressing messages to the rascal of Isin and impress upon him the urgency of my commands."

I am surprised. The rascal of Isin is Ishbi-Erra, the influential and powerful governor of the city. Ishbi-Erra has drawn the ire of the king, for he has proclaimed himself king of Isin, separating himself from the central rule of Urim. Why send a junior scribe like me when Inim-Nanna, the chief-scribe himself, can go, or one of the senior officials?

Again, it is as if the king has read my mind. "The rascal does not entertain any military personnel, and he speaks to our older officials with great disdain. He may lend an ear, even if in humor, to a young Scribe, for you will be no threat. But remember, Nemur, a threat and entreaty you will deliver."

Wonderful. The king's son may have had a hand in my wife's end, and the king will have me hanged in Ishbi-Erra's courtyard.

The king continues, "Inim-Nanna says you are temperamental, argumentative, and refuse to accept things as they are. I saw that too. And that is the fire I need in my scribe as he stands before Ishbi-Erra. You shall nag him like a wife, harangue him like a grandmother, and speak eloquently, expressing a case like a scribe. Can you do that?"

Should I fly like a crow, Your Majesty, annoying him with my cawing?

"I am honored by the responsibility His Majesty entrusts me with. And I beg the chief-scribe's indulgence, for my behavior is not with malice but curiosity."

Inim-Nanna, who is standing behind the king, scoffs but says nothing. No doubt the man is smarting from yesterday's humiliation. But I have the king's patronage. For now.

We prepare for a dictation. I use a sharp reed quill to etch the script on a wet clay tablet placed on a clean stone platform. I carefully cut into the clay, holding the pen at an angle, and let the cuneiform lines take shape as I cut deep enough for the letters to hold. It is a time-consuming process, one that involves taking an initial draft and then refining it—either on the same tablet, should its composition allow, or on a fresh one, for which clay is brought in by the palace servants. Once the etching is complete, they take the tablet away to dry in the sun before placing it in leather and sealing it with a royal wax imprint. The king inquires of my welfare in the meanwhile and suggests that many young women would be willing to marry a scribe. I nod without commitment.

The chief-priestess Geshtinanna is present on this occasion. She says it is common for people to reconsider their position when ready to travel, for such is human nature for the preservation of self. She then gives me a long lecture on healing from grief and leaving it behind in pursuit of duty and devotion. As if that would bring any solace to me. I accept their lectures without argument. What I find odd, though, is why the chief-priestess is adamant that I put this behind me quickly and find someone else. The commoners are flies to royals, flicked with a finger and forgotten.

What is her role?

But even as we wait for the tablet to return dry, a messenger comes running to the throne room. It is about the Martu. A new group has deliberately defied guard orders and is squatting near a fertile segment of the river, not far north of Urim. This is an alarming development— for we know that the Martu are sometimes like a pestilence. It appears a military garrison has managed to surround them, but the raucous bunch, armed with clubs and slings, has been creating unrest, much to everyone's surprise. The commander is seeking the king's direction on what to do. King Ibbi-Sin calls for another clay tablet and delivers a hasty order.

"You will first go immediately to this garrison, deliver the order and ensure it is executed, and then leave for Isin."

I curse having to go on this distasteful mission. I hope no one slings a rock at my head. I am thankful that the king orders a small royal detachment to accompany me to the site of unrest, and then that four guards, instead of two, will come with me to Isin. It is about a five-day walk from Urim, in the north-westerly direction, to Isin on the other side of the Euphrates River. I have barely recovered from my long walk and return from Larsa, and I will be on my way again, on an exhausting march to a scary man who is so bold that he defies the current king of Sumer and sees himself as king. Father Enlil laughs at me and shows no pity.

After rest, waiting for the dried and sealed tablets, we determine it is too late in the evening for me to be on my way, but I will be leaving as soon as the sun makes his presence felt. The long walks will do good and bring clarity to my thinking. If the royals think I will forget my wife's death and the circumstances surrounding it, they are sadly mistaken.

It is both a pathetic and sordid sight—a group of beastly-looking people, semi and completely naked, women and children included, sitting in large groups while surrounded by armed soldiers.

I can see the impact of the corralling. Dead are littered around, a result of unarmed men fighting soldiers. But there has been no slaughter. The local commander has done a commendable job in controlling this incursion, but we can see the exhaustion in their faces and postures, having held this group for more than three days at least, as they waited for the king's orders.

There are two hundred to three hundred people, with about a third being women and children.

The whole place stinks of feces, urine, sweat, bloating corpses, and marshy mud, as expected when unwashed humanity is forced to stay in place. No doubt many are hungry, for I hear children crying and screaming, mothers lamenting and begging soldiers for food to feed their children, men arguing from a distance with stone-faced soldiers. This is a plain land near the marshes. One can hear the river flowing. The mangroves and reed clusters and palm tree are abundant. The soldiers have separated the sheep and the cows that came with the Martu nomads.

One of the royal guards speaks the language of the Martu and will act as the interpreter. I have been asked to convey two things: an order to the Martu, and then an order to the garrison commander.

This is going to be unpleasant business.

For most of my life, I have been in Urim, which has been peaceful under the king even as he waged wars in our frontiers. I have traveled many times to neighboring cities—but it has always been to governors' courts where I have been received respectfully, where the people are my own, and where there is no danger of violence. This is the first time I am confronted with an unwashed mob of the Martu. Now, I know that the Martu are not known for culture. These are people who go without a bath for a month, unlike us, the cultured people of Urim who find the time for ablution at least once in six days.

I first ask the interpreter to find me the chief of this group. After much shouting, a tall, elderly-looking man finally makes his way before me. All he wears is a loincloth, and his body is full of dark splotches and scabs. His hair is knotted, and his remaining teeth are rotten. Even from a foot away, his odor is overpowering. We complete short and curt introductions, and I tell him that I am here as the messenger of the king to convey his orders. The man nods and accepts. He says he is the chief, and that he represents the will of the people and those he is commanded by, meaning the nomads have a chief-of-chiefs. This is a surprising development.

"The Martu have invaded our pastoral lands. You have been ordered by the king to stay west, and you must leave."

The chief shakes his head. "Gods give land to all. Our people will die without access to the river. Your king gives us no quarter."

"You squat and do not leave. You destroy fertile land. And you have fought our men."

"They have prevented us from taking what is ours. Our chief demands we take what is ours."

The hubris of the man! Or the sheer stupidity.

"I am not here to negotiate, chief of this tribe. I shall now read the king's order."

Men of Martu, hear the voice of the king of four corners, Ibbi-Sin, who tells you this:

You may seek comfort in the lands that I, king of four corners, lord of all this land and Akkad, allow you to. And you shall leave all others.

And so you shall do, or none may live to see their children grow or feel the embrace of another.

It is a short, pithy order. Get out and go where we have allowed you to be, which is not a lot of places. I understand the Martu plight, but it gives them no authority to invade our lands and put our farmers and tradesmen in misery.

The Martu chief listens quietly. And then he does the most inexplicable thing.

He spits on me. The vile bastard drenches me in his foul expulsion, causing me to stagger back. He screams something, and suddenly his entire clan, emaciated as they may be, rise to their feet and rush toward our soldiers.

What is driving these fools?

I run back to safety and am covered by the guards.

The stones are flying from Martu hands, and one barely misses my head as I duck.

I hear the garrison commander scream orders, and then suddenly, this is no longer a standoff.

I watch in horror as close-knitted soldiers keep their leather-and-hay shields up and begin to hack the attackers with axes. This is no match, and there is no mercy. A soldier grabs a wildly screaming, charging woman by the hair, yanks her to the ground, and then hacks off her head with one mighty swing. The screams rent the air, and limbs pile on the ground as axmen hack off the hands, heads, and legs of people, whether they are charging or lying down. The gray-brown grassy land is drenched in blood. Even children are not spared—soldiers drive spears through them right into their mothers' chests, or smash their little skulls with the back of the axes. The frenzied attack suddenly turns into a great mass of lamentation, with the men trying to fight but the women pleading for the soldiers to stop. I have never been so close to violence before—I have heard of great tales of valor and wars, but this is none of that!

They are not stopping. Their bloodlust has exploded. Our soldiers attack defenseless people lying on the ground in supplication, stabbing or hacking them. Soldiers drag women to rape amidst bloody limbs and body-less heads. I am horrified at the scene. This was not the king's order. No one was supposed to be massacred! I frantically look for the garrison commander, who is standing on the periphery and shouting at his men. He is excited, and his orders are encouraging them to continue.

"Tell them to stop!" I shout at him, for I have never felt a greater kinship to these foolish people whose demand is simply land for them to live. They are no soldiers. Barbarians they may be, but they bleed the same, they cry the same, and their mothers try to protect the children the same. What gods sanction savagery? Why not beat them and have them leave?

He looks at me like I am mad. "Stay back, scribe! This is not your domain to order!"

I do not relent. I have seen enough. "The king has not sanctioned this massacre! You are wasting valuable slaves when we need them, and the king will hear of it," I bluff. It is true that those captured can make good slaves, and those we do need. Whether the beastly Martu can be tamed enough is a question, but we have seen many Martu live harmonious lives in Urim, having converted to our ways.

He snarls at me and raises a hand to strike, but then he stops, knowing that to inflict violence on me when on a king's errand will mean certain death. His bloodshot eyes blink a few times, and he steps back. He turns toward the murderous scene, and I can see him dithering. What man enjoys the pitiful cries of dying innocents? In one corner, two sadists hold a boy as a third hacks off his leg, shouting with glee.

"Stop them! Or I will report this to the king!"

Finally, the commander pulls out a whistle from his waistband and blows it loudly. It takes a few more orders and whistles before the bloodthirsty soldiers stop what they are doing and step back. Most of them are painted in red, their faces mad with crazed violence, and before them lie the majority of the Martu, butchered like pigs.

A few remain—huddled, shaking, crying in a corner.

I know that the injured will be left to die on these fields. My face feels hot. I swoon but manage to control myself. I have to try not to vomit–

A gush ejects from my stomach through my mouth as I empty the morning's contents. I hear someone laugh. These men are beasts... these are not the civilized men of Urim and our land. Since I have never been to a battlefield or a raid, it may be that we have always been like this. I have heard that the Akkadians and the rough men from further north, the Assyrians, are even worse. What could be worse? My cocoon of safety as a scribe has been shattered today.

Summoning my courage and knowing that I hold authority as the messenger, I pull out the other tablet. I know what it says.

I speak to the commander, saying the words of Ibbi-Sin, your king!

The destroyers of our lands must not go unpunished. Beat them away, as you must, but so shall you make an example of fifty, and have

them hung and scourged to their death. May
there be laments of their women and children.
This you shall do. Those alive shall be brought
to Urim in fetters as slaves.

I pretend to read it silently, and then I tell him loudly.

I speak to the commander, saying the words of
Ibbi-Sin, your king!

The destroyers of our lands must not go
unpunished. Beat them away, as you must, but so
shall you make an example of fifty, and those
you shall beat thrice and then brought to Urim
in fetters as slaves.

The commander looks puzzled, but then there is no man
here who can read.

To change a king's message is cause for immediate
execution, but I am not returning with this man to Urim,
for I am away to Isin, and I can always feign ignorance if
questioned. I do not care if this vicious monster is executed
himself. But then, it is unlikely the king will ever speak to
this brute and ask what happened. The slaves will vanish in
the underbelly of Urim, sold with a nice profit rendered to
the palace. The Martu, by nature of their backward ways,
do not make good slaves, for it is like teaching dogs. Few
show signs of intelligence—or at least, that is what I am
told—and that is why we do not take too many Martu
slaves. But this is a sad caravan of poor people. The Martu
chief's words give pause—what did he mean by saying his
chief expected them to take what is theirs?

I address the commander. "There is something the chief
said that requires me to understand more. Have you ever
had these nomadic groups organize themself on behalf of a

higher power? Or have a purpose other than occupying foraging land?"

He looks puzzled. His anger toward me is now somewhat cooled. The excitement has worn off, and he is looking at what he has wrought. "No. They come in small groups, settle where we allow them, and leave when we order. We even trade with some of them. But I have heard of them being more aggressive further east."

"Can you have a soldier find the chief for me, if he is alive?" I ask. I can barely even look at the field of death with the bloody stumps and lifeless bodies.

He reluctantly orders his lieutenant to find the chief, and as we wait, I ask the commander, "Have they resisted this way previously? With violence?"

"I hate them. They are animals, but no, they have never pushed violence. They are belligerent, dirty, argumentative, and we find a way to settle them without killing too many."

Too many he says, unironically.

I must convey to the king, whom I saw as one with lofty ideals but not much anymore, that something is changing with the Martu. They are beginning to take the shape of invaders rather than foragers. This is a dangerous sign, for the Martu are many, and we know they control towns far north. Does the king know about how the Martu are organizing, or does he think the enemies are all within, or from the far kingdom of Elam?

It is a strange choice—to help the king against our invaders, or to go after his son, who had a hand in my wife's death. The last few days have been a curse, but the gods have kept me useful and alive for a reason. There is a new fire burning within me. My zeal cools when I realize the king has his network of spies and advisors and priests and shamans to give him guidance. Who am I to tell him about the Martu developments?

"Their chief is dead," says the lieutenant, who has returned from his inspection.

I am not surprised.

The commander begins the mop-up operations.

Those injured and lying down are put to death with a quick stabbing or an ax to the head. The horrifying part is what they do with the little children—for they are no good as slaves, and they cannot be cared for, and the soldiers suddenly do not want to take their blades to them. Instead, they haul them to the swampy waters and drown them.

I can barely look at the thrashing little legs and hands.

The whole affair is a disgrace. They tie up the remaining twenty Martu men and five women, all bleeding and naked, and whip them until angry red welts rise on their bodies. The captives barely have the strength to wail, and a few collapse to the ground. The soldiers tie ropes around their necks and line them up. They will be dragged to Urim, where some will survive and others won't. We do not treat our slaves harshly, but then the Martu are treated worse than many others, for the people see them as barely human.

I am not done, for my curiosity is piqued. I walk up to a healthy-looking man, in his middle age, and summon the interpreter.

"Why did your chief tell you to fight, even though you have no weapons?" I ask him.

He looks at me with his dark, shining eyes. "What Atturapi demands, we obey."

"Your god asked you, unarmed men and women, to fight our soldiers?"

"He is no god, but god he is," the man says cryptically. "And him we obey."

"Is Atturapi here, with you?" I ask.

The man shakes his head, *no*.

"Is he the chief-of-chiefs?"

The man signs a *yes*. It reaffirms my theory that the Martu are evolving in their tactics. Someone yanks the rope in the front, and the slave train begins its miserable journey. And it is time for me to move, to go north, to governor/king Ishbi-Erra, the scoundrel who calls himself king. And I, a lowly scribe, am supposed to negotiate with him.

I break the king's order tablet to pieces and throw it away. There is now no evidence to argue about. I order my four guards to join me, and they drag our ass along with food, water, medicines, clothes, money. I hope that the routes are safe. The lead guard holds an insignia of the king's seal, which means we are to be afforded safe passage and shelter.

I try to shake away the grisly scene before me, traumatic and no doubt to haunt my dreams in the days to come, adding to my miserable state.

I gesture for my men to follow me. It is several days from here to Isin, and we do not have time to lose. As I pick pace on that dusty path, my mind is a frothy ocean of uncertainty.

CHAPTER 13

NORTH OF URIM

THE WATCHER

The man looks at the distant figure of the scribe Nemur speaking to one of the tied slaves. *What is the scribe doing?* he wonders, for a messenger must give his message and move on.

The ways of the learned men and their arrogance for knowing how to hold a reed pen annoy him. The scribe is a healthy man, but he is no soldier. His slim limbs have never held an ax or run a few miles while pursued by violent attackers.

It amuses him that the scribe had vomited copiously at the scene of the Martu violence. But the man has his orders, and he will follow the scribe to wherever he goes. It is warm, and the air shimmers in the heat, causing the figures to dance. The man has dressed like a merchant, and his six soldiers look like innocent cattle herders. The route from Urim to Lagash and Isin is a well-trodden path of many a trade caravan, and their presence would not be unusual. The route is desolate and with few people.

He checks his scabbard and scratches his beard. There is something odd about this scribe—he is defiant. He had not shown cowardice when he had been arrested or when he had been thrown in the dungeon. The eyes showed fire. The man does not know what the scribe had done, for the stories about him are strange—that he suspected someone of having caused his wife's death, but that his wife had traveled, and the scribe's fellow from his school had been murdered. What has this man done?

The man is perplexed by the scribe's stubborn argument on behalf of his wife.

But those questions are not for the man to resolve, for he has his orders.

And so, Enkidu, the Akkadian who has made Urim home and sworn loyalty to the crown of the land of Sumer, flexes his muscles and begins to move once Nemur finally gets on the road.

But Enkidu's guilt gnaws at him, for he has a secret that is creating an unusual kinship with this lanky scribe.

CHAPTER 14
ON THE WAY TO ISIN
NEMUR

I decide to stay far away from Lagash, choosing to avoid another crowded city where I might come to harm. I no longer know where the governor's loyalties are and whether he will be kind to a man who bears a message from the king. The risk is Governor Nawirtum thinking I am on the way to Isin, to seek Ishbi-Erra's cooperation to punish him. One never knew with these men and their ambitions, and they would extinguish me like a cockroach.

The long, quiet walk is helping me.

It has cleared the cobwebs in my mind and allowed me to examine all facts around the death of my wife, the conduct of the royals, the politics of my land. And it is all discomforting.

But when I prayed to Father Enlil in the night, it occurred to me that the universe has given us a certain purpose and influence. A marsh can only go so far from the river. Even the sun lasts half a day before he rests. A king has control of his domains, and those domains shrink and expand. A woman serves her husband, and a husband does what he can to bring beer and barley to the house.

The woman does not ponder all day about becoming queen, nor the man a king, the fish a dog, the priest a general.

Likewise, the twinkling stars and the chirps of birds tell me a message—that I must commit myself to what I can control. It is my duty, as a husband sworn to protect my wife, that I seek the truth behind her demise. It is not in me to change the course of my land's history or resolve the disputes of its kings. And once I return from Isin, I shall throw myself into uncovering the truth with unwavering focus.

I may be a scribe with no training to fight, but a will is a powerful tool.

The guards accompanying me this time are more serious men. They are respectful, watchful, and maintain a careful distance.

Once we cross the river to the east, the land is harsher—the roads are rougher, the ground rises and falls, and there are numerous bluffs and small ravines. The earth turns a greater shade of orange, and there are fewer patches of green. It is a hostile land, and lonely men may disappear, never to be found again.

We pass a few traders who offer friendly courtesy, and even a few straggler Martu who glare at us but go about their way. I have only been to Isin once, years ago, on a scribe visit. I had not seen Governor Ishbi-Erra then, or heard of his ambitious nature.

We stop at a small watering hole belonging to an old farmer. It was a nice business for the man and his sons—we paid for the water, ate thick soup and pieces of goat meat, and I had a chance to wash. It was invigorating after days of dust and dirt. I was surprised that we had not been beaten or robbed yet. Perhaps the kingdom is still safe.

The next portion of the walk takes us along a narrow dirt road through low-lying barren hills. I fear these places, for they are perfect points for an ambush. Robbers lay low in these areas and confront unprepared travelers. I am tense until we pass this region to more open ground. The guards sometimes tell me to hold up a wicker shield over my head in protection—I cannot figure out if they do this for their amusement or whether they are serious, but my shoulders begin to ache terribly by the end of that march.

That is when I notice something far behind. I thought I had sensed something before and dismissed it, but I am more certain now—a slight rise of dust, indicating a group trailing us. When we are on higher ground, I make sure to turn back and peer into the distance. I am sure there was a gang coming behind us, keeping a distance. Who were they? I am suddenly afraid. I knew that we would soon enter an area known as the cow's graveyard. It is so called because it is a desolate place, barren, without any life or sustenance, and if one takes a wrong turn from the rough, barely visible path, one would be lost in shrubbery and stony wilderness, never to return.

My anxiety rises, but I am helpless. All I can do is tell my guards to hurry and to walk fast, pushing forward the recalcitrant donkey who shows no joy in this journey.

The cow's graveyard is upon us sooner than I think. Why would someone name this a cow's graveyard? I wonder, for no cow in its right mind would bother venturing into nothingness.

They say that if you turn east, go past the wilderness, and climb the formidable mountains far in the distance, you will be closer to the Elamite kingdom. I have never been there. Someday, I hoped I would take my wife to their city, so that she may bask in that language and ways of life. Such a day will now never arrive.

The cow's graveyard lasts half a day of walk, and we are halfway through. I am desperate to get out of this place before dusk, so that we may find comfort and lie hidden among the bluffs looming at a distance. "Hurry, hurry," I tell the guards, even as I am tired by the walk and exertion. I am also certain we are being followed, for the distant, barely-visible figures continue to trail us. Maybe they are just traders, for they have not gained ground. Am I worrying too much about nothing?

We cross the cow's graveyard without dying in it, and I am immensely relieved. The orange orb is beginning to set, for it is time for the god to rest. The wind is cooler, and the bluffs afford shelter for us to sit, eat, and rest. We have carried firewood and firestones for warmth and to cook the meat with water and salt. I make small talk with the guards. One of the men is from Urim, and he has never left the city since his birth. The other is from Eridu but has left his parents and now lives in Urim. The other two are hovering nearby, watching the now-darkening bushes and growing shadows. Where did that trailing group go, I wonder? I am certain they have not passed us. And looking back from here, from a higher point, I can see the trail, and no flickering lamps or a sign of anyone.

They have not lit the lamps yet.

Or they passed us as we were busy setting up our rest, away from the trail.

Or I imagined them.

I am tired.

We eat our bare meals, and it is tasty for our hungry stomachs. It brings energy back to me, and while I am tired, my mind is restless, afraid, and vulnerable. A scribe knows to wield a reed pen, and yet here, in these savage lands, what most understand better is the language of the sword and ax. My father once tried teaching me how to fight with an ax, but I found no pleasure in those arts. The royal school for scribes teaches its students basic sword skills, but the teacher had little interest—and I, as a student, had no wish to seek more from him. And after the revolting affair with the Martu days ago, watching the blades of axes slice through breasts and necks, seeing the impact of swords on legs and bellies, any desire to master the art of human butchery has died a miserable death. But mine is an exalted position right now, with guards around me all the time. I will have no luxury after the mission, and I am certain someone seeks to harm me.

My mind calms down as I lie with my leather bag as a support for my skull and look up at the sky.

The wondrous blaze of the heavens is a sight to behold. They teach us little about these stars in the sky. What they are, how they came to be, and whether they are lights from cities in the heaven where the gods keep those who have left this earth, or whether they are abodes of the gods alone, with the dead toiling in the netherworld.

My eyelids feel heavy, as if the gentle hands of the god of sleep are pulling them down against all my resistance.

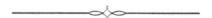

The sudden pain and shock is stunning.

I open my eyes in terror in the darkness.

Something or someone is pulling my hair and trying to drag me.

NO!

The night flame is burning, but there are frantic figures darting in the darkness. I try to scream, but my throat is parched, and barely a sound comes out in the moment of horror. As if by instinct, I kick around and try to fight off the grip on my hair, but my hands flail in the night,

116

grasping nothing. I come to my senses and realize that we are under attack. Bandits? The followers? Where are the guards? I hear swords clashing, and screaming, and the person lets go of my hair. My elbow hits a rock, and pain shoots up my shoulder.

I clamber to my feet.

Do I flee? Do I fight? I have no weapons with me, nor the skill. Suddenly a powerful arm grips me around my throat and pulls me back. I try to shout, but nothing comes out.

Is this it? I am about to die like a butchered goat in the middle of nowhere! Father Enlil, help–

"Be quiet. Quiet!" the voice hisses in my ear. It almost sounds familiar. Not one of the guards! I relax and trust the voice, for if he wished to kill me, he could have done so moments ago, smashing my head against a boulder or driving a knife through my heart. He pulls me back behind a large stone formation, even as my feet graze against sharp rocks and rip the skin. I keep my mouth shut until we are in almost complete darkness.

"Stay here," he whispers. "Go nowhere, and don't do anything stupid."

I can barely see the man, except that he is powerfully built.

He moves like a cat and vanishes.

My heart thunders so loudly in my ears that I can barely hear the shouting and fighting at a distance.

I take a few deep breaths to control my anxiety even as I mutter prayers. I think of running—but where will I run in this darkness? This place is not only deserted, but there are ravines and ditches everywhere. It would be laughably easy to stumble and fall into one, and then die of thirst and hunger while lying down and lamenting my life and my broken bones. I put my back on the rock and hide like a woman waiting for someone to save her. Oh, if only I had learned to fight! But my feet at like stones—they do not move, and I do not have the courage to dash into the fight and lend a hand in any way I can. I gulp several times, trying to wet my parched throat. And then, to be safe, I stumble around in the darkness until I find a nice, fist-sized rock and hold it in my hands for safety. This is my sad weapon, but it is better than my writer's fist. My eyes have adjusted now to the soft but very dull light of the half-moon. I can see the outlines of boulders and shrubs all around me. The fight is going on.

I wait for the sounds to subside.

What do I do if our assailants win? What if they come looking for me? Do I fight? Surrender? Run? I do not have to contemplate for long, for I hear a rustle near me, and suddenly a short man springs from the darkness. I can barely see him, but his murderous intentions are clear, for the blade in his hand glints in the moonlight. His knife nicks my forearm, but it does no more damage as I jump to the side. I swing wildly and sense the dull *thwack* of the stone contacting his body. I do not know where I struck, but he stumbles and grunts. My whole body feels like it is now alive, in fear, anger, rage. I lunge at him, and this time the stone in my hand connects with his skull. I hear the *crack* and his legs give out under him. He collapses in a heap. I hunch over him and smash the stone again on his head, and it makes a sickening sound as it splits his skull open. I can barely see him–and I am thankful for the darkness and that I do not have to witness his brain matter, or the blood. My legs begin to shiver now that the danger is over.

It is quieter, but are there more men looking for me? I take a few weak steps back to the darkness near a large boulder and wait there. I hunch and place my palms on my knees to recover—breathless, frightened, and hoping there is a kind end to this episode.

Where did I drop the stone?

I bend to find another one.

"Scribe, are you alive?" I hear that voice again. This time firm, louder. What if he is with the assassins and trying to trick me? I squat on the rough ground and do not answer.

"This is not the time to shit, scribe. Get up," he says. Blood rushes to my cheeks, and my heart is light with relief. I rise slowly, tracking his silhouette, waiting to see if he will attempt anything. The man has a sword in his hand, but he is standing there waiting for me.

"If I wished to send you to the netherworld, you would be dead long ago, scribe. Come with me to the fire."

I begin to shiver.

I muster my strength and walk toward him, but with my stone concealed in my hand. He says nothing and instead turns and begins to walk towards our campsite. It is a short walk, and when I arrive at the fire, the scene is chilling. Five men mill about near the fire. At least six bodies are strewn around, visible in the light, and I am sure there are more beyond my sight. One man is lying injured near the fire, groaning.

"You were of interest to someone, scribe Nemur," the big man says. I know I have heard his voice recently. And then it flashes to me! This is the same man who had arrested me at my house, and then dragged me to the dungeon. I may have heard his name, but it eludes me.

I say nothing. He makes a dismissive gesture to his men, who then fan out, ostensibly to keep watch for any other misadventure. My heart has quietened down, and strength returns to my throat. "Who are you?" I finally ask.

He appraises me. "You might have a word of gratitude for those who have bled to keep you alive, scribe," he says, his voice with a sharp edge like a finely crafted blade.

I have no idea what has happened, and yet he thinks I must offer gratitude. "I can offer what you deserve if you tell me who you are, and what happened here. Perhaps you killed my guards and planned to kidnap me."

He laughs. "For a man almost dead, your mouth has no fear, scribe," he says, "but I assure you that we have just saved you from a murderous gang. Two of your guards are dead, one is injured and unconscious, and the remaining one is with my men, patrolling the perimeter."

I nod at him. He walks toward me, and I am tempted to run. But I will not be laughed at today, for I have not only survived the attack, but also killed a man with a stone.

No sooner had I had these thoughts then I throw up again, and this is the second time in a few days. I hear him chuckling. After living for years in peace, with harmony and happiness, in just a matter of days I have lost my wife, been accused of murder and thrown in a dungeon, witnessed a massacre, escaped an attempt on my life, and killed a man with my own hands. Enlil and Inana have great plans for me, though they have laid that path with nothing but pain.

"Calm yourself, scribe. We will speak when you are ready. But you must hurry, for if you want to know who is behind this, we will have to squeeze that information from this man here," he says, pointing to the injured man lying near the fire. He is awake and has a large gash on his thigh, now partially bandaged to stem the bleeding. I do not recognize the man, but I understand the need for urgency.

"Let us proceed," I say bravely. "But for me to participate in his questioning, you must tell me what happened."

He nods. "We followed you from afar, and we have been tracking this group for the last two days. They were clever, concealing themselves away from the path."

"I may have seen you for the last two days, but at a distance."

He laughs. It is a disdainful, guttural laugh. "Those that you speak of were barley traders. They had nothing to do with this, and we are not fool enough to be seen."

My face burns with embarrassment. I was followed—not by one, but by two groups—and the one I worried about were grain traders. But why was this man following me?

"Who are you, and who sent you? I must know that."

"I will tell you all you need to know later, scribe. We must speak to this man first, before his life ebbs from him. Do you care to find out who tracked and tried to kill you, or do you want to know my life and purpose? My name is Enkidu, and that is all we will speak of about me now."

Enkidu? His name is Akkadian. I am intrigued, but this is not the time.

Enkidu is right. We must find out the purpose behind this attempt on my life.

We sit by the injured man's side. Enkidu is an unpleasant-looking man, and he looks like a dangerous criminal in the flickering glow of the flames. His large profile, big arms, thick face and a nose like a hawk's, dark dense beard, large eyes, and curly dark hair give him an aura of power.

"Who sent you, cockroach?" he asks the man.

Cockroach grunts and turns his face away.

"We have been following you for days. You are no highway robbers. Your men are dead. Good soldiers, but not good enough. Who sent you, and what was your purpose?"

The man mutters something but does not answer.

Enkidu slaps him hard across the face. The sharp sound cracks like lightning in the air. I flinch.

"Who are you? Who sent you?"

Blood drips out of his broken lips, and his stained teeth glisten in the light. "Money. Money."

Enkidu sighs. He pulls out a dagger from his belt. It is wet and glistening, coated with someone's blood. He holds it in front of the man's face and waves it. "Whether you wish to die quickly or slowly is up to you. Who sent you, and who are you?"

But the injured man is stubborn, no doubt having spent years in violence himself, and he grunts.

Enkidu's men have tied the man's hand behind his back and secured his legs as well. There is not much he can do. He suddenly grabs the man's legs, drags him, and throws his feet into the fire. I am horrified by the loud, horrible screams and the revolting smell of charred flesh. The man tries to roll, but Enkidu does not let go. The flames burn through the leg, and I cannot bear the howls. "Stop it, stop!"

Enkidu drags the almost-unconscious man's legs out and waits for him to regain his faculties. He is delirious with pain, and I can see the whites of his wide-open eyes and hear the tortured breaths of agony.

Enkidu leans toward his ears. "You will speak now, and I will pray for your family and end your life quickly and mercifully. Resist or lie, and I will take each limb and burn it to the bones, and then chunks of your flesh. I can go for a long time."

Does torture work each time? Do those under pain not tell whatever a man wants to hear?

The man's resolve shatters. He gasps and nods frantically. "Paid, paid by a senior man from the palace. Do not know the name. Do not know why," he says as he grits his teeth.

Enkidu nods. I am not surprised. "Go on," he says.

"To kill the scribe. Do not know why! To kill him quietly, away, make him vanish! That is all I know," he says. His lips quiver and he tears up. "Please, mercy."

Enkidu looks at me. I address the man. "Does the man who paid you have a name?"

He shakes his head vigorously.

"Did you recognize him? Can you describe him?"

A small gust of wind blows hot smoke from the flames toward us, causing my eyes and throat to burn. The *fpat pfat* sounds of exploding seeds in the wood feels like a welcome diversion.

The man speaks haltingly. "Tall. Big. Had an accent. Was hooded, dark, cannot describe much. Had an accent."

Accent?

"What accent?" I ask, puzzled. This could be important. A non-resident of Urim, employed by someone powerful in the palace, would not be commonplace.

"Elam. A slight accent of Elam!"

My heart jumps a notch at hearing it. *Elam?* My world is getting muddier by the hour. I know that the various things I have experienced are connected, but the gods do not reveal how. Like a complex puzzle of shell boards, I have all the pieces, but no picture emerges from them. And I do not even know why Enkidu rescued me.

We ask a few more questions that bring us nothing more substantial—these men were mercenaries, and they had been recruited by their handler, who had been summoned by this powerful man with the accent of Elam. He intersperses his every answer with prayer and begs for a quick death.

I finally nod to Enkidu, who places a hand on the man's forehead and makes a prayer. The man looks almost relieved and glad when Enkidu places his dagger on his chest and plunges it into the man's heart, ending his life as fast as a butterfly's flutter.

My legs are shaking from everything I have experienced and seen. I sit quietly for a while, even if my mind desires more answers...this time from Enkidu.

He is sitting on a flat rock, sharpening his knife nonchalantly, as if this savagery was a boring episode of his life. There is no question that if I cross this man, he will kill me with the same consideration that he might give an insect.

Such are these beastly men. And somewhere, in a dark recess of my heart, I wish I had the same skill with a dagger and the same bronzed will to fight an enemy without fear. It takes a while for me to recover and regain my faculties, but I am bolder, more determined, and now with a hunger to resolve the unknowns and bring to justice the perpetrators. Even if it is the prince, in his sickly bed and sicker mind.

I do not know where we are in the hour of the night and if dawn is further away, but I am now awake.

"I owe my gratitude to you for saving my life, Enkidu," I finally say. He makes a curt bow but says nothing. "And I have questions for you."

He nods. "There is much to say."

I take a deep breath. "Who sent you, and why?"

He smiles. The man can smile, I realize, thinking that there are happier emotions in his heart.

"The king. His Majesty Ibbi-Sin sent me."

CHAPTER 15

SUMER

NEMUR

I am shocked at what I hear. The king? I splutter, "The king sent you? Why?"

The mystery deepens, for how would I ever guess that His Majesty, who cavalierly dismissed my sorrow, would send someone to protect me? But then I realize in an instant that it could be that he wished to ensure my message to Ishbi-Erra would be delivered without disruption. It had nothing to do with my situation or well-being, or the kindness of his heart, but because I carried an important message.

But then another flower of doubt blooms in my mind. If he wished to protect me, then why not send a larger contingent with me so that no one would dare attack? Enkidu and his men could have traveled with me from Urim.

Enkidu watches me quietly. "I do not know why, scribe. I do not ask the king *why*. I obey orders."

Of course.

"But I can tell you what he desired for me to do."

"Go on," I say.

"I was asked to trail you discreetly and observe if you were being tracked and to protect you from any ambush. The king did not say why, except to order me to protect you. And so shall I do."

My head is spinning from the developments. Enlil has woven a unfathomable web. He tests me at every step, and yet he keeps me safe. What is all this supposed to mean? I do not know. I aim to pray in the morning and seek favorable omens—but there are no chickens to sacrifice, and the sky is bare in this region, so no clouds or birds to give messages. Though in secret, my heart does not believe these omens much, for I have rarely seen an omen foretell anything of value. Perhaps the priestesses infer things better than scribes.

"Did His Majesty say anything else?"

"His Majesty does not need to say much else to his guard. He said to protect you, and that is all I need."

I let his words sink into me. Why would the king do that—unless he suspected that there was truth to my words? The king of our land himself thought something nefarious was afoot! His Majesty's tacit support infuses a great strength within me.

"You must sleep," he says. "The king has told me to break your bones if you do not deliver the message to the governor of Isin."

CHAPTER 16

ISIN

NEMUR

The governor of Isin, Ishbi-Erra, the one who calls himself king of the city and the towns nearby, is a pudgy, clean-shaven, bald-headed man whose oiled skin shines like bronze on a bright day. He fancies himself an emperor, for on his head is the finest lambswool shepherd's cap adorned with a shining lapis-lazuli and carnelian studded tiara. He makes himself tall by sitting on the tallest Syrian cedarwood chair with carvings of bull faces on either armrest. Enkidu and I remain kneeling until we are told to rise. My knees hurt on the coarse floor, and for the miserable trudge of the last few days.

"Rise. Rise, messengers from my brother Ibbi-Sin," he says.

Brother? The gumption of the man to no longer see His Majesty as king of all our land and Akkad.

I am unsure whether to call him with a royal honorific title or just governor, but my loyalty, even more hardened now, is with the king. For him, I will risk my head.

"We are honored to be in your presence, Your Excellency," I say. He nods and does not seem offended. Perhaps the governor of Isin is not full of himself, like a frog after a full meal, even if he resembles an unpleasant toad.

"And what does my brother wish for me?" he asks. Governor Ishbi-Erra has a soft, raspy voice, one that carries in a quiet room as if a corpse is dragging itself over it.

"His Majesty sends a message, Your Excellency, to be delivered with the utmost urgency."

He rubs his chin and takes a sip of wine from a clay cup resting on the wide armchair. His senior council all sit around him in an arc. I do not know any of them.

"Read it," he says.

I pull out the clay tablet from my bag. It is carefully wrapped in thick leather and secured by a wax-sealed rope. I break the seal, and Enkidu makes a show of slicing the rope. I have brought the brute with me to demonstrate to the governor that the scribe of Urim has the royal guard with him. I bow to the governor and to the tablet, and begin reading.

Speak to Ishbi-Erra, saying the words of Ibbi-Sin, your king:

The omens speak ill. Father Enlil tells me so through darkened skies and louder crows that the Martu monkey is preparing to descend from the mountains,and that his nomad hordes will ravage our lands and yet you, Ishbi-Erra, have not paid heed to my orders to fortify the frontier and build your forces. I have sent you silver for the purchase of grain through unhindered routes, and you have only sent me partial supplies and no men that I have sought. Your duty is to me. Where are your warriors who should have come to me to join my army?

The man from Elam shakes his fist. I have heard that he seeks to kiss the Martu monkey on his mouth and together to take the lands of Enlil, so how can you ignore my missives? Without haste, I ask you to send me one thousand men, 30,000 kors of grain, and 1,000 kors of exotic spices that you so readily trade with the far lands. And without delay, send scouts to the frontier to report to me the movements of the Martu and any signs of the army from Elam.

How is it that they know our inland routes, our weak towns, and the easiest ways to get to the Euphrates? Do not be weak on the spies in your city!

The scribe brings you my words, and through him, you shall speak.

I take a deep breath and look up. This is not a friendly message, and I hide the sadness behind it. I know that the king is desperate and feels besieged, for he is slowly becoming a king in name only, defied by his governors and losing his domains one by one. Ishbi-Erra's dark eyes show no emotion. His generous jowls are tight, but at least he has not ordered anyone to seize me and cut my tongue out. I have heard that the Assyrians in the far north do ghastly things.

"How is my brother faring, scribe? Why is he fearful?"

I realize that I must now offer an opinion, and I stand before the governor as an envoy and not a messenger. After all, I cannot keep saying that I have nothing to proffer.

"His Majesty glows with energy and has the heart of a lion, Your Excellency, and he wishes for the safety of all under his domain."

Ishbi-Erra nods and grunts. "Fear not my presence, scribe, for I am no Martu beast to injure a messenger in my person, and one sent to me by my brother. Speak your mind before this throne, and no harm shall come to you. If my person must respond to my brother, I must have answers to my questions."

For all his raspy voice and toady appearance, the governor sounds like a man of reason and not one given to uncontrolled passion. I have misjudged him.

With the power of my king before me and with the permission of the governor, I decide to speak what Enlil brings to my tongue.

"The king worries for the safety of Urim, for we are facing increasing incursions and news of even greater hostile presences planning to arrive at our gates. Blessed by the gods, he thinks that those loyal toward him have turned their backs to him as they seek their own pleasurable destinies, unaware or unwilling to recognize that what threatens His Majesty threatens them."

I exhale. But I feel immensely proud of my wise words. They are such that an experienced envoy—

Ishbi-Erra laughs suddenly, breaking my thoughts. "It appears my brother sent a minnow to a wolf! You think of yourself as an ambassador, scribe?"

The men around him laugh, and my face feels hot. But I have spoken plainly, and there is no reason for him to mock the truth.

But once the sniggers calm, Ishbi-Erra appraises me coolly. "As presumptuous you may sound, thinking that those who rule cities would not see it so, you speak as plainly as the Assyrian lands, scribe. That I do not dismiss."

I bow, relieved and somewhat proud that even my immature attempt has resonated with him.

"Now. He says he is in trouble. I know the incursions increase by the day. We have had large Martu hordes invade our grain fields and unexpectedly demonstrate belligerence when asked to leave. And this they would not have done without being induced by a different power."

Martu belligerence in Isin?

Ishbi-Erra nods thoughtfully and looks mildly surprised when I describe a similar situation near Urim a few days ago, when the king's forces massacred a field of Martu. But he does not offer commentary on my story; instead, he continues. "And yet, even as he confronts this menace, the great king of Urim, my brother, has he thought how smaller cities must feel if asked for support?"

The men around him watch me intently. There is nothing for me to say in response.

He continues.

"Isin is an island of strength, and strength it has, for I have fortified it," he says, flexing his flabby biceps and slapping them, "and I have fed and trained my men to be warriors. I have armed them with the finest copper and bronze, I have built my barges for trade, expanded my fleet, created guarded corridors on land for merchants to travel unmolested, heightened the walls, dug deeper moats, and stocked my granaries with enough to last a long siege. I do not allow the dead to remain in ditches, allowing foul demons to enter our world and cause sickness and deplete our fighting men."

His ample chest heaves as he says this, and as much as I arrived with disdain for the man, I am coming to appreciate his views, though I am no king or governor and have a superficial understanding of matters of kingdoms.

"And these I have done in the isolation of my city, with discipline, with the right offerings to our many gods, and with cunning. My brother has neglected his city. He has squandered away Urim's power in meaningless wars in borders, on expensive ceremonies Father Enlil and Nanna never desired, and by surrounding himself with fools who think with their cocks rather than with their heads."

I have to control myself from nodding, for then it will not be Ishbi-Erra that takes my head, but Enkidu soon after we leave the city. The direction of the governor's response is clear—no help will be forthcoming. Suddenly, the governor stands, and all the men around him scramble to their feet. I am suddenly afraid. An excited king, or one who purports to be one, can be dangerous, and I hope that he regards me as a messenger.

But the governor continues talking. "And to do all that takes time, money, sweat, and blood. Not something to be given away to those who squander it."

My face remains stony, but a debate rages in my head. *Am I allowed to speak with what little knowledge I have on the affairs of Urim?*

"Now, read that message again, and remember what I speak in response. You will craft a message in the end," he says and gestures for someone to prepare the writing clay.

With trembling hands, I read the message again as he paces the stone platform on which his throne sits. He looks comical as his belly shakes, but it is how many underestimated him, as he grew through the ranks in King Ibbi-Sin's army until he became a powerful governor who sees himself as king of his domains. *Do not be fooled by the ample jowls and large bellies,* I tell myself, and control a snigger that rudely rises up my throat.

"Now, listen to these words," he says. "The price of grain has more than doubled, and he expects his silver to deliver it at half the price. He seeks exotic spices and yet does not realize that his marauding troops have shut the routes that come along the southern land from the sea. I have sent scouts to the frontier, and there is now no sign of men of

Elam, but there is increasing hostility of the Martu—but he knows that. He speaks arrogantly of spies in my court," he yells, his voice cracking as he points to himself. "He must watch for those he surrounds himself with, for the boat that leaks is on his waters and not mine!"

I bow to him, waiting for a chance to speak. He then makes me repeat his assertions to ensure I have received them correctly. Satisfied, he returns to his throne and takes a long sip of his wine.

"I have granted you permission to speak. And I am a man of honor. What say you, scribe, speaking the words of the king?"

Many thoughts have swirled in my mind, and if I am afforded the freedom, then the bravest scribe of Urim will speak his mind and either go back a man with accomplishments—or walk the paths of the netherworld to join his wife, having kept his pride, though his work unfinished not having caught his wife's killer.

"His Excellency illuminates my little scribe's mind with thoughts I have not considered, for you are the great ruler of Isin, and I am a messenger and dust beneath your feet. And I kneel to His Excellency for giving this messenger his voice, for it must be allowed to speak on behalf of its king."

He nods and looks mollified.

I continue. "It is true that King Ibbi-Sin seeks the support of those that hold his land close to their heart, but the king's struggles are not all his making, for those who have lived in Urim, and traveled wide and far, know that Urim has always been more vulnerable."

There are no guffaws from the audience. Enkidu stands beside me, stone-faced.

My voice finds strength. The blessing and power of Enlil courses through me. "We are further south of Isin, and our eastern quarters have always required greater manpower to defend against lowland incursions. Like a woman scorning her lover, the river Euphrates has moved away from us, causing difficulty in harvest. And the recent droughts, the omens have shown, are not caused by the king. The oracles have examined goat's livers, the shapes of clouds, and the movement of fishes in the water, and none say that the king is to be blamed."

"You speak with conviction, young scribe, and I will allow you to continue," he says.

I bow and resolve to make the strongest case possible. I notice that even Enkidu looks at me with respect—he sees that the sword alone is not one that demands veneration.

"The king has sadness in his heart. He sees Urim as the mother cow that has nursed its calves, and now that those have grown and no more need the teats of their mother, they no longer come running for her call. She is in peril, and yet her lament is unheard."

I realize that I have gone from terming the king as a lion to suddenly representing a sad cow. I hope Enkidu reports none of this to the king.

Ishbi-Erra scoffs. "You speak the words of a poet, scribe, and yet I assure you Urim is no cow, the king no sad man, and the peril is of his own making. To heed his call now is to weaken our own defenses."

There is a certain quiet satisfaction in my heart that the exalted governor speaks to me as if I am a senior envoy. My boldness has appealed to him.

"The advisors say that without the combined power of the northern and southern cities of our people, the evil from Elam, with the help of the Martu, might drive a wedge in-between, cutting the regions off and then overrunning them," I say. This is something that was discussed in the council before I came here. If an enemy positions himself in the middle, the river and land trade will grind to a halt, putting everything at risk.

"That may be. And yet, does my brother not see that if the large cities do not maintain their strength, then Elam will begin by chopping off heads in the north, starting here, and then proceed south? Would it not behoove us that Isin, Lagash, and other northern cities remain strong, Urim finds its strength, and then we smash the enemy that comes in the middle?"

So much for my attempt at conveying strategy, for the governor has a point. I am no military advisor, and I do not know enough to counter what he says, except to bow and be quiet. There is nothing else for me to convey. Ishbi-Erra paces around the room. He has not dismissed me yet, and he is not the odious man I imagined him to be, as those in Urim made him out to be. I must not keep my blind faith in my royals.

"My brother seeks my help, and by the guidance of Enlil, An, and Inana, I do not wish to bring him greater sorrow. But I cannot give all that he asks. Has he messaged Nawirtum of Lagash?"

A gentle wave of relief washes over me like a pleasant waterfall on a hot day. If I go back with something, *anything*, I will have gained more royal favor, for the king is of the opinion that he will receive nothing.

"Governor Nawirtum has expressed his inability to help in any manner," I say, with much indignation in my voice.

"The scoundrel thinks of no one but his own hide," Ishbi-Erra says, "and he must be taught a lesson."

Yes, crush the cockroach.

The governor asks us to rest and return the next day to take his message. I am thankful for his generous hospitality, for it has been many long days since I have enjoyed a room, a soft bed, slaves who are at my call, hot meals, and a hot water bath. Enkidu joins me for dinner, along with many officials from the governor's court.

Governor Ishbi-Erra has not joined us.

At dinner, I learn new things that cause concern.

There are swirling rumors that the king of Elam himself has attempted a raid on a remote frontier town. And that he has met with a man of the Martu, though no one can confirm it. If this is true, then it further lends credence to the king's worry that Elam is up to mischief.

There is more—Ishbi-Erra suspects that there is a spy in the king's court, sending sensitive information on routes and fortifications, allowing for the Elamites to plan. Though no one can confirm anything, a good jug of wine and beer makes men speak of many things they would otherwise not—for example, one of the governor's young wives is known to expose her breasts to the guards and tease them, causing them great discomfort in their loincloths.

I learn that the governor is an able administrator, harsh with criminals, and has begun issuing tablets in Isin that proclaim his era as if he were a king.

Enkidu tells me that I have served the king and that even as a scribe, after having gone through harrowing episodes for days, I have maintained my faculties.

That night, sleep comes comfortably, though my dreams are haunted. I am chased by wolves and ripped apart. My wife is kidnapped by masked men, and I laugh as she is taken away. She is sinking in quicksand, and I drink beer as I wave goodbye to her. A beastly, haired monster drags her by her hair into the tombs as she begs for my help, but I am busy carving a message to the tablet. I wake up more than once, but eventually, the exhaustion takes over, and I finally sink into a deep slumber.

CHAPTER 17

URIM

ENKIDU

The return to Urim, with Enkidu's men and Nemur's remaining two guards, promises to be uneventful.

Governor Ishbi-Erra has given the scribe a message to deliver to the king, and while it is a fraction of what the king had asked for, it is something rather than nothing, which is what that scoundrel Nawirtum of Lagash gave, as per the scribe.

Nemur is an intriguing man, Enkidu thinks—younger than himself, but of much difference in his upbringing. Enkidu never knew his parents, for he was abandoned as a child to be brought up in a temple, first in Babiliim, and then in Eridu, and finally Urim. He knew no school, nor did his destiny belong to the priests. What he learned was to fight, and that is what he had done all this time. And now, he is part of the king's royal guard, feared and skilled. He is proud of his role, and while he has watched scribes from a distance, Nemur is the first he has interacted with.

Enkidu looks as Nemur walks ahead. The scribe is a slim man, tall, but he has the lithe limbs of someone who could be trained as an archer or a swordsman. He does not have the constituency to wield an ax. He speaks firmly, slowly, and with that irritating superiority of a learned man. There are a great many who can draw blood with their blades, but there are few who can wield a reed pen and carve words that convey meaning. Enkidu muses that while he sees himself as a warrior and superior, the reality is he is a bodyguard to the scrawny scribe with an interesting story. They have not spoken much, but the return walk looks more conducive for conversation. The few times Nemur has attempted to speak to him, he had to warn the scribe to watch the road ahead and let him fulfil his duties. But now, in these vast plainlands, where there is nothing as far as the eye can see, one might let down his guard.

He ambles up to Nemur, who has his head down in his thoughts. The scribe is a quiet man—eloquent he may be in a court, but outside it, he speaks little. Whether that is his nature or whether the events of these days have given him great distress, Enkidu is unsure.

"Scribe. Do you wish to rest?"

Nemur looks at him. "My legs are tired."

There is no place to call shelter, but Enkidu's men have the supplies to stand up a flimsy, basic tent. Nemur and Enkidu sit underneath it, shielded from the stare of an angry rising sun. No matter how small or large the offerings may be, Utu, the god of the sun, is relentless in his punishment during the day.

"The king has found a bold messenger. I have never seen a scribe speak up to governors—they grovel on their knees or hang their head low when harangued," Enkidu says.

Nemur smiles. He has a gentle demeanor, even with his curly dark hair disheveled like a man who knows no home. "I care less for my life than I once did."

Enkidu realizes that the scribe is battling his inner demons, and no one has lent an ear. All he has received are blows, imprisonment, and admonishment. He rubs his itchy beard. It has been more than ten days since he has washed. Just as dogs find it distasteful when their owners rinse them in water, Enkidu has no great love for wetness.

But his commanders and the royals have admonished him more than once that they would not have a man smelling like a carcass around them.

He turns to the scribe. "Do you still mourn your wife?"

Nemur looks at him. His eyes are sharp, like one whose thoughts have greater meaning. "You find it strange, do you not, Enkidu?"

Enkidu is surprised. *Do scribes have the power, by the hand of Enlil, to reach into another man's mind?* "Love for a woman is not unusual, scribe. But as your wife, she was property, and property can be replaced. Your wife is dead, but wives die all the time. Why not find another woman? Cattle die. Sheep die. Dogs die. Everyone dies. Men where I came from have so many wives, they do not even know if one of their wives has died. My wife and three children live in Urim. She serves me, as she should, like any wife, but should she die, I would mourn her for a day and find another woman. It has been many weeks for you!"

Nemur looks at him strangely. "Property she may have been, but she was the one for whom I held deep affection. Do you not remember your love for your wife when you were younger, Enkidu, or has all that bloodletting burned away any gentle emotions that may have been in your heart?"

The scribe's words sting. But Enkidu scoffs, "I do remember. I do not understand how those feelings linger when someone has departed. If I were to die, I have no doubt that my wife will receive permission to control my belongings and find another man."

"But it does not mean she does not pine for her departed husband, even a brute like yourself," Nemur says, smiling.

Enkidu struggles to respond. *How long can I keep up the lie?* "It is my brutishness that has saved you, scribe. And while you were given hints to put the past behind you and forge a new path, you do not seem like the type who might willingly accept such suggestions. You may be invested in your ability to read and write, making such men soft in nature, but there is a certain fire in you."

Nemur shakes his head as he squints and looks into far nothingness, where there is gray-yellow sand in unending desolation. "You understand my intention," he says.

Enkidu finds Nemur's case curious. "If you were willing to tell me what has happened, I may be of help. If His Majesty seeks to protect you, and by now it appears there is a desire to murder you, then the more I know, the better I am prepared, should the king ask me to be in your service."

Nemur looks surprised. "But this is not a situation where you can go and stab someone, Enkidu, for this needs a man who can think and investigate."

Enkidu laughs. "You think of me as nothing but a beast with a blade, do you not, scribe? In your mind, a man without a reed pen has no capacity for thought. Or those who live a life of violence have no ability to consider informed decisions."

Nemur looks at him strangely. "Your words are wise."

"I may be royal guard, scribe, but I have been an investigator for His Majesty on matters that have required delicate maneuvering, not force alone. They say I have a keen mind to uncover follies and dastardly deeds, even if I cannot etch a word on clay or read treasury logs."

The scribe smiles. It is a knowing smile. The smile of a perceptive man who can infer the thoughts in others. He looks at Enkidu and asks, "You have always longed to learn to read and write, have you not?"

Enkidu is surprised again. This scribe must be a shaman! That is a revelation Enkidu has never confessed to anyone.

The deep ache to *learn* to read and write! How much he longed to do it, and it was a strange feeling for a man who lived his life in the path of harm, deception, and cruelty. And now, attached to the scribe who does nothing but write and read, Enkidu's jealousy has reared its head and seeped through his mind for this man to astutely catch his desire.

Suddenly embarrassed, Enkidu stammers, "Read and write? What? You live in a fantasy where every man wishes to do so. I live in a world that has more practical demands, and those I fulfill with my swords and axes. What use is walking around with a tablet and a pen?"

Nemur does not respond. He smiles. He changes the topic and asks where Enkidu lives, and is surprised by Enkidu's description that his quarters are not as luxurious as he imagined them to be. Nevertheless, Enkidu lives in a prosperous part of Urim, though not inside the palace walls.

Finally, Enkidu surprises himself when he tells Nemur, "Should you need assistance, scribe, find me."

CHAPTER 18

URIM

NEMUR

I look at this fearsome rough man whose words have a certain erudition in them. He is not the fool I thought he would be, and the more I speak to him, the greater my opinion grows. He describes his background and the many trades he is an expert in, and I can see that he enjoys sparring with me. I am quite certain that he burns with a desire to read and write, for that is a skill that brings great dignity and aura, and yet he is too embarrassed to admit it.

"Why do you wear that strange helmet?" I ask him. It is rare for the fighters of Urim to wear copper-plated circular head protection. Most caps are leather and lambswool.

"I like it," he says as he adjusts it. It is irritating, as sunlight glints off it. "Besides, when you have many people swinging at your head, a metal-and-leather helmet is a better option."

I cannot argue with that explanation—it is a preference. I prefer a certain length, weight, and texture to my reed pens. Not all are made the same. Not all etch the same, and anyone who thinks every reed pen is the same is a fool or an idiot.

He then switches topic, and I do not begrudge him doing so. Enkidu is insistent that I tell him my story from the beginning of what happened when I returned to Urim from Lagash. We resume our walk, and with him beside me, I describe the chain of events. The empty home (*no, it did not*

seem like it was ransacked, but a few valuables were missing),
the revelation (*did your wife look beaten or abused in the
lineup? I do not believe so*), the supervisor's description (*we
may need to speak to him again*), Iddin's death, my
imprisonment—and then I reveal to him what Princess
Ningal said. He knows the rest.

"The prince? He..." his voice trails off. I know what he is
thinking: that the soft-spoken, well-intentioned prince
hides a monstrosity within him. Whether he was directly
involved or someone attached to him was, we know
nothing—for it is all speculation.

"It is an unusual situation. Sending a pregnant woman
to her death through the most devious means!" he says. I
am pleased with his words, which means his heart is
warming up to the theory that she was sent unwillingly.
There is much to realize, but this is a start.

"Will you be assigned to me permanently?" I ask.

He shakes his head. "It is up to the king's wish. But I
would not reject that idea," he says, smiling. "I can teach
you how to hold a sword."

"And I can teach you how to read a few words," I say
cheekily. He protests loudly at the uselessness of it all, but
the more he does it, the more I am convinced that the gruff
soldier would not mind a pen and tablet in his hands.

"Oh, what a comical sight it would be—the fearsome
Enkidu sitting daintily on a wooden board, balancing a clay
tablet as his bushy eyebrows focus in concentration while
he carves the phrase *I am a gentle scribe* on the tablet," I say.

He shakes his fist at me. "More jokes, scribe, and you
will enjoy a fractured bone!"

The return to Urim takes a lot more time than I wished,
for a storm puts us at a standstill, causing several days of
delay. With two days left to reach Urim, and with the

corridor protected by our garrisons, Enkidu takes leave of me for another task. "We will speak again, scribe," he says, and I watch as his strange copper-and-leather helmet vanishes behind a low, barren hillock.

As I continue to trudge home, I cross paths with another scribe. He is on the way somewhere, with the standard complement of an unwilling ass and two guards. I know this man—he is a senior to me, and we have respectfully acknowledged each other in many sessions. He is a slight man, and his face is full of pockmarks, a result of a dreadful affliction that Enlil cast upon us long ago.

"Nemur," he smiles as we near. The bells on his donkey make a pleasant sound.

"Another errand, teacher?" I ask respectfully, using the honorary title for more senior scribes.

"His Majesty wishes for me to meet the governor of Nippur. Where are you coming from?"

"Isin," I say, "meeting His Assumed Majesty Ishbi-Erra."

He sniggers. "Everyone is an assumed Majesty these days. The gods have taken your wife, I hear. May she enjoy the fruits in the garden of Enlil."

The man sounds sincere. Has he not heard, or is pretending not to have heard, all the sordid stories and the rumors surrounding her death? I thank him and say I am now looking for another wife—that is the easiest way to quell more questions.

"Are the roads dangerous?" he asks. "I have been to Eridu and several smaller garrison towns in the south, no sign of Martu incursions or impediments."

"The paths to Isin and Nippur are clear. You will come across the occasional Martu herdsman or trader groups, but none hostile."

He sighs with relief. "I am tired. Tired of all these missives from the king that bear no result. And he expects me to behave like an envoy and conjure favorable outcomes. I barely escaped with my life twice. Our ranks are decimated, Nemur. Not many of us left. Some have died, some have left, and the few remaining are being flung to the far corners of the kingdom on various useless missions."

I laugh. "Such is the story of our life, teacher. We must save the kingdom, and all we get is an ass and two guards."

He rubs his stubble and shakes his head. "I worry for our great Urim. The city is restless with all the rumors. And yet outside it, the land is as yellow and flat as it has always been, the river flows like it always does, and the night sky blazes as ever."

Only if you did not witness the Martu massacre as I did.

"That may be true, teacher, but you know that the grace of Enlil and Nanna can change at any moment and with any slight."

He nods. "I am jealous that you are returning. It is not safe to the west of Eridu. The governor there has complained that someone in Urim's royal court leaked a grain deployment schedule, leading to an ambush by a Martu gang."

I am surprised. Ishbi-Erra complained about spies in Urim. "Ishbi-Erra mentioned loose mouths in Urim. I will be conveying a similar message to the king."

"He is tired. He does not listen to wise counsel. And his son," the man says and clucks. "Enlil has not blessed him."

We both stand there, contemplating our lives. Finally, it dawns upon us that we both must leave and carry our burdens. I wish him well, and we part ways. The important learning for me is that my value has increased. And that means the king will care more for my safety than ever before.

The rest of the trip to Urim is uneventful, and for that, I am grateful to Father Enlil.

I am once again in front of the king. We have not yet revealed the attack, for the message from Ishbi-Erra is of greater importance. He has inferred from my deflated demeanor that the message is not one that brings much relief, but I hope that the meager assistance Ishbi-Erra has promised might provide succor.

"Read it," he orders. I observe the eager eyes of the council—the chief-priestess, the prince, his wife, a few other priests, General Nigir-Kagina, and Inim-Nanna, the chief scribe. It is as if all the luminaries of Urim are here, waiting for me to deliver magic to assuage their concerns. I briefly cast an odious glace at the sickly prince. What does he hide? And what is he inflicting on his wife, who has been kind to me? Or is the clever Geshtinanna, who wields much power as the chief-priestess, behind something? But a scribe must be careful before he points the finger at a royal, for it is like a lowly goat looking at a cub in a pride and hoping to convince the other lions to kill the cub.

I remove the tablet and read.

```
Speak to Ibbi-Sin, my king, saying the words of
Ishbi-Erra, your servant:

Your orders have come to me, and I have sought
the guidance of Father Enlil and his prince
Enki. May the inglorious Martu and the evil
Elamites not step into the king's lands! I have
```

fortified Isin, and the storehouses have grain
to sustain the cities, for us, and for you.
Your commands, my lord, bring much
consternation, but as your servant, and yet the
governor and protector of lands north, these I
offer:

One hundred of my best warriors will leave soon
to join the forces of Urim, and I have approved
10,000 kors of grain to be loaded onto new
barges and delivered to Urim at the earliest.
These I offer immediately, and then together as
we repel the Martu and Elamite danger, with the
blessing of Enlil, I will release more from my
storehouses.

I have dispatched scouts to far frontiers and
bring troubling news. Evil is on the move, and
he wishes to swarm us like locusts, with the
rat and the snake coming together, and for that
reason, every city, north, and south, must
maintain their own strength, for if one breaks,
so will others. Isin and Nippur will not be
broken by the Martu hordes or the Elam
slingshots, and may the great king protect his
cities. I have also heard the news, and Enlil
has told this for the favor of his son Ibbi-
Sin, that there is a wandering mouth in His
Majesty's court, and its words reach the ears
of the enemy, exposing the weaknesses of Urim.
That mouth, or mouths, must be shut.

Enlil surely blesses his son Sin, and may your
strength crush the dogs who seek to bite us.

King Ibbi-Sin stays silent for a long time. He mutters and
taps his fingers on the armrest. I can see the dark skin
below his eyelids, and his face is gaunt with stress. He is

receiving more frightening news of invaders from all sides. I do not know how bad it is, and I had not discussed it at length with Enkidu, but it is clear from Ishbi-Erra's and the king's behavior that the Martu incursions are rapidly getting worse.

Finally, the king speaks. "You have done well, scribe Nemur, to extract what little you could out of him. How willingly did he part with his offer?"

I make sure to take advantage of this. "Not much, Your Majesty, but with the authority and power of my king, I was able to use words guided to me by Father Enlil and convince the governor to do something, unlike the scoundrel Nawirtum."

He spends more time interrogating me on my time in Isin, learning of Ishbi-Erra's preparedness. He then turns to no one in particular.

"Ishbi-Erra is no gentle lamb. He points to spies in my court, and yet he knows much of the Martu movement, knows when to fortify, and has had no incursion in his lands. What is to say he does not seek to sow seeds of doubt here, even as he aligns with the enemy and strengthens his own hand?"

No one dares speak a word.

The king is getting noticeably angry.

"Here I sit, king of the land, lord of the people, even as the ugly Martu and the vile men of Elam knock at our frontiers, and my governors dare defy my ask! The hubris of men shall cause Enlil to smite their homes and burn their walls once I destroy the enemy," he thunders, and then suddenly turns on General Nigir-Kagina. "You! You have let them become too powerful, for if they feared that the general would be by their door, dragging them by their hair and lashing them for their impunity, I would not have to deal with rascals who speak much but do little!"

The tall and dignified-looking general looks flabbergasted. I know nothing about the relation between the general and the king, but to be lashed at in the full court is insulting. The general scrambles to his feet and gets on his knees, as is customary when receiving admonishment. But he says nothing and keeps his head low as the king rants.

"New sightings every day! Hordes from the east, from the west, like rats scurrying to destroy everything in their path, and no frontier city has stopped them!"

Who can point out to the king that he is responsible for keeping those cities in his control and ensuring that the incursions stop?

"How are they learning of our garrison locations? Our temporary checkpoints? Ishbi-Erra is behind this!"

These are becoming the ravings of a man losing his control, and it bodes poorly for us all. If we had the blessings of Enlil, then his son, the prince, would take power—but then he is sick in his body and mind, and I wonder if he is the one leaking information to the enemy for an unknown favor. Cure? Safety? *Succession?*

The gathering winds die down with little commentary from the rest of the council. The prince has barely uttered a word. His wife, Princess Ningal, has not moved her eyes from her feet, and chief-priestess Geshtinanna looks worried as she chews her lips—what are the gods whispering to her? The others, it is clear, are waiting to leave as fast as they can. I have not had the opportunity to mention that I had been attacked. Had the king forgotten why he sent Enkidu behind me?

I muster courage before the king begins to rise. "Your grace and protection have saved me from the cursed forces that have followed me, Your Majesty," I say, kneeling before him.

He looks puzzled. I clarify, for Enkidu has not yet returned to Urim to convey the details of the journey. "Enkidu, the royal guard who you sent for my protection, saved me from an attack," I say.

His Majesty's eyes narrow. I am hoping that the king will assign men to protect me and at least launch an inquiry, based on what we learned.

The king does not say much for a long time, and then he finally sighs. "It appears you will have to watch your own back for something you or your wife did, scribe. The kingdom has other concerns," he says, his voice tired and his eyes lacking energy.

With that, he turns and walks away. Despondency and anger fill me, but there is little I can do. I watch with dismay as the court is dismissed, and not one senior official looks at me as they leave in a hurry.

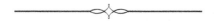

Exhausted, defeated, I return to my house.

I am thankful that it has not been ransacked—for everything appears to be where it should. The house is once again dusty and smelly. I leave all concerns of the world aside and spend time cleaning the floors, wiping surfaces, bringing water to wash, and arranging the few belongings. Neighbors peep in to inquire about my well-being and to inquire if the Martu hordes are nearby. The news of the incursions has spread in the city, and people are anxious. The worries are a reflection of the people's loss of confidence in the king, who they believe, and rightly, no longer has the strength to protect the kingdom. I give watered-down responses that while I have seen signs, none point to great danger, and that it is no different from the past when we waged war or fended off adversaries.

I have no work at the palace the next day, for twice every twelve days, I am afforded the freedom to stay home—and for that, I am thankful. I fall into a deep slumber for the night, for my mind and body can no longer bear the burden.

I wake up late into the morning, fresh from a dreamless sleep, and my mind feels invigorated.

A strange sadness returns, for the house is empty, and there is no comforting voice of my wife as she foes about her day. There is no one to ask if I am ready for food, or if I wish for a drink, or whether I need another fresh gown to wear, or if my hand is aching.

There is no teasing, laughing, nagging, or arguing. The silence is deafening in its message of loss. But I am filled with purpose. Enkidu was right—I am not a man who will forget and move on. But there is one major problem: I have no idea what to do next, except to pursue vague hints.

But as I sit to eat coarse bread, another frightening thought begins to form, like a dark, ominous cloud.

Elam.

That is all I have. A hint that the man who sent my killers had an accent of Elam. Why would an Elamite send someone to kill me? What connection may that have to my wife, who, as I know, has blood from the Elamite lands? My mind runs rampant again, for this connection creates many uncomfortable possibilities, each as mysterious as the other.

Was my wife having an affair with the Elamite man and killed by him or someone he knows? The prince? What is their connection?

Did my wife have anything to do with the question of spies in the palace who sent messages to Elam?

Did being a woman with an Elamite past bring her under suspicion, causing her to kill herself?

The threads are connected, but I do not know how.

Even as I contemplate my situation, I am suddenly startled by something that I never considered before. I scramble to my feet and rush to the corner of our little house, where we have a pedestal with the idols of our gods. Enlil and Nanna bless this corner. But the pedestal is a stone platform not affixed to the ground. I kneel before the platform and offer quick prayers, and then gently remove the stone idols and put them aside. I place my palms firmly on a notch on the side of the stone platform and push it as hard as I can.

It barely budges.

I push it again with everything I have, even as the coarse stone bruises my palms. The slab moves with a grinding sound, revealing the hollow beneath it. This is our secret hollow—not the most effective, but one that cleverly conceals another hollow beneath a thinner slab. In the upper hollow, I have kept a few carnelian beads and a silver ring as if to let a robber take what he has and leave, leaving the more precious chamber below unmolested. My intentions behind checking this are to ensure my valuables are intact, and to see if there is anything here, placed by my wife, that might provide any clue to what happened to her. A gift from a lover?

When I lift the lower slab slowly and peer inside, I see the usual objects first. Our small wooden box with silver and a precious ring of gold, a carnelian necklace, a lapis-lazuli ring, a basalt idol of Enlil, two ivory reed pens, a tablet contract from the magistrate asserting that this house belongs to me. These are all familiar items, for we peered into this every few days.

These were our savings.

But below them all, I notice something else, and my heart leaps. *Another tablet!*

I remove everything from the hollow, and with trembling hands, I lift it up gingerly, being careful not to break it.

It is a tablet, one that I have never seen before. It is not the fine clay that I use but a more coarse, hastily made slate. The ivory pens have clay stuck to them—I would never leave them that way. I have never used ivory pens to write, for they are my prized possessions.

Ninshubur! Ninshubur! It must have been her!

My hands shake as I lift the tablet.

And there, etched in Ninshu's hand, in her immature writing, are two sentences.

CHAPTER 19

EAST OF URIM

ATTURAPI

He looks at those before him—the haggard, the hairy, the old and the young, the women and the men, the fat and the thin. No matter how tired their bones and battered their bodies, their eyes speak a different tale. One of resolve, of belonging, of desire.

He has shown them that the Martu must have a place in the history of men, and that they deserve to be treated not as beasts, but as people. That their way of life, wandering and finding their pastures, is no more offensive to the gods than the ways of the people who build their cities and forts and claim those to be theirs.

He has seen, from the days of his grandfather, that their own way of life is threatened as the rulers of the empires near the life-giving rivers create their rules, preventing the Martu from living their lives. Where they have peacefully arrived, they have been threatened, beaten, deliberately kept corralled, cheated in trade, harassed on the roads, imprisoned for minor infractions, spit at, laughed, and scourged, as if they are no more than beasts. But under Atturapi, all that has been changing—they have been able to run over small towns and control the granaries, and he has introduced his people to the better comforts.

But he has started. Now, with officers from the camps of the king of Elam, who stays hidden in the mountains and will not return with an army until another two hundred days when the weather is more forgiving, he has been able to create a legion and equip them with crude but effective weapons. A few weeks ago, he had sent a group to test the garrison near the great city of Urim, his target, and those brave men and women had fought and died. It has given Atturapi the confidence that his people will fight, even without him at the helm.

"Glory will be ours!" he says as he raises his sword. "The city of Urim will be beneath our feet, their gods shall bow to ours, their women shall be beneath us, and their men will toil for us!"

A great roar arises into the cloudless, clear sky. "The king of Elam, glory be to him," he says, knowing that the officers of Elam are in his ranks, "has lent his powerful arms for our cause. And together, the Martu and Elamite shall put an end to the arrogance of the black-headed people!"

"We bow to the great chief of all chiefs!" shouts one of his lieutenants, to much approval. Atturapi raises a hand to silence them.

"In two days, we march. Our bravest, the first of their kind, beloved by the divine Belu-Sadi, blessed by the milk that flows from the breasts of his wife Belut-Seri, shall strike fear into the hearts of the men of Urim!"

There is much bellowing and celebration. For them to even conceive of the idea of invading the heart of Sumer is beyond anyone's imagination. There are many men of the Martu—clustered in various pockets along the river, near Babiliim, on the desolate far west beyond Eridu, pockets in the east near Tigris—and they have all received orders from him to be ready. Many have sent their representatives for the first wave. The weapons the first five hundred will take are crude stone axes, stone blades, wooden spears, leather-and-stone slingshots. He has not yet had the chance to secure a reasonable supply of copper and bronze, or to access enough capacity to forge weapons made of them. But that day shall arrive soon, he is hopeful.

Atturapi turns to a man beside him. "The king of Elam must know that it is Martu blood that will spill in a few days for the benefit of the king, and that must never be forgotten."

The man's cracking voice is a whisper. "His Majesty does not forget those who have strengthened his hand. Our glorious Inshushinak grants favor to those who worship him and those who help his people. And that is why I have more good news for you, this time about the routes that are unmanned and which side of Urim's outer wall is least protected."

"You seem to be able to come when you wish, with impunity, as you expose the innards of Urim," he says to the man.

"Powerful I am, and protected by the powerful, for my mission is sacred," he says with hubris.

So they say, until they are one with the ground, Atturapi thinks. But for now, any intelligence from inside Urim, and any help from Elam, are all welcome. He does not mind shedding blood, but only in quantities that do not harm his ability to fight.

The man continues, "And this sacred mission I shall continue until the doors of the temples of Urim are broken with battle axes, and the laments of their women fill the air!"

Atturapi grins at this man. He hates those who betray the lands they live in, but in this case, this man is giving Atturapi what he wants. Once Atturapi has it, he will snuff him like a bug, no matter what his allegiance to the king of Elam.

CHAPTER 20

URIM

It is dark and secluded. A perfect location for their union.

He grunts as he thrusts into her, and she stifles her moans. He is what she has waited for, for days, and while there is much to talk about, the heat of her desire must be cooled first. He grabs her breasts and kneads them, and she almost screams with pleasure but bites her lips. She digs her sharp nails into his back, digging in, cutting his skin, and drawing blood. She likes to do this, for it excites her greatly. The pain. The desperation. She wraps her legs around his waist, meeting his urgency, arching her back, and the considerate lover he is, he allows her to explode with her orgasm first. She is hot and burning, and she lets him continue until he is spent.

He falls away from her, and they wait for a few moments to recover. He reaches back and touches his back, checking how much he is bleeding on this day. With her mind now clear and free from the fires of passion, she turns to him and asks, "How is he not dead yet?"

In the darkness, all she can hear is his breathing. She gets impatient and scratches his shoulder with her sharp nails. He winces with pain. With her, there is never only pleasure.

"It is difficult to kill a man who has the king's grace without drawing any attention. You never know who is watching!" he whispers close to her ear.

"But you know much about the king's guards!" she says. "That man is dangerous. His mind does not rest, and he speaks with impudence. You thought he would forget his wife, yet he clings onto her memory like a dog to a bone."

"How did a lowly scribe become a threat?" he says, almost whining. "I should have had him stabbed as soon as he arrived from Lagash, even before he found about his wife."

"Can we not haul him in on a charge of sedition? Ensnare him in the fact that his wife was a woman of Elam's blood? And then execute him?"

He shakes his head so hard that she can feel the bed beneath them shake. "No, no! He is a royal scribe. He cannot be arrested and tried without the king's presence. It does not matter what the charge is—sedition, blasphemy, murder, rape, freeing another man's slave, whatever it is. That is the law, and the king, in particular, favors him."

"What use is complaining about it now?" she says, cross with his stupidity. What should have been a non-event threatens her. That stupid chief-scribe who arrested Nemur caused the whole mess of him appearing before the king, making him a protected man.

"It was your idea to send her as a traveler," he hisses. "It might have been easier to have her kidnapped."

She finds his stupidity irritating. While he brings her pleasure on the bed, his thinking leaves much to be desired. "She was a priestly maid of the palace. No one would be willing to kidnap her. Besides, violent death or disappearance would have caused the palace guard to get involved. And you know that."

"I control the guards."

"Not all!" she scolds him. Even in her exalted position, there are limitations and lines she is not allowed to cross.

And situations she should never be tainted with—being implicated in the murder of a pregnant woman, a maid of the palace, and in service of the gods, is one of them.

They are quiet as she contemplates what to do next. She murmurs, "It is too risky to have him attacked and not draw attention. Who knows what else he has been saying, and to whom? We have to be exceedingly careful. We have much to lose."

"Your ambition burns hot, my beautiful!" he says as he pulls her hair and smells it. She hates it when he begins his endearments, for she cares little for them. When this is all over, she will discard him like trash.

"You must exercise the utmost control, or find yourself hung from a wall and flayed," she warns him. She wants him gone, not tortured and dead.

"Of course, of course," he says.

"The scribe needs to vanish. The gods sanction it, but how shall we do it without more noise?" she says as he rubs her belly.

She looks at the darkness above and hears him breathe. She has little confidence that he can come up with an original idea, but he is a faithful servant when it comes to carrying out her wishes. As her body begins to cool, her mind ignites with a new idea.

She taps his shoulder. "Is it true that the Martu are preparing to move on Urim?"

"What do you mean? They have been conducting raids and minor incursions for a while."

She controls the urge to lash out at his stupidity. "No, you fool. A larger armed attack on the city. That is what is being discussed these days," she says, her voice rising in anger at his ignorance.

"Shh. Keep your voice low," he tells her. "Ah, yes. That one. Yes. I do not know when."

"Is their army big enough to bring down the city?" She would be surprised if he said yes.

"No," he whispers. "They are not anywhere near that strength."

"But if they appear by our walls, will we be reacting with force?"

"Yes. The king must show strength."

"I know that," she says impatiently. "Will the king send all his forces?"

He shakes his head. "The king wishes to preserve his standing army for larger battles ahead, of which he is sure will happen, and you know that. No, not all his army for these minor battles."

"He has not been discussing the plans in the council I have been in."

He runs a finger along her cheek. "But he has, in the ones I have."

They have the advantage that while she is in some confidential gatherings, he is in others. And together, they are privy to much detail of the inner workings of the kingdom, even if his station is lowly compared to hers.

She runs her finger on his chest. "I have another idea..." she says as her hand moves down.

CHAPTER 21

URIM

NEMUR

I stare at the letterings on the tablet. There is no question it is Ninshubur's, for I have taught her to write, a desire so strong in her that she never tired of nagging me and would not heed my words that women had neither the intelligence nor the right to learn to write. And when I made progress with her, I was surprised that her capacity to learn was no different from the men in my school, thus putting to question another statement relayed to us by our teachers as fact.

The sentence is crude, as if written in a rush, but it is clear.

The poisonous moon sends honey to the one-horned bull

O my beautiful Urim, may you not be under his wicked leg.

I stagger and sit, stunned. What was this? When did she write this? It takes me several minutes to regain my faculties and think calmly. I am certain that she did not write this and hide it from me. She wrote this when I was away, and she hid it for she feared something, and she died before she could see me.

I am certain. As sure as Father Enlil is the lord of this world and that the sun rises every day. Even before I begin to decipher the meaning, I am sure that she wrote it in fear and kept it cryptic to evade the comprehension of intruders. A tear forms in my eye even as I break into a laugh, as this sentence takes me back to a lesson I gave her long ago.

Sometimes, Ninshu, we couch our words in vague statements, allegories, and metaphors so that someone who intercepts it may not understand the true meaning. But those who have spent years in the art of reading and writing can see the true words beneath the surface of what is written. They know that to separate the fruit from its stem means to decapitate, to fold the hands for the skies means to obey the order of the king, to pour poison means to speak ill or—

It dawns upon me. I remember what I told her. *To pour poison means to reveal secrets of one to the other, to be treasonous.*

My heart begins to beat harder. What was she trying to say?

I read the sentences again, trying to decipher the meanings even as blood rushes in my ears. I run my fingers along the etchings, feeling her presence. It is as if she has reached out from the otherworld and is speaking to me.

"What happened to you, Ninshu?" I whisper, holding the tablet to my face. It is warm to the touch. She is talking to me, telling me to seek justice.

Father Enlil has kept me alive for a reason, after everything I have witnessed and experienced. An evil has descended in my life, and I will seek to drive it out.

Or I will die trying.

I am certain of a few things. That she did not kill herself. That she was murdered. That her killers seek comfort in their titles. That this has something to do with a spy in Urim. It is now a question of justice for my wife and the safety of this kingdom. With these absolutes, I will forge ahead—except I must now be exceedingly careful, for whoever is trying to hide her death is trying to kill me, to put to rest any investigation or uncovering of this danger.

But where do I begin?

And how?

I fantasize about being a stealthy, powerful warrior, cornering certain highborn and threatening them with a blade, extracting the truth, killing anyone that fights me with a lethal display of warcraft. But I have none of those skills, and my reed pens and lanky limbs scare no one, and I have no illusions about that. I am the man whose stomach heaves at the sight of massacres and whose legs tremble after an attack on his life.

My brief fantasy comes to a grinding halt, replaced by impotent rage. But Father Enlil has given me a keen mind, and my teachers have taught me patience, for no good comes of mad actions. No justice will be served if I am killed on a foolhardy mission with no thought. How do I get to the truth? How do I warn the king? I must think.

And then, for the next ten days, I do nothing except hide in my house and eat and think and engage in casual talk with my neighbors. There is no immediate mission, and the palace has asked me to wait for a summons. I send word to the chief-scribe that I am taken by illness and wish to rest, and my absence is granted. No doubt the unctuous bastard is happy not to see me.

CHAPTER 22

URIM

NEMUR

I know little of what is happening in the outside world. For all these days, I have kept my head low as I decide what to do next. I am sitting and drinking a cup of a hot herbal drink when there is an urgent knock on my door.

"Who is it?" I ask.

"We here on behalf of the general of Urim, and I am a captain of the Urim garrison."

What?

I am confused. What does the military have to do with me? I open the door to find three armed soldiers.

"Nemur, scribe of Urim?"

"Yes."

He makes a show of looking at a tablet. I know that these men are taught how to recognize names on a slate. His finger trails the tablet and stops midway. "Here," he says, as he taps on it.

I peer at it, and yes, I see my name.

"And?"

"By the laws of the Urim, by order of the king, by the authority of the general, you are one of the citizens who has been called to service immediately. Urim needs you!"

My posture surprises him. "Do you not know, sir?" he says, respectfully, knowing I am a royal scribe.

"Know what, captain?" My head is spinning—I have no idea what they are here for. I am not under arrest for something new, which is a huge relief, but what service is he referring to?

"An army of the Martu is nearing Urim, and the king has called a portion of the army along with a roster of private citizens to confront them beyond the walls."

It takes me a moment to digest everything he says. The Martu are getting ready to invade? A cold shiver runs up my spine—the boldness of those wanderers to approach the beating heart of our kingdom! But what else— what does this have to do with me?

"Our powerful army will beat them, no doubt! Am I expected to act as a mediator or pass messages?" I ask, realizing I have been called to service. Even as we are speaking, I can see more soldiers rousing and taking others with them. People are out in the street, for the news of the impending attack has spread. A dreadful thrill washes over me—I have never seen Urim attacked!

"No, sir. No messages. Our orders are to slaughter them all, but we will preserve the bulk of the army, for we believe this is a test battalion."

"Then what do they want me for?"

He looks at me like I am an idiot. His demeanor changes from one of respect to that of command and anger.

"You have been designated to be part of the citizen army," he barks at me.

It is as if someone has slapped my face. I stammer, "What do you mean, citizen army?"

He looks irritated and angry. "You are now a soldier, scribe, and under my officer's command. Leave with us now. You will receive a spear or ax at the gates. Now!"

His two men step around me menacingly. I am utterly flabbergasted. They want me to be a *soldier*?!

They have no patience for my loud complaints, for one of them canes me on my buttocks and screams in my face, "You are designated by the king's law, and those who resist can be summarily executed. Do you want a dagger in your gut and to die howling like a dog, without honor, with your body thrown for animals to eat, or do you want to serve?" the captain shouts at me. My face is hot, but I know I have no escape. I am aware of other conscriptions—and in fact, in small towns that are besieged, everyone, women, children, the young and the old, become soldiers.

Why did I think I was an exception?

Except that Urim has a large standing military! These are men sent on frequent missions, they are paid out of the royal treasury and the loot from conquests, they receive subsidies for their weapons and armor, they have ranks and even receive property and money after many years of service. The citizen-soldiers are randomly recruited men from the city, based on need and urgency, and we receive nothing. It is law and required in service of king, that's all.

How did I end up on a citizen-soldier list?

I have no time to ponder as they prod me to wear a knee-length tunic and a belt and leave with them. I hurry inside, ensuring that my valuables, including Ninshu's tablet, are hidden. I wear one of my runner tunics and tie a worn leather belt at my waist, and change to thick sandals I use for my long travels. By now, other men are walking with soldiers as their families wish them goodbye.

There is no one to see me away. Fear grips me like a vice as I trot with them. It is not a long walk to the southeast corner of the city, where the outer wall is about ten feet tall and the ramparts are narrow. There, as we near, are hundreds of men—a mix of soldiers, with their pointed, leather-and-wool hats, and citizen-soldiers who are milling about, looking anxious, waiting for orders and weapons.

I care barely talk as my throat chokes.

I am rudely shoved into a waiting group. The tall and heavy wood-and-copper doors of the southeastern wall are right ahead, and a formation of ten times fifteen or twenty is standing in front of it. I see archers, axmen, spearmen, and swordsmen. They are all dressed in ankle-length feathered skirts, leather breastplates, and shoulder protectors. The stench of sweat and urine is strong here, for many relieve themselves on the sides as they wait, and rivers of piss flow on the yellow-gray mud.

I know the section of the wall here, for I had been the one bringing messages from the palace to the contractors. This section is not as tall as the others since the terrain beyond it is rough, sloping, and gives the structure an advantage over any invaders. And for that reason, the palace had decided to save money and reduce the height and thickness. It was after the exhortation of one of the military commanders that the king agreed to finance the heavy double-door that is as formidable as the twelve other gates. The large, heavy crossbars are made of bronze. No one else has such doors—of that, I am certain, for it is us, the blessed of Enlil, who created it. Mixing copper with tin creates a product that shines and is harder and sturdier. My fear is assuaged by the fact that we have powerful defenses, superior weapons, and skilled warriors.

And now, standing and waiting as the sun inches into the sky, bringing the heat on our backs, I begin to think. How did I end up on this list when I belong to the rare and dwindling class of scribes? This is preposterous. It is like taking a rare mountain-donkey, the beast called *the horse*, on a swim in treacherous waters instead of keeping it on land. I am no elite soldier, and to waste me on a battlefield is beyond comprehension. Was the inclusion of my name random? Was it premeditated? Does the king know?

I catch a glimpse of a senior official—I have seen him in the court but do not know his name. I am certain he knows who I am. I push aside a few men and manage to get near him, even though he is surrounded by soldiers and is issuing orders to them. The crowd here is increasing, and the atmosphere is stifling.

"Lieutenant, honorable lieutenant!" I shout, jumping, raising my hand. I am taller than many of these men, so getting his attention is not that difficult.

He looks at me with a scowl, irritated by this intrusion, and then I see that his eyes light up with recognition. He gestures for one of his men to step aside, letting me near him.

"I beg for your consideration, lieutenant," I say as deferentially as possible, bowing.

"What is it?" he asks curtly. "You are a scribe, are you not?"

"Yes, I am. The king uses me for messages to the governors. I do not know why I am here?"

He looks puzzled. "Are you part of the citizen contingent?"

"Yes, sir. I am a scribe."

"Was your name on the recruit list?"

"Yes, but—"

He exhales. "Do you think you are special compared to the farmers, metalsmiths, grain sellers, bakers, and roadmenders who are here today?"

I stammer, "But the king—"

"Scribe, your messages will mean nothing if Urim falls. Now get back and follow your instructions."

"Lieutenant! I—"

"Back!" he screams in my face. Two of his men shove me back and glare at me. One whispers, "Make no noise. Those who protest here die bad deaths. Go back and wait!"

My skin is hot, and I walk back to the citizen-contingent. We are about two hundred strong, by the measure of it. We are packed here, in one corner, as the soldiers continue to form rectangular patterns and stand in formation. No one has told us what to do or expect. Far behind me, a line of armed men are standing across the pathway, ostensibly cutting off anyone who thinks of running. I crane my neck to assess the situation—by my rough estimation, there are about four to five hundred in all. Nearly half are citizens.

We wait.

I am too nervous to engage those around me in chatter.

They look frightened.

We *still* do not have weapons!

Are they expecting that we charge like mad bulls down the sloping rocks and attack the Martu with our flopping bellies? Are we being sacrificed?

At one point, I realize that I must forget any embarrassment and do what must be done, and I let loose a yellow stream of my own against the eroding wall. Staying among others and absorbing their nervous energy, I feel somewhat better, even if worried and angry about how my name made it onto the list. It has an eerie semblance to how my wife was taken to her death.

A farmer next to me finally cannot control himself. He looks at me with wide eyes. "I will die. I have seven children, and my three daughters are not even married. My wife is too weak," he says, his voice quivering. "Why could they not take the soldiers?"

I have nothing to offer him. There is no one to mourn me, but that does not mean I deserve to die. "Our soldiers will protect us," I say, with no conviction in my own voice. For all I know, without the omens guiding me, the soldiers might push us as shields.

I begin to get tired of waiting, and that is when we hear a shrill whistle. Soldiers push us into an even more dense group and then create space for a stand where several slaves and ox carts bring heaps of crudely and hurriedly fashioned spears and stone-head axes and knives. They then push us in threes to pick a weapon. By the time it is my turn, I have axes or stone daggers.

I know for certain I would be useless with an ax, so I pick up a stone dagger. It is clear that it has been carved only recently, and I am horrified by the thought that we are not even being given copper or bronze blades. What good are stone daggers against the enemy? I look at the distressed faces of the other citizens as they pick their weapons.

We all arm ourselves and wait.

Finally, there are several whistles, and the contingent goes quiet. I watch as someone appears on the rampart— my guess is this man is the commander, going by his thick leather corset and bronze-tipped wool helmet. He is a muscular man, not tall, but his dark beard and bushy eyebrows convey great seriousness.

Someone yells as they get clubbed for making noise. The commander looks down at us, unsmiling. He begins, "Listen! The Martu now wait beyond the slopes, threatening the temples of Enlil and Nanna! These godless heathens, these primitive beasts who know no land, who eat no cooked meat, and who foul all they touch, these impudent barbarians think they can intimidate the lions of Urim and its gods."

I have heard loud proclamations before, but what are we faced with? What are we supposed to do? I wish I was Enkidu—fearless, powerful. But I am Nemur, the man with a reed pen.

The commander continues. "They wait below the slopes, and to them we shall show the power of our gods and men. Them we will slaughter, and their blood will seep into the ground and grow harvest, and their meat will be rich pickings for all the foul creatures. We will show no mercy!"

The soldiers roar in support, and the citizen-soldiers make a smattering of unenthusiastic noises.

"Soldiers! When we exit the gate, you will receive orders on formation. Our brave citizens will fight alongside you and bring glory to Enlil and His Majesty!"

We will be alongside? Not behind?

I hear soldiers hoot and laugh.

No doubt these bloodthirsty hounds will go home and speak of entertaining tales of how the citizen-contingent fought and died. My hands shake involuntarily, and my legs feel weak as the various unit leaders begin to arrange the men. I can barely see around with the shuffling and shouting, but it is not long before several shrill whistles rent the air, and the great gates begin to open to the beat of heavy drums.

I do not know my position yet. As the mass of men begins to exit the city through the gates, I get on my toes to see if I can see something, but since we are on higher ground, all I see is men's helmets and flat land ahead before it slopes. Blood rushes into my head, and a sense of purpose fills me. Maybe there is glory for me, putting down a beastly Martu and dying like a warrior.

The stomping of feet, the clatter of weapons, the rising yellow dust, the noise of orders and whistlers and conch shells and the rhythmic power of drums, all meld into the background as I emerge from the gate into the open.

The orders comes quickly as we begin to spread, and as clarity emerges, I look beside and behind me in horror. I am on the front lines, the fourth block from the left, with soldiers in their feather-adorned skirts and bronze breastplates to our left and to our right.

With me is a ragtag of peasants and other workers, some so old they can barely stand, and boys barely into their teens. It is a mix of anxiety, thrill, fear, and desire to bring a great name and go to the gods as their beloved and brave. Such is the heady effect of conflict—it brings quiet violence even in men who have never held a weapon.

The dust settles.

I look down.

And there they are.

The enemy.

The Martu horde.

They are spread out in no specific formation—it is a large group, much like our citizen-contingent, and armed similarly with poorly manufactured weapons. A few women are amidst them, a most unusual sight. Or perhaps they are no women, but men dressed as such. One never knew Martu customs.

Is this how these fools seek to bring down Urim?

The commander of our unit walks the length, exhorting everyone. "At my order, you will charge down. You will face the animals and drive your spears and daggers into them.

The archers will unleash fury from the skies even before we clash with them. Show no pity. Do not let the fear in their eyes or the spittle on their lips fool you! Cockroaches they are, and shall be treated as such!"

I wonder what the Martu chief has said to his people. My heart beats with a steady rhythm, and perspiration builds on my eyebrows and lips. The sun is behind our heads now, looking down, and the gods are telling us to bring glory. There are no birds in the sky, so the omens cannot be deciphered. Someone kills a lamb and extracts its liver for signs, and I hear that the augurs say this is the most auspicious hour to fight the Martu.

And then a loud conch shell fills the air, and the captains in front of lines yell at us. "We will go down, but we will not attack the enemy. They are too far, and we will tire if we run for long. We go to the bottom of the slopes and wait for the final order to rush!"

They turn and lead us down—it is a long slope, dusty and gravelly, and we all follow the captains like cattle.

The weapon feels heavy in my hand, and I fear that the stone blade may dislodge from the wooden handle, leaving me defenseless. But it has stayed firm.

By the time we arrive at the flatlands, I am out of breath, heaving and gasping. My shoulder hurts holding the weapon, and my mind is utterly confused as to how I came to be on the frontline of an attacking contingent. When I straighten, I can see the Martu now. They make a loud cry and brandish their weapons, and they spit and scream expletives which we do not understand. Several of their men, large specimens, come to the front and thump their chests, stomp their feet raising dust, slap their skulls, and let out loud roars. Our men do the same, and soon I do that too, overcome by the blood-fueled madness around me. I shake my dagger, screaming for blood, and kick dust. It feels like entertainment, as if we are in a noisy festival.

And then one man comes forward holding a large leather shield, aware of our archers who, for some reason, have not let loose their bolts. There must be a reason we are now waiting to attack the Martu, who now stare at us, standing a voice away. The two small armies stare at each other, but quietly now as we wait for this man to do whatever it is that he is planning to.

He speaks haltingly in our tongue. "Fear us, you black-headed dogs! We piss on Urim and your gods! The heavens have called for Martu!"

Our soldiers let loose expletives and scream, calling them pigs, rats, beasts, barbarians, motherfuckers, sisterfuckers, and cockless mice, but the man is smiling as we make noise. When the clamor dies, he makes a gesture to someone behind him. The men part and his "soldiers" drag six men and a woman to the front. *Our people!* It is clear that these hapless innocents have been captured on a raid on a distant town. The bruised, naked, beaten captives barely make a sound as they are dragged to the front.

"This will be your fate!" he screams like a mad man. "Leave Urim, run, or you will cry for your deaths!"

The men holding the captives suddenly draw their blades across the bellies of the condemned as I watch, horrified, wondering why our commanders have not asked to charge.

The captives scream and kick as blood spurts from the gashes.

The perpetrators then thrust their hands into the wounds and pull the entrails out.

I shout, almost involuntarily, cursing them. "Let us charge! Kill them!" I scream, surprising myself. A great roar of anger erupts from all around me.

The Martu bastards rip the livers and intestines out of their victims and drop the parts to the ground, to the bellows and cheers of their men.

One of the men chomps on an extracted liver, smearing his face with blood and grinning at us—disgusting!

What are we waiting for? Kill these bastards! Kill them!

Then they push the poor captives to the ground and launch at us. I am almost ready to sprint when I hear "wait!" I control myself from running. My blood chills seeing these animals rush at us, imagining our fate if we are captured.

I will not die this way! Why are we not charging them?

"Archers!" comes the shout and a whistle, and in an instant, I hear the hair-raising whine of arrows from behind me. The murderous bolts darken the sky over us and descend on the Martu. The impact is horrifying as it is satisfying, watching as the short bronze-tipped, feather-winged arrows slam into the enemy runners and throw them to the ground. The strum of the bowstrings and the *swish, swish, swish* of the arrows continue on, dropping the oncoming Martu. They do not have archers, and they care little for the slaughter.

What do I do? What am I supposed to do? Panic gushes like a fountain. Those not felled by the missiles are running at us, screaming, their hair flying in the hot wind and their mouths open wide.

And then, finally, I hear the word "charge!" accompanied by whistles and conch blows. As if Enlil himself has picked me in his arms and raised me to the wind, I run like a crazed bull into the enemy. The soldiers charge ahead.

if I die, I will die a warrior, and meet my wife with pride!

I scream in terror and let the hot, miserable wind envelop me in its ugly embrace. The Martu beasts are a sprint away, and before I clash, our soldiers ram into them, thrusting their spears, swinging their axes, and slashing with their blades. *This is what battle feels like!*

It is utter chaos, and the man rushing at me is a wild-eyed, bushy-haired, thin Martu. His mouth is wide open, and I can see his yellow teeth. His hand holds a crude stone ax, and I crash into him headlong with my elbow pushed out. All sounds feel like I am underwater, and my senses all mix into utter cacophony. A sharp pain explodes in my ribs, and I howl. He is below me, sprawled on the dusty earth, snarling and struggling to get up. I backhand his face with all my force, and he barely grunts. He begins to push up, trying to throw me off, and intense fear and anger grip me.

Wait, there is a weapon in my hand!

I plunge the dagger into his open mouth with as much force I can muster, breaking his teeth and smashing his tongue to a pulp. His eyes open wide, and he makes a guttural noise as blood spurts, hitting me on the lips. Revolted, I shake my head, but I hit him again, this time fracturing his eyebrow and puncturing an eye.

A man I no longer am. Not a scribe. I am an unhinged savage in the throes of bloodlust. I smash his face again, crushing the nose and causing an eyeball to pop and a transparent liquid to ooze from his socket. His hands go limp. It is madness around me. With the back of my hand, I wipe the foul blood from my face. Around me is a tapestry of brutality—a sword severs a hand, and it falls on the ground; a head rolls in the dust, staring at me with unblinking eyes; a man writhes on the ground, howling, his red intestines spilling from his middle; someone is kneeling, blood pouring from his mouth like a river, drenching the dirty yellow ground. There is mud and blood in my mouth, and part of the skin on the side of my elbow has peeled off.

I try to get on my feet to find someone else to maim, to kill. My head hurts, and my ribs cry out in agony—I do not know if I have been stabbed or beaten. A man staggers towards me—one of our soldiers—with an ax-head embedded in his skull. He collapses in my arms, and I stagger back, letting him collapse.

Where do I go?

Do I run?

Are we winning?

There are no answers.

My ears unclog, and the sounds are becoming unbearably loud—the screaming, shouting, vomiting, clash of stone and metal. A hairy, large man charges at me. I turn to face him at the last moment and raise my hand in protection. His stone-ax connects with my dagger, and pain shoots up my shoulder as I drop the weapon.

My feet give out under me. *Not now, no, Father Enlil! Nanna! Not now!*

I fall to the ground. A desperate scream comes out of my mouth, and I bring my hands above my face in a futile attempt to protect myself.

The man looms over me, his face scrunched like a maniac. His arms raised high, holding the sword. The sun glares at me from beneath his armpit.

He stomps my belly with his leg, and his sword swings down even as fresh agony blooms in my middle.

This is an end that no god—not Enlil, not Inana, not Nanna, not Enki, not wife or parents, not those in my school, not the chief-scribe—no one who knew who I am would imagine.

But the gods desire it.

CHAPTER 23

URIM

ATTURAPI

Atturapi watches the mayhem from a distance.

This is a test of his strategy.

To see if his people have the fortitude to face armed soldiers and lay down their lives for the Martu cause.

And they have not disappointed!

He is hidden behind a bluff. The battlefield is ahead, and Urim's wall looms over the slope. There is a ravine starting on the left edge of the battlefield. Atturapi wonders if the men of Urim will run into the ravine to escape or draw them into another ambush. The dust in the atmosphere is obscuring the view—but a few things are clear. The clever ruler of Urim has decided not to expend his army. He has sent half of it with wretched, untrained fools. Nevertheless, his own fierce people are no match for the trained and experienced soldiers of Urim who, even outnumbered, are butchering his untrained men. But his heart is filled with joy, for this is a testament that his people will rise to the occasion for their glorious gods, Belu-Sadi and Belut-Seri, and drown the enemy with their relentless push for a domain.

His own reserve of a hundred hardy men with battle experience and twenty Elamite elite guards are watching.

"If anyone runs from the battle and heads in this direction, catch and impale them," he says. On this day, no one from his attack contingent will walk out alive. They knew that, and they shall keep that promise.

The picture becomes clearer as time passes as the sun moves further west. The yellow tunics and bronze caps become more prominent, indicating the thinning of his contingent and even the citizen-force of Urim. The battle is coming to an end, but systematic slaughter has begun. The soldiers move with purpose, crushing the heads of the injured or stabbing them. Atturapi wonders if they will take prisoners, but even if they did, there would be no use. Not one man in this advance attack knows anything about Atturapi's plans. No matter how hideous the torture, they can say nothing if they know nothing.

"Do you believe in the value of my information?" the man beside him asks, irritating Atturapi.

"Of course," he says. "You will be richly rewarded by your king, and by me when we put our feet in the sacred chamber of Nanna atop the Ziggurat of Urim."

The man smiles. "I have risked much to be here. I will find my way back to Urim once darkness falls."

Something has been nagging Atturapi. He points to the edge of the battlefield. "A ravine starts there. It is ripe for mounting an ambush, or for the defeated army to run and vanish in its spiderweb. You should have told us about it."

The man scoffs. "It is too steep for anyone to rush up for an ambush, and anyone descending it will die there if pursued. The only thing it is good for is to dump the dead and let the wilderness consume them."

Atturapi lets go of the topic. There is no use dwelling on it now, as the battle is underway.

"Your safety is important to us all," he says, turning to the man. "Next time, give us better information, like the strength of the archery squad."

The man bristles at the insinuation. "There are limits to what I can poke my nose into, Chief Atturapi. The general of Urim is a suspicious man, and there are plenty of rumors of spies inside."

"The gold we pay you is not for you to only fuck your woman and have her mouth moan the secrets of the council, but also to deal with men like the general," Atturapi says.

"King Kindattu values me, Chief Atturapi. May you watch your words and insolence," he says with an edge in his voice.

Atturapi hides his scorn. *These Elamite scoundrels. They wish for the Martu to bleed for their cause until it is time for them to come when Urim is weakened.*

"I recognize the harshness in my words, and for that, I bow to your king. If our attacks must be more lethal, we will need more information on the weaknesses."

The man nods. "And you will get more."

They both turn to the battlefield. It does not look like a single Martu man is standing now. He notices a few soldiers pushing around his men, laughing as they harass them, stabbing them in various regions of the body, and letting them bleed to death. But this is no surprise, for such is the nature of this violence. The enemy may have even spotted him and his men, but they watch and make no move. With a small contingent, it would be foolish for them to pursue and risk an ambush.

"The Martu have become beloved of the gods, but they fought bravely," the man beside him says.

Atturapi nods—tonight, there will be a feast and prayers for those who have laid down their lives. He gestures to an Elamite messenger who has accompanied him.

"Tell the king that the Martu have shown a lion's heart and an elephant's resolve. We will conduct a few more raids to test Urim's resolve, but the king must move his army in a few months if he wishes to rule this land. Remember that these are no fools, and the longer we wait, the more time the king of Urim has to reconcile with the other governors. They are not aligned with him yet, is that not true?" Atturapi says, looking at the spy.

"They do not yet agree to King Ibbi-Sin's exhortations, but all that may change. It is important for the Martu not to attack Nippur or Isin, for that will force them to hold each other's hands."

The messenger summarizes the conversation and agrees to leave for Susa to convey the developments to Kindattu, the king of Elam. They watch as the soldiers of Urim and the few remaining citizens signal something to the men on Urim's wall parapet. Soon, men stream from the partially open gates to come to the battlefield and collect the dead. Atturapi is conflicted between leaving his own men on the field, to be offerings to vultures and other creatures, or to pay respects. He finally decides that when the field is clear and it is dark, he will have his men gather the bodies in one place and set up a pyre worthy of their sacrifice.

CHAPTER 24

URIM

She waits quietly, anxiously, for him to arrive. She is not longing for his body today, but she desires to hear his voice, to know that he is safe, *that their plan is safe.* The benefits of her position afford her privacy when she desires. There are many locations in this vast complex to meet unobtrusively under the guise of official business. It is practice for princes, princesses, priestesses, queens, generals, and even high-ranked royal maids to confer with members of the royal guard and the army for various reasons.

The day has been momentous—the Martu had finally appeared beyond Urim's wall, where she expected them to be. There was no doubt about the outcome, for several hours ago, there had been loud celebrations in the city announcing the city's victory over the beasts of Martu. The jubilation of the crowd in the form of music with lyres, drums, harps, bells, whistles, conches, claps—all that noise outside the inner walls was so loud that she could hear it here in the far corner of the palace. She had to go to the temples of Enlil and Inana to conduct her official duties, something she hates but is compelled to do, for she has no great love for these gods anymore. And now that all the ceremonies are over, she is tired, and it is time to find out if their brilliant machinations worked.

At last, the curtain to the room separates with a soft *whoosh*, particular of his style to throw it to the side, and she sees a silhouette. He strides toward her with purpose, with his arms open, ready to embrace her and throw her on the bed. But she is in no mood for any of that—although when he nears, his sweaty smell mixed with that of the blood stirs a sexual sensation in her. What they are doing is dangerous in many ways, and yet that is what saves her life from the humdrum of her existence.

"Not now," she says. "Not today. My blood flows, my belly hurts, and the divine laws demand separation." That is a lie, but it is an excuse that keeps him away from his forceful lust.

He grunts in disappointment. He has not been understanding in the past when she has said no, but such is the nature of these men that they assume they deserve what they want and will get it regardless. She sighs with relief.

"By the grace of Enlil, you are back and safe. For that, I am grateful!" she says as she makes signs to ward off evil and then touches his lips and chest.

"Those fools. All slaughtered like dogs."

"But for a worthy cause," she says, smiling. "And the warrior is back."

"I did not fight today," he says. "I stabbed two runners. How I longed to be among those who fought, but today was not the day."

They are quiet for a while as she leads him by the hand to the bed so he can sit. Finally, she cannot wait. "Tell me more about it. You know I like to hear!"

"You are a strange woman drawn to blood and death," he teases. "A dangerous woman."

"And that danger draws you to me and gives your phallus a strength it has never had before."

He laughs. "And yet you deprive me today."

"There will be another. Now, what does my warrior have to say?"

He runs his hand on her cheek and settles comfortably on the bed. She sometimes finds his casual demeanor, ignoring her status and rank, irritating. But it is a matter of time.

"Atturapi was pleased with our information, though the bastard demands more. The king of Elam will receive reports of today's attack and be told that he must hasten his plans. The longer he waits, the greater the chance for the governors to clasp Urim's hand. But it will be some time before we know what the king of Elam does."

"How committed are the Martu?" She is surprised that these barbarians were willing to receive orders, follow them, and lay down their lives in a futile attack. They are not as beastly as she has been told.

"Atturapi is a convincing man. The many tribes follow him like sheep, and he is an effective shepherd. The king of Elam must not underestimate him."

"His head must roll if he is insolent."

"And it will. They are oxen, and we are the farmers, and he sometimes forgets that. Your loins turn moist at the talk of murder!" he says, moving his hands toward her thighs.

She swats his hands. "Not today, I said," she says, her voice cold. "Do not forget who you are."

She cannot see him clearly in the candlelight but can make out that he is upset. So shall it be, for sometimes these men must be reminded of their station. "Now, tell me what else transpired. What of our threat?"

He takes a moment to compose himself. "The Martu fought bravely, but they are all dead. I do not know the count, but I heard that about half of our citizen-contingent is gone, and about twenty of our soldiers. Riots have broken out in Urim. People have been dragging the Martu traders and settlers out of their houses and setting fire to them."

"It is clear the Martu need more training or reinforcement," she says.

He does not respond to her tactical assessment. Instead, he turns to the other topic of interest. "The scribe."

"I have been waiting. Was he on the citizen-contingent?"

He chuckles softly. "Very much. My informant tells me that the fool looked frightened and lost as he stood in the frontline outside the walls."

She grins. The thought of that tenacious pen-pusher standing with terror on his face makes her excited. She hopes he was butchered like a pig, slowly, and his skin flayed off before he died, screaming, wondering what happened to his wife. Her loins *do* feel wet at the thought. She chastises herself for having lied to this man—it would be a heavenly pleasure imagining the day and the future as he had his way with her, but this is not the time to expose her excuse. She will take a cold bath later and pray to her gods to calm the heat that rises in her.

"And?" She controls the excitement in her voice.

"He said that the scribe went to fight, and the last image of him was as he became part of the dense fighting. He could not see what happened, as he was not next to him."

She is disappointed, though she knows his informant could not have been next to the scribe. But the inevitable question is next.

"And he has not returned," he says, chuckling. "He walks the molten rocks of hell, searching for his nosy wife!"

They both laugh. But she has to ask. "Did they find his body?"

She feels him stir beside her. "We piled all the bodies and burned them. I am certain I saw his battered face."

"You are sure?"

"As sure as Inshushinak imbues life in us all. His head bashed in, teeth broken, tongue smashed to pulp, and his knee smashed."

She is relieved. Finally! There will be no royal investigations into the deaths of citizen-soldiers. And with the bodies burned, one could argue that he vanished. The king has too much on his mind to investigate a lowly scribe's death, no matter how valuable those pen-wielders are. A fine warmth fills her cheeks and bosom. She turns to him.

"A battle-worn warrior needs his reward. But you must describe the savagery in all its glory," she says as she moves her mouth toward his ready erection.

CHAPTER 25

URIM

The garden is beautiful. There he walks amongst the pond lilies and roses. The date palms line the path paved with smooth pebble stones. Little gold specks shine between the pebbles. Beautiful marble pillars line the path, and coiled plants embrace them. Thick bunches of ruby-red grapes hang from the curling greens, ready for picking. A stream flows next to the path—it is a rich blue, reflecting the surface beneath, and the tinkling sound is melodious to the ears and calming for the nerves.

Where are you, Ninshu? I am here for you!

There is no one on the path. It is strange. No boars or sheep, no dogs or cats, no snakes or birds. No people. The cobblestone was cool to the feet when he started walking, but it's becoming warmer now. He feels as if an invisible force is pushing him forward. He tries to stop, but it is as if god's hand is compelling him to move. The cobblestone is getting warmer, and now his cheeks feel the heat too.

Where are you, Ninshu? I had hoped you were waiting for me in Father Enlil's garden!

There is a huge bush in front of him. He cannot recognize what it is, but it has massive deep-green leaves with sharp thorns on it. A bright red sap drips from its thick veins. The smell is noxious, like death itself, like the putrid stench of a bloating corpse. His stomach heaves, but his cheeks are even warmer, and with trepidation he pulls aside the leaves, ignoring the sharp pain of its needles in his palms.

The scream in his throat never leaves his mouth, for something has sewn his lips shut. There, in the center of this noisome bush, is his wife, tied to a pulsating central stalk. Her eyes are open but full of blood, and she is moaning in agony as fire burns beneath her feet.

No, no, no, no! Why, Father Enlil, why? What have we done? Why? He shakes in utter desperation and torment.

He jumps forward, trying to free her from—

"Don't make noise, you bastard!"

What—

"Shut up, or I will suffocate you!"

Where am—

Ninshu?

"Shh. Quiet now. You are alive, you stupid, sorry bastard."

My eyes open to darkness and flickering flames. I almost shout in terror at the looming face of someone near mine. My mind is a marshy mix of confusion and fear. Am I in hell, cast away by Enlil? Or am I alive? Everything comes crashing into my being—that I was in a battle with the Martu, having been recruited as a citizen-soldier, and that I killed at least one man, and the last thing I remember is a monster descending upon me.

Who is this man looking down at me?

Enkidu.

It is Enkidu staring at me with his big eyes. Just that he hasn't put my feet into the flames. I try to get up, and a sharp pain shoots up from my side, causing me to gasp and lie back on a linen pillow.

"Water," I groan. He pulls out a smelly leather water pouch and pours into my mouth. I gulp it greedily until I quench my thirst. My throat feels less like someone has poured sand in it. My grogginess slowly melts into the darkness, and everything comes into focus. We are alone, in what appears to be a canyon, and there is a small fire beside me.

Enkidu is watching over me.

There is a bandage on my torso.

"Where are we? What happened?" I ask. My voice is hoarse and strained.

He does not answer. Instead, he extends his hand and gives me a piece of roasted lamb meat dripping with fat. It tastes heavenly—though all it has is salt and nothing else. I chew hungrily, ignoring the throbbing ache when I move my jaw. I become aware of other points of pain, apart from my ribs: my shoulder, my knee, the back of my head, my nose. What happened to me? And more importantly, how am I alive and here?

"I cannot decide if the gods want to kill you or keep you alive, scribe," he says as he squats by the fire and chews on the meat.

"The gods are toying with me, and I have given up on guessing why," I say, grimacing. The water and meat are bringing life back into me. That I am not dead is further testament to a new theory—that the gods are trying to kill me, but they are the beastly gods of the Martu or the Elamites, and mine are keeping me alive. I feel a sense of comfort with this theory, for what chance would I have if my own gods wanted me dead?

"Sacrifice a goat and look at its liver. You can infer the omens," Enkidu says, chuckling.

"You know as well as I how often those omens come true," I respond. "This is the finest lamb meat I have ever eaten."

"I am waiting," he says. "I am a man that receives many orders but not much gratitude."

"I bow sincerely to you, Enkidu. You have saved my life, and for that, I am eternally grateful."

He grunts in acknowledgment. "I cannot kill you now. Tell me, scribe, what went into your mind," he says, pointing to his head, "that you decided to charge the Martu while holding a stone dagger?"

Does he believe that I volunteered?

"And do you think I," I say, pointing to my head, "would do that? Pretend to be a soldier?"

"You were enlisted as a citizen-soldier, were you not?"

"Of course."

"And no scribe has ever been put on that list, as you might be aware. But your name entered the list."

Enkidu is a perceptive man.

"Do you now believe that there is a conspiracy to kill me while making it look like something other than an overt murder? They did the same to my wife," I ask.

He wipes his fingers on his tunic and moves closer to me. He sits on a small rock nearby.

"You are a curious situation for me, scribe. But there is something different about your case. By the grace of Nanna, you are alive—you may be telling the truth when it comes to a conspiracy."

Finally, someone believes me!

"Was the battle today?" I ask. Not knowing what had happened, there is much to ask Enkidu.

"Many hours ago," he says. "Why don't you rest some more before you ask me questions?"

I sigh and touch my tender side. My ribs are bruised. But here I am, not dead, and now with greater resolve to find those who have consigned me to this miserable fate. Enkidu seems to have a supply of food, for he roasts another large piece of meat and begins to eat. My appetite is satiated. I make myself comfortable and wait until I am of sound mind to speak. It does not take long for the food to work its magic.

My mind needs its answers.

I demand that Enkidu tell me what happened.

He tells me. "I was part of the elite rear guard of the attacking contingent to make sure we returned victoriously. I noticed you when we advanced, and it took me several glances to determine that it was you, but it was too late for me to take you out of the line, for that would need the general's permission. I was certain you had been coerced into this—I did not know how, but I was sure."

"And you protected me?"

Enkidu nods. "I made my way hastily to where you were. I saw you kill one man. Very brave of you, for you did not run away squealing like a girl. With Enlil's blessing, I managed to reach you in time and stab the attacker who was about to kill you. And then, during the melee and the chaos, I grabbed you and had you run with me into the ravine."

"I ran with you?"

I remember nothing.

"Enlil did not give you wings, scribe. You were disoriented, bleeding, but you managed to keep your feet with me as I dragged you away."

"You dragged me away while fighting off the Martu?" I ask, incredulous.

He pats his biceps. "You fought Ishbi-Erra with your words, standing before a governor while knowing your head may roll if the wrong words flowed from your tongue. I fight men with swords."

His humility is surprising. "No one pursued us?"

"Maybe someone tried, but I doubt it. I know this ravine and its various branches, and when you finally lost your senses, I carried you until I could not, and then let you rest in a cave."

"But we are not in a cave."

"I went back to Urim and returned, and then moved you to a safer, deeper section."

"What if I had woken up?"

He clucks. "You are not a flower, scribe. You might have realized you were saved and waited, or you would have ventured out and died."

"That you valued me enough to save me..." I tell him, feeling certain respect for the man.

He slaps my shoulder hard enough for me to yell in pain.

"I do not know what your value is, scribe. I am a man who obeys the king, and he is my master and god. He thought you were valuable enough to save on the journey to Isin. And knowing that, I took it upon myself to execute his unsaid wish and save you."

I do not believe him.

"If you follow the wishes of His Majesty, does it mean you will follow my orders?" I ask, even as I wince with the pain that radiates from my torso with every movement of my body, including my mouth.

Enkidu laughs. He has a raspy grunt. "You may be a man bandaged and at my mercy for your life, but that does not stop you from running your mouth."

I grin. "Well, Enkidu, here we are. If I were to return to Urim, there is no question that I will face certain death. And by association, you will become a target."

He points at me. "You are not going to Urim, scribe. You are coming with me."

CHAPTER 26

URIM

NEMUR

"What?" I am perplexed.

"If you cannot go to Urim, where will you go?" he asks as he takes his bronze sword out and begins to rub it on a rock.

There is nothing for me to say. Where would I go? I am injured. I do not have my guards or my supply donkey. There is no telling how our guards or outpost soldiers may treat me if I am found wandering alone. There is no question that the Martu attack has heightened security and suspicion inside Urim. I would starve to death or be eaten by wild animals long before I found safety in another town, assuming they would even let me in.

"You have nowhere to go, and you will die if you try," he says with finality in his voice. "Which is why you will come with me."

I look at Enkidu. His story about following the king's desire appeals to me at one level—for men who swear their life in service of their masters will do anything for them. I have, myself, undertaken arduous and dangerous journeys in His Majesty's service. Even with my misgivings about my wife's death and His Majesty's unwillingness to help, I have conducted my official business. And therefore, a man of the royal guard and a soldier sworn to serve King Ibbi-Sin might conduct himself in ways beyond my understanding. But I struggle to see why Enkidu did all that he did to save me. The king would have many other missions of far greater import.

"You said you returned to Urim. Does the king know what happened?"

He clucks. "The king was busy with other matters."

"You saved me from certain death on account of His Majesty's desire to keep me alive, and yet as a royal guard, you did not see him and recount this?"

Enkidu looks away.

"Captain Enkidu," I say, finally using his title, "surely there is another reason. It appears to me that you have gone rogue, and if we are to travel together, then I must know why."

Enkidu nods. "You are a perceptive man, scribe, and you keep proving that. If you laugh at what I say, then I will ram my first to your hurting ribs."

I laugh at that, and my ribs hurt. "Why do you see the need to threaten me at every juncture?"

He smiles. "I told you I was an investigator for His Majesty, and yours is the most interesting case. I have never heard of a woman sent to death as a traveler, and from everything you said, my curiosity has grown stronger as to who is trying to keep you from uncovering the truth, and why they are going to such great lengths."

"That is not all," I say, as I have heard all this before. My case is a strange one, and Enkidu knew that as we walked from Isin to Urim.

"You are like a nagging wife, scribe," he says as he points his sword at me. The sharp blade glints in the dancing flames.

"If we must work together, Captain, you must reveal the truth behind your actions."

Enkidu struggles with what he wants to say. He gets up and tends to the fire, using a stick to move the red, glowing embers, causing them to break and light up the fresh twigs on top of the pile. The fire rises higher, bringing much-needed warmth. He sits that way for a while, and I do not force him.

Finally, he turns to me. The golden-yellow flames reflect off his face. "I told you about my wife and three children."

"Yes, what about them?"

"My wife, whom I held in great affection, is no longer with me."

I am surprised. "Where did she go?" *Did he not say his wife and children live in Urim?*

He makes an odd sound, like a bull snorting. "She did not go anywhere. She was falsely accused of magic and burned to death."

Could he see the shock on my face? "My heart has leaped with anguish, Enkidu. I did not know! May she be walking in the garden of Enlil," I say as I make many gestures to the gods.

"She appears in my dreams, accusing me of not bringing to justice those who perpetrated this act, for I believed that my loyalty to the king was greater than my pursuit of her murderers and a distraction from my duties. She is not walking the gardens of Enlil, scribe. She haunts the burnt forests of the underworld, screaming for justice."

At that moment, a low howl of wind sweeps through the ravine, causing a chill to run up my spine and my hair to stand up. Enkidu falls to his knees and repeatedly taps the rock with his forehead, a sign of seeking forgiveness. I am surprised by his anguish.

"Her accusers and murderers have long vanished, and yet the guilt has grown in me like a monster, gripping my heart, squeezing my innards, and it grows stronger every day. I cannot sleep a single day with peace."

"And you saw how I lost my wife—"

He cuts me off. "She says in my dreams that I must atone by seeking justice for your wife when there is a chance. And that alone will free her from the torment, and she, with your wife, can walk the gardens of Enlil like sisters, holding their hands and waiting for us."

His eyes are glistening, and I am certain I will make no humor at his expense, at least not now. But the thought of Ninshu and Enkidu's wife walking together to a place of happiness brings comfort and greater resolve.

"What was her name?"

It takes him a long time to respond. I wait as the fire crackles. "Admu-Isha," he says. "I knew her since she was eight. We were married by the arrangement of our families when she was eleven. I paid a hefty dowry to her father," he laughs. "But she was worth it."

Enkidu then talks about Admu-Isha, his long-gone wife. Her curly hair. The dove-like eyes. The tinkling laugh and dramatic tears. He speaks fondly of his children, two boys and a girl, working as farmhands and maids under the custody of a guardian. I let him speak about her at length— and the big man sounds nothing like himself, reminiscing softly about her cooking, arguments, kisses. He suddenly looks embarrassed and stops talking.

"Who killed her?"

"I did not find out!" he snarls. "This was during my early days in the royal guard, when I was filled with the self-importance of a man whose only duty was to his king. I made my heart cold and hard and pretended that her death meant little. I even spurned her parents and sent them away rudely by giving back the dowry."

It is common for men to discard their wives. But it is not uncommon that some men have great affection and adoration for them, and that Enkidu was one of them, like me, and we are now bonded in a strange and macabre kinship.

He talks about how his anguish has grown as he grew older, and that his duties gave him no chance at redemption. But it was his involvement in my case that lit the fire beneath him and increased his torment.

"Then justice we will bring to Admu-Isha, and to Ninshu. But you know that we must operate exceedingly carefully, for there are far larger forces at work."

"How?" he asks. "Have you learned anything new?"

"Did you know I taught my wife to read and write?" I say as I look up to the heavens blazing in their gemstone glory.

"Your wise mind is bold to try," he says. "I have been told women do not have the capacity."

"We are told many things, Enkidu. Many things. Have you forgotten that your ancestor Enheduanna, the chief-priestess and daughter of the great Akkadian king Sargon, was a great poet herself?"

Enkidu did not know who she was. I decide to keep my history lesson for another day.

"I have never seen our chief-priestesses or princesses read or write," he says stubbornly.

"Does not mean they cannot. My wife learned it as any student at the school."

"She defied the odds, scribe. But what more do you know?"

"Be patient, Enkidu. That is why I told you my wife could read and write."

He looks confused.

Before I relay the message, a painful cough shakes my body, magnifying the agony. Enkidu knows a thing or two about being a physician, for he forces me to lie on my side, and it helps subside the attack. I take several miserable breaths and wait for the unpleasant sensations to subside.

But he is relentless. "What about your wife knowing to read and write?"

I raise a palm and ask him to wait. And finally, when I can muster a sentence, I tell him. "She left me a message."

CHAPTER 27

URIM

He walks quietly into the night.

His heart is restless, for he has lied to her, hoping she will never find out.

Nemur had vanished from the battlefield. He has visited the piles of the dead along with Atturapi to conduct a cremation, but he is unsure if the scribe was dead. Many bodies were mangled beyond recognition, but the scribe has a particular look. He is tall, scrawny, and he has a distinct dark discoloration on his chest. No one like that was in the corpses. He is certain that Nemur had been on the battlefield. He had personally ensured that the name was on the list, he had seen him in the citizen-contingent near the gates, and his informant had sworn many times that Nemur was at the front line and had charged into battle. The man was able to describe the physical characteristics and behavior accurately enough for him to believe.

Then where has he vanished? Did he miss identifying the dead body? Two men on his receiving force have assured him forcefully that Nemur had not returned. Then why is his heart palpitating? How has this lowly, inconsequential scribe become a risk?

He is worried about her reaction. She is a clever woman and drives him wild in many ways, and there is no question she would have his throat slit and throw him into a ditch if he did not deliver on his promises.

Much is at stake for both of them.

He has spent years in service of the king of Urim, even though he detests him. He has prayed to the gods of this land, though he would gladly take a pick-ax to the temple of Enlil and Nanna. King Ibbi-Sin's predecessor, Shulgi, had attacked his home in Susa and murdered his entire family, and enslaved many of his relatives. The great King Kindattu has given him a new life. A purpose. He will not allow a bedbug with a reed pen to spoil the plans he has crafted with great care and finesse.

He hits a dog, and it whimpers away, and then he passes a ditch with the smoking bodies of a few dead Martu attacked by rioters.

The scribe's house is some distance away, and he hates walking here in the filth and congested streets. Not many lanterns are lit at this time of the night, and the two men accompanying him are stealthy and deadly, walking quietly behind him, unseen in the darkness. When he finally reaches the scribe's house, he notices that the door is unlatched, but the neighborhood is deathly quiet. He places a hand on his scabbard and opens the door. It squeaks, and he gingerly steps in, peering into the darkness. As things stand, it appears that no one is home. Or the scribe is clever and is assisted by the eyes of god, that he is hiding quietly, waiting to ambush him. One of his men enters to join him, as planned, and the other stays outside to keep any curious visitors away. They step quietly into every room, and there's not much space to cover. The house is deserted and unkempt. The poor fool must have been dragged out to fight, he sniggers. He looks around to see what he and his men can take with them, but there is not much.

"Hold up the candle," he whispers. The man with him lights a wick, and they inspect the corners of the house.

Nothing suspicious or strange. It is the uncared-for house of a man. He feels somewhat relieved—if the scribe was in the battle and has not returned, it is almost assured he is dead. There were no prisoners in the battle. He makes a gesture of prayer at the lovely little statue of Enlil in the prayer corner. The smooth stone reflects light off the lantern. As he is about to leave, he notices something on the floor.

What is it?

There appears to be a drag mark on the floor, like a stone rubbed on a softer surface. He kneels and follows the mark to the stone platform on which the gods' idols sit.

He smiles.

"Give me a hand," he tells the guard.

The two of them heave the stone platform from the opposite direction of the drag mark. Unsurprisingly, the platform moves, much to his delight. Beneath it is a hollow—it is a disappointing find, and there is not much there to his benefit.

Why go through all this trouble to hide useless, low-value items?

He puts his palm on the floor of the hollow and feels around the edges. *Aha!* There is a notch. Once he has found a good purchase, he pulls it up with force, and the slab detaches, revealing another hidden hollow.

The clever bastard.

In there, he finds more of what he wanted. Gold and silver and even a deed for the house. When he is about to finish checking, he realizes that there is another flat tablet at the bottom. He can read the script of this land.

He pulls it out and holds it against the candle light.

And when he reads it, Num-Assina's blood turns cold.

CHAPTER 28

URIM RAVINES

NEMUR

"A message? A message before she died?" Enkidu asks. He clears the rough, muddy ground near me, moves a rock, and sits leaning on it.

"Yes. She left me a tablet and hid it in our secret place in the house."

"You are a wise man, scribe, to teach your wife to read and write, allowing her to reach you even after her death. She has the blessings of the gods!"

"Where were the blessings when she was sent to her death?" I say wryly, but the divine work in their mysterious ways and their intentions are not always understood. I hasten to correct myself. "But evil has harmed my wife, so the gods are doing what they can to keep me safe and find justice for her."

Enkidu nods. "What did it say?"

I can remember it as clear as the noon sun and a full moon.

The poisonous moon sends honey to the one-horned bull

O my beautiful Urim, may you not be under his wicked leg.

Enkidu is flummoxed, but he recognizes the nature of the message. He agrees with my explanation that the message was cryptic to hide its meaning from prying eyes. And after some back-and-forth, I explain my theory to him, with the hopes that Enkidu's own experiences will help bridge the gaps in my understanding. He knows the palace intrigues and what certain things might mean. The energy from the rich meat and the warm fire has given me strength.

"My wife worked in the palace. I firmly believe that she saw or heard something that put her in danger. Since she worked for the royals and influential priests, they did not want to risk a blatant murder, but instead tried the most insidious way. She must have sensed peril, but I was away, and she had nowhere to turn. She feared someone. And what she feared, she wrote."

"What do you think it meant?" he asks.

I have thought about it for days, trying to tie everything—all my experience and theories, and I think I know.

"It is the second sentence that tells me more, and from that, we must decode the first."

"Go on," he says, and then he pulls another piece of the lamb meat from his bag and hands it to me. He is like a magician with an inexhaustible supply. I chomp on it greedily, inhaling the aroma and enjoying the flavor, even if the meat has no herbs on it.

"Can the glorious Urim be under the leg of anyone except another ruler?"

"No."

"The prince, weakling that he is, is plotting against the king. There have been rumors that the king would declare someone other than the surviving prince as his heir, on account of his feeble body and mind."

"I have never seen the prince as capable of turning on his father," Enkidu says. "But you are convinced."

"What hides in wicked men's minds is not always easy to see, Enkidu, and you know that. The prince cast his immoral eyes on my wife, and that I know. And he had the means to send her to her death, without drawing suspicion from others like the king."

"Why would the crown prince go to such lengths to kill her? It would be easy for him to accuse her of something and have her executed."

"She was my wife and a servant of god, entitled to a hearing by the king and an explanation why she must be executed without my being there to answer on her behalf. The kings of Urim have long granted us scribes protection and privileges on account of the sensitive tasks we undertake. That is my guess—it is unusual that they took that route, but in times of panic or other considerations, men make all manner of decisions that may be strange in hindsight. Perhaps he is in no longer in the grace of his father. You fought off attackers and saved me."

Enkidu clucks. It is his way of saying that I had a compelling argument. "We must assume at this point that the prince was threatened by your wife for reasons unknown, and then tried to have you killed. The manner of her death indicates great care on his behalf, to keep it as quiet as possible, knowing that he was in the wrong."

"Correct."

"And the reason is not that he may have lusted for her, in which case all this is too elaborate. It must be that she uncovered something he was plotting against the king himself, because of which he did not want a death recommendation to come before the king. Fearing her actions, he chose to end her."

"That is what I believe. Whether I am correct, and how far, Father Enlil knows."

Enkidu goes back to stirring the embers. Once the flames have gained muscle, he turns to me. "If we agree that she did not want Urim to be under the foot of the prince, how does that connect to the first sentence?"

I have thought about it much, and it's a different theory, but I respond to him. "I do not know. What she is saying is that someone, the moon, is a malcontent, sending information to the one-horned bull."

"I think she is saying the moon is a spy, sharing information with the one-horned bull."

Enkidu's simple explanation is striking, and it brings clarity to the thinking. But then he continues. "If we believe the first sentence to be alluding to a spy sharing information, and second to a ruler over Urim, then that exchange of information is to benefit the one who will take over as a ruler."

"Yes."

"Why should the ruler be the prince alone?"

I am flummoxed by the simple question. In my blind hate toward the prince, consumed by the thought of seeking revenge on him, I had never considered that it might be someone else.

"It does not have to be," I finally say.

Enkidu is drawn into the theories now. "I believe something else, scribe. That the spy is sharing information with the Martu, and it is the Martu ruler that your wife lamented about."

"The Martu have no rulers," I say. "They are a bunch of loosely connected tribes."

He shakes his head. "They are no longer wild nomads. The Martu have taken over small towns in the northern periphery of Sumer. There is plenty of intelligence now that they see a man named Atturapi as their principal chief— and it is a matter of time for a chief-of-chiefs to become a king."

I remember the conflict near Urim on my way to Isin. It is becoming clearer that the Martu are coalescing, and their ambitions are becoming greater than finding and foraging land. Is this Atturapi trying to become king? Do we have a Martu spy in the court?

"Is Atturapi known as the one-horned bull?"

He is unsure. "They do not worship bulls. Their god is a shepherd. I do not know what or who the one-horned bull is."

I ponder all the possibilities, but I am tired. My side begins to hurt again. Enkidu senses it. "You must rest, scribe, for we have a long walk."

What does my future hold? What do we do? "What is the plan, Enkidu?" I ask nervously.

He looks at me and grins. "Well, scribe, if we are to accomplish what we must, you will teach me to write, and I will teach you to fight."

CHAPTER 29

URIM

NUM-ASSINA

She is furious. Her cheeks are red with heat, fist clenched, and when she rages, she is both a beautiful tempest and a frightening goddess. He is trying to calm her, but his clumsy attempts have been met with nothing but derision and insults. He cannot let this situation lose control.

"Please calm down, I beg you, O fine divinity of Urim, I have apologized for my lies! I did not know what to say!"

She looks at him with contempt. Those dark eyes fix onto his. "How stupid can you be to attempt dishonesty with me, knowing how dangerous this could be, you fool?" she admonishes him. "Now, not only are you not sure he is dead, but his fucking bitch wife left him a message that is more than obvious!"

"Obvious to us, but not to anyone else! We do not even know if he read it. And even if he did, if it made any sense to him. And even if he thought it a message, his wife made it vague enough that no one would be able to decode it!" he says, mustering strength. It is one thing for her to be angry, but she must put aside her passions as a woman and think like a man, like him.

Her bosom is heaving, and her jaws are tense. She calms herself by breathing in and out. "Do you know what they do to those condemned as spies?"

Of course he knows. He has overseen those executions. But he must let her expel the anger, even if it means repeating things he knows.

"They are scourged with metal hooks. The men are hanged upside down on the walls and have their balls cut off. The women are impaled and have their breasts sliced off. Is that what you want to happen to us?" she hisses.

He musters the courage to grab her hands and place them on his chest, and does not let go even as she fights him. "No such thing will happen. You are a divinity! He is dead, or injured, or running. How can a lowly scribe infer that you and I are behind this, when he knows nothing and has no one to help him? The king is too distracted, and he will continue to be, as the Martu attack Urim again and again. The king of Elam will descend from the mountains in a few months. There is nothing this Nemur can do. Nothing."

She relaxes in his arms. "You say nothing," she says softly, "and yet here we are, after multiple attempts to kill him, and he evades us like a rat in a granary."

"And he will die like one, if he is not dead already. He is no danger, he is insignificant, and there is nothing for us to fear!"

She pushes his chest and moves back. "This is why you think with your shriveled cock, Num-Assina. There does not need to be an army coming after us. All it will take is a tenacious man, a big mouth, and a willing ear from anyone in the royal council. How stupid are you?"

He watches with concern as her rage morphs into sorrow. She sits on the bed, and her tears flow. She sobs, and her body heaves as she laments. "Years. It has been years, dealing with my life. We have worked so hard, by the grace of my gods and yours. So hard!"

He sits by her side and places a hand on her shoulder, and she slaps his hand. "It is difficult for a woman, no matter how royal! All my desires and ambitions are dying. You will not destroy my chance of becoming queen!"

"No, no. Have I not done everything for you? Have I not negotiated your bright future, *our* future? Your glory will reach the heavens, shining like an ocean of rubies, like a sky of gold, for you will be all that you have desired!"

She sniffles and wipes her nose. "All those promises will mean nothing, Num-Assina. Brave one. I am no longer satisfied by your words. Find him. Find him and kill him. If what you say is true, there will be more chaos, and no one will care if he was ambushed and chopped to pieces."

"You are sure he is alive?"

"I do not underestimate him. You did not find him on the battlefield, did you?"

He is silent. There is not much for him to say.

"Send your scouts. You are a man of war. You should know how he escaped the field and where he went. Find him, and do not return until you have his desiccated head in a bag. Make him scream with agony before he dies, for all the anguish he has caused me," she says, and the coldness in her voice kills any ardor he had for her affection this evening.

CHAPTER 30

SOUTHERN SUMER

NEMUR

My respect and gratitude for the gruff Enkidu have grown immeasurably. It has now been seventeen days since our escape from the ravines by Urim. Enkidu knew the secret paths that branched in directions unknown to me, and yet he, ever guarded, watching for pursuers, managed to get me out of the ravine into the rough terrains south of Urim. We sneaked during the day and walked during the night, having crossed the Euphrates in a rickety abandoned boat and used the increasingly vast marshland as cover.

He is confident that with the ever-increasing tumult in Urim and the scarcity of military patrols, no one would come in pursuit of me, assuming someone even thought I was alive and important enough to pursue.

The marshes grow wetter, the reeds taller, the roads quieter, and the weather more humid as we travel south, and it will not be long before we arrive at the great southern sea.

Enkidu is taking me on a path that stays away from the ports or traveled areas. My progress is slow due to my injuries, and we often have to wait hours before we can procure food, either by killing the random bird—a marshland pelican or a heron—or by buying from traders.

My tender side is healing, and I am lucky that no bones are broken. But while my body still suffers, my mind is much happier away from all the intrigue and stresses of

Urim. The sense of solitude is powerful, and my banter with Enkidu is as delightful as it can sometimes be infuriating. *No, writing does not make your penis shrink, just as fighting does not make it stretch from Urim to Assyria.*

We have a sense of purpose.

A destiny to fulfill.

A justice to pursue.

And we both agree that just as one needs to apply the right heat and force on bronze to forge it into a weapon, patience and cunning are important, even if it one must wait. To try to find our way into Urim would mean death, and Enkidu is unsure how powerful his influence is to protect me.

We finally arrive at a marshy wetland, where the Euphrates, to my right, is wider than what I have seen before. I have never been here, though I have heard much about where the great rivers become one with the sea. There is no sea here, or at least nothing that looks like a sea, for I have never seen it.

"Are we at sea?"

Enkidu laughs. "No amount of reading can help if you have not been to what you have been reading about!"

I sometimes wish I could cane the man for his assumed superiority because he excels in areas that I do not. But if he teaches me to fight, I might one day have the last laugh.

He points to the deep-green reedy region in front of us. From this flat area, there is not much I can see.

"There. That is where the Euphrates meets the great river Tigris," he says, though I cannot see anything except bushes and swamps. "We do not have a boat to venture into the waters, but we will soon have to cross either the Tigris or the Euphrates to get closer to the sea."

"I cannot swim."

He looks at me like I am an idiot. "Once we cross the river, we continue south for two days until we come to the great sea. Then we turn west to go to a settlement I know to be safe and away from everything."

"How do you know this place?"

He picks a small stone and throws it at a crow that flutters away, *kaa*-ing angrily. "When one works for a king as an investigator, one goes to many places one never imagined."

I am sure he has stories from these places, but for now, the focus is to get where we will find safety. We walk several more hours until he stops and says, "Now we build a raft."

It is a fascinating thing to watch Enkidu work, starting with the reeds and other wooden detritus. "Is there anything you cannot do?" I ask.

"Well, I—"

"Oh, do not answer. You cannot read or write," I say.

He chuckles. "That mouth of yours," he says, pointing a stick at me. "What is keeping you alive now, scribe? Your tiny little reed pen, or my big sword?"

We men never tire of comparisons. He makes me run around and fetch like I am a dog, but there is not much else I can do to help except to follow his instructions. It takes a few hours for him to fashion a raft, and as frightening as the experience was, I am relieved to have crossed the Euphrates to the west to continue our onward journey.

The mosquitoes here are relentless, buzzing and covering one like a blanket, causing red itchy welts to rise on the skin. We do not have the sap of the bur tree to keep them away. All we can do is wait for the night to arrive to set up fire and smoke.

We are back on a dusty path away from the reed clumps. The land here has a lighter yellow texture compared to further north. They say that if you keep walking west from here, you reach the great desert, and then beyond that, the land of the pyramids and pharaohs. Someday I may be able to explore all these fascinating lands.

"What about your absence, Enkidu? Someone, the king even, will notice that you and I have been missing. Will no one look for you?"

"Royal guards come and go. We fight. We die. We are forgotten. Someone will enquire as to my whereabouts. Someone will say I was in the attacking contingent. There may be questions as to why I was sent to the frontlines. But then a conclusion will be made that I died, and that will be it."

Such is the value of our lives.

Our plan, assuming Enlil is not laughing at me from the audacity, is to join the settlement where Enkidu is taking me. Then, spend a few months in intense training. And finally, return in stealth to Urim, assuming that Urim is standing. We have discussed this many times on the road, and I continue to refine it as we trudge the lonely path.

We share stories of our childhood, the canes on our backs, the girls who were married away to better men, the sellers who chased us for thieving apples. His circumstances took him to military service, and mine to a royal school.

"Why does it take so long, scribe? After all, it is a few words and learning how to carve them," he says, curious about the time for education.

"We learn not only letters and words. We spend much time learning previous works, understanding their meaning, learning mathematics, philosophy, agriculture, politics, arts of omens and premonitions, consecrations, and even variants of letters as used by Akkadians."

He nods sagely. "Those are big words, scribe. We will be skipping that."

"I will teach you the language of our land and the basics of reading and writing. And, as the years progress, if we are alive, I can teach you more. What will you teach me?"

He grins and slaps my shoulder hard enough that I almost stumble and fall. "Oaf!"

He laughs. "Much, scribe. I will forge you into a fine weapon worthy of the gods."

My mind immediately conjures a scene of me taking on an entire army, all by myself, swinging, flying in the air, chopping off heads.

The sea is a sight to behold. I have never seen one before. They say that it envelops the four corners of this world, extending in all directions, and no man has ever sailed to the end. It is a magnificent view—the blue color is unlike the green and gray of the great rivers. It extends as far as the eye can see, the waves rippling endlessly under the warm wind. I have read that the waters are so deep that a thousand men may stand upon each others' shoulders and not appear on the surface. And unlike the river, the water becomes frothy near the shore, which is full of welcome and soft sand, and then washes one's feet with a gentle caress. To stand and to let the wind whip the face while inhaling the strange weedy and salty smell is an experience I have never had, and I must say I enjoy it immensely. Enlil is throwing this temptation at me to see if I will remain resolute to my cause, or decide to forever shun Urim and live here, in this watery garden of temptation. And as if he reads my mind, Enkidu asks me. "Tempting to live here, is it not?"

I smile even as I bend to scoop wet mud.

"There is a beautiful garden near the junction of Euphrates and Tigris. We did not have the chance to see it. But they say that when the gods created the world, they put a man and a woman in that garden, and the beauty tempted them to couple, creating the first children of the world."

I scoff. "Do you need a beautiful garden by two great rivers to want to sleep with a woman?"

He makes a few thrusts with his hips. "You have a point, scribe. I would fuck a woman even if I were surrounded by pig shit."

"No doubt," I say as I walk further into the water, letting it lap my feet. It is a delightful feeling.

"How far is this settlement?" I ask.

He points to a location not far off. "We walk along this beach for a day, and we will be there."

CHAPTER 31

THE SETTLEMENT

NEMUR

The settlement that Enkidu takes me to has about a hundred people, and it is called Surimmu.

It is fishermen and reed exporters, and these people are a hardy stock who have lived here since their ancestors. Some of them remember Enkidu, for when he came here, years ago, he saved them from the savagery of a gang of regional bandits who were impacting the trade routes.

Enkidu has alluded to how he helped this community, but I am surprised by the gushing endorsement of the town chief—a wrinkly, dark, and joyful old man to whom I have taken an immense liking. His wife, five sons, and four daughters all live in the same settlement and have a remarkably similar countenance to that of their father. They are affable, generous, and of such good nature that I have questioned Enkidu more than once if this were not all an act to lull us into complacence. He has assured me repeatedly that outside the hustle and competition of Urim and other big cities, distant settlements have people who behave in the way the gods intended it to be.

We are given a hut and offerings of women to wed, which we decline. Enkidu tells them that I am a relative of his who has vowed to leave the violence of the kingdom. We manufacture a compelling story that they believe. They see that I am an eligible bachelor and are astute enough to say that the manner of my speaking and the softness of my fingers suggests I am a man of words and culture.

There are two girls who live in a hut nearby who show interest in me, and one widow who has taken a manner of liking to Enkidu. As tempting as these propositions are, I know we must be vigilant and focused on our purpose—but that has not prevented us from taking a few days of rest, partaking in many festivities, and indulging in a few minor flirtations, even if there was self-admonishment for having entertained such behavior.

With the town physician's help and the powers of the salty air, light exercise, and labor in assistance of the chief, I heal quickly, and the tenderness in my side and the numerous bruises and pains all vanish, bringing a certain freshness and power back into my being. And for this, I pray and thank Enlil every day, and make offerings of food and beer without failure.

But this day is momentous, for it is now, with the omens perfect for what we are ready to embark on, that we both take an oath before a crudely fashioned clay figure of Enlil that by the glory of the gods I will bequeath my knowledge to Enkidu—and he, warrior skills to me—and together we will bring down the dark forces that have haunted me and threaten Urim.

Even as I busy myself in these pursuits, there are days when the memory of my wife comes rushing into my head, drowning me in a powerful waterfall of sorrow. I hide in a corner or behind a tree, and I let the sobs rack my ribs, for no man must display his tears.

Death, when it comes in a manner of life's normal course, is not resented, for that person has lived their obligations to this world and then walks the path to the gardens of Enlil. But what if that death is unjust, when those that we love are snatched away by the whims and cruelty of others? May no one look down upon me for my tears, for Ninshu's death was unjust and a cruel slap to me once again, as I have endured a similar loss before, having lost my first wife at childbirth. And then again to lose the woman with whom I shared stories, laughed and argued with, and the one who would bring my glory by our child. There is no justice in that! I let my sorrow wash over me, and I let it out as one lets out poison, thus cleansing oneself and hardening to the tasks ahead.

After the prayers, I sit before the idol of Enlil, holding a fresh clay tablet with that wet earthy smell, and ask Enkidu to pick up his.

He is a big man, but to see him anointed with ash, wearing a fine white loincloth, and gingerly balancing his own tablet on a wooden platform, is an amusing sight. The widow, who goes by the name of Burutur, little bird, has been of assistance in this ceremony and in the preparation of fresh clay. Enkidu basks in her attention, and I have once before had to tell him that I will not tolerate a student sitting with an erection before a deity. He is wearing a linen girdle to prevent any disrespect. We have agreed to our manner of interaction.

When I am teaching him, I am his teacher, and he shall accord respect to me as if I am his school-father.

And when he is teaching me, he is my captain, and I shall obey his commands as a soldier.

I have warned him that learning requires patience, diligence, and long hours of recitation, learning by rote, sitting cross-legged, hunched, receiving streams of abuses and commands, and then rejoicing when a sentence can be read and a word written. He tells me it is similar to learning how to fight, except that I would not be sitting or hunched over, and what is in my hands would not be a clay tablet.

I ask him to pray to the tablet, wet and soft on a wooden board, and speak the first letter: "U."

Enkidu is a harsh tutor. I am not a man given to early mornings, and he never forgets to deliver a painful *whack* on my thigh with a wooden board to wake me up. He says I am a focused, clumsy, yet willing learner. The day is structured for my physical training in the morning, rest and meals, and then reading and writing until we are tired and ready to sleep after social mingling with the locals.

It has now been fifty-four days since our arrival.

My muscles have become tighter, my palms are calloused; my forearms, shoulders, thighs, and back show signs of bruises and battering.

But my mind feels better and more powerful.

There is a thrill when I hold a knife or an ax or a sword and swing, move, dodge, duck, run, pivot, thrust, slap, throw, and twist.

Enkidu is like a singer with weapons, and there is beauty in his methods. He brings me to tears sometimes with the yelling and admonishment, combined with the slaps and kicks if I repeat my mistakes. *If I make mistakes with a pen, no one dies, but if you make a mistake with a sword, you will walk the gates of hell!* he once said, though I countered it with, *a wrong word can end not one man, Enkidu, but entire kingdoms.*

He says I am a worthy pupil, and that the punishment I take as part of learning is what will make me strong.

I feel it.

I see it.

As I hack the bark of a fallen tree with a sword, or cut the branches with an ax, or slice a thick linen pad with a knife, I know that the manner by which I do it is vastly different than what it was months ago.

We fight, we read, and we write. I have prepared various tablets with writings in them to teach him. I even read poems to him, one that is popular from the north, and it features a tyrant called Gilgamesh. It is a short poem, though I think in the hands of more poets, there could be more to the story. I tell him that the tyrant is missing a sidekick, and they should call him Enkidu.

He makes me run on the wet sand of the beach—it is at once exhilarating and exhausting, causing my thighs to feel like they have been beaten mercilessly and my lungs like they are on fire.

But I have gone from running a thousand feet to ten thousand, to twenty thousand, and Enkidu says that I must reach the ability to run thirty thousand.

He says I am turning into a lean, fast, fighting beast. He teaches me how to fight without weapons—using hands, grappling, pushing, shoving, kicking, slamming the torso, and it is these sessions that are brutal. I am bruised by the end of the session—I think he relishes the joy of beating and slapping me senseless. Therefore I return the kindness during my sessions when I unleash a torrent of insults (*a slug living in cow dung has more intelligence than you, dumb idiot*) that I hope will somewhat compensate for the pain I have experienced. They are not comparable, and he knows it, for he laughs my insults away, but I cannot laugh my painful welts away.

In this training, I have learned the vocabulary of a soldier. Gone is the refinement of the language taught in the school and spoken in the halls of the palace. I have never been one to swear, and now here I am, putting myself to shame as I rain invectives. Fucking frog-cock, big fat thundering cunt who devours dead cocks, ball-less melon boobs fit to be a eunuch, sheep-fucking rotten-dick, corpse-breath with rotting foreskin, and so on, are all part of a comfortable language.

Occasionally, we sit by a campfire in the night, in the company of those we have befriended, and we regale them with tales real and concocted.

The girls blush at my erudition, and Burutur cannot get enough of Enkidu's rugged bawdiness. These simple folks have never been to Urim, and the stories of the palaces, the great Etemenniguru, the temples and gardens of Enlil and Nanna, are utterly fascinating to them.

I impart to them the glorious history of our kingdom, of our forefather Ur-Nammu, and then the powerful lineage of Kings Shulgi, Amar-Sin, and Shu-Sin, before our own King Ibbi-Sin.

The fact that I have met the king causes such excitement that a few folks force me to accept their prostration, for I am a divinity having met the king. Enkidu does not receive the same treatment, for he is a soldier, but I am a "learned" man—though no one knows that I am a scribe on the run.

Burutur's affection for Enkidu does cause worry—would he abandon our mission to remain with her? This is a subject we have touched upon several times, but he has assured me that he has not kissed her (he has), not fondled her ample bosom (he has), or attempted to have intercourse with her (of that I am undecided).

I hope his wife comes in his dreams and scares him—I know that is an unkind thought, but one necessary for our cause. Burutur says she is twenty-two years of age, though she looks thirty to me. Her husband, she says, became one with the sea and now rests in the bottom.

I have resisted my temptations, but Father Enlil knows how long I can, for the power of Inana is great here, and Igigina, with her beautiful eyes, is bewitching in a manner I have never imagined. I hope my beloved wife will forgive my transgressions, should I commit one.

I am thrilled by the fact that one of the traders has been to the land of the *Misr*, that place of the pyramids and pharaohs. He tells us his astonishing tale and what he saw. The pyramids, he says, reach the sky, and they are brilliant white with limestone coating, and golden caps adorn their top. Now, these pyramids, unlike our ziggurats, are not dedicated to the gods, but they are tombs of the kings for their afterlife. Their kings are gods like ours, but their divinity is more interwoven in their lives than ours. He talks of temples with beautiful pictures, the ways of their life. Their great river, while not as great as our Euphrates, is a powerful, life-giving force. He says that their desert is harsher with vast, lonely stretches, and that when one goes toward the direction of the setting sun, the desert never ends.

Such are the fascinating tales I have been able to hear, over the sounds of the waves, by the crackling of the night fire, far away from Urim and Elam where kings and ministers plot, and where the murderers of our wives lurk in the darkness.

PART II

CHAPTER 32

ZAGROS MOUNTAINS

KINDATTU

The king of Elam waits for his visitor. This flat but high position offers a sweeping vista of the lowlands and the beautiful snow-lined mountains around him.

The weather is becoming warmer, and so is the urgency from his messengers.

His own army is now ready, supplied, and on a slow march through the formidable Zagros range, several days behind him. The wind is cold, and his thick wool blanket affords comfort even as his eyes tear up. He inhales the crisp air and takes in a deep breath before walking back to his tent. He is irritated by the delay of the Martu chief, but before the irritation turns to anger, he notices the Martu contingent straining their way up the grassy incline.

It takes nearly an hour for the Martu to arrive before him. Atturapi has lost his flab, but it amuses him to see the Martu chief huffing and gasping as they near him. Atturapi finally comes before him but does not kneel, much to his annoyance. The sweaty man bows to him and grins. "I am pleased to see the king of Elam again."

Kindattu raises his palm to tell the Martu chief to stand straight. The man is perspiring even in this cold weather. "The walk must have been strenuous."

Atturapi nods. "We are people of the lowlands, Your Majesty, even if our god is the lord of mountains."

"Join me, chief of the Martu," Kindattu says as he directs Atturapi to his tent for a hot meal of roasted mutton spiced with myrrh and sprinkled with salt. They speak little, as they first pull chunks of meat and drink a hot brew of his home.

Once the stomachs are half-filled, he decides it is time to discuss matters of import.

"Is the meal to your satisfaction?"

Atturapi laughs with his mouth full of chewed mutton. "Heaven, Your Majesty. You have fed me heaven."

Kindattu smiles. "Then we shall speak of how we bring hell to the land of the black-headed people."

Atturapi stands and stretches his back. "Much has happened in the last few months, king of Elam. But for more to happen, His Majesty must descend from the mountains."

"My army is moving. Brief me on the current situation, Atturapi, for my messengers can only know so much."

Atturapi is pleased by the attention. He nods thoughtfully. "The Martu have proved that we have the hearts of lions. We have now attacked Urim four times, and Uruk twice. The cities hold fast, but they are weakened from within and outside. There are now frequent riots inside Urim by people afraid and angry that they can no longer trade without fear, travel with wind in their face, or barter with favorable terms. There is frustration about the king's Inability to end the attacks. The prince is weakening, making it impossible for the aging Ibbi-Sin to put his son in charge."

Kindattu nods appreciatively. "What of their military capability?"

Atturapi scratches his belly and yawns. "Weakening. Urim is trying to preserve its forces by mixing its attack contingents with their citizen-forces, and that is creating much unrest and anger. They have pulled back their border garrisons to strengthen the city. Do not look down upon them yet, king of Elam, for they are a formidable force with commendable defenses."

Kindattu remembers all from his failed attack months ago. "What about the king's alliances with the governors?"

Atturapi takes a small piece of wood and pecks his teeth. The lack of formality irritates Kindattu—this is a sign of the man assigning greater importance to himself, and he will have to be shown his station. Not now, though; not when his people are shedding blood.

"The most formidable governor of them all is Ishbi-Erra of Isin. And I have news that is blessed by Belu-Sadi, for he smiles upon us all, that Ishbi-Erra, like a tortoise, has decided to hide in his shell and protect himself."

Kindattu is pleased. His own missive to Ishbi-Erra has received no favorable response. The governor of Isin will ally with no one.

Atturapi continues. "Nawirtum, governor of Lagash, that coward who spits on his own king, will not only not lend help to Urim but has proposed trade deals with us. The snake has no loyalty, but for now, he serves our purpose."

"Uruk? Eridu?"

Atturapi scoffs. "Those cities have little influence or objects of interest. It would be a foolish endeavor to waste our resources on fighting them. They are weak, but they are fortified, and they can withstand our siege for months."

"How do you know that?"

"Your spy, Num-Assina, the royal guard captain of Urim, has been of considerable help, Your Majesty. He brings us news that is of great strategic value."

Kindattu is pleased. He is surprised by the elevated thinking of the Atturapi chief—the man is no beast. "The important question, chief of the Martu, is whether Urim can withstand a siege. And how long."

Atturapi tugs on his earlobe. "Urim has several granaries, though they are not all full. After much recriminations, Ishbi-Erra has supplied many barges of grain, which means the city can withstand five to six months."

"That is too long!" Kindattu exclaims. He knows that the problem is not the ability of his hardy men to hold the siege, but how to maintain supplies and logistics.

"May His Majesty be comforted by the knowledge that my tribes will be able to give his army all the wine, beer, barley, rice, mutton, and even women when needed. The large, fertile lands between Isin and Urim are no longer guarded as they once were, and once His Majesty's army arrives at the gates of Urim, we can then take control of almost all those lands."

"You will be richly rewarded, Chief Atturapi. The gods of Elam and I will not forget the services rendered."

Atturapi bows. He looks concerned as he frowns and nods to himself.

"And yet something bothers you," says Kindattu.

After hemming and hawing, Atturapi finally addresses him. "Your man, Num-Assina, is missing. This is not the time for the spy to go on personal expeditions."

Kindattu is surprised. "What do you mean, personal? Where has he gone?"

"We do not know where. It is such that he sent a message that he had to attend urgent matters on behalf of the woman who gives him information from inside the royal house, and that he is obligated to carry it out. He does not say who she is. Does His Majesty know?"

Kindattu controls his expression. He knows. He knows much about the woman Num-Assina gets his information from, and she is a demanding woman, dangerous even. But her spirit excites him—and he longs to meet her when the time is right.

"I expect my faithful servant to conduct his affairs, and a king does not need to know the details. If he is away on a pressing matter, then it may be of importance."

"I do not know. There is rumor about a personal vendetta against an unknown scribe. It barely seems like a matter to pursue."

Kindattu is surprised. "Scribe? What scribe?"

Atturapi shrugs. "We do not have much in terms of intelligence of how your man operates, Your Majesty. What we hear are whispers. A scribe appears to have offended him, or her, greatly, and he has vanished. Num-Assina has left in haste. We need him to return quickly to plan our move. Does His Majesty have someone else inside who can assist in the meantime?"

There are many from Elam inside Urim, but their value is low. Kindattu assures Atturapi that Num-Assina is a man who knows who he serves and why, and that there must be a compelling reason, though he is both frustrated and curious now as to what caused Num-Assina to vanish.

"There is no more time, as you say, Chief Atturapi, for us to wrestle with these trivial problems. We have done enough to weaken them, and we shall attack, spy or not."

Atturapi looks relieved. "What is His Majesty's plan?"

Kindattu stands. "Come with me," he says and leads Atturapi on a short walk in the north-easterly direction. From there, they can see the glorious mountains stretching as far as the eye can see. He points to a narrow winding path between the hills. "My army is on the way, Chief Atturapi. And when the sons of Elam set foot on Urim, they shall remember the indignities heaped upon them by King Shulgi, they shall remember the laments of their forefathers, and they shall wreak destruction upon the wretched black-headed people. And when the pick-axes tire and the fires burn themselves out, I shall be on the throne, and you," he says, gesturing to Atturapi, "shall be beside me, as the king of the Martu."

The big man puffs up his chest and surveys all the land around him. "The sun gets warmer in two months, King Kindattu, and we should not ignore the powers of their gods on their land. When His Majesty's army descends from these mountains into the plains of Sumer, my people will be there to greet them and fill their bellies with fresh meat and barley, heady beer and toddy, and we shall break the walls of Urim as brothers!"

Not brothers. Never.

Kindattu nods but says nothing. When the cold wind caresses his face, he fantasizes again how it would feel to bring down his ax on the idol of Nanna in the great Ziggurat of Urim.

CHAPTER 33
THE SETTLEMENT
NEMUR

One hundred and thirty-two days.

That is how long it has been since I woke up in the ravine with Enkidu staring at me.

I am no longer the man I was. A scribe I came here as, and a soldier I go from here as. Enkidu has transformed me, and when I see my reflection in calm pools of water, who stares at me is not who I knew it to be.

My muscles are hard and sinewy, I can run twenty thousand feet without effort, and I can grapple, swing, and strike with lethal force and accuracy. Enkidu says he is proud of me and that what is inside me is a warrior-scribe, a type that he has never encountered before.

He is proud, for he sees me as a younger brother and a force forged by his own methods. I wake each morning praying to Enlil and Inana, to Enki and Nanna—and I have added Enkidu to that list, for what he has done to me is beyond expectation.

My skill is as a shortswordsman. I wield a short sword—it is not as long as the traditional weapon of the army, but it is not as short as a dagger or a knife. Enkidu prefers this weapon, for it is lighter to carry and more dangerous than a knife. There is no forger in this settlement, and we have had to make many trips to a place two days from here, closer to the ports, to find a man competent enough to create a few for us for a reasonable payment. But I am an expert at fighting with it, now certainly faster and nimbler than Enkidu, who is a large man, and his years create a certain strain on him.

We started with wooden planks, then wooden swords, then crude copper plates, and now we practice every day with beautiful swords, taking care not to injure each other. But the truth to my skills has been tested in our job—we act as protectors to tradesmen who walk the lonely paths. They were often robbed, and it is on those roads that I have finally confronted, fought, and honed my skills against bandits.

I have killed three, after narrowly escaping death once.

I am no longer who I once was.

Enkidu has spent considerable time to teach me the art of concealment and deception. The ability to stalk quietly, to observe those around me, to move stealthily like a cat, and to appear near people without their knowledge. We have used this to great effect, and it is the most favorite of all my skills. I have made Igigina scream with fear by appearing behind her, made entries into many a rich merchant's homes without their knowledge, acted as a guard for practice, and challenged Enkidu himself in who can outwit and evade the other. I have won sometimes, and the others, but we take pride in how good we are—a testament to the god's position that should a man pour his efforts into the development of certain skills, then no matter what his station or who he prays to, he may achieve ability far greater than those who do not put the same focus and work.

But I am proud of Enkidu.

The gruff and brutish man remains gruff and brutish, but it is a sight to see him sit with the tablets and read them effortlessly.

It is a joy to watch him gingerly hold the reed pen, paint delicate strokes on soft clay tablets, and fashion beautiful sentences. His latest masterpiece is an extension of the Gilgamesh poems, and in this, he has inserted himself as a henchman of the king, and he has named himself in it. These poems will survive, and someday, in the times of our great-great-grandchildren, people will marvel at the stories of Gilgamesh and Enkidu.

He assures me vigorously that I am no Gilgamesh and nothing like him, and I have been pressing for him to give me a role in his poems. Enkidu sometimes serves as a priest for local ceremonies, with his newly acquired knowledge of sophisticated hymns and his ability to carve blessings for the devotees. In these ceremonies, Enkidu sings the great hymns of the flood in his terrible voice. How long ago, the gods, angry by the behavior of the men of our lands, chose not to save us from a flood of the river. And then Zi-ud-Sura built a great ark in which he gave refuge to men and women, and then he placed all manner of animals—sheep, ox, bulls, cows, cats, and many life-giving plants—and took them to safety. An and Enki are pleased, and the clouds part. His renditions invite equal parts guffaw and adoration. In private, these songs take a less holy tenor. Zi-ud-sura becomes a pimp, and he saves prostitutes first, and by the time the flood ends, there are so many babies on the ark that the gods can no longer sleep in the night due to their cries, and they end the floods. These versions earn much laughter and many rebukes, forcing him to pray to An and Enlil to pardon him for his silliness.

As much as our desire to seek justice and fondness for the ones we have loved and lost has remained, it is but the order of life that there must be other changes.

Burutur is no longer a widow, for she now calls Enkidu husband, even knowing that his destiny is uncertain and that we might leave soon, never to return. Her father has accepted that Enkidu has no dowry to pay, and Enkidu toils in his modest farm two times a week as repayment for his daughter's hand in marriage.

And me? I have vowed not to wed until my mission is complete, but I have declared my affection for Igigina and sworn to return if the gods keep me alive. Her parents are not pleased by this, for they do not want to keep their beautiful daughter unwed, and many richer men have asked for her hand. Her father has told me that I have a year, and that I must bring four shekels of silver if I am to call her my wife. That we are immensely popular in this settlement has helped our reputation, though we have had our friction with a few who have not been happy with our presence. Such is the situation for any outsider.

Disturbing news has begun to trickle in from travelers from Urim, and this we learn from our trips to the port. The king has withdrawn most garrisons, leaving the roads unguarded and open to bandit raids, which have increased in frequency. There has been no Martu incursion in our region, and one group that ventured far to the south was lynched and set on fire. They say Urim is now heavily guarded, and all entries and exits have been sealed, and everyone is inspected. The most disturbing news is that the Martu have launched more attacks—at least four more— from different corners, as if testing the defenses. They have been repelled, but the ferocity of the attacks, the size of the Martu units, and the duration of the sieges have all increased, creating significant stress on supplies and trade.

There is news of riots in Urim and Eridu, a massacre of Martu traders, the murder of innocents fingered as spies, and increased brutality of the king's soldiers. It is as if Enlil is forsaking us. My heart aches at this news, and Enkidu and I have started speaking of our duty to return to defend Urim—not only to find my wife's killers and those who are after me but also to uncover a conspiracy that may be putting Urim at risk.

There are rumors that the prince is either dying or dead, chief-priestess Geshtinanna is forcing the king to hand her partial responsibilities as overseer of the army by the authority of her divine connection to the gods, and that the general is frustrated and impatient with the king, who appears to be paralyzed by the crises he faces. Governor Ishbi-Erra has not lifted a finger to help. There are many other outlandish stories about how the Martu eat the dead soldiers, and that they grow larger with every heart they eat, and how they are poisoning the rivers. It is my knowledge of the workings of the palace and the government, and my years of study on various subjects related to people and medicine, that help me separate the nonsensical from the realistic.

In between our practice, Enkidu and I stroll on the beach. I have concluded that the shores of the sea, with its soft sand and salty wind, with seagulls causing a ruckus and waves lulling one's senses through their unending *swoosh*, is the most favorite place in all that I have visited. Someday, I pray to Enlil that he will let me return and live here.

"Urim is in danger," I say. "We have to plan to return, Enkidu, or I fear we will lose the city, and with that, what we vowed to do."

He nods. "I am surprised at the Martu boldness. What has possessed them to behave this way?"

I look at him like he is a fool. "They have instigators behind them, Enkidu, I am certain. I sense the hand of Elam. The Martu were never this sophisticated in their thought."

He sighs. "When shall we return? I will beat my chest in sorrow on the day, for I love Burutur! And the affection I have for her, I convey to my dead wife when she visits me."

"I know. But those dreams will not end, and neither will my heart rest, if we do not complete what we did all this for, Enkidu. It is time."

We both sit on the wet sand and let the warm water lap at our feet and thighs. A flock of seagulls flies overhead, making a great noise. They circle over our heads, and as I watch, they fly in the direction of Urim.

He looks at me, and I tell him, "The gods have spoken. The omens are clear. Urim calls us, and we leave in five days."

CHAPTER 34

SOUTHERN SUMER

NUM-ASSINA

Excitement courses through Num-Assina's veins. It had been days since he had been on the scribe's trail, like a hound. After her admonishment, he had found time to return to the battlefield. Followed by three trusted men, they had contemplated where the scribe may have vanished if he were not dead. Num-Assina had given himself twenty days to find the scribe or return, for his services were needed by the Martu, and then when King Kindattu arrived on the plainlands, he would be expected to present himself before the king.

He had first led his team through the ravines, and there, still fresh, were the trails of one or more men having stayed there recently. He had then found pieces of a bloody tunic. Knowing that an educated scribe might realize that going north where the Martu were more numerous would be a mistake, Num-Assina had emerged from the ravines to take a road south and begun to question travelers. His first luck was a traveling food vendor who had positively identified a large man and a lanky, thinner man, injured, on the way south. The description of the thinner man left little doubt, and the silver shekel he had paid the vendor was far more worthy in its weight. The days since had been frustrating and rewarding, with a smattering of intelligence suggesting that the two—and he did not know who the second man was yet—had moved further south along the river.

Armed with the knowledge of two men, distinct in their appearances, Num-Assina finally struck gold at the port near the southern end of the Euphrates where he learned of two men who visit from time to time, from a nearby settlement of Surimmu, and they are soldiers. He is surprised that they talk of the scribe as if he is a soldier, but these simple men may be thinking that anyone with a soldier is also a soldier. Num-Assina is sure that the man traveling with Nemur is a soldier, and it greatly piques his interest as to who is helping Nemur, and why. The heat is getting worse, and in these marshy wetlands closer to the sea, it is oppressive with the humidity, the mosquitoes, and various pestilences that inhabit the region. His story has been remarkably effective—armed with the seals of the royal guard, it has been almost childishly simple for him to tell the people that the king desires to find these important men, and have people give him the information and comforts he needs. He is excited to quickly complete this mission and take the scribe's head back to her. The men at the port have told him to go to a settlement called Surimmu, and its huts are visible now.

He feels a sense of accomplishment as he lies on a low dune near the settlement, observing the comings and goings. "How many huts do you think are there?" he asks a lieutenant.

"Thirty to forty, sir. The men at the port were right... we may be looking at a village of about two hundred."

"I am surprised they made it this far, and disappointed that they are stupid to remain in Sumer."

The other man sniggers.

"For harboring these men, we will have to return and teach this village a lesson," he says, excited at the prospect of the pillaging, burning, raping, and torture. He would bring her along for a show, for she is greatly excited by such acts.

"How do you plan to find them, sir?"

"We have to be careful. If they get even the slightest whiff of our presence, they will vanish," he says. "Besides, we do not know how dangerous they are."

"Imagine the scribe fighting, sir. Him pissing his tunic and waving a reed pen at me threateningly!" he says, and they begin to laugh. The man stands up, parts his gown to expose his penis, and then waves his finger in the air, shouting, "Do not come near, or I will stab you with the pen or cut you with my cock!"

They all have a good laugh, imitating how he would scream when they put out his eye or cut off his penis, or when they sodomize him with a thorny branch and pull out his nails. It is good entertainment, until he tells them to stop. Num-Assina knows that he and his men cannot be seen in the morning. But they would need to capture someone to reveal their hideout, and then strike at night.

He and his team will wait until it is dark, and when the right opportunity presents itself in the form of a lone fisherman or farm woman walking back to the village, they will seize them for information and plan the attack.

As he lays in the night, looking up at the bright moon and starlit sky, Num-Assina returns to the one thought that has bothered him greatly—and that is regarding the man accompanying Nemur. The description of the man resembles Enkidu, the one he hates with the passion of a thousand burning suns, the one who has repeatedly impeded his efforts to rise up the ranks. It was Enkidu who

King Ibbi-Sin sent to guard Nemur on his way to Isin, thus frustrating his cause of trying to assassinate the scribe. Could Enkidu have been involved with Nemur? That would make everything more complicated, but give him a unique opportunity to finish both of them.

CHAPTER 35

SURIMMU

NEMUR

As usual, after a long day of training, teaching, and helping the town chief with errands, we decide to sit by the beach next to a campfire. We have begun planning our return, and today Enkidu and I decide to once again discuss all the details. Our near and dear ones from the village will join us shortly, for they must not be privy to our conversation lest they put themselves in harm's way. Burutur, Enkidu's wife, knows somewhat who we are, though she does not know that I am a royal scribe on the run. My lovely Igigina thinks I was a schoolteacher who decided to leave Urim out of frustration. They have been aware that we plan to return to Urim in service of the king, out of honor and duty, having explained to them that such are our ways. Honor is dear to Enlil and the gods of our land. They understand our actions and have made prayers in the temples for our safety.

The sand is pleasant to the legs, and the waves are calm and reassuring. There are no bad omens in the sky, which is clear, allowing us to gaze at the magnificent jewels above us. We are bathed in the white milkiness of Nanna's benevolence—for today is a full moon, and he shines gloriously in the sky, shaming all the stars around him, drenching us all in cool and wonderful moonlight. It is so bright, we needed no lanterns as we came here.

"Three days," I say. "The beautiful life here will come to an end, but my heart aches to return to Urim, to finish what we came here for."

Enkidu nods. He writes on the sand. It is Burutur's name. "Never had I imagined..." his voice trails.

"Are you going soft, Enkidu? The warrior soldier whose heart flutters—"

"Oh, stop it," he says gruffly. "You are insufferable now, scribe. What monster have I created?"

"Think of it, great Enkidu. I can now stand on this soft sand, pull out my sword with lightning speed, and pivot like a dancer as I let the flashing blade swing so fast that an eye cannot track it. And you, the warrior Enkidu, sit daintily on the sand, writing his wife's name on the soft sand as he whimpers her name and makes kissy noises."

He begins to laugh, shaking his head and clucking. Enkidu is a brother and father to me, and we have forged an unlikely relation—nothing that Sumer has ever seen.

"Have you had your fun, Nemur? Because the only one having fun in the night is me, but all you do is tug your cock and fantasize about Igigina."

"Burutur says no matter how much she tugs yours, it stays asleep."

We snigger and insult each other more before settling to discuss matters of greater seriousness.

"You are certain we can enter undetected if we scale the low south-eastern wall?"

He nods. "It is the lowest in all of Urim's outer walls. Few know that there are notches in the mud bricks on one corner that you can use to climb. It is rarely guarded, for the rampart is too narrow and the wall is not easily accessed from outside due to the harsh terrain. The two of us, a rope, and a grappling hook are sufficient."

It is a risky operation but one we must consider, for it is too dangerous to attempt to enter the city through a gate, posing as anyone. We do not know what orders have been issued or who is seeking to harm us. How has Enkidu's absence been received? No one knows. But I am certain the king may have inquired about his absence, and by linkage, mine. Surely they may have sent search parties? Though no one has arrived in this settlement representing the king. Enkidu was right—we are insignificant, forgotten, and with no one to care if we live or die.

"And you are certain of your desire to find a way into the palace to interrogate the maids, and seek presence before the king?" he asks. It is an audacious plan. Once we are inside Urim, we are confident that we can take advantage of the tumult and find people who are allied with us, and with Enkidu's connections, find an audience with the king directly. This is a possibility that would have been impossible months ago. We believe with all our hearts that the king is not corrupted, and neither is the general. If we can find a way to them with the appropriate message of the threat to Urim, they might be willing to grant us an audience. It is a risk we will take, and a risk that may lead to premature death. But if that is how I will finally die, then it is as Enlil desired.

We are soon joined by our neighbors and others from the settlement. About twenty-five hardy men and women, whom we bring together for an enjoyable late evening of fish, beer, and mirth. The chatter drifts from topic to topic—the challenges of other growing settlements impinging on our water for fishing, the impudence of tax collectors who not only demand the portion required by law but want some on the side as a bribe, the rudeness of traders from Elam who have settled here for years but are unwilling to learn the language, the misbehavior of the youth and their disrespect to elders, the improper behavior of certain girls—all debated with much vigor and passion.

That is when a frequent trader to the ports slides between Enkidu and me. We call him *big-paddle*, for he takes a boat from the Euphrates port to get to Surimmu. It is much faster than taking the winding road, as we did.

He taps me on the shoulder, and then Enkidu. "Boys, come closer," he says, and he looks sinister with his sunken eyes and the reflection of the flames dancing on his hollow cheeks.

"What is it, big-paddle? Are you cooking up a new scheme to rob your buyers, and you need our help?" Enkidu asks.

"Hush. I should be charging you a shekel for this, but since you have helped me before, I offer this for free," he says.

I am puzzled. What is this character up to? "Out with it, big-paddle!"

Enkidu and I lean close to his face.

He rasps with his stinking breath, "Someone from the royal guard was in the port inquiring about you, and they didn't look happy."

CHAPTER 36

URIM

IBBI-SIN

King Ibbi-Sin stands on a section of the rampart in the north-eastern section of the outer wall of Urim. From where he stands, if a crow were to fly from his hand and head in a straight line in the direction of what he sees, it would fly over the Zagros Mountains and arrive at Susa, from where the threat to his land has emerged. General Nigir-Kagina is giving him an appraisal of the situation, even as the closest members of his family contribute to the discussion.

"We anticipate King Kindattu's army arriving at the footsteps of Zagros in a few weeks, Your Majesty. And then, the most logical path is for them to take the same road our illustrious King Shulgi took in the opposite direction to Susa when he conquered them."

"And why, General, are we unable to stop them before at the footsteps?" he asks, though he knows the answer. It is an utterance of frustration, not one that seeks a response.

The general stands tall. He has been by the king's side for as long as he can remember. Nigir-Kagina responds, "We must preserve the army for defense, Your Majesty, and where we are strongest and can maintain supplies. The governors have all retreated within their walls and will not help us."

"What is the latest from Ishbi-Erra?"

"He will no longer answer our missives."

"That scribe? What is his name, the one who extracted some concessions last time—where is he?" he asks. Where are those that have talent at the time of need?

"As you may remember, Your Majesty, he was inducted into a citizen-soldier unit and did not return after one of the attacks."

Ibbi-Sin is annoyed. There was supposed to be a rule against inducting scribes, or maybe it had changed. He can no longer remember.

"Did I not have someone watch over his back?" he asks. "The royal guardsman, Enkidu?"

The general looks grave. "He is missing, Your Majesty."

"Those scoundrels. I hope they are dead and died valiantly, and did not run away like traitors," he says bitterly.

"When hardships are at our doorsteps, the weakest run first, Father," says Geshtinanna, the chief-priestess. "And the general has not shown himself to be ready to face the challenges."

Ibbi-Sin is surprised at this sudden assessment. The general's face reddens, but he knows not to object. Geshtinanna is not only a revered priestess, but she is a princess. He looks at his son, who is sitting on a stool, looking emaciated, his face gaunt and with an unhealthy pallor. Prince Emmu-Sin wheezes but says nothing. His wife, daughter-in-law Princess Ningal, nods at Geshtinanna's words. "The chief-priestess is right. We would not be in this situation had the general planned better from the beginning."

The general looks at her as if to say *what does this woman know about planning?* but she stares at him defiantly. Ibbi-

Sin is surprised at the attack on the general by the two senior women in his court.

"This is not a woman's role. Be quiet until I appraise the situation!" he admonishes them.

Why has Enlil forsaken him, he wonders? A benevolent god would have given him a strong and capable son who could lead the army and smite the enemy. And yet his son is close to death, getting weaker by the day, even as the son's wife struggles to care for him. If his son were worthy of the crown, his daughter-in-law would have made a magnificent queen, for she is radiant in her beauty, sharp in intellect, and bold in her manner of speaking and thought. In many ways, she is like a sister of Geshtinanna, the daughter who could be king if she were a man!

Ibbi-Sin laments his misfortune before turning back to the general. "Harden your heart from these painful words, Nigir-Kagina, for I know you have spent nights without sleep and made many threats to prevent the current situation. But the gods have looked the other way as the storm has gathered."

The general bows and intentionally avoids looking at the two women. The prince, now racking up a cough, is of no use.

"How soon will they be here?" Ibbi-Sin asks.

"The latest message indicates that Kindattu is on the high points near Zagros, and that he will descend in a few weeks once his army catches up with him."

"Why can we not attack him if his army is not near him?"

The general rubs his beard. "A large contingent of the Martu, armed with metal spears and defensive ditches, now blocks the entryways to the mountains. We can defeat them, but it will erode our army, tire them, and it will be too late for us to mount an assault upon the mountains without logistical support."

Ibbi-Sin is frustrated. *How did the Martu become so powerful?*

"What about our frontier garrison? The one we deployed stealthily to capture the routes?"

Nigir-Kagina flinches at the question. He lowers his voice as if to keep it contained to the king. "Their plan was betrayed, Your Majesty. Their path was blocked with significant resistance. We had to withdraw."

Fucking treasonous bastards! He had had many senior officials executed in the last few weeks on suspicion of high treason, though many had complained loudly that they had nothing to do with the steady leakage of information from war planning sessions. How was information going out?

Suddenly, Geshtinanna speaks out. Her voice is cold and clear. "General, how do we know that it is not your senior staff that is behind leaking military intelligence to the enemy?"

The general clenches his fists, and his eyes narrow. "If there had been even a dust grain of suspicion, Your Highness, they would be hanging upside down from the walls. My men are above reproach! There is someone else privy to our conversations."

Ibbi-Sin stops short of airing his suspicions. He has considered his family among the potential spies. The king of Elam would put them all to death or enslave them, so why weaken the kingdom to their own doom? He has thought hard about his own son, his daughter-in-law, his daughter, his chief-scribe, his generals, other priests related to the royal family, overseers of the treasury—anyone that even might be related to him. He has even had two nephews sentenced to death, and a distant cousin sold to slavery. But nothing has staunched the bleeding.

He has a nagging feeling that the scribe's story of his wife being sent to death being a conspiracy is linked to all this—and now he has vanished, and so has one of his long-term royal guards. Is it all related? His mind hurts. He dismisses the thoughts.

"Continue to look for mischief-makers, General, and put them to death if there is even a hint of suspicion!" he orders the general. He will make sure to pull someone from the royal guard to watch the general and members of the family.

"Conflict is near. Send orders to all remaining garrisons to retreat and arrive at Urim. Dig protective ditches at all vulnerable points. Ready the oil drums and pitch, ration grain, and let all citizens know they must be ready to fight," he says, knowing that the inevitable will be here soon.

"When are we calling a war council to plan the final details?" comes her voice from the background.

CHAPTER 37

SURIMMU

NEMUR

My heart thunders in my chest as I lie quietly on the cold, soft sand on the low dune near my hut.

Enkidu is nearby, crouched, and I can hear his breathing. The moonlight is bathing everything around us—soft, milky, gentle. This is the second day. We were here last night, and nothing had happened. Today has passed with no incident, except that one of the men who returns home every night has not returned. We do not know if it means anything.

We have been here for hours, and I begin to wonder if our fears are unfounded. What if the king has sent a genuine party to find me because he needed my service? But Enkidu and I have argued this endlessly, finally settling on the theory that it is better to be careful than to be foolish.

The fingers of sleep slowly begin to tug at my eyes; that beautiful sensation that causes men to surrender to the sweet embrace with little fight. From here, we can see my hut and Enkidu's at a distance. Our meager self-constructed dwellings of grass-roof and mud-walls are close to the beach. A few lamps flicker outside homes nearby, and dogs roam around. I blink my eyes several times and shake my head to ward off the sleep, but it feels like a futile exercise. When I—

Something pokes me, and I open my eyes in fear. Enkidu is close, giving me an angry stare. "You idiot, keep your eyes open. You started snoring!" he hisses at me. I nod, ashamed at my conduct. Enkidu has told me how soldiers on guard duty In the night are subject to surprise inspection, and those who are asleep are flogged until the skin on their buttocks peels off, or even sentenced to death if a garrison is in a dangerous enemy zone. He slaps my face twice, until my sense has returned and I am awake. We return to our positions, and my anxiety increases again—which is a good thing, for it keeps me awake and alert.

Enkidu slaps my shoulder. Why is he—

He is pointing at something near the beach. It takes my eyes adjusting to the darkness beyond my hut, where the hard earth turns to sand before vanishing under the sea. But I can see something—someone—moving.

By the grace of Enlil!

There, hunched low, are at least four figures.

They are laying low, crawling—the moonlight glints off a blade in the hands of one.

The figures become clear when they near my hut. Then they spring to their feet and move swiftly like cats, and two men take position near the rear, and two others circle to the front. Everything they are doing fits with Enkidu's explanations of how experienced soldiers maneuver and conduct raids.

From my position, I cannot see the front of the house, so I watch quietly to see what they are doing. Several moments pass with nothing happening, and then finally, the two men who had vanished in the front walk Into my view. They whisper animatedly, and it is clear from the postures and behavior which one the leader is. I look at Enkidu, who is watching the scene with concentration—

and as much he has trained me in the art of conflict, we are clear that it is he who leads here, and it is his command I will follow.

The men are far enough that whispers do not carry in this wind and over the sounds of waves. Enkidu slides closer to me. "They are not here on a friendly visit, Nemur," he whispers.

"That is obvious."

"This is the time, scribe. They are here for *you*. And if they are here stealthily and for you, then they are the ones who will give you what you need."

I know what Enkidu is saying. It is now or never. If we run, or if we let them go, then we may never have the chance to find or surprise them. To fight them here, where we have the advantage of time and surprise, is a far better option than to take our chances in Urim. But Enkidu is placing the burden of choice upon me, for after all, this is *my* battle, even if he has his own salvation entwined within it.

The men are talking, looking around, pacing nervously.

Will I be able to fight these soldiers? Am I ready?

What if they have come in peace but wanted to meet me quietly?

What if I die here, without finding anything, after all this?

Enkidu nudges me furiously. "Now is not the time to let your mind wander to a thousand places, Nemur. Are you ready?"

His tone and demeanor suggest that there is no other time for us to act.

But am I? "Give me a moment," I tell him.

Then I pray to Enlil—*father help me, may you who rules the four corners and blesses us with bounty give me the strength. May he who bows to you and worships you with a reed pen have the strength to wield a sword, for the cause is just. Help me, goddess Inana, may you imbue me with the spirit of war, a war waged for the sake of love and justice.*

"This soldier awaits your orders, captain," I whisper.

Enkidu smiles. I realize he relishes this. This is what he does best.

"Listen to me carefully," he says.

CHAPTER 38

SURIMMU

NEMUR

The men are milling about, pondering their next move, when Enkidu and I rise from where we are and walk toward them, my heart thundering in my chest, boxing my ribs so hard as if it wishes to break out from the barrier and explode. I control my breath. My muscles are tense, and my hand grips my shortsword until my fingers hurt. They are immersed in their conversation and have not realized our presence.

The figures are now closer. The sand is soft beneath our feet and makes that *squish, squish* sound, and the brilliance of the moon shines upon all. The men are near my hut, between the mud wall and a dirt mound. There is plenty of open space for them to run, but I know the obstacles in each direction. The only way for them to get to an open flat area is to run through us, toward the beach.

Enkidu shouts loudly, "It seems the king's men prefer to act like robbers when visiting their subjects!"

The shock in the group is evident as they almost jump where they are, turning to face us. The leader, clear from his demeanor and the deference the others have been paying to his gestures, places a hand in front of a man ready to charge and stops him. I cannot yet see his face, for he has a pointed lambswool cap with an extension that casts a shadow on his face. They are all wearing protective leather corsets, belts, and runner sandals with threads that tie them to the calves. Nothing about them indicates a friendly visit.

The swords in hands glint under the moonlight, and the men begin to spread out slowly, menacingly.

I address the leader. "Looking for me?"

At first he does not respond. But at the same time, I notice a fifth man emerge quietly from the shadows and stand with them. Enkidu was right. There is a spotter—and we were lucky he had not seen us before. There is no point in throwing a ruckus or drawing attention, for no one in the village would touch royal guards. They know what retribution looks like. We have told them not to jump to our support for their own safety. The hour is here, and it is five against two, of which one is a scribe who has learned to fight but never employed it in combat. If I die here, I am confident Enlil will walk me to his gardens to reunite me with Ninshubur, for my heart was valiant, my attempt brave, even if futile.

It is as if Father Enlil has swooped into my being with goddess Inana, filling me with a sense of powerful calm. My breath slows, my heart calms, and my mind is clear like a cloudless bright sky.

Then the leader steps to the front, even as his men fan out. From the corner of my eye, I wait for Enkidu's signal, but he has remained motionless. I will move when Enkidu does.

"You have many lives, scribe," he finally speaks. It is a high-pitched voice that cracks in places. I have no doubt anymore that this man is linked to all my travails. An anticipation grows in me—as dangerous the situation is, I will have all my questions answered before I kill him, or before my death.

"Num-Assina!" Enkidu exclaims. *He knows the man!*

"Who would think an ambitious royal guard like you would trail a lowly scribe like a dog, Enkidu," Num-Assina says. It is an Elamite name. I may have seen this man amongst the royal guard contingents behind the king, but I cannot remember.

"We are all dogs, Num-Assina, and the king is our master," Enkidu says and spits to the side. Num-Assina does not respond. His men are watching us quietly, waiting for the flick of his wrists to pounce on us.

"You are going to bleat like a sheep and howl like a dog when we flay you, scribe. It is an exquisite sensation," he says, and his men laugh. It enrages me that not only are these men here to kill me, but to torture me for seeking the truth about my wife. Surely Father Enlil would not allow such injustice? I will drive my sword through my chest if I must, but they will not take me.

I decide not to entertain silly insults. "Why, Num-Assina? What did my wife do?"

He scoffs. "She complained too much when I fucked her. The bitch smelled, and she was no fun."

Enkidu is quiet. My cheeks burn with anger, but Num-Assina will not provoke me.

"Instead of juvenile insults, you could show the dignity of a royal guard by telling me the truth before you kill me," I say, calmly, quietly.

My demeanor and words take him by surprise. It seems to kill his ardor, for he is used to other men taunting increasingly ugly insults before they lunge at each other. But here I am, letting his poisonous arrows fly by my ear.

"She should have minded her own business," he says cryptically. "The ears of a palace servant must stay away from the affairs of those above their station."

He has the light but discernible accent of the Elamites. I recognize how they roll their tongue, for my wife did it. One may spend years elsewhere, but the hints of our roots never go away. I decide to take a leap of faith, tying everything together.

"What is the Elamite king giving you in return for your treachery to the king?"

He flinches and gathers himself. "Treachery? Your bastard ancestors made slaves of my people in Elam. And soon, your people will walk with ropes around their necks. I do not call it treachery, but justice."

So, it is true. This man is trading secrets. But royal guards are rarely in confidential gatherings, especially war councils.

"I doubt the value of a lowly royal guard giving information to a king, Num-Assina. You overthink your value."

He is quiet, and then he laughs. "The fool is you, scribe, for your lowly mind cannot comprehend the access—" He stops, recognizing what he has given away.

He has access to someone high. I have Enlil's guiding hand, helping me with making connections. I decide to push it once more. "The prince is a weak failure, and the words in his mouth have no value."

I hope to finally get confirmation of who is behind the treachery and my wife's death.

But Num-Assina laughs. "The prince? He is a dying, miserable cockroach. He can barely even sit straight. And—"

Enkidu's arm moves at lightning speed, and a stone flashes through the air and smashes into the face of the man to the right of Num-Assina.

The man clutches his face and staggers back.

We now have four.

The men all shout and charge us.

A raw power surges through me. In my left hand, I have a hard stone. Enkidu has taught me many times how to throw with accuracy—and I launch it with all my strength. The stone sings in the night wind and smashes into another man's skull with an audible *crack*, and he staggers and collapses.

This is it, Father Enlil!

Num-Assina is almost on me, his eyes wide and full of fury, even as Enkidu's heavy sword clashes with the two men engaging him. The attack pattern is not surprising—to Num-Assina, I am the prize, a weakling easy to catch, and Enkidu is the danger and therefore needs two men.

We both crouch and face each other. My sword is held low, ready to thrust, and I have been told and trained many, many times not to swing wildly at an experienced opponent. May Father Enlil remind me of every rule Enkidu has taught me. I know that fights end quickly, and all it takes is one powerful contact on the body to cause enough injury.

"You fucking son of a whore," he sneers. "You think you can fight us?"

I do not respond.

I watch his hands, as I have been taught.

He tries to kick sand at me, but it is futile, for this ground does not have much loose land. He looks like a petulant child throwing a tantrum. He thrusts his blade at me twice, but I step back, avoiding it. It is dawning upon Num-Assina that I am no longer a reed pen pusher. He finally makes up his mind and lunges at me.

Our blades clash with impact, but the force does not hurt my shoulders anymore.

The parries and thrusts, the clang of metal, and the exertions of the dance of death no longer exhaust me. It is as if goddess Inana's great power is in my every fiber, and every time Num-Assina raises his hands and swings at me and is rendered useless, his frustration rises.

I make small mistakes, and he draws blood—first by the nick of the tip of his blade on my shoulder, and then a scrape on my elbow, a cut on my thigh—but none enough to bring me down. But as he gets wilder, my aim gets better, and I draw my first blood by thrusting the sword and cutting deeply into his side. He grunts, and the surprise on his face is evident. A *scribe* cutting his skin?

Num-Assina is enraged. My mind retains its focus, as Enkidu has taught me in the many days of training. My true advantage is not my combat skill over this man, but his surprise and under-estimation.

He lashes at me, shouting, swinging wildly, crossing his sword in a circular pattern.

I jump back and parry the onslaught like a nimble monkey, avoiding getting hit. I do not know what is happening with Enkidu, but the fact that no other assailant is upon me and there is no searing passion of a knife in my back means they are engaged. Then Num-Assina overarches, and I take advantage of the situation and bring my sword down on his arm. The sharp blade severs Num-Assina's arm at the elbow, hacking it off, causing the rest of his arm to dangle like a limp piece of hung pink meat. He bellows in shock and stumbles, and instinctively, in the heat of the moment, I act on my training, *thrust the sword and kill*—only to realize that I want this man alive. But it is too late, for the tip of the sword rams into his torso below his chest. I pull it out quickly, but the wound is deep. He collapses on the ground, writhing in agony, his almost severed arm pumping blood and moving like a headless snake as he rolls.

I am at once thrilled and repulsed, but the months of training has saved my life in violence that has lasted a minute.

With Num-Assina on the ground, I turn my attention to Enkidu. One of his assailants is on the ground, headless, while the other is engaged, circling Enkidu and trying to stay alive.

I have had enough.

It barely takes a butterfly wing flutter for me to cover the ground, and even before Enkidu reacts, I stab the man from behind, right between the ribs as I have practiced many times with a wooden stick. He falls dead, his legs giving out under him in an instant.

Enkidu is breathing hard, and he shakes his head in acknowledgment. "I had him," he says between gasps—the man's pride has been somewhat wounded by my intervention.

"Yes, you did. I thought to shorten the encounter."

Enkidu drops his sword and places his hands on his knees to recover. He has told me before that only in plays on stages does a man fight four all alone and win. "Is he alive?"

"He is rolling around," I say, looking back.

Enkidu rises and places a hand on my shoulder. "You have proved to be a warrior, Nemur."

My chest swells with pride. But we do not have time to waste. I gesture to Enkidu, and we rush to Num-Assina.

My tormentor's face is contorted in agony. He is on his side, with his free arm clutching the upper portion of his injured one. I have no pity for this man. Enkidu grabs him beneath the shoulders, and I hold his legs. He fights futilely but gives up quickly as we carry him inside my hut. We light a few oil lamps and quickly examine him. He is bleeding, and the injury below his ribcage is deep. We do not know how long we have. Enkidu casually severs the tendon connecting two parts of Num-Assina's hand, and he screams in pain. Enkidu takes a piece of linen nearby and wraps the bloody stump to stem the bleeding. The business of violence is grotesque.

I lean forward into his face. "Who are you getting your information from, Num-Assina? What is the reason for my wife's death? Who was behind it?"

His eyes are unfocused as he looks at me. A small smile appears on his lips.

I press on. "Why? You are about to walk to the netherworld, and we will wish for the gods to give you a benevolent passage and kind judgment if you tell us the truth!"

He groans. He tries to say something, but blood is filling his lungs and his throat as it sputters out of his mouth. I lift him from behind to help ease the pressure and to let him spit blood out. I speak to him from behind. "Why? What does the prince have to do with this?"

My desperation shows. Enkidu watches quietly, letting me talk.

"Prince?" he says through his bloody lips. "The prince can't even get his cock up!" he says and begins to laugh, and the blood sputters out in small jets. "Slaves," he wheezes. "You made my forefathers slaves. Now you will all live under his feet."

What is this man's history? I do not know. "My wife was murdered, was she not? What did she do?"

"I told you," he says angrily between his coughs. He rests his head on my chest and begins to make a strange whistling sound.

"His lungs are full of blood. He will not be able to breathe," Enkidu says.

"My wife did not go willingly to her death," I say.

He nods weakly.

"Someone made you kill her, didn't they?"

He nods again. They say that a quiet acknowledgment at the time of death is truthful.

Perhaps in his final moments, he wishes to do good. "Who was behind her death? Tell me, Num-Assina! How did you manage it?"

Enkidu lifts his head and slaps him hard, trying to bring him back to his senses. "Who are you conspiring with?"

But Num-Assina does not respond to either of us. His body begins to shake as he tries to breathe. I let him go, and he falls to the side, twitching, in his desperate death throes. This was a man who had a hand in my wife's unjust death, a man who would relish in my torture and execution, a man with intentions to stab his king in the back as he sold my kingdom to a hostile enemy.

I watch dispassionately as he wets my floor with his blood and vomit, and soon his body stops shaking.

My legs begin to wobble, and I collapse. We both sit quietly for a long time, not speaking, as I let the fear, disgust, sorrow, and anger all dissipate slowly. I crawl outside, retching and expel the meager contents of my stomach. I have killed men before—but the bandits were nothing like fighting trained guards. My fear here was intense, and so is my relief. My body feels weak for a while before it regains its strength.

"Death came to my doorstep today, but you helped me from becoming a victim of its jaws," I tell Enkidu.

He grunts. "You did well, scribe. You are now a true man."

I do not retort to him that true men do not need to kill and perpetrate vicious violence to prove their manhood, but these are the thoughts of men who know nothing but violence. Yet he has saved me. My hut has bandages, herbs, oils, ointments, and even a half-cup extract of the joy flower to numb pains. We spend time inspecting our wounds, none serious by the grace of Enlil and Nanna, and apply ointments. I tie a bandage around my torso, and Enkidu on his thigh.

"We have much to converse, but first, the bodies. We do not know if there is a rear-guard on the way," he says, knowing how they operate.

"What do you suggest?"

The sea is a terrifying place.

I sit white-knuckled, clutching the sides of the wobbly boat, even as the fishermen laugh at my distress. Ahead of me is nothing but a vast expanse of water, with waves lapping the boat and wetting my body. This is not like the great Euphrates, which feels tiny and insignificant. I never realized how large waves were and how they come toward us with an unending rhythm. My teeth chatter in the cold wind blowing from the west. These men say that the water is so deep, they have never been able to find a rope long enough to attach to a rock to determine the depth. They say terrible monsters lurk in the deep, and if one is in the water for long, they come from beneath to devour them. Whether they tell these tales for their amusement, I do not know, but my lips are not turned up in a smile.

"Relax, Nemur, the jaws of the murder fish take a moment before they cut you into two. Nothing to worry about!" one of the oafs yells at me, even as he shakes the boat with his two legs as he stands balancing himself. *Stupid bastard.*

"Many tales of men lost at sea, circled by demonic tentacled snakes for hours before they are dragged beneath. Not fun at all!" says another, and they share a hearty laugh. I ignore their childishness.

Enkidu is on another boat nearby, and he sits calmly, like he always does, as if he is on an excursion. My boat carries two dead men, and his carries three. They are wrapped in linen, and we have tied rocks to their feet. It is imperative that these men vanish, and there must be no trace of their arrival, assuming that there was no other spotter who witnessed the clash and then ran away to warn anyone else. But in the past day, there had been no visits, and the vigilant townsmen have helped us with an expanded search which yielded no sign of others on the way. We have stripped the bodies of all the belongings, burned the clothes, taken the silver loops, and erased any sign of Num-Assina and his men's existence.

We finally reach a point far enough from the shore where the men say that the currents will not bring the bodies back. It takes the three of us to lift the bodies from the boat floor and heave them into the water. The bodies float briefly before they sink and vanish into the dark and murky depths.

Num-Assina's end partially answers certain questions, but not all. I have not had the chance to sit with Enkidu to discuss it, but my mind is a whirlwind, trying to remember everything and making sense of it.

I watch noisy seagulls fly over us as we return to shore. I finally muster the courage to reach down and feel the water, letting my hand cut through it. One of the men has a change of attitude. He smiles and nods approvingly. "The sea is a beautiful thing, and it gives us food. Don't worry. You can keep your hand there!"

I enjoy the sensation as I immerse my hand up to the elbows, and I push away seaweed floating in the sea. What a marvel this magnificent body of water is! With my mind calm, I begin to think about what we must do next, and it is clear to me that it is time to return.

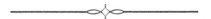

The departure from Surimmu is bittersweet. These wonderful people have given us sanctuary, and I pray to Enlil that no harm may come upon them, even if Urim falls to the Elamites or the Martu. May their generous hearts continue to beat as they always have! Enkidu leaves a tearful Burutur, and I, a hopeful Igigina. My terms of marriage for her have not changed, and if I do not return, her father will give her away. The chief of the village ensures that we are supplied with dry fish and goat meat, fresh cucumbers, figs, and even rare apples. We have an ass to carry the supplies. We receive ointments that guard us against mosquitoes, joy flower extracts, and herbs to patch and heal wounds. We have chosen to take the land route again, for my fear of the sea is great and has not reduced since my last trip. Enkidu and I have a plan to stay away from the worn paths and keep a vigilant eye for anyone else on the way to murder us.

"You will promise to return!" Burutur presses on Enkidu, forcing him to kneel before an idol of Nanna and pray to it multiple times. "Do not be the second husband who leaves to the abodes of the gods without his wife!"

Enkidu, sheepish under the approving glare of the townsmen and knowing that this display of affection adds to my arsenal, nods and comforts her.

I stand before Igigina, looking at her lovely eyes and glowing face but unable to embrace her under the burning glare of her father. Her lips are sweet, but I cannot taste them today. My whispers are low enough to keep the words of endearment away from the ears of her father or Enkidu.

The chief of the village bids us goodbye, telling us to conduct our duties and to return as men blessed by the gods and the king. If only if they knew what we were trying to do.

With a heavy heart, we begin to trudge the dusty road back toward Urim, back on the yellow-gray gravelly paths surrounded by dull grey shrubbery before we arrive at the dense mangroves of the marshy banks of the rivers. The walk back is uneventful, but the tell-tale signs of the conflict are abundantly clear. The tax collection posts are deserted. There are no army patrols on the main path running parallel to the Euphrates toward Urim. The southern garrison mud wall ramparts are empty. There are not many traders on the road, and those who we see are no longer going to Urim. Some are leaving the city, and they tell us a tale of fear, worry, riots, and an impending clash with the Elamite army.

The journey affords me the unpleasant opportunity to engage a few highway bandits, much to their detriment.

The number of men I have killed with my own hands has risen, and the gore and violence no longer deter me. I have accepted it as a way of life for which I am now better prepared.

It takes us another thirteen days before the imposing structure of the great Etemenniguru appears in the hazy distance, beckoning us to fulfill our destiny.

We have plenty of time and solitude during our return to talk about what we should do next.

By the grace of Enlil and the wisdom he has bestowed upon me, I am sure I know who is behind all this.

CHAPTER 39

URIM

KINDATTU

Kindattu feels the warmth of Inshushinak's blessing on his face as he looks up at the glorious sky and lets the wind caress his face. Behind him stands the army of Elam—fifteen thousand men, eager to follow their king to the four corners of the world, to bring glory to Elam and Inshushinak, and to break away the shackles of shame of having once been under the feet of a king of Sumer.

He surveys the land around him. Behind him, parched earth, dry without a shrub, a result of the gods' anger that has caused drought.

Ahead, the abandoned farmlands by the river which has narrowed in its majestic width due to the lack of water. The mangroves and reed clusters have lost their density due to the receding waters and the machetes of greedy men. And then, far ahead, beyond the river, rises the ghostly orange-brick structure of the Ziggurat, on top of which is the temple of their gods.

He clenches his fist.

It is time to bring down this city, this kingdom, this king, his people, and return to his home with its citizens in fetters, its gods made subordinate to his, and the riches of the land claimed for Elam.

To be able to control vast tracts of arable land around the great river and become the lord of the waterways and the ports would make his kingdom the most powerful in the four corners of the world, and Kindattu wishes to be known as nothing less than the greatest king of Elam.

Having descended from the mountains, he has been on a march for days and has finally rendezvoused with the Martu chief, who has gathered his people in impressive numbers.

His army has been supplemented by five thousand Martu.

Kindattu has been impressed by these hardy nomads and their ambitious chief. He will have to ensure that the Martu stay in line, deferring to him, seeing him as their king, for their hunger cannot impede his plans. But the Martu have taken control of many pastures and large cattle herds, therefore providing ample supply for his army. They have demanded a higher price for their service and food, but such is the nature of war, and Kindattu is confident that the riches of this kingdom will more than pay for itself.

"The walls of Urim are before us, Atturapi, and I can hear the cries of their women!"

The Martu chief laughs. "His Majesty thirsts for their men's blood and the pleasure between their women's thighs, and by the grace of our gods, it will not be long!"

"I will need your men to join my engineers to construct bridges to cross the river. It will take long to cross on boats," he says. The floating bridges, made of logs tied with thick hemp ropes, are a fast and efficient way to move men. He has used them to great effect on his army's journey across the Zagros.

"They are ready."

In a few days, his men will be on the other side, advancing toward the walled city. After much consideration, he has decided not to send units to try to close off the routes to Urim, for that would spread his forces thin—and not knowing enough about the latest maneuvers, he does not want to be weakened through surprise attacks and ambushes.

His father has told him many times that he who lasts the siege will win, and while the Martu can supply him, it does not compare to the strength of full granaries in a fortified city. Far away from his own capital, it is critical for Kindattu to preserve everything he has to last the campaign. But there is one element that bothers him. At the most pressing hour, when the needs of receiving critical intelligence are most beneficial, his man, Num-Assina, has vanished. Not that he is critical anymore, having given him much intelligence on the operations of Urim and having fed a steady diet of details that have helped the Martu wage a war of attrition and create a chokehold on the city. But if Kindattu can get intimate details on the latest defenses and weak points of the fortification, then he can defeat the city with minimal impact on his men, leaving a significant force for him to attack other cities.

"Have you heard anything from my spy?"

Atturapi grunts. "No. No one knows where that whoremonger has vanished. We have sightings that he was seen with a few men, headed south."

Why? What caused him to leave?

"What is the latest estimate of their forces?" he asks Atturapi as his eyes dart between the translator and the Martu chief.

"About ten thousand men, drawn from Urim's own force and a few towns nearby. The biggest cities have all locked down—Uruk, Eridu, Lagash, and importantly, Isin."

"They are vastly outnumbered. And you are certain there are no patrols and garrisons outside?"

"None that we know of," Atturapi says. "But we have all coalesced. We do not know the latest around Urim."

"How trained are their men?"

Atturapi shrugs. "We do not have more news since your man last sent his assessment, Your Majesty. Urim's is a well-trained, experienced force, but their numbers are smaller. Defections are few. If we must fight, and we do not know their weakest points, then we should expect the loss of men."

Kindattu looks at the long wall of Urim and ponders the vanishing of his informant.

It is time to signal the man's second-in-command to do his duty.

CHAPTER 40

URIM

NEMUR

After vacillating between walking up to the massive Syrian cedarwood doors of the southern wall of Urim and asking to be let in, or scaling the lower section after sunset, we finally decide that scaling may be the less risky option if the sentries are fidgety. The surroundings of Urim outside the wall are deserted—an extraordinarily rare thing. On a normal day, enterprising hawkers line the paths outside the gates, selling lucky charms, drinks, travel leather bags, walking sticks, incense, barley, beer, fresh bread, lentils, tents, and flowers and fruits. Even prostitutes waited to offer a quick behind-the-bushes action as travelers began their long, lonely journeys. But there is nothing outside the walls except desolation.

On the ramparts, we see soldiers lined up at regular intervals. This is an alarming sign. Soldiers rarely show up on this section of the wall. *Why are they there?*

"The enemy is nearby. Their army is here," Enkidu says as we stay hidden in a dense cluster of grass, watching the wall, outside any archer's range.

"Are you sure?"

"I know the protocols, Nemur. We do not draw up our army and get them on these ramparts if the threat is not imminent."

"Another Martu raid? We've heard that they have since attacked Urim four times since we left."

"That would not lead to these signs. This is worse. Much worse," he says, staring at the wall. "If I were to bet a shekel, the enemy has entered our lands with an army. Has to be Elam. They're getting close."

I take a deep breath. As much my heart desires to turn away from impending conflict and needless violence, my duty is justice to my deceased wife, who was egregiously wronged, and to protect Urim from the diabolic conspiracy. And for that, I must go to the king.

When the sun finally sets, the torches light up along various sections of the wall. But not everywhere, for the wall is long, and there are areas where the duty commanders have determined that there is no utility in having torches. Our plans have had to change. The section we originally planned to scale is no longer a viable option. We wait until there is a dim light from the partial moon in a cloudless sky. The rugged landscape near the wall is excellent for our clandestine trip, and soon we are at the base near a poorly guarded section. The flickering lights are much farther to the right and left, and while the barrier here is over twelve feet tall, we might be able to climb by Enkidu hoisting me on his shoulders, and then me helping him with the aid of a rope. We have the barest of belongings now—our weapons, packed food, money, and implements to climb. The ass fetched a good price days ago.

Finally, Enkidu signs for me to get ready. He stands flat with his back to the wall and interlinks his fingers to provide a platform for me on his palms. I hold his shoulders and climb—Enkidu is an extraordinarily strong man, and he pushes me up with ease. I grip the upper edge of the wall while shakily balancing my legs on his shoulders and find purchase. With effort, I manage to scale the remaining height and roll onto the rampart.

The silhouette of a guard is not far away!

Lights flicker at a distance. I hear the low chatter of men.

I bend to look down and see Enkidu's figure waiting for me.

The coiled rope is hanging from my belt. I unclip it and prepare to throw it down for him to grip and climb. It is going to be a difficult one—he is heavy, and while I have strength, we have seen through our training that there are limits. My hope is to be able to haul him up with one powerful tug and let him grip the edges.

"Who are you?" I suddenly hear a voice.

No!

The dark outline of the guard is getting closer. He must have seen my body obstructing a light source. Do I kill him? It is a strange immediate dilemma—to kill a man of my city, one who is doing his job to protect it, for no fault of his own, so that I may find justice for the one killed unjustly.

My mission requires me to follow a code—that I will not kill innocents.

I straighten and stand quietly. My heart thuds in the chest, hoping that Enkidu does not get impatient and call my name.

He must know what I am doing.

"On an inspection round! Why are you moving from your post?" I say loudly. *Hopefully, Enkidu has heard me too.*

The figure stops. "What inspection? No one told me of any."

"Do you expect General Nigir-Kagina to send personal invitations to all guards with his plans?" I say as officially as

I can sound. "This section of the wall is poorly guarded. My job is to check if it must be reinforced. Now go back and stay where you must!"

The figure hesitates. Will he advance on me? Will he call someone else?

Enkidu and I have discussed these scenarios. If I am at risk, he has asked that I flee into the city, and said that he will find a way to enter eventually.

Finally, he mutters. "Fine. But next time, announce your presence before you near a new guard post. I thought you were an intruder."

"What Elamite or Martu scum speak the beautiful language of Urim, my friend?" I say casually. And for added effect, I throw in a few names of our gods. "May Enlil bless you for standing guard, and may Nanna feed your family with plentiful grain."

He bows in friendly acknowledgment, and the silhouette fades back into the darkness. I let out a big sigh of relief.

Enkidu is standing below, impatiently. I wrap my palms with linen and throw the rope down to him. We do not want my palms to be bruised and bloody trying to bring him up. With much effort, Enkidu finally manages to get on top and lies on the rampart briefly, panting from the exertion.

"You did well," he whispers. "Let us find a place to get down. Keep your profile low."

We both hunch and take small steps along the narrow rampart, adjusting our eyes to the million glittering lights of the city behind the wall.

"Hey!"

Not again!

It is him. Didn't that bastard go away satisfied?

"Stay where you are! Is there someone else with you?"

I tap Enkidu's shoulder. "We jump."

He nods.

We both quickly squat, grip the edge, and pivot ourselves to hang from the wall on the inner side. I do not know if the man is racing toward us, but we have no time to find out.

I let go.

Please, let me not break my leg!

With the grace of Father Enlil, the ground is not far from the top. My legs painfully impact on muddy ground as I fall. I try to minimize the impact by rolling, but it is painful. I hear Enkidu grunt nearby as he crashes. There is a shout from the top, but we scramble to our feet and make a mad dash toward the narrow paths between a cluster of houses.

I hear no whistle. There are many reasons why a lonely guard might not attract attention to himself. I am thankful to the gods to have let us back into the city.

Now it is time to bring down my rage on the people who casually determined to destroy my life.

And that of Urim's.

It is a perverse joy to see chief-scribe Inim-Nanna's terrified face in the flickering light of the nightlamp. No man wishes to wake in the darkness of the night with two men by the side of his bed. Enkidu's hand is on his mouth, and my blade glints in the darkness. Inim-Nanna's wives died long ago, and he lives alone in a large home within the inner walls, inside which we have been able to get with relative ease through the employment of the right words and casual confidence.

"Shhh, chief-scribe. If you call attention, the next sound will be that of the air hissing out of a gash in your throat. Do you understand?" I ask.

He nods fervently.

Enkidu partially removes his hand, and Inim-Nanna keeps his mouth shut. *Excellent.*

"Do you recognize me, chief-scribe?" I ask. My appearance has changed since I last saw Urim. A dark beard and luxurious mustache adorn my face, my hair is longer, my chest is no longer hollow, and my shoulders are wide and strong. His eyes open wide in recognition, and he gulps.

"You will whisper, chief-scribe, do you understand?"

He nods again.

Enkidu removes his hand from the man's mouth, and he takes several breaths.

"What is the meaning of this? Nemur, they said you were dead!"

"Is that what you wanted?" I ask menacingly, pressing the tip of my knife to the hollow of his throat.

Inim-Nanna whispers urgently. "What? No. No, no, no. Please do not kill me! What do you want?"

"The truth. You know why I am here," I say. "Who made Iddin put my wife's name on the traveler list?"

It takes him a few moments to come to his senses. He looks frightened.

"Now, or never," I say. "I have little patience left. And with everything around us, no one will waste time investigating your untimely death."

"Fine!" he hisses. "Iddin is a lowly scribe. I do not watch over what men like that do!"

"Liar! My wife's death did not come from the hands of lowly men. Num-Assina came to you, didn't he?"

Inim-Nanna flinches. I know. I know he knows. He knows that I know he knows. He clasps his wiry fingers on his blanket.

"Num-Assina is a womanizing scoundrel. Why would he come to me?" he rasps.

I take my knife and place it on his thigh, and before he can utter a word, I draw a deep, bloody gash running up vertically from his knee.

He tries to scream, but Enkidu clasps his mouth. Blood wells up from the wound, and I wrap it with his blanket.

"I am no longer a soft, dainty-fingered scribe, Master. The next target is your testicles."

He clutches his damaged thigh and curses me, but I do not care. "I know about Num-Assina. If you lie again—"

"Okay, okay," he gasps. "That bastard came to me when it was time to finalize the list."

I am surprised but quickly calculate that it was possible Num-Assina was using his henchmen. Did it mean there was a second man within the palace in this treasonous pact?

"What did he say?"

"That he had orders to have Iddin draw up the final list for certification. I was surprised, for we had finalized the names, and another scribe was carving the names."

"And you let him?"

"He invoked the prince's and chief-priestess' names, and said I was in danger due to the conduct of one of my scribes. Said if I went to any of them with a question, I would be dead within a day. Offered me gold and a good word in the ear of the king, who was not favorably disposed toward me."

"You, the exalted chief-scribe, listened to a royal guard?"

"He is with the royals and the chief-priestess all the time! The king was unhappy with me. I did not think too much!"

This greedy idiot could be telling me the truth.

"Did you check the final list?"

He looks at me with irritation. "What? No. I assigned Iddin."

"But you knew why someone might ask for such a request."

He does not respond first. Finally, through clenched teeth, he says, "I did not know it would be your wife."

He gasps and mumbles in pain, but I believe him when he says he did not know. "If you speak a word of our presence, the entire city will know what you did, and we will find you and make you wish you were dead."

He nods desperately. I know that this weak, craven man will do anything to save his hide.

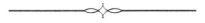

We lay low for the night, seeking refuge in a brothel where no man is asked for his history. The women are puzzled that we are willing to pay but do not wish to partake in any sexual activity, though they say this is not unusual. Men come to them all the time seeking simple affection, they say, for they have not received any for long. My mind is a hive of activity, but I am thrilled at the progress.

Will Inim-Nanna scream and run to the royals?

When a man is ensnared in a scheme he does not understand, he will be quiet lest his stupidity is exposed. Besides, he is no longer favored by the king. I am emboldened by my bravery and strength and what we are uncovering.

But time is running out.

Since our entry, we have learned the most distressing news. The Elamite army is here, and we are told that they are visible from the northeastern wall, amassing in great numbers beyond the Euphrates. It is a matter of time before these locusts swarm us. No hint of help from the other cities, and Urim's men have been called to take up arms. We have to find our way to the king, but how? Getting in front of him and screaming names will do no good—and besides, he is likely livid at our absence. We can go to no one else, because we do not know who else is infected with this rot.

But to confirm the theories about my target, I must first find myself before the king.

And that is when I get an idea based on what I have been hearing, and it is almost as if Enlil has blessed us with this opportunity.

The great ceremony to Enlil and the gods is scheduled today.

This magnificent event is an offering to the gods to beg them to bless us with victory.

The procession starts at the rising of the sun, amidst a great din of hymns by a hundred priests, the clanging of copper cymbals, the strumming of lyres, the blowing of conches, and a rhythmic beat of thunderous drums. The king leads the mass, along with all his court, distinguished citizens of the city, priests and priestesses, senior military officials, traders and merchants, and selected commoners allowed within the inner wall gates for a limited time.

My newfound skills have helped us corner two hapless priests and steal their attire—and we are now one in this crowd that is bursting with noise and colors. The soft white of lambswool mixed with the orange and blues of lapis-lazuli and carnelian, the red limestones interspersed with the blinding clarity of topaz, the patterns of flowers and plants mixed with artistic renditions of Enlil and Inana, all create a heady atmosphere of devotion. The hypnotic chants fill the air, and no doubt the king and everyone around him hopes that the sounds carry across the walls to the fields beyond the Euphrates, to frighten the godless armies of the Martu and Elam.

Hope that we will subdue them.

Enkidu and I are wearing identical priestly garb—crisp white linen tied to our waists, covering to our knees, ash on our shoulders, blue makeup beneath our lower eyelids, a copper ring each on one of our forefingers, and grass blades in our left fists. No one has recognized us, and it is difficult—for I, with a clean face before, now have hair on it, and Enkidu has shaved away all his mustache and beard. Even I would miss him in the crowd. One thing distinguishes us from the other priests—we have daggers expertly concealed in our tunics. We walk barefooted on the cobblestone paths that lead to the great Etemenniguru looming in front of us.

Enkidu and I jostle for space as we walk with a foul-smelling group of traders, pushing ourselves further into the crowd.

We ignore the angry looks and returned elbows to get ourselves to the front of the crowd. This is where it becomes challenging—the king is protected by rings of guards, not to mention hundreds of senior officials walking behind him. But the man with me is clever and knows much about how these security arrangements work. When we get forward enough, behind the military cordon that separates us from the royal and distinguished citizens section, Enkidu leans to me.

"Keep walking. This is my area of expertise now," he says. We do not have a backup plan. What he does now is all we have. At best, we can hope to escape from the crowd if the situation turns on us and hope to escape without being caught.

Enkidu walks away from me, squeezing through the walkers, and soon I can barely see his head at a distance. My heart begins to hammer in my chest, and I wipe sweat from my eyebrows. *What should I expect?*

The Ziggurat is looming in front of us. It rises high in the sky, the orange bricks of the massive bulk of the structure shining in the morning sun, reflecting the golden light. From this angle, it appears that the sun is almost on top of the temple on the Etemenniguru, making it look like a magnificent mountain which is adorned by the glowing sun orb. The path now curves to our right, taking us to the broad stairs that rise up to the top of the structure, where the chief-priestess Geshtinanna waits for the king to conduct ceremonies to Nanna and Enlil. On each end of the stairs are yellow-colored flags fluttering in the morning wind. More priests stand on the staircase, at regular intervals, singing hymns. It is enthralling, but my mind is filled with anxiety. *Where is Enkidu?*

Suddenly, the soldiers in front of me part, and Enkidu reaches his hand to me, grinning mischievously. A senior man, by the looks of his attire and the ornate belt, is looking at me sternly. I bow and step inside the military ring, nervous.

Enkidu leans to my ear and yells to be heard over the deafening noise of cymbals and drums. "Let us say I created much amusement and horror in this man, a long-time friend and a senior commander. He will take us to the front."

"He trusts you?"

"I saved his life twice."

"How do we get near the king?"

He grins again. "You will find out!" he says, and then vanishes.

What is this monkey up to?

I walk in step with armed men around me and inch forward. They defer to me. For now, I am a priest in their midst, and if I am here, then I am automatically considered to have the right to be here.

Enkidu reappears again, this time holding two sets of giant copper cymbals, each set tied together with orange-dyed hemp rope. He hands one set to me.

"Bang them as loudly as you can, be loud in your incantations, and move quickly behind me."

Ah, this rascal. Why hadn't I thought of it before?

The ear-splitting clang of the cymbals is irritating enough that the soldiers part for me as I push forward in the group. Soon, we are almost in the front.

I see many familiar faces.

I keep my head down, and while making an unholy ruckus, we both advance through the crowd. There are gold-necklaced, ruby-wearing fat traders and merchants here, along with elegant, transparent-gowned high-priestesses and wives of senior officials. The crowd is less dense, and ahead, not far away, are the divinities of this land. The king walks alone, wearing a loincloth and a lambswool cap with a gem-studded tiara. Behind him, on a litter, is the prince. He must be sick not to be able to walk. Next to him is Princess Ningal, his wife, along with other relatives of the royals, and General Inim-Nanna and others walk right behind. The chief-scribe is missing. No wonder why. I have no pity left for the man.

Enkidu walks next to me.

"Move forward with purpose. Ignore the dirty looks. We are priests, and people know that religious procedures change all the time. Do not get close to the king—we both should walk wide aside from him and get in front. And then we turn and prostrate before him. This is our chance. Make loud noises!"

A risky but brilliant plan—one with no conflict, death, or any utterly stupid maneuvers requiring killing scores of guards and scaling palace walls.

I resolve myself to the terrifying task ahead. I nod to Enkidu, and we both make signs of prayer. He moves further right and I to the left, far enough to break out of the cluster of people onto the edge of the broad cobblestone path. I raise my head to look up at the top of the Etemenniguru and begin to clang the cymbals so loudly, it makes even my ears ring. With my head held high, I make loud lamentations to Enlil and Nanna. From the corner of my eye, I can see the puzzled faces of a few, but none concerned—for in this din and ceremony, I am another person of the process. A few even bow to me as I pass them. After all, I am a man of god in a holy event.

My legs make quick progress, and I near the litter on which the prince is sitting on a low chair.

I manage to look at him.

He looks deathly pale.

His eyes are half-closed.

The man is emaciated—his ribs and the bones of his shoulders jut out. He can barely sit.

Princess Ningal walks beside him, her fingers on the edge of the litter, a dutiful wife by her dying husband. Her face is a study in stoic bravery—her long nose turned up with resoluteness, her sheer robe floating as she walks by the prince. Chief-priestess Geshtinanna's figure is barely visible on the top of the Etemenniguru, but in her resplendent orange robe, she is a brilliant speck on the abode of orange bricks.

I have questions for her. Many questions.

But first, I must speak to the king.

My legs feel weaker as I near the figure of King Ibbi-Sin.

Even in his physically and mentally enervated state, with his allies deserting him and his governors paying no heed to his words, the king is a supreme and divine figure.

He has been on the throne for fifteen years, ruling this great kingdom through all its tumult and challenges, giving its subjects peace and prosperity. He is clean-shaven and walks with purpose, his back straight, his tiara shining in the sun, sitting on the finest lambswool round cap. I stay at a wide distance from the king, making a ruckus, looking with trepidation for Enkidu to appear on the other side. The oaf finally appears, and it takes effort for me not to laugh, for his behavior is dramatic as it is attention-seeking. He is contorting his body like a talentless dancer, clanging the cymbals with each pivot. I cannot hear his voice in all the noise, but no doubt he is mouthing nonsense that sounds like a hymn.

But the space in front of the king is clear. It is not far from the broad stairs that lead up to the one-hundred-thirty-foot tall structure. With my heart thundering in my ribcage, I leap back to the main path and take a few steps ahead of the king. I see Enkidu from the corner of my eyes. He jumps onto the path and nears me.

No guards are reacting. At least not yet.

I turn and stand, looking straight into King Ibbi-Sin's gaunt and leathery face. But his eyes shine brightly—he furrows his eyebrows, unclear what is happening.

As planned, we both dive to the ground in prostration before him, causing him to almost stumble. I see his feet before my face, and as quickly as we can, we both rise to our feet.

Two royal guards run to his side.

The king sees our faces for the first time.

And his eyes open wide in recognition.

CHAPTER 41

URIM

KINDATTU

Kindattu watches as his men begin to cross the floating bridges.

It is a chaotic affair, for some are too excited, and they fight and jostle on the swaying logs—a few fall into the river and drown. But the crossing has begun and should be over by the next day. There appears to be a ceremony proceeding in the city.

The tight lockdown of the city has posed problems for him, along with the vanishing of the spy. What about Num-Assina's assistant? Has he seen the fire arrows in the night? Has he connected with Num-Assina's woman? What is he doing? As the day of the battle nears, Kindattu is getting increasingly worried. While previous intelligence from Num-Assina has been helpful in identifying general weak points in Urim's defense, sections of the wall susceptible to breach, areas likely to catch fires if fireballs are launched, and so on, he does not have the *latest information.*

Kings and military commanders are no fools.

They change strategies all the time.

Areas considered easy to attack can be ambush points, paths easy to traverse can be full of unforeseen dangers, an innocent-looking attack unit can be full of bristling spikes. He has harangued Atturapi about the chief's failure to bring more information out of Urim, but the man has angrily responded that almost all the Martu inside Urim have been murdered by the mobs, and with an absolute lockdown, there is no way to get anyone in—and even if they did by scaling quiet sections of the wall, the odds that those men would learn something useful *and* get out undetected would be next to impossible.

Kindattu prays to Inshushinak for a breakthrough, but none has been forthcoming.

On the other side of the river, his army has begun to assemble tents, kitchens, lavatory ditches, ox pens, areas for funeral pyres, dispensaries, and defensive ditches.

Would the attack last a day?

Would this be one big battle that leads to victory, or would it be a grinding, punishing war of attrition and siege?

Great offensives can leave nothing to chance, which is why he is ensuring that they are ready for a long wait, should a powerful push fail. He has sent another missive to Ishbi-Erra, this one gentler, more cooperative, less threatening, asking for the governor of Isin to join him. His scouts have begun making discreet trips around the great wall of Urim, looking for weak spots, understanding the terrain, and mapping attack points. A few of them have been victims to arrows from the ramparts, so he has had to order them to stay out of range. Kindattu does not have an inexhaustible supply of good scouts who have the exceptional ability to remember minor details and provide invaluable information to the battle commanders.

He is losing patience, and it will not be long before the clash of these two great kingdoms.

CHAPTER 42

URIM

NEMUR

It is a credit to the perspicacious nature of the king that we have our heads on our shoulders. After the initial surprise and listening to both of us urgently spelling Elam and that we have critical information, the king realizes our ruse and asks us to walk beside him. I do not know yet if those behind us have realized. But we get on both sides of the diminutive king and keep pace with his energetic walk. It is not far yet to the steps, and we hope he will let us walk the stairs to the temple.

"Speak. And if you are here to deceive me again, you will hang upside down from the walls," he says.

"Yes, Your Majesty," I say. "And I beg for his Majesty to listen to what we say, however preposterous it may sound, for ours is a tale worthy for His Majesty to listen to."

His piercing eyes look into mine as if reaching deep into my being to ferret out the truth. He finally nods his assent. Enkidu, meanwhile, continues his comical contortions, and the king, irritated by the noise, tells him to stop it. Emboldened by the king's willingness to listen, I quickly take him through critical elements of my story, making sure he remembers parts of it.

"As you recollect, Your Majesty, my wife was supposed to have traveled, but many questions lingered. I came before His Majesty accused of another's death, but the hearings led to a conclusion that I was not behind it, and that her death was suspicious."

"Yes, I remember. And I told you to consider your duties."

"Indeed. And you remember, Your Majesty, that you sent Enkidu to watch my back on the way to Isin, and I was attacked on the way."

He frowns. "Yes. There was an attempt on your life."

"You, and the chief-priestess Geshtinanna, and the others, asked me to put aside my grief for my wife—"

"Yes, Yes, I know all that, continue," he says impatiently. I am chastened by his tone, for I may be speaking of a wife's death, but he has the fate of the entire kingdom in his hands. Even if his grip on it is tenuous.

"Please, Your Majesty, I beg of you to heed my words, for this story of my wife becomes something bigger than my domestic troubles."

He looks at me, puzzled. "Go on."

The magnificent staircase is now about fifty feet ahead. The stairs are twelve feet wide and rise to the heavens. The priestly hymns are louder, and on top, Geshtinanna awaits us. The noise of the following mass has lessened, for they have been stopped from proceeding further. They will remain behind, praying and participating in the rituals.

"After I left His Majesty's presence, I stayed home. But I was drafted into a citizen-contingent for the first Martu attack. Scribes were not to be recruited."

His eyes show recognition. He may have heard I had been recruited. But he does not say anything.

"And before I left, I found a hidden message from my wife."

He is surprised to hear that. This is now becoming more interesting for him. "What message?"

I describe the finding and the message behind it, including the insinuation that it may be a clue that a spy was sending information to the enemy.

Now I have the king's complete attention. We have many steps to climb. We are at a level where our heads are above the roofs of structures nearby.

"Continue, scribe," he says, and his climb slows down.

"I fought the Martu, but it was Enkidu who saved me again and hid me in the ravines."

We arrive at the steps. He does not stop us. It is now the three of us on the stairs. It is a strange sensation—to be here, on these sacred steps, with the king of all Akkad and our land, telling him a tale. We climb a few steps, and he stops to look behind.

I look down.

And there, two attendants are helping the prince to his feet, but he can barely climb. It is a sad sight, for when the grace of Enlil is lost, even the sons of divinities are not spared from the ravages inflicted on their bodies. General Inim-Nanna tries to clamber up, but the king gestures for him to remain behind. A few other senior courtiers realize who we are. I can imagine them trying to make sense of it all.

I turn away quickly. The king resumes the climb. "Continue."

"We ran away from Urim, knowing the danger on my life and that a conspiracy was afoot which caused my wife's death for something she knew. Something that imperils the throne, Your Majesty."

The wind is picking up—it is cooler here, and the view spectacular. We are not even halfway up, and yet the view before us reveals all Urim and beyond: every building, every palace, granary, temple and road, the tombs, and the walls. And on one side, the reflection of light from the snaking river is blinding.

Beyond the river, the sight is chilling. The distinct dark clusters of the army of Elam are visible.

I continue. "Enkidu and I escaped to a settlement to plot our next move, knowing that we must someday return to warn His Majesty."

He grunts.

"That was when a group of murderers, headed by a man of His Majesty's royal guard, tracked us to the settlement with a desire to murder me."

He pauses. "I believe the conspiracy afoot, scribe. We have seen information leaked repeatedly, and many have been put to death, to no effect."

Innocents.

"The man was Num-Assina, Your Majesty," I say, hoping he recognizes the name. "And my wife either heard or saw something she should not have."

His eyes furrow, but he shakes his head. "I do not remember them all. I am sure Nigir-Kagina would know him."

"We killed him. But before he died, he confirmed that he had a hand in my wife's death, and that she had to be killed quietly in a manner that would not arouse any suspicion or investigation."

King Ibbi-Sin places a comforting palm on my shoulder. My body shudders, for it is as if I am touched by god himself.

"May Enlil give you comforts in his gardens, scribe, for the manner of her death go against all rules of Urim and justice."

Tears spring to my eyes. This is the acknowledgment I wanted. I fought for. I lived for. I blink them away. We continue climbing.

"By the grace of His Majesty, I know she will. Which brings us to the subject of the spy, Your Majesty."

We are now nearly three-quarters up on this *é-temen-ni-gùru*, the glorious stepped seven-level structure that creates an aura, and the world is visible from here on this day. The orange flags on either side of the stairs flutter and create a sacred symphony with the hymns and cymbals. Chief-priestess Geshtinanna is looking down upon us, and from here, she looks like an embodiment of Inana, the goddess of war, with her bright-orange partial gown that exposes her proud breasts, adorned navel, and smooth thighs. Her hair is cascading down her shoulders, straightened with oil and shining in the morning sun. In one hand, she holds a sword, and in the other, a plate with burning incense. Blue makeup adorns her eyes, and her lips are bright red. It takes little time for her to recognize us, and she gives me a deathly stare.

My eyes briefly turn to Enkidu, who gives a knowing nod. Far below, as if we are looking down from a lofty mountain, I see the mass of people looking up in devotion and hope—hope that they may not be taken away as slaves or murdered in the savagery of war. The fragrant aroma of frankincense, myrrh, and balsam, mixed with the valuable secretive ingredients from Meluhha, is strong and heady in the air. The outline of the eight-foot basalt statue of Nanna is visible in the shrine behind Geshtinanna. I hear the sounds of the rest of the royal court a few steps behind me, with Princess Ningal calling out, "May we come up to be by your side, Your Majesty, my father?"

The prince coughs.

King Ibbi-Sin turns and signals for them to stay. "I will tell you," he says firmly. Their irritation is palpable.

I whisper to the king. "May His Majesty stop here, for my words are for His Majesty."

He stops. His eyes are narrowed in concentration, and his jaws tight with anticipation. "Have you learned the identity of the traitor who sits near me?" he asks.

From here, by the steps of the shrine of Nanna and Enlil, where gods sit and watch over my land and city, with my chest constricted, I propose a preposterous idea. "I do not know yet for certain, Your Majesty," I say, as I turn to look at the chief-priestess, "but there may be a way we can find out."

CHAPTER 43

URIM

KINDATTU

Kindattu watches as the third delegation from Urim approaches his army.

He is growing impatient with the impasse.

A day ago, men from the ramparts had raised flags and sent two unarmed messengers requesting him for a parley. Desiring to subjugate Urim without much loss for himself, Kindattu had received them cordially, preparing to make clear demands for their surrender in return for saving the city from destruction. But the first delegation was utterly useless, mouthing platitudes and suggesting strong cooperation between the two kingdoms, improved trade, and so on and on. None that Kindattu had any interest in. He had tried to extract details of the strength of Urim's defense, but the messengers had repeated what they were told—that it was indestructible, impassable, inviolable, and so on. He had sent them back with a warning: Urim must surrender, the king must abdicate his throne and throw himself at Kindattu's mercy, and be spared of violence.

Then came the second delegation—better than the first. This came with more concessions. Offers of a significant amount of gold, one hundred healthy ox, five hundred sheep, accession of a strip of land near the Zagros Mountains, the withdrawal of Sumer's garrisons from a major trade route in the east, free access to facilities in the southern ports, one hundred slaves, and the handover of two border towns to Elam. Kindattu had conveyed the Martu chief Atturapi's needs, and he had received concessions there: the Martu would receive uncontested pasture fifty-thousand-foot by fifty-thousand-foot between Urim and Lagash, along the Euphrates.

These were excellent allowances. In fact, so good that the fool Atturapi had dared to suggest that they abandon the invasion and return with these favorable terms.

That is the problem with men who were never kings. Their understanding of empire and kingdoms, and what divinity conferred upon kings meant, is limited. Kindattu had laughed at Atturapi, and then warned him never to suggest settlement for things that might look great to a low governor or a chief of cowherds, but they were *nothing* to the king of Elam. *Nothing.*

He had the messengers lashed and sent back on litters. The king of Urim would see his mercy, for he had not had the messengers impaled and paraded before the walls.

That sent a strong message, and there is now a third delegation. He will allow no more. If there is no surrender, then Kindattu will prepare for an attack. The scouts have been bringing him favorable news on access points and ramps to launch the siege. As much as Urim has prepared, and as much of his army's blood they will spill, he is confident the city will fall. The more they resist, the greater the destruction will be.

The delegation has three men this time. Their fearful and pathetic faces betray the news—the king of Sumer is a stubborn and stupid man.

The leader, an aged man, stands before him like a supplicant, his back hunched, hands folded, old eyes full of fear. Kindattu has an urge to strike and end him, but he has been told by his father and his priests that Inshushinak frowns upon his children who inflict death on those whose sin is carrying the unfavorable words of those above them. Even lashing this old bastard would kill him.

"Lord of Sumer and Akkad, king of four corners—"

"He is no king of four corners! Speak no more of your king's glory, or I shall have you impaled. What is the message?"

The chastened man looks around, afraid and uncomfortable. He speaks haltingly. "The king wishes to convey that he is saddened by Your Majesty's refusal to agree to a hand of friendship."

Kindattu scoffs. The only thing left is to cut off King Ibbi-Sin's hand. "And?"

"He reaffirms his commitment and his offers, and in addition will give Your Majesty a hundred shekels of gold. He asks Your Majesty if there is another wish that Your Majesty wishes to convey in return for the avoidance of war."

Kindattu controls his anger. The *insolence* of these fools! "I would have you beaten to death, old man, crush you like the cockroach that you are, for bringing a foolish message from a position of weakness!"

The hapless man stammers and falls to his knees. "Such is my king's order, Your Majesty, and I am but a humble servant."

Kindattu kicks the man on his shoulder, and he goes sprawling on the dusty ground, whimpering. His temple pulses with anger, but he restrains himself from lashing out further. But then, the man beside him, a general, speaks softly. "Your Majesty. We have news."

He turns and looks at the general, puzzled. One of the messengers is standing quietly behind the general, and there is a slight smile on his lips.

CHAPTER 44

URIM

NEMUR

I had insisted on being here, on being proved right. It has taken much convincing and pleading. We are in the darkness, by a specific section of the western wall, where, on the other side, a narrow pathway ends at the wall buttressed by two mounds. The wall here is thick and tall, and no military commander, as per Enkidu, would bother to attack here.

But there is something unique about this location.

There is a narrow tunnel cut through rocks that goes underneath the wall and emerges on the other side, and is concealed in the cleverest manner. Only a few know about its existence—the king, the general, a small number of the most elite royal guard. Clearly, Num-Assina had not known it. There was no indication of any intrusion which indicated that the treacherous bastard had divulged its location, and no one else was up to mischief.

We wait quietly. The pressure is immense. The distinguished General Nigir-Kagina himself is here to oversee this operation. On our side of the open mouth of the tunnel, to either side wait men with axes, buckets of resin, fire-arrows. The ramparts are empty except for one scout lying low and looking outside—the soldiers have been pulled away, and the torches extinguished.

The partial moonlight is all we have, and the unnerving deathly silence is oppressive.

Enkidu is standing beside the general.

"You better be right, scribe," says the general, his whisper at once hopeful and ominous.

I bow to him. "Nanna graces us all, General. I am confident," I say. My voice feels hollow.

"He is a brilliant man, General. And he has been right several times before," Enkidu says helpfully.

What if I were terribly wrong? What would happen to me? I try not to dwell on these thoughts as I look up at the sky with Nanna looking down upon us, smiling, gracing us with his light.

"Should we send some through the tunnel to check?" I ask.

I can see the general's expression from here. It is one of irritation. "Be quiet, scribe!"

Chastised, I keep my mouth shut. I must not mistake my skills of deduction and basic fighting with knowing how to plan attack and defense strategies.

He continues. "A clever enemy will be watching us from the other side, looking for signs of an ambush, for noise and pin-pricks of light, for anything that is contrary to the message they have received."

"Yes, General."

"They are watching. They are waiting to move. And we have to wait."

"Yes, General."

"Don't ask me again if we should go into the tunnel, or I will have you sent in and sealed."

"Yes, General."

But I smile inwardly. He believes me. The great general of Urim believes in my theories.

"The twig has snapped!" a captain says urgently. A thin rope runs from the inside bronze handle of a rock-cut door on the far end of the tunnel. The rope is attached to an arrangement of twigs that would snap if there was sufficient pull—one indicating a significant movement of the door.

It is time.

The general clears the men in front of the mouth of the tunnel and positions his men along the walls, invisible to the intruders crawling through. The tunnel can hold two to three men at a time.

I watch with anxiety and fascination at the dark opening, waiting, worrying. *This is it.*

The deathly silence grips my neck like a vice, and the only sound is that of blood rushing to my ears. For several minutes nothing happens, but this is expected. The tunnel runs a distance from the wall, through the mound. And then, finally, we sense movement through the rustling of gravel.

The first head peeks through the hole.

I watch terrified, thrilled, and elated, as the figure of a man emerges slowly, and until he comes out and turns back and adjusts his eyes, he would not see the rows of men standing behind him near the wall. We need a few men alive to confirm details. He seems pleased by the emptiness ahead and makes the mistake of rising to his height and taking a few steps before he realizes the trap, seeing figures rush at him from the corner of his eye. But it is too late. Two men seize him, close his mouth, and drag him away. The next man realizes what is happening and hesitates to come out, but two soldiers jump into the ditch before the tunnel's mouth and drag him out—though not before he screams.

Archers jump into the ditch by the tunnel mouth and launch a volley of lethal arrows into the darkness. The *twang, twang, twang* of the bowstrings makes my hair rise, bringing memories of the Martu attack. I hear screams inside. The archers empty their quivers, and then the men with resin buckets and flaming arrows take their turn. The archers dip their cloth-wrapped arrowheads into the resin, an attendant lights it on fire, and they shoot it into the tunnel. These arrows are known to set their targets aflame like human torches, and since the tunnel gently descends all the way to the other end, the bolts scream down in a straight path striking the hapless men inside. I hear more commotion, and my nose burns due to the acrid smell of the fire.

"Now!" the general orders.

Gangs of men move to seal the tunnel with large boulders.

Someone blows a whistle.

Along with a few others, I run toward a ladder set on the wall and climb up as fast as I can to get to the rampart. At the same time, a group of archers has materialized, almost magically, and raised their bows.

Even in that darkness, under the gentle light of the moon, what I see is alarming. At a distance, in the shallow crevice leading to the wall, is a line of soldiers now in disarray as they realize the ambush. But before they can do much, our men rain down arrows upon them, all within striking distance. I am filled with purpose that I almost want to jump down from the wall and go fight them. That advance contingent would enter and create havoc, opening the doors for the enemy to rush.

And what it means is that the army of Elam has moved during the night, quietly, to be closer to the gates.

It is a frightening development.

The air fills with conch sounds and more whistles, and while I do not have a good understanding of the meaning of different sounds, the figures scramble, and soon we see no one. But the torches all along the wall are ablaze, and soldiers make a great noise as if to indicate that they are alert and ready, and trumpets sound to bring the city to alert. As I look behind, lamps light in houses, and the great city is suddenly alive, like a beating heart.

With the city on full alert, the general believes that the enemy will not attack, not knowing if there are other surprises in store.

We climb down—it is time to talk to the men.

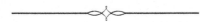

What I have learned from Enkidu's words and from my own experience is that no man, no matter how hardy his countenance and strong his soul, can withstand torture for long.

The first man is writhing on the ground, three of his fingers and an ear lobe sliced off with a knife. We are in a hut nearby, under the light of lamps. The man is a soldier of Elam—it is clear from his patterned long-gown and threaded beard, now wet with blood that has sprayed from his pulped lips.

"What were your exact instructions?" asks the general, seated before him. "Exact. We know much, soldier. Do not lie again."

The translator kneels on the blood-splattered ground and speaks to the man's good ear. They seat him again. He clutches his hand and looks around, his eyes wild with terror.

The torturer, a short man with a skirt, is now holding a thin copper needle and advances on the man. He struggles as two soldiers hold him tight, and the torturer pinches the right cheek and then stabs it with the needle, driving it deep on one side of the pinched cheek and pushing it out the other. The man screams again.

"Next time, it will be your eyes," the torturer says. "And I enjoy this very much."

I can barely watch. Enkidu's expression is passive.

The man's lips quiver, and spittle flows from his mouth. He is praying to his gods. The torturer has a clamp in his hand that he suddenly pushes into the man's mouth and, as he kicks around, wrenches a tooth out by its pink, glistening roots and throws it out. A gush of blood fills the man's mouth as he makes horrifying sounds, thrashing in agony as men hold him.

The brutality is sickening, but they have brought this upon us when they could have acceded to our demands for peace. Still, I pray for the man to tell us and walk the gardens of his gods.

"Now. Before it gets worse," the general says as they help the man spit the blood. He finally shakes his head and begins to whisper to the translator. After a few brief words, the translator looks at the general.

"He says they learned the secret of the tunnel from a spy."

"What spy?"

The man mutters something.

"He says a man from the last delegation told them about the tunnel."

There. The final confirmation.

"We have what we need, General," I say, unable to control my mouth. "This man should be given a merciful death, for he only carried the instructions of his king."

The general glares at me. But he knows the accuracy of my assessment and the cleverness of the mission. He nods. The man calmly accepts his death as a soldier drives a dagger through his chest.

By then, the second man has no desire to resist. He corroborates all the details and tells us more, and from all that, the direst picture emerges—the king of Elam has no wish at all to arrive at a settlement.

With the armies of Elam at our gates, the king and his generals have their mission, but I intend to pursue mine and then perish, if I have to—for this kingdom, this king, and for the woman who was wrongly sent away to her lonely death. Enkidu has his own demons to pacify.

Enkidu and I look at each other. It is now time to finish this journey and bring the wretched criminal to justice.

CHAPTER 45

URIM

KINDATTU

The king of Elam is in a rage. The messenger who gave him news of the secret tunnel lies dead before him, his every bone broken, his eyes punctured, his tongue cut out. He screamed and begged that he had no idea the soldiers were walking into an ambush, but how could this dog be believed when his best men were roasted alive in the tunnel? How promising the previous night looked! If they could get through the tunnels, they would be able to set fire to many structures, cause confusion, open a gate and allow his garrisons to enter before launching the full attack.

All that has been accomplished is that he has been made to look like a fool. And for that, they must pay.

They say great wars can last months, years even. But not always. Not when he had attacked cities near Susa. He has heard of many battles that were over in a day. They may lead to huge losses, and they may bring much suffering, but they are concluded. A grinding siege-and-wait leads to disease, starvation, and death, and gives many opportunities to the defenders to destroy everything—which would deprive the attacker of the riches, both material and people. If that is Urim's wish, he has no intention to grant it.

He has decided.

After months of stressing Urim through Martu incursions, Kindattu is confident that the people and army of Urim are tired and weary. Many will be wishing for all this to end and desiring to come under the rule of a new, powerful king.

He looks at his vast army with its disciplined units grouped in hundred each, the archers and slingers, the axmen and swordsmen, expert wall-climbers with rope and grappling hooks, ladder-bearers and spearmen, all backed by battering rams that will break the gates, launchers that can shoot flaming linen-wrapped stones into the city, and ten horse-driven chariots that can wreak havoc on enemy units that come outside the wall.

Yes, the horse-driven chariots. They are Kindattu's secret weapon. These beasts of the northern steppes are rare, expensive, and to be used in the most pressing conditions. The black-headed people call the horse a mountain-donkey, not realizing its power and potential. They have not learned to tame these beasts to become weapons of war, but Kindattu has been taught how to use them by the horse-riding merchants of the north. When the army of Urim sees his display of these wonderful animals, they will be discouraged of their chances.

He has given his orders.

Today is the day. It shall come as a surprise to the fools of Urim.

There will be no prolonged siege.

There will be a decisive battle, and it shall end this kingdom.

As the sun gently rises in the east, Kindattu finishes his prayers to Inshushinak, wearing his thick rich-brown leather corset, the king's spectacular one-horned bull helmet with gold plates, an ornate scabbard with his jewel-crusted sword, shoulder and knee pads, a thick ox hide sandal tied to his ankles, and two snug lapis-lazuli bracelets. He sits with augurs for the omens of the day—the brightening sky is clear of clouds, birds fly from east to west, and the river has not grown muddier. All these, the augurs say, suggest to the king that the gods will not be in the way. There are no dead fish floating in the river, and no bird has dropped from the sky. The king must launch today, they say, for the tidings are favorable.

The wall of Urim is a few hundred feet away as his men array in battle order. The mass of his soldiers is in the center—the battering rams and wall climbers in the front, archers and slingers next, and then spearmen and swordsmen forming the bulk of the infantry. On either side of his army are five horse-driven chariots with their solid wooden wheels, with cutting swords affixed to the center. This terrain is not conducive for chariots, but they are here more for intimidation than utility. On either end are the Martu—their army, if one may call it that, are making much noise, bellowing, excited at the prospect of loot and plunder, and eventually, unrestricted access to land. They are an untrained horde, and Kindattu wonders if any will even survive to enjoy the fruits of victory. But it is not his concern, and the Martu will have to be shown their place eventually.

The formation of the army is like a crescent moving toward the north-eastern section of the wall, which is about fifteen feet high and now protected with a dense cluster of soldiers on the rampant. There is no question that columns of soldiers wait behind the gate, if it were to be breached. Kindattu has decided to concentrate all his power on one gate, for spreading his forces in multiple sections, attempting to break through other gates, would spread his forces thin and make them vulnerable to surprise attacks. The battering ram units all carry tall lightwood shields to protect themselves from the arrows that they know will rain down upon them. It is critical for his own archers and wall-climbers to counter-attack, to allow the rams to slam into the gate uninterrupted. What Kindattu does not know is whether the enemy will open the gate and rush his forces to repel the attacks.

When the sun finally comes behind the nape of his neck, Kindattu, the king of Elam, signals his armies to move forward by whipping his hand across his chest and thumping his feet.

And then, in one great unison, the combined army of Elam and the Martu begin to advance on the north-eastern gate of Urim while making a great clamor.

From here, even at a distance, Kindattu can see the famous archers of Urim raise their bows to the air and wait for them to be within his range.

Blood will flow today, he thinks, but if there is one body that shall stand alive at the end of this day, he believes it will be his.

CHAPTER 46

URIM

NEMUR

Sun rises in the east, gently suffusing the great city of Urim with his orange blanket.

The city is tense, quiet, and ready. The battle is imminent—the army of Elam is standing a few hundred feet away from the north-eastern wall, and it is a large, well-equipped force.

I have learned that the king has arrived near the north-eastern gate to exhort the troops and prepare them for the impending battle. General Nigir-Kagina has accepted my argument and allowed Enkidu and me to leave without being conscripted. Instead, we will act as defenders of the palace, should there be a breach. He knows what I am planning to do, though he wishes to have no part of it. For him, certain lines are not crossed, and it includes any manner of attack on the royals. But I care for no line.

We both leave the hut and gingerly step over the two dead Elamite soldiers who have been unceremoniously dumped outside the door. I try not to think of last night's violence, for there is much more to come. I am fresh, energetic, angry, and filled with a sense of impending doom. If the day ends with my death, so shall it be. King Ibbi-Sin, having heard my theories on the steps of the *Etemenniguru*, has given us a royal seal for unrestricted access to any place in Urim.

Enkidu and I rush through the deserted markets, locked granaries, and empty brothels, and arrive at the inner wall.

A garrison of about five hundred men is now stationed here—it is the last defense, and the men are trained, hardy soldiers who will lay down their lives without hesitation. They have dug ditches in the front and filled them with sharpened wooden spikes. The ramparts are busy with archers and spearmen in their bare upper bodies and feather-adorned skirts. It takes us effort and argument with a captain before he lets us through the cordons. The massive gate slowly opens for us to enter the inner city. I am surprised to see a large contingent of forces here—but I should not be surprised. The king would seek to protect the most magnificent and holiest sections of this great city. The palaces, the temples, the *Etemenniguru*, the royal tombs, all with their riches, ripe for picking and the eventual target of the enemy. There are elaborate traps and trenches behind the wall, and the soldiers are arrayed in formation.

My mind questions the strategy of dividing our forces and keeping many here when the king could have thrown all his strength to the front and prevented the enemy from entering in the first place. But I am no general, and I do not seek to claim expertise in tactics of war. My world is smaller.

"Why are you not with the forces?" another captain barks at us.

"Perhaps you wish to ask the king! We are here on a sensitive mission," I say, showing him the royal seal. He holds it close to his eyes and examines it carefully while staring at us both. He finally grunts and lets us pass. Once we break through the lines, it is suddenly quiet and empty. The palm trees planted by the side of the wide graystone path sway gently in the morning air, the flowers in the well-maintained beds have bloomed to their pink, orange, and white beauty. There are few guards in front of the palace entrance walls, and there is no sound from the temples adjoining the main complex. The *Etemenniguru*, which rises to the sky, looks quiet. I wonder if there are soldiers there, in the shrine, waiting for the last stand.

We finally arrive at the main palace, the abode of the king, the seat of the ruler of our land and Akkad. The vast structure with its hundreds of rooms and hidden passages would be impossible for me to navigate, if not for Enkidu's help. He has roamed these ochre- and mud-colored halls before, and knows the meaning and significance of the many rooms. Where people meet, where they pray, where they are buried, and so on. Guards watch us as we make way, and there are a few slaves and palace maids serving the affairs of the palace.

The palace, while it appears to be one giant structure, is a complex of multiple sub-sections attached to each other through long corridors with arched doorways running through small gardens. When we cross several large, sparsely furnished rooms, we arrive at a corridor that Enkidu tells me takes us to the next sub-section of the palace, with the chief-priestess's quarters on one side and the prince's on the other. But four men stationed at the entrance of the corridor block our way. This is not the king's guard, for they are all now away with the king.

"Halt," the leader says, raising his hand.

Frustrated, I show him the king's seal. "Let us go. Orders."

He does not budge. "The prince's orders are not to allow anyone beyond this point."

Of course.

Enkidu advances menacingly. "Move out of the way, guard. Do you defy the king's order?"

The man bows but does not budge. "When the king is away on the battlefield, the ranking royal in the house has the power to determine who may arrive and leave, sir."

Enkidu bristles at this rule, unsure of whether this is made up. Who are these guards?

I do not want to cause harm or spill blood on the palace floors. At least not the blood of these men who are doing their duty.

"The king is lord of all our land and Akkad, guard. His word is law, and no one can supersede the king's words!" I say, imploring. "We are here on his word, and we must be allowed to proceed."

The man looks unsure. His eyes soften. But his demeanor is firm. "The king is my lord, and yet he has defined laws that I must obey. If I let you through, Enlil will see my dereliction of duty, and the king will put my family and me to death."

It is futile to argue. If we threaten them, there is a risk that he will call his backup, assuming they are nearby. All this ending with a stupid skirmish in the palace corridor? I think Enkidu and I can take on these men, but to what end?

"Should we find another way?" I whisper to him as the guards watch quietly.

He shakes his head. "There is no other way. This part of the complex has high walls on all sides."

Frustrated, I mull my options. Unable to control myself, I yell loudly, "You are defying the king's orders! We have to see the prince!"

The man looks at my waist. "Then hand over all your weapons."

This fucking son of a roadside whore!

"Are you an ass in human skin, idiot? We are about to battle Elam, and you want us to hand over our weapons and run around? Do you want me to go naked?"

We then get into a shouting match, yelling at each other but not drawing our weapons. I can always wait and return—but return to what? Who knows what the battle today will bring to us? I look around the vast and empty hall behind me. There is no one. The long corridor is empty. My hand reaches behind my leather belt to grip a short and heavy club. Enkidu gives me the slimmest of nods. Father Enlil has kept me alive for a reason, but he also wishes that I spill no blood that must not be spilled, and this I have resolved to on the way to the palace. I know that my wife watches, and so does Enkidu's. Like a gazelle, I sprint across to the leader, and before he can reach, leap into the air after pivoting off the wall and strike his head with the club.

Even as I land on my feet and spring on the other man, Enkidu has held him in a choke and Is squeezing his neck— it is a technique that causes one to lose consciousness. The remaining guard looks at us with terrified eyes, unsure of what to do.

I tell him gently, "No harm will come to you, soldier. But no guard is allowed to defy the messengers of the king."

He nods fervently.

Enkidu and I drag the unconscious men to a nearby room and drop them there. The remaining guard heaves a sigh of relief when we tie him up and leave him with a warning. It does not matter how long they take to wake— we will have gone to where we want by then. I no longer care about what happens after. With them out of the way, the corridor is empty. There will be more later, but not every guard will be as stubborn and stupid.

We walk briskly, keeping an eye out for any trouble. Once the corridor ends, it opens to another large room, painted all in dull blue, with a few benches. I wonder if the rooms are bare because the palace has begun to clear the more expensive items and hide them elsewhere. There are two ornate doors on either side, painted with pictures of lions and ox.

Enkidu studies the two doors. "That one," he says.

I hope he knows where we are going. It is an unsettling feeling, walking these halls and corridors that once hummed with activity and energy but are now quiet and ominous.

The door is locked from inside—Enkidu taps on it. "Open! Messengers from the king!"

There is a small peephole at eye level, and someone looks through. Enkidu raises the royal seal. The door opens without questions this time. Two men are guarding it from inside, and they say nothing as we show the seal again and tell them we must hasten to the prince's royal quarters.

"Are there guards stationed there?" I ask.

"Five," he says. "And four litter bearers for His Highness."

"Is he in his quarters?"

"He is. And so is the chief-priestess."

"We have a message for him. You stay here and let no one in," I say confidently, as if I am an authority from the royal detail. He nods.

As we walk toward the prince's quarters, Enkidu smiles at me. "The deer has become a lion," he says, and I grin. "If we die today, Nemur, know that we did everything we could, and you will have died a proud, brave man."

"And I am eternally grateful to you, Enkidu, for it is your guiding hand that brought me here."

He is pleased by the acknowledgment. We have discussed the next part several times, but reality lays to waste the best plans.

The first royal quarter to our right is the chief priestess', which is unmistakable based on the entrance. Two stone statues of Enlil and Nanna greet the visitor, and the door is exquisite Syrian wood with paintings of the *Etemenniguru* and the shrine of Nanna. Should I see her first? I wonder.

No.

We continue down the corridor—the prince's quarters are right ahead. The ornate double door is affixed with two beautiful bronze bull masks, a silver wreath, and the insignia of the prince: an upside-down sword with supplicants on either side. It is a sad symbol, for the man has not raised a sword in years, let alone smite his enemies. My entire being is now infused with a sense of anxious energy, and I am propelled by anger.

There are no guards in front of the door.

We rap a large copper ring affixed to the door, following a protocol I have observed in the courts. After a silence, a small rectangular slide window opens at eye level. "Yes?"

"Urgent message from the king. The battle is imminent."

"Who are you?"

The stupidity of these men! We have come through all these rings of protection, and they want to check!

Enkidu barks with his gruff voice, "Senior messengers from the royal guard, and we bear the seal of the king for passage. This is urgent, you fool!"

I sense hesitation. Muffled voices. "Show the seal."

Dear Enlil.

I hold it up.

More muffled noises. "The prince does not—"

"Tell the prince that this is the king's word! Do not waste our time!" Enkidu yells. "We did not come all this way to scratch our balls by the door, you idiots. Urgent! Your heads will eat dust!"

Enkidu raps the ring many more times. He knows how to enact drama, though he does not know when to stop. I signal him to be quiet.

Finally, I hear the creaking of the door. The moment there is enough space for us to squeeze through, we push in, entering the comfortable chamber with several reed stools, a cushioned bench, and copper and bronze lamps and ornaments. Two guards close the door behind us, *rightly*, and stand on the side. We glare at them, holding the seal in front of their faces and telling them not to intrude.

"He rests with Her Highness Princess Ningal, his wife, sir."

I nod. The deferring title is good. They see us as authority now.

Enkidu parts the curtain.

I enter the royal bedchamber.

There, in front, is a wide bed. The prince is propped up on a pillow and looking at the door, having heard the commotion. His wife, Ningal, is holding a cup, helping him to drink it. Two maids stand in the far corner, looking nervous.

Their eyes open wide in surprise. But before either of them speaks, I address them.

"For a form so lovely, a face as radiant as the moon, and a voice so sweet, who knew the poison that courses through your veins, Princess Ningal?"

CHAPTER 47

URIM

IBBI-SIN

The deafening noise fills the air like a thousand drummers in a marriage hall. His men raise conches and trumpets to make a great clamor, even as the enemy marches, making loud commotion of his own. King Ibbi-Sin, lord of this land and Akkad, stands on a high platform protected by shield-bearing soldiers, a distance away from where the bulk of Elam's army is advancing toward. On this day, his fifteen years of rule shall reign supreme and continue, or fall, bringing down the great dynasty of Urim. How would his forefathers, the great kings Ur-Nammu, Shulgi, Amar-Suen, all look upon him from the gardens of Enlil?

On this momentous day, he misses his dear son. The boy who never showed mettle for battle has grown weak, and Ibbi-Sin wondered if his own determination that the prince was unfit to rule had led to his deterioration. But he puts those thoughts behind him as the enemy's relentless march fills his vision.

The king of Elam has amassed a considerable force.

The Martu barbarians baying like diseased dogs have lent a hand. He watches as the battering rams, made of thick heavy wood with metal fronts, are wheeled toward the gate under a hail of arrows. They are prepared—the thick leather shields in the front are protecting the pushers, and their own archers are returning a punishing volley of arrows on his men, who are inflicting but also receiving terrible damage. Arrows come with such force that they lift men off their feet and throw them backwards. Behind him, on the ground below, are dense columns of his own army waiting behind the gates. *How long will it hold?* he wonders.

The archers change tactics. They begin to launch fire arrows dipped in resin. The bolts thud into the battering ram and the shields, but the flames do not spread. Arrows slam into the oncoming mass of men, lighting them on fire. They scream and run around, burning others, looking like fireflies in daylight, but the wall of shields and men advances inexorably.

He knows that no number of arrows can halt a dense infantry protected by shields. He wonders if his army can hold them near the walls and grind them down, causing heavy losses. And whether they can do it again, and again, and again, until the demoralized enemy gives up. But the battle would not be over. He would have to send his army out in the open then, repelling and driving these unholy beasts from his land—and for that, as king, he will need to shed copious amounts of the blood of his people.

General Nigir-Kagina is pacing along the rampart, dodging arrows, yelling orders. The catapults begin shooting fist-sized stones with deadly force at the oncoming invaders. The rocks pulverize many heads, wetting the gray and gravelly ground with blood and brain matter, but the enemy keeps coming. Ibbi-Sin watches as Kindattu's infantry bring their own slingers to the front and begin to counter stone with stone, breaking the skulls and jaws of his own, who clutch their destroyed faces and collapse on the ground, writhing. His guards force him to squat as they protect him from the hailstorm of death.

The general runs up to him and peeks through the cordon. "They will begin battering the door in minutes, Your Majesty. Do you wish to open the door and attack them, or wait for it to be broken in?"

He considers the question calmly. "Do you think you can repel them if you open the door?"

The general sighs. "They are too great in number."

Ibbi-Sin curses and looks up at the protective shields. *Why have you forsaken me, Father Enlil?* The betrayal in his own household has caused enormous damage through the revealing of garrison deployments, weak points of trade routes, incentives of governors, manner of defenses. He has half-heartedly believed the tenacious scribe's words. His heart is heavy, but without absolute proof, how can he raise the dark finger of accusation against her who cared for his son like a dutiful wife? He has left her in the palace, proceeding to the battle, letting the gods do justice as they choose, for they have shown no consideration to him. If it is their desire, then for Ibbi-Sin to condemn his own daughter-in-law would be an even greater affront to them.

A powerful shock reverberates through the rampart, and he stumbles where he squats.

"The rams are on the gate! Climbers!" somebody screams. There is more running, and the screams, shouts, and taunts of men, the clang of metal, the dull thuds of wood, the twang of the bowstrings, the ear-splitting sounds of cymbals, whistles, and trumpets, the bone-shattering impact of stones hurled over the wall, the sound of flames from incoming burning linen balls—it is nothing like Ibbi-Sin has ever encountered. His own battles were on open ground, and the great city of Urim had never been attacked in this manner. Even the skirmishes with neighboring cities were limited to small armies facing each other in the fields. No one had ever dared to arrive at the walls of the city blessed by Nanna.

Until now.

A captain peeks through the shields. "The general says it will not be long before they break the gate, Your Majesty. Their rams are too powerful!"

Ibbi-Sin wonders if he should rise, away from the shields, inspiring his men, exhorting them to fight, even as he, as their god, stands in front. "Take those shields away! Away!" he swats at his guards, and their bewildered expressions annoy him. "Take me to Nigir-Kagina!"

They form a protective barrier as he races across the rampant, making way through men hurling javelins and stones now that most of the arrows are depleted.

Thwack! An arrow barely misses him, but the soldiers are energized to see their king amongst them. "Do not give up, fight! Kill as many as you can before they breach!" he shouts. The leaders shout his message, but he knows much of it is lost in the pandemonium.

He pulls out his ornate sword and holds the bronze-studded, blue-painted shield in front of him as he raises his weapon. "For Enlil and Nanna, we fight!" he roars in his gravelly voice, and the soldiers around him shout with gusto. Nigir-Kagina comes running to him, ducking behind the rows of men with their shields up.

"Your Majesty, it does no good to anyone if you die here," the general says, his voice firm. "To fight, they need their king alive. They will lose the will should His Majesty take a strike in full view!"

Ibbi-Sin is about to admonish him but knows that the general is right. "I have to be here! Keep me protected, so they feel my presence."

The general's look tells it all. "Their wall-climbers are getting ready, Your Majesty. We cannot hold them for long. The Martu have spread to either corner, trying to climb. I have to thin the lines on the wall, Your Majesty. You have to get down!"

Suddenly, someone shouts, "Breach! wall-climbers!"

Ibbi-Sin looks on in horror as several men leap from the edges onto the rampart, swinging their swords in one hand, an utterly foolish and suicidal attempt. Who are these fools! His men quickly drag the assailants and stab or crush their heads with the maces. But that is just the first wave. Even as the thunderous sounds of the ram bashing in the door get louder, more men come over the wall, and there is now a mad scramble to push them down.

"You have to leave now, Your Majesty!" Nigir-Kagina implores. "You have to retreat to the inner walls with an extra contingent, to protect the divine palace and Etemenniguru!"

Cannot let the gods' shrine be fouled!

"Please!"

Flustered, Ibbi-Sin signals his men to lead him down the wall. But the ladder is a distance away. He runs along with his men, his shield to his left, even as they hack and push the wall-climbers now clambering over in larger numbers. A man's hacked head bounces off his legs and he kicks it to the side, even as he steps over the dead. When he reaches the destination, Ibbi-Sin looks back from the wall, and his eyes catch a figure hunched among a heavily armed, shield-bearing protective guard.

The man from Elam, wearing a gold-plated, one-horned bull helmet.

And even with his fading memory, Ibbi-Sin remembers what the scribe told him about his wife' message.

The poisonous moon sends honey to the one-horned bull.

O my beautiful Urim, may you not be under his
wicked leg.

CHAPTER 48

URIM

NEMUR

"For a form so lovely, a face as radiant as the moon, and a voice so sweet, who knew the poison that courses through your veins, Princess Ningal?

Her eyes are ablaze. They are usually dark as coal, but now they are fiery embers. She stands straight and appraises us, royal in her bearing and as haughty as a princess can be. Her eyes dart to the entrance—is she expecting anyone?

"Watch your insolent mouth, scribe!"

"You know who I am," I say. "How many princesses can recognize a scribe, when his appearance is no longer what it was when she saw him first?"

Her eyes flutter at the first mistake.

"I come with a lineage to the gods and remember all who have stood before me," she says, and she turns to her husband. "What man tolerates intruders in his quarters where he lounges with his wife?"

The prince is slumped on his pillow. His face is white, as if drained of blood, and his eyes track us weakly. He tries to say something ,but saliva drools from his mouth. It is in that moment that Father Enlil sends a lightning bolt through my mind, bringing clarity to an otherwise murky affair.

"How can a kindly prince, he who has done nothing but to serve his father and given you the comfort and protection as a husband, do anything when you have been poisoning him?"

She flinches as if touched by a branding stone. That is when I know that my guess has hit her like a bolt with dreadful accuracy. The prince's languid eyes open wide—I know he can hear, but his limbs have lost strength. Did he know? Has he given up? I look at the cup near the stool.

The two maids begin to sniffle, and then suddenly, one of them bolts toward the door. Enkidu moves swiftly to block her, but my hand shoots out and grabs her by the hair. She wails as I pull her to me and put the dagger to her neck. "The cup is tainted with small traces of poison, isn't it? By the grace of Nanna, I shall not hesitate to spill a woman's blood. Tell me!"

Enkidu walks toward the door to check on the guards stationed in the other room. Even as the woman whimpers, Enkidu returns and quietly closes the inner door.

We now have the time to deal with any attack. And if I were to die here, I will take this unholy woman with me.

"You are running out of time," I say as I press the blade to her neck while watching Ningal. She has a strange look on her face. Her face is flushed, her eyes dilated, and she shows no fear.

"Yes. Cut her throat. Fuck her if you want. Do it. That's why you are here!" she says, taking me by surprise. "Go on! Let me see if you have the strength, you lowly pen-pushing cockroach."

What a foolish thing to say. I whisper to the woman, "The princess has no regard for you, but the gods will favor if you tell me the truth. I seek to do no harm to you."

She nods, and her voice is barely audible. "Yes, every day. A little. May gods forgive me," she says and begins to wail. It is a heinous act, no doubt under duress and orders from the madwoman in front of me, but justice must come to all. Enkidu drags her away and ties her hands and feet, and even as the princess and prince watch, he ties the other woman. The maids make no noise and accept their fate.

With them bundled in a heap, I return my attention to the princess, who stands firm with a twisted smile on her face.

"You are poisoning the prince, and you had my wife killed. It is you, is it not, Princess, that conspired with Num-Assina to pass secrets to the king of Elam?"

The prince grunts. I can see his distress. The sense of betrayal. The monstrosity of what his wife has wrought.

She wrinkles her imperial nose and scoffs at my words. "You make unfounded speculations, and for that, you will be flayed before me, begging for mercy, and hung upside down from the city wall."

I laugh. "The ears of those who listen to this, here in this room and hiding elsewhere, shall recognize that you did not vehemently denounce my accusations. If Urim falls, it will be because of you! Why?"

Suddenly, her face contorts in a fury. "How dare you ask why?"

At that moment, five men emerge from the side chambers, armed. They take position behind her—her guards must have heard some commotion or raised voices. We have made the mistake of not closing all doors to this room.

I turn to the prince. "Your Highness, she does not outrank you. Tell the men to stand down!"

But he is unable to speak, frothing in his mouth. The pieces of this diabolical conspiracy continue to form a shape. Enkidu gently pushes my arm, distancing himself, creating clearance as he takes a fighting stance.

"The woman you protect has betrayed the loyalty of His Majesty. You all know the penalty for aiding her. Arrest her!"

She laughs. The guard beside her, a tall, powerfully built bearded man with a long sword, walks by her side and kneels. It is a strange gesture. He raises a palm and slides it up her naked thigh on the parted gown. He rises and whispers something in her ear, and she grins. The entire demonstration disgusts me.

Enkidu spits to the side. "Not a princess. A whore!"

She ignores his taunt. "Are you wondering why they haven't attacked you yet? You stupid fools coming into the royal chamber, taking advantage of the battle outside. You don't know yet, but the army of Elam has breached the walls and broken the gate. They are pushing inside."

Enkidu and I share surprised glances. But should we be surprised? We knew that our army was outnumbered and outmaneuvered, and with no help forthcoming from neighboring cities, it was a matter of time before Urim fell.

"Soon, Urim will have a new king."

And I complete the sentence. "And you have conspired with him to be one of his new queens."

She pauses and looks at her husband with disdain. "What he cannot give me," she says, pointing to the suffering prince, now dying of poisoning, "King Kindattu will."

"So you began to conspire the moment King Ibbi-Sin declared that his son was not ready to succeed the throne."

She curls her lips and swings her palm, as if to suggest, *is that not obvious?*

"And my wife, why—"

Her eyebrows knot in anger and her nostrils flare. "That stupid bitch. I should have gutted and drowned her in the river instead of giving her a gentle and glorious end."

Gentle? Glorious? I resist the rising anger in me to strike her, for that would be a mistake. This is now as much a conversation to learn the truth as it is to bide our time and hope for the right circumstances to strike and escape. I know we do not have too much time, if the battle is now raging in the outer walls—it will arrive at the inner walls soon.

"You sent her to her death for no reason!" I say. I have a strong guess, but I will let her speak.

Her eyes are cool, and she rubs her arms. "No reason? A little mangy donkey shouldn't interfere with the workings of those far above her station. She was sneaking around Num-Assina and me, and then she had the audacity to try to counsel me. *Please do not let the pain of your marriage stray you from the path of righteousness, Princess!* I remember the sheer impudence, gall, brazenness for a lowly palace priestess to not only overhear my words, but to try to tell me what to do. I should have kicked her like the dog she is!"

Even as I listen to her, astonished, she murmurs, as if justifying the act to soothe the conscience, to unburden herself of her conduct. "I sent her to walk the gardens of Enlil. No one would suspect, I thought, and besides, she would travel to the abode of the gods. But you had to be a rat, unwilling to let go."

I sigh. So that was why. My wife had heard them conspire and had made the terrible mistake of trying to tell this vicious princess. It was not surprising. She had from time to time talked to the royals, including the chief-priestess, as part of her duties. Sometimes it was telling them about new processes, incantations, or mundane subjects like procuring worship materials for their quarters, clothes, makeup. She had overstepped once, from the gentle duty of her heart, and walked to her death. I blink rapidly to hide the tears forming in my eyes. She must have perceived her mistake and the danger to her life soon after, which was why she left the message. I would never learn of everything that led to it, but I knew enough.

Enough for me to die knowing I had finally found the truth, and the perpetrator.

"It was you who made Num-Assina do what he did."

"It was his cock," she says crudely. The eyebrows of the men behind her rise in surprise. But the tall man beside her grins with his yellow broken tooth. No wonder he is the next *cock* fooled by his desire for her.

I try another tactic. I address them. "She will discard you all like trash. You are too stupid to see it."

The leader snarls, "You know nothing about what she will do. She has nurtured us, fed our families, brought comfort to our lives with her rewards. And to her, we are indebted."

"And not to the royal house to which you swore fealty? Or the prince who is your true Lord?"

They do not respond to that accusation, avoiding my eyes.

"Num-Assina was an idiot," she says derisively. For this treasonous monster, everyone else is stupid.

"Num-Assina is dead," Enkidu finally speaks. "And his desire to torture the scribe was driven by your orders."

She laughs. "Why do you think my men have not cut off your heads? I want to see you both die slowly, screaming. I will enjoy it. And one day, when I sit beside the throne of the man with the one-horned bull cap, I am sure to find a lot more entertainment than under the weak king."

The desire for more and the ambition for power is ruthless and terrible.

"And you have no remorse for poisoning your husband."

"Remorse?" she says, twirling her bangled wrist. "He has given me nothing but sorrow since the day of marriage. He could not give me a son. He gave me no pleasure in the bed. And finally, he deprived me of the tiara of the queen. What was there for me?"

"You could have left him."

She laughs. It is a mirthless, hollow laugh. "Leave? Leave a prince, and go where? This is how cockroaches like you think. I would be sold as a slave or a noble's whore if I had not done what I did, once this kingdom falls."

"This kingdom will fall because you weakened it!" I shout. I can feel the heat in my face. Not only did Ibbi-Sin have to contend with unending incursions, but the worst blows were attacks on trade posts, outposts, confidential garrison deployments, unguarded areas—all of which contributed to a war of attrition, along with the drought and intransigence of neighboring governors.

"It falls because the king is useless, and his seed has no strength!" she says, her every word a poisonous arrow to the prince, whose fists are curled up in balls, his eyes wide open, and his face contorted in helpless fury. How did I not see it when she first cast aspersions on him and tried to make it look like my wife's death was due to his amoral debauchery, when it was she who indulged in every manner of conduct that violated every trust, duty, and loyalty?

"Urim will fall and rise again!" she spits. "The king, his son, and even his scribes are weak, spineless bastards!"

Oh, the rage of a woman who lost her chance to be queen.

"And you thought that letting Urim fall was your wisest move, that the king of Elam would have you in his harem?"

She has a faraway look in her eyes. "He saw me years ago. He lusts for me. And he has promised to have me by his side for the services I have rendered."

"No king will desire a wanton harlot as his queen," Enkidu helpfully opines. I cannot control it. I snigger at the comment.

It throws her into a towering rage. Her face red with anger, eyes full of fire, she screams at her men, "Get them! Don't kill them! Get them!"

This is it. You have brought me here, Father Enlil. Is it your wish that I die here, or is my life worthy for this earth?

It is as if the hand of god is guiding me, and the world around me becomes a blur of blue, red, and orange. The shouts and screams are barely in my ear as I run, jump, swing, dodge, duck, and slash. I feel the squirt of warm blood on me, the sensation of blade cutting through soft flesh, the distinct *tuk* of the sword's impact on bone, the sharp pain of the edge of a knife scraping the skin. Someone is pushing, a woman or women yelling, sounds of brass lamps crashing, the glistening velvet blade shining before it penetrates something soft, the moans, and the slick wetness of blood on the floor causing me to slip and fall.

Then the sharp pain of a vicious kick to my ribs, the *thud* of a sandaled foot on my back, and the blinding white-hot pain of a club on the back of my thighs. I try to lift my head, but the foot slams down on my skull, causing me to smash my teeth on the hard ground, breaking a tooth and causing my mouth to fill with the warm and acrid taste of blood. *Bring her to justice, Father Enlil, even if I should die! And let me die before the torture!*

My head is spinning from the attacks, and my vision is hazy. I cough a few times, spitting out blood. Someone is cursing. Two hands grip me under the armpits and drag me. *Am I being saved?* My dragger shoves me into a chair and ties my hands to the sides of the armrest. *Not being saved.*

More noises. My vision slowly comes into focus, since I've been left alone for a brief period with no one hitting me and me not trying to kill someone.

I look around.

Enkidu is struggling with two men as they kick and pummel him. They drag him toward the bed and tie him to a bedpost. Ningal is standing on the bed, her hair disheveled, her long luxurious gown open at her breasts, and there are scratches on her face and belly. I do not remember attacking her. I do not remember much in the red haze of pain. My hearing slowly returns.

"Tie them securely! Hard! Don't let them wiggle!"

Once satisfied that we are both securely restrained, she gets down from the bed and walks up to me. Two men remain with her—the tall leader, who is injured, for he limps toward me, and there is a deep gash on the side of his torso which he has tied with a cloth. His grimacing face is full of hate. And one other man, unscathed, tries to help his leader, who angrily swats him away.

The prince is on the bed, but they have tied his legs. Why? Where will a poisoned, dying man, go?

What happened to the guards outside?

The guard brings Princess Ningal a stool, and she sits on it demurely in front of me. What a strange perversion of life that I must be taunted by a *woman* and hurt by her, as if she has not done enough. Is this Father Enlil's strange sense of humor? To bring me on this long journey so I can die like a whimpering dog at the hands of one who has wronged me? I control myself from blaming my gods, the ones who have watched over me, fed me and kept me alive.

"Bring him to his senses," she orders. *I am in my senses, you fucking rotten pig.*

The guard slaps me hard, causing my ears to ring. But it does shake the lethargy and make me alive and awake. A volcanic fury erupts in me, and I begin to fight my restraints while raining them with a torrent of abuse. She leans back and giggles, and the guard punches me savagely in the stomach, causing me to gasp and double up in pain. I realize there has to be a way to save myself, but *what?*

Once I manage to regain my breathing, they lift my head again, and I finally face her. She enjoys this—this ugly, monstrous woman who has fooled every citizen with her gentle outward demeanor, her beautiful face, her pretense of devotion to the prince. Hideous terror lies within her, and no one saw it.

She raises a knife, and I flinch. She slowly drags it along my arm, cutting the skin, causing a small drop of blood to ooze and flow down my restrained hand.

"You are a learned man," she says, "and you know much about the various peoples that inhabit the four corners of the world."

I say nothing.

"I should kill you for all the misery and anxiety you have caused me. You would not be in this situation if you had moved on. Found another woman. Or a mistress, or even a young obedient slave. How pathetic that you pine for your dead wife."

Does she have no remorse? I have heard of people—we call them those without the touch of god—who are strange in that they do not have the ability to empathize, they feel no softness in another person's touch or words, and they have no sense of someone else's pain. They are cursed, and I am sure they will not walk the gardens of Enlil after their death. But when alive, they bring great misery to those around them. I have seen cruel men. But a woman, and amongst the royals who come from the lineage of gods? It is shocking.

I have decided, foolishly, that I will endure the pain. Whether I fight or not, I know she will do what she wishes to do, and if that is the case, why not say what I want? "You know nothing about affection. You are nothing but a mad bitch, foaming in her mouth, desecrating everything that is holy, bringing great shame upon this land and herself," I say evenly.

She slices my right upper thigh, enough to draw blood but not deep enough to cause death by bleeding. I wince and grunt. My whole body is pulsing with various kinds of pain, and I never thought I would withstand it all and continue. I will not give in to this beast.

"I was telling you about the peoples of the world, was I not, scribe? Far to the north, even further north than the land of the men of Akkad, are a people called the Assyrians. You have heard of them, have you not?"

Her eyes have a strange glint of excitement in them. She is breathing shallowly. I nod, unsure what she is trying to say.

"The Assyrians know how to inflict pain on their victims. They have learned many methods, and I was told of one in particular."

My heart begins to race. This is no happy story about the Assyrian people.

She rubs her finger in the blood on my thigh and wipes it on her gown. "The Assyrians have mastered the technique of flaying. We do it, but rarely. Only for the most heinous crimes."

No.

"I have never tried doing it. I am a princess, not a butcher. Not a torturer. And I am a woman. Has a woman ever flayed a man?" She looks at the leader by her side, and he smiles through his pain.

"And I will try it on you today, scribe. And my new king will be pleased."

No.

"You first, and then him," she says, pointing the knife. What otherworldly demon spawned her?

I begin to struggle against my restraints.

"They say some live for days after being skinned. But the masters can do that. I am sure I will be clumsy, and you will die sooner, which is unfortunate. I will wear your skin as an ornament," she says, rotating her wrist.

Fuck you.

I look at the man beside her. "Your fate will be like mine. You wait, you treacherous scum."

He raises a hand to hit me, but she stops him. "Don't. Let me relish this. I will wait here until King Kindattu's men arrive. Let them see what their new queen is made of."

Mad woman.

"Or I should first castrate you?" she says, her demonic eyes twinkling.

Oh, Enlil. He who has blessed the lands with fruit and flowers.

Thy name proclaimed around the world.

To thee, I pray to give me fair judgment in the netherworld.

She makes another small cut on my inner thigh, drawing more blood. "Or not. What pleasure is there in skinning a eunuch? Oh, your wife was a fine woman, a good servant, but nosy. She had no reason to peep into an otherwise unknown, deserted room while I rode my lover, or to hear our discussions."

To your abode I verily go.

Oh, Lord of the world.

"Enough about her. I should cut off your fingers and let you live. What a fine end for a scribe!"

My father, my benefactor, the one who has given me life.

He who dwells in the shrines of Uruk, he who dwells in our hearts…

"Are you praying, scribe? No prayer will save you from Inshushinak. He who is your new god."

My body feels like it is on fire. The little cuts burn.

Take me to your arms, Enlil, Nanna,

Me who is your servant, one who toils for your name, son of your glory.

"Hold him. He is shaking too much."

Lord Enlil, to you, I raise my hand.

"Once you die, you will roam the netherworld as a demon—desperate, lonely, eating clay and sand, for a worthless bug like you would never receive consideration from the judges."

For you, I lift my foot.

And to thee I bow my head.

I close my eyes, let the tears flow, and wait for the slicing to begin.

CHAPTER 49

URIM

IBBI-SIN

King Ibbi-Sin despairs as he watches from the rampart of the wall of the inner city. The battle is near him, with the enemy having fought through the defenses, killing large numbers of his army and the valiant citizens. Thick black smoke rises from the many houses, granaries, offices, outer city temples, shops, villas, trees, and shrubs set on fire, either by retreating soldiers hoping to slow the attackers, or by the attackers bent on laying to waste everything they encounter.

Barbarians.

Men with no regard or civility. Backward sons of mongrels. Beasts.

He knows that rape and plunder will follow if the women and children do not escape through the now opened gates in the southern sections—this was his explicit order, let the people flee with their belongings, through the gates far away from conflict, and get out if they can. Once the ardor for blood and lust has cooled, and the new army has settled, life returns to normal, as the new lords need to restart trade and agriculture. When he invaded the lands of Elam, bringing their men and women in fetters, he had never burned their cities down.

He was a man of this glorious land, a king borne amongst the divine lineage, full of culture and intelligence. Not like this scum of the earth, working together with those who are nothing more than feral pigs. The defense of the inner wall is managed by experienced troops, but the king knows that in the end, it is the numbers that matter.

Even the best five hundred cannot face an untrained horde of five thousand.

And the army of Elam is not an untrained force. They have shown surprising skill, maintaining their discipline in the center while the idiots of Martu die like flies, flailing about on the side. Perhaps it was all intentional, to use them for wearing his city down and then let them die and wither away. After all, Kindattu *could have* kept the Martu legions *behind* his army.

The noise and panic are palpable, and his soldiers, ready with their bows and slings, spears and swords, watch the paths through dense clusters of houses that eventually lead to the gate of the wall where they stand. The fires are getting nearer, and soon, they spot their own army retreating. Ibbi-Sin's heart sinks when he finally sees what is happening—his men are hopelessly outnumbered, fighting with incredible bravery, and falling as they are struck by advancing spears and swords. Suddenly, like rats exploding from a hole set on fire, the two forces spill into the open area near the wall, within the archers' range. And again, the bolts fly with stunning accuracy, pinning many enemy troops and his own, and then the return arrows begin. It is a recurrence of the battle near the outer wall.

Soon this wall will be breached, scaled, broken, and all his men will die. And those who surrender will either face execution or live as slaves. Ibbi-Sin does not know much about the treatment of slaves by the Elamites—but in his own kingdom, slaves have been treated with justice and kind laws, and while they will never be the same as the citizens, they are not butchered at a master's whim.

Oh, Enlil, why have you condemned your children? How have I wronged you? Oh, Nanna, patron of this city, is there no tear in your heavenly eye for those who have worshipped you be murdered, tied, dragged away, and your temples desecrated?

The smoke begins to blow toward the wall, causing his eyes and throat to burn.

He turns to a senior commander by his side. "This cacophony will lead to my death, and I shall become an unrecognized corpse burned in the fire. If there is a chance for negotiation, then I have to be alive."

The man nods.

"Gather ten of your best men and take me back to the palace. I shall wait there for the king of Elam while seated on my throne. And I shall die there, if I have to."

The man bows.

Ibbi-Sin continues, "And once I have turned the corner to the palace, tell your men to retreat, and they may run if they desire."

The man recoils in horror. "Our lives are to protect His Majesty and the land that god Enlil has given us. Please do not ask us to run!"

Ibbi-Sin places a palm on the man's head. A gesture of blessing. The king then turns without a word and walks toward the ladder.

CHAPTER 50

URIM

NEMUR

I can barely breathe as she crudely tries to scrape the skin on the other thigh. Her men have not only restrained me, but they are holding me down, pressing from the shoulder to prevent me from shaking and toppling over. I can barely hear anything over my own screams.

Please. Father Enlil. He who shows mercy. Why?

This woman will find her justice in the courts of the afterlife, and that I have accepted. Blood is roaring through my ears, and everything is muffled.

Commotion.

I blink my tears.

What is—

A man topples over me.

The blurry figures in front spring to their feet.

Movement.

Screams.

The sounds of struggle.

Suddenly someone is slapping the tears off my eyes. *Feminine* hands.

Heart pumping wildly, but by the grace of Enlil, the mind regains clarity!

A figure materializes in front of me, clear.

Geshtinanna.

"Wake up, scribe. Do not weep like a woman. It's just a few cuts!" she yells at me.

I let out a spittle-flying laugh of relief and wince at the pain. *A few cuts*, she says, but it is as if my being is enveloped in incandescent agony. My thighs are slick with blood. Jagged cuts ooze blood, and layers of peeled skin hang grotesquely on the side.

There is more commotion. More guards.

"Tie her up," Geshtinanna says. I turn to see Princess Ningal screaming and fighting with two guards.

The leader of Ningal's guard lies dead on the side, an arrow through his torso and eyes.

Where is Enkidu?

I spot someone giving him water as he groans and comes to his senses. He has been spared from damage.

The chief-priestess, the one who I detested for many reasons—for her imperial behavior and sharp words, for not seeing the doom upon Urim—how can I begrudge her for saving me from a horrifying death?

"Bring the salves and bandages," she orders someone. "One of the benefits of being tortured in the palace is that the instruments of healing are readily available."

She grins, and I smile back. I greedily drink water, bringing succor to my parched lips and throat. But it tastes of blood. I spit it to the side, cleansing my mouth before drinking again.

She keeps watch over me through it all.

A princess, daughter of the king, chief-priestess of all Urim, and she is tending to me!

Someone has tied a scarf over Ningal's mouth.

"Elamite army. Where are they?" I ask, slowly, fighting through the pain.

She smiles sadly. "They are near the inner walls. My father is arriving at the throne room soon, and there he will await the king of Elam."

The king's way.

"How did you...?"

She waves her hand. "One of my messengers brought me the curious news of two men rushing to the prince's quarters. From the description, it was clear who it was. I remembered your gesticulations to my father, though he never divulged it me, and now I know I was under suspicion. But I had to investigate."

"The guards outside?"

She laughs. "I am the chief-priestess of Urim and the king's daughter. Do you think they would defy me? I sent them off and listened to the conversations from outside the door. Once I determined that you have been truthful and correct all along, I had to call for my own armed guards and wait until they arrived, even though I heard the clashes inside."

Finally, someone thinks to cut my restraints and free me. I wipe my bloodied hands on a linen pad. "You have saved my life, chief-priestess. Nanna has sent you."

She looks at Ningal, thrown to the side with her hands and legs tied. "You tried to warn us. You tried to save my father and this kingdom, and we did not listen."

It is an exceptional acknowledgment coming from a princess. I bow to her.

A palace physician comes over to me with salves, cleansing liquids, and more bandages. It stings, and pain shoots up my legs like needles through a foot as he washes the wounds and tightly bandages them. Not only do I have bruises from the fight and multiple swellings, but I am told that I have cuts on my torso, thighs, arms, shoulders, and back, and if I do not take great care, evil will enter the wounds and cause putrefaction and death. It is a common occurrence among soldiers who are wounded in battle.

Two men hold me below the armpits and raise me to my feet. I wince and limp around, trying to bring energy back. But my mind is clear again, even with all the pain—and Enlil, in his own inexplicable ways, has kept me alive again.

Enkidu has recovered, lightheaded but immensely relieved that I am alive. "She cut you like a butcher's lamb, scribe. Did it make you hard?" he asks. Geshtinanna gives him a disapproving look.

"You missed the joy, Enkidu. The pleasure of a princess carving you like a pig is forever lost for you."

But we are running out of time if the Elam's army is on the way. I limp up to the tied Ningal and stare at her. There is no remorse in those eyes—only hate. Hate that her despicable act has not borne fruit.

"Her justice must come from my father's hands," Geshtinanna says. "And you must deliver the story to him. Let us go."

A burly guard helps me walk, and Enkidu stays by my side as we leave to the throne room, with a struggling Ningal carried on the shoulders of two men. As I pass the open quadrangles, I realize the great tragedy that my city is experiencing.

Smoke.

No doubt the dwellings and people are on fire. The dark tendrils are reaching into the palace and portending an ominous future.

I struggle to keep pace and hop on my better leg as my helpers drag me along. We soon come to the throne room, which is busy with the king's guards, some of whom recognize Enkidu. King Ibbi-Sin is on the throne and looks surprised at our dramatic entry. His daughter, Geshtinanna, walks up to her father and whispers something. The king nods at a man nearby, and he announces loudly, "An emergency court is in progress. The king asks the scribe Nemur and the guard Enkidu to present their case!"

Geshtinanna nods at me. Shaken, surprised at the sudden announcement but ready for this day, blessed to be alive and for justice to be done, with the grace of Father Enlil and glory to Nanna the patron god of Urim, I step forward and kneel before the king. I struggle with the pain and discomfort. The salves have an extract of the joy flower. A comforting drink I was given was infused with joy flower as well, reducing pain and bringing a dreamy clarity to my mind.

The men carrying Ningal unceremoniously dump her by the king's feet, her mouth restrained with a gag. She is an unsightly presence—with her hair wild like a feral hog, her breasts flopping out of her gown, her legs twisted in defiance. The king looks at her with disdain.

King Ibbi-Sin's voice quivers as he addresses me. "The sun sets on Urim, and a great pestilence finds its home in our hallowed temples, scribe, and you seek justice for which you have persevered for months." Even in the face of this crushing defeat, he maintains his dignity. He looks small on the throne—his body has shrunk in the last few months from the stress, his eyes are hollow, the lambswool helmet with the tiara is loose, and his body shows several bruises.

I clasp my hands in prayer. "To our lord and king, my heart aches at what the wretched men and women have wrought upon this land. But even as we lament for what we lose, by Enlil's permission, we can bring justice to she who drove a spear into His Majesty's back and has led to the despair of His Majesty's noble son, the prince."

346

He nods. This is a small council now. There is no chief-scribe, the general is missing, the prince is being attended to, and his wife lies on the ground, foaming in her mouth. There is no pomp and splendor.

It is a dark hall, quiet, with the first wisps of smoke filtering in from outside.

"Speak," he says.

I have thought about this day many times.

"And treat your words as gold."

What he means is speak little, be precise.

"The princess Dumumi-Ningal came to the lap of Urim with one desire—to be queen. To her, this land mattered little, the king mattered less, and the prince mattered none. When His Majesty declared that the prince, noble in his being and gentle in his heart, but without the blessing of a strong body, would not be His Majesty's successor, her dreams of sitting by the throne of Urim vanished like the morning mist burned by the sun. Her gods—and one can no longer be sure who they are—have gifted her with a keen and cruel mind. Under the guise of caring for the prince, she found her way to the most intimate and confidential military planning meetings. She seduced and gained firm control of a man from the royal guard, one with the blood of Elam and full of grievances about the treatment of his people by His Majesty and our illustrious kings."

I pause. No one is speaking. Princess Ningal is attempting to speak through the restraint over her mouth, and everyone ignores her. The king nods. "Go on."

"Blinded by her ambition, she established contact with the king of Elam through this man, Num-Assina, and him having seen her before, made an unholy proposition. The promise of marriage and to be by his side, in return for critical information concerning the kingdom's defenses, weaknesses, routes, deployments, and relations."

He looks down at her but says nothing. I notice a glistening tear in the king's eye.

"Even as His Majesty showered her with affection and access to sensitive conversations, she betrayed you at every turn. While there may be others, she was the one who assisted the Martu in their precise and strategic incursions, and Elam's attacks. But when my wife, a palace maid and messenger for priests, overheard a tryst between Num-Assina and the princess, with great innocence, she approached the princess and cautioned her. And soon after, in my absence, my wife began to fear that her life was in danger. The princess conspired with Num-Assina to sway the chief-scribe and his assistant to put her name on the list for unknown transgressions, knowing that any other method of the murder of a woman of palace temples might draw the full investigation of the royal guard. They thought sending her to a quiet death as a traveler would silence any wagging tongues. They did not predict my behavior."

The king smiles. He knows much of the rest of the story as I recount how I was sure that my wife would not travel willingly, the attempts on my life, the message left by my wife, the escape to Surimmu, the hints from and death of Num-Assina, and our return to Urim.

"When Your Majesty finally let us plant the seeds of false information, only Ningal was in the meeting with you and the general."

I stop and wait for the spider web of pain rising from my thighs and torso to subside. It gives His Majesty time to make the connections.

The king then addressed me. "You paint a compelling picture, scribe, and yet one might say it is all speculation.

What is to say that Nigir-Kagina was not the informant, and his actions at the tunnel were a pretense? The rest, one might say, are speculation."

"His Majesty seeks the truth and justice, even as he bears the pain of treachery," I say, and then I recount the happenings in the prince's room, and chief-priestess and princess Geshtinanna recounts the rest. When it is all over, there is nothing but deathly silence, and the fury in the king's eyes is palpable.

"How did you decide it was Ningal?" Geshtinanna asks. While the story is perfect, what led me to her in the first place?

I take a deep breath and control the pain.

"I always suspected the prince," I say, honestly, and tell them about how Ningal pointed the finger of accusation at her dying husband. "But as time went by, Enkidu and I considered the possibility of someone else. We often say it is women with the beautiful face of the moon, and my wife's message alluded to a moon. When Num-Assina attacked us, he said something—that the prince could not perform sexually, though his choice of words was crude. Now, how would Num-Assina know that? When I then chose Ningal as my prime suspect, other things fell into place. That the prince might not accede the throne meant she would never be queen. That trading secrets for a place by the king of Elam could give her that position. That an insidious scheme to send my wife to death as a traveler has the signature of a woman, Your Majesty, for our men rarely resort to subtlety. But even after all that, a doubt lingered that it might be your daughter. The selective planning session finally revealed that it was Ningal, corroborated by her behavior when we confronted her. That final act exonerated general Num-Assina."

He interrogates me more, but our sequence of events, and his daughter's affirmation of the incidents in the prince's quarters, all finally quell his doubts.

"You are a remarkable man," he says finally. "And one with true affection."

But before he speaks, I say what I have always wanted to. It is a bold and foolish move, but has that ever stopped me before? "For the reasons of my pursuit, and by law to dispense justice, I beg the king to let me administer punishment to her."

The watchers are stunned. Enkidu looks at me like I am mad.

The king speaks. "Betrayal requires her to be executed. I should cut off her head here!"

"She has had a direct hand in my wife's death, the pursuit of my execution, and my torture. By law that His Majesty has instituted, and by Enlil's grace, he who has kept me alive to seek justice, it should be I who delivers it."

I feel the eyes of suspicion upon me. What nefarious designs do I have? Do they think I wish to ravish her? Or torture her to death? It does not matter.

Geshtinanna starts to speak, but the king raises his hand to silence her. He finally speaks. "Laws that I have decreed have had their power, for they are applied no matter to whom. The scribe's expectation is just, even if her actions have impacted us as a whole. But her direct hand is evident in her violence against him. And for that reason, I grant the wish. What else, scribe?"

"And I ask His Majesty to order me on one last mission to Governor Ishbi-Erra. Urim may fall, Your Majesty, but there is a chance for me to take your message and gather forces to eject the enemy."

He smiles. "You have valiant intentions, scribe. That scoundrel retreated long ago. What good does another message make?"

We can now hear the faint sounds of clashes, even if far away. The army of Elam is getting closer. The smoke is becoming darker, and soon there will be red eyes and coughs.

With Geshtinanna's support, I convince the king that a message would not be in vain. With Enkidu and an additional soldier, along with a supply donkey, we will leave by a secret path behind the palace, enter a tunnel that goes through the royal tombs, and exit near the presumably deserted north-eastern gate of the city. Deserted because the terrain to come near that gate, from where the army of Elam was, is exceedingly difficult. It is a strange feeling as we discuss logistics and our departure. A departure that may never see me return to Urim.

The council decides its own fate.

King Ibbi-Sin will wait on the throne, and the chief-priestess will be by his side. They have refused to leave. They will bring the prince to the throne room.

A few remaining attendants scurry about to bring ceremonial garments and makeup for them to wear. They light lamps and burn incense to bring fragrance to the smoky and dark hall. Geshtinanna announces that it is time. I prostrate before the king and chief-priestess to receive my blessings.

I have a question to the chief-priestess. "Will my wife be at peace, chief-priestess? Is she languishing in the dim corridors and bleak rooms of the netherworld? How can the gods punish her for a blemish-less life?"

She smiles at me. "Our understanding of the netherworld has changed, scribe. Her good deeds on this world, her unjust end, all have given her kind consideration from the judges. She walks the gardens of Enlil, and her food is delicious. The rooms are bright and the flowers bloom in her world. May you live in peace in that knowledge, and when it is your time, you shall lead a gentle life."

"What about mine?" Enkidu asks. We have had the time to brief her on Enkidu's life and his involvement with me.

She nods at him. "The netherworld is nothing like what the poets wrote in the poems of long ago. Those who have suffered injustice in the world, will find greater pleasure in the afterworld. Your wife now lives in peace."

My great momentous journey is about to end—by receiving dictation from the king to go on a mission.

The king rises from the throne. While Geshtinanna is the chief-priestess, the king is the true supreme priest of the land, and his recommendations carry great favor with the gods. He blesses us. "I seek the intervention of Nanna and Enlil, and while they may have looked away from my fate, that they shall forever bless your wives and give all the great comforts afforded in the netherworld of Ereshkigal."

I control my emotions. I may have failed in protecting her in this life, but I have finally managed to give her comfort in the netherworld. When I pass the seven gates after my death, I shall care for two wives.

The king asks us to rise. He looks at my sorry being and asks, "Do you have the strength to carve a message on a dry tablet? There are no other scribes."

"Your Majesty, my palm and fingers are too hurt to be able to place enough pressure on a stone pen on a dry tablet. But we have a scribe."

The king raises an eyebrow.

I grin at Enkidu. "It is time to put your skills to work, big scribe."

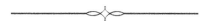

The journey through the tunnels is quick, and the battle is far away now as we move in the opposite direction.

I insist that we make a stop by the queen's sealed tomb—not because I wish to pay respects to the queen, but because that is where I kneel and weep for my wife who was taken away in so unjust a fashion, away from her unborn child's love, from her husband's arms, alone, afraid, and not ready to travel. But I am confident that she is happy in the gardens of Enlil, where I am certain she is—because not only was she of the cleanest heart, but her deed was so pure that it led to her death. I hope that she is proud of me, knowing that when I join her, I am Nemur, the *leopard*, even if a limping, miserable leopard.

We take a deserted, dusty path among low muddy mounds, keeping ourselves hidden behind abandoned tenements until we reach the wide-open gate with nothing and no one near it. The princess has been bundled in a coarse hemp sack and left on the ass. She has stopped struggling. Enkidu carries the king's message, very proud that he was able to sit before the king and take dictation. If we survive and reach Governor Ishbi-Erra, then it will be I who will speak for the king. We quickly enter a rarely taken rough path within dense reed clusters by the river and begin walking north. But I look back one more time at the great Ziggurat, the *Etemenniguru*, abode of Enlil and Nanna, and hope that one day I can return and pray there again. I pray for the safety of the king and his daughter Geshtinanna, for they have given me justice even in their darkest hour.

As I limp along and look back, the glorious tops of the many structures of Urim, visible behind the wall, slowly vanishes in a swirl of black smoke.

CHAPTER 51

URIM

KINDATTU

The screams of burning people and the piles of dead before him bring joy to the king of Elam. Here he is, walking the paths cleared for him, finally *inside* the great city of Urim. He has waited for this day for a long time, since the armies of the black-headed people came to Susa, debasing his gods and people. This is an impressive city, he thinks, for the houses are far more numerous, the granaries larger, the cattle pens bigger, and the temples grander than his own glorious Susa. But not anymore. He is of two minds—whether to burn everything down in spite, or to preserve what is left, so that he can dwell and rebuild this as a new city of Elam.

He finally issues orders to his men. "Loot as you please. Round up and tie all the men, women, and children. But do not burn the dwellings, we will need them."

Kindattu marvels at the layout of the inner city as he walks in front of the senior commanders of his army and a few Martu men, including Atturapi, who is gloating at this victory. The beautiful wide central walkway, the many large government structures, villas and palaces of the nobility and royalty, are all around. He wants these preserved for his enjoyment.

"Anyone entering these buildings and caught stealing will have their hands cut off."

He issues more orders. Systematic loot and plunder is necessary to ensure those who must be rewarded first, are rewarded first. "Which is the king's palace?" he asks the man beside him, someone with intimate knowledge of the city.

The man points to a wide, flat-roofed complex far ahead, to the left of the towering structure of the great Ziggurat. He looks at it in disdain. The abode of their gods. Ones who blessed the subjugation of his own people. A great sense of purpose and energy fills Kindattu. "Give me an ax!" he orders, and receives one. In front of his men, he runs up the wide stairs of the Ziggurat, covering two steps at a time.

The king of Elam does not stop until he has reached the top, his lungs burning, his thighs on fire, and his back shooting pain from top to bottom. He looks around—the entire city is beneath him, parts burning, stretching in every direction, but it is *his*. He swings the heavy ax and smashes the wooden door, once, twice, relishing the splinters flying and the *thud* of cracked wood. It takes a few more until an entire middle section of a board breaks and crashes.

He kicks the broken door in.

The entrance is dark and musty. The floor, made of cool stone slabs, is devoid of any patterns. Kindattu is surprised at the sparseness of it all. The walls are bare except one, on which is a beautifully carved relief of their moon god, with his flowing robes and beard, cow-horns on his head, blessing a seated king. There is a stone pedestal in the center, but the idols of the gods are missing. Where are the treasures of the temple? Where is the gold, silver, lapis-lazuli that was supposed to be adorning the shrine? The bastards have cleaned the temple and hidden the riches—but he will find out where.

Enraged, he takes the ax to the wall relief and damages it, chipping off the sections of the wall.

Finally, spent of all his energy, angry at the emptiness but happy at having conquered the city, Kindattu comes out to stand atop the Ziggurat. He inhales the fresh air here, away from the acrid smells and smoke, and looks down on his expectant army.

It is now time to find the king of Urim, for he has not been felled in battle, and captured men have told Kindattu that the king of the black-headed people waits for him, in his palace, seated on the throne.

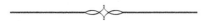

The king of Elam stands proud in front the defeated Ibbi-Sin, seated like a fool on his throne, with his daughter, a priestess, by his side. His men, all unarmed, lie on the ground, prostrate, signaling that they will not shed blood. They are all tied and led away—whether their heads will roll or whether they will toil as slaves is to be decided. The Martu chief, Atturapi, stands beside him, his face full of excitement.

Kindattu has seen Ibbi-Sin, long ago, at a receding distance. But now, here he is, in front of the man who calls himself the king of his land and Akkad, and now king of neither. The man is small, lean-limbed, with a gaunt and hollow face.

But there is a certain satisfaction for Kindattu in hearing what this defeated man has to say, whether he will beg for consideration, for another life.

"Speak," he says, firmly, loudly. "Speak before the new king of the four corners, Ibbi-Sin, for your forces are dead, your city laid to waste, your cattle-pens open, and your land beneath my feet."

Atturapi grunts with agreement. "You are no more king, Ibbi-Sin, and your insolence toward us has come to an end!"

Kindattu is irritated by the Martu chief's interjection. Ibbi-Sin ignores Atturapi, and instead he addresses the Kindattu. "The king of Elam must know that kings come and go, fortunes ebb and flow, as surely as the moon rises and the sun rests for the day. And as such, the king who departs asks the new king to spare his new abode, his new citizens, and rebuild this great city, for it belongs to the world and not only to the king of Elam."

Kindattu scoffs. There may be truth to Ibbi-Sin's words, but who is he to lecture the new king?

"You are no one—" begins Atturapi. Kindattu's hand shoots up sharply, indicating for the Martu chief to *shut up!*

"You are in the presence of two kings, Atturapi, and even if one has been vanquished, he is king. Be quiet!"

Atturapi looks mortified. He looks around, but Kindattu's royal guard stare at him menacingly. He mutters and recedes to the background. Ibbi-Sin stoically refuses to look at or engage Atturapi.

He looks at a slumped figure by the side of the woman who looks on defiantly. Kindattu considers what he must do with her. A man whispers to his ears. "She is the chief-priestess, Your Majesty. And the slouching figure is his son, the prince."

Kindattu points at the prince. "He must die."

Ibbi-Sin nods. "Then I ask the new king for a merciful end to an ailing son."

Long ago, his father had counseled Kindattu that while a vanquished ruler must never be allowed to raise his head and become a threat again, kings must be accorded respect, for the gods look down upon kings who treat those that are as themselves with cruelty, and may heap cruelty upon them in the future. When the kings of the black-headed people had attacked Elam, they had not burned the cities or desecrated the temples and tombs. Kindattu feels a spark of guilt for what he has wrought upon this city, but dismisses it quickly.

Kindattu nods. "That I shall grant a father, but time is of essence. It must be now."

The priestess offers a prayer as Kindattu watches. One of Kindattu's royal guard walks behind the barely alive prince and waits as the priestess struggles to hold him in a seated position. Irritated, Kindattu orders another man to hold the prince and keep him upright. Once the prayers are complete, as Ibbi-Sin watches, the guard drives a dagger through the hollow near the shoulder into the princes' heart. The priestess weeps silently, her hands and arms drenched in her brother's blood, as their father and king Ibbi-Sin watches without expression.

Kindattu then points to the priestess-princess. "You will remain here, as the priestess of your gods, and you will proclaim to your people that they shall peacefully subject themselves to my rule."

Geshtinanna looks surprised but says nothing. Kindattu knows the power of using the priests for his bidding. A quick return to peace is required for him to establish his rule and move to conquer new worlds. Ibbi-Sin places a palm on her head in blessing.

"Rise, Ibbi-Sin. Your people shall see you in fetters. Once king, now nothing."

With much flair, four men walk up to Ibbi-Sin, who stands and waits. They tie his hands with silver cuffs, place a thick hemp rope around his neck and tighten it, and restrain his legs with manacles to prevent running.

"Where is she? Princess Ningal," he says, looking around, surprised that she has not come to receive him. He has seen her long ago, enchanted by her beauty and resentful when she was given away to the prince of Urim. He has heard much about her, that she has captivated the people of Urim, and with her in his bed and by his side, and Ibbi-Sin's daughter as his priestess, he would be able to reign over all Sumer and Akkad with little resistance.

The chief-priestess answers him. "Your spy has no honor, King Kindattu. Her deception was uncovered by our men, and in accordance with our laws, we have burned her and spread her ashes in the gardens."

Kindattu stares at the priestess, looking for deception, but she does not lower her eyes as she looks back with unflinching steadiness.

"We have learned that she aimed to poison you, as she did my brother, and declare herself eternal queen. And while she may have caused our weakening, Your Majesty, she has failed to reap the sweet fruits of her treachery, and she shall languish in the prison of the netherworld for her unjust deeds."

Kindattu is surprised. Could that be true? That Ningal would try to poison him? He has heard things about her—about her strange fascination with cruelty, her ambition, and how insistent she had been on getting what is hers. He knew that she was slowly poisoning the prince. It was true, a woman who knew no loyalty or affection could turn on him. And he long suspected that his spy may have been having immoral relations with Ningal—in which case how could he, as king, accept her?

"She is but one piece of all that has aided me, and her end gives me no pause," he says. "Spies, like kings, come and go."

There is nothing more to say. Kindattu nods at his men and they lead Ibbi-Sin away, and as Kindattu looks at the receding figure of the frail king, he thinks of him as a sparrow that has flown its city, never to see it again.

CHAPTER 52

URIM

NEMUR

This desolate stretch by the river has dense mangroves and reed clusters, with the channel narrow and muddy, but deep. We have walked without pause until nightfall, and it is now time to rest before completing one act.

We bring down the princess from the donkey and remove the knots on the sack. She gasps as she is exposed to the cool air of the night. Gone is the glamour on her face, the shine in her hair, and the power in her eyes. Under the flickering lamp lights, she is a pathetic and exhausted figure. She wobbles when we let her on the ground, and I let her fall after she trips on stones. She collects herself and regains her posture.

I tell the two guards to watch the periphery. She looks around, her eyes wild, realizing she has no idea where she is in this darkness. The sound of the nearby Euphrates is crystal clear from here, and so is the buzz of the many critters of the night.

She finally turns toward me. "What are you waiting for? Did you bring me here to rape me? Go ahead!" she says, ripping the gown on her upper body.

I control my breath. "I have no desire to touch you, Ningal," I say, dropping all honorifics. "My skin crawls like there are a hundred cockroaches on it at the thought of even being close to you."

She looks offended. "Then what? Do you want me to be your slave?"

Enkidu watches quietly. We have spoken little on the way, focusing on the path ahead as I tried to preserve my strength from the many injuries I have sustained. The tight bandages and the salves have kept the agony in check. I fervently pray for no fever and suppuration of my wounds, because it can lead to a painful death.

"A slave does work and brings value to his master. Having someone like you as a slave is like having a pig guard a house. All it will do is soil the yard and eat the food."

Realizing there is no desire for us to engage with her, she changes tactic. Gone is the defiance. Tears flood her eyes, and she sobs, and her chest heaves. "You know nothing about a woman trapped in the prison that was the palace!" she says. "And what it did to me!"

I control the urge to laugh. "Sit down," I say. And she obeys me this time, meekly. Enkidu has set up a small campfire.

We offer her meat and water, and she eats greedily. Her composure improves as the food fills her belly and the fire warms her body. She explains to us her terrible life, the abusive prince, the horrible king, all determined to reduce her to nothing.

She argues with me when I contradict her, making it a point to tell me that I am a commoner who knows nothing of royalty. What is remarkable is the delusion that she thinks I believe anything she says. Her tears may be copious, but they drip with utmost insincerity.

"Enlil blesses you for the kindness," she says, smiling, after finishing the last morsel. "If you do not believe my words, we can arrive at an arrangement."

I say nothing in return.

But she speaks again. "I have a proposal. One that you might find most beneficial."

Enkidu and I look at each other.

Let her speak, he seems to imply.

"My ears wait," I say.

She leans forward, and her face assumes the stern and composed look of a princess sitting in the court. "Ibbi-Sin's land is lost. But I can give you a new life. You are hereby appointed as my scribe, and Enkidu shall be my guard."

I do my very best to control myself from beating her.

She continues, "Take me back to King Kindattu. I shall tell him that you have saved me from certain death, and also reward you with enough shekels to last a lifetime."

She is serious.

There is no humor in her voice.

She really believes in her words.

It is the blessing of darkness and the sitting position that she cannot see Enkidu's incredulous expression.

The moon appears from behind the clouds, and the effects of my repeated doses of a concoction of the joy flower are wearing off. The pulsating pain from my many limbs begins to remind me of what I have been through.

Enkidu nods at me, and I return the gesture. He suddenly seizes her from behind and gags her. Her eyes are wild, and now they show fear. She tries futilely to scream. We seat her near the fire so we can all see each other, but we tie her securely to a stump.

"Listen to me, Princess," I tell her. "It is time for me to speak."

I remove a blade from my sheath and show it to her. She begins to struggle and continues to shout into her gag.

"Listen!" I say harshly, and she quietens down.

"I come from a mother whose words of wisdom were followed by beatings from love. She walked the gardens of Enlil before her chest could be filled with pride at my employment as a scribe. I wedded a devoted wife who was taken away with my first unborn child at childbirth. For their passing, I blamed no one, for that is the nature of life. I lost Ninshu to nothing but greed and treachery. At the hands of a woman! One that the people saw as a goddess, but with so dark a heart that no blood pumps through it."

She breathes heavily as she watches. Her eyes are dark with the deepest black.

"You spoke of the Assyrians. I have heard that they burn the women who cavort with other men, and you, a princess, deserve even worse. It should be I who will scalp you."

Silence.

"I was a scribe, princess. I knew no violence. All I did was in service to the king, walking from city to city, conveying messages. With the blessings of Enlil and Nanna, that was what my life would be, forever."

Silence.

CHAPTER 53
SOMEWHERE NORTH OF URIM
DUMUMI-NINGAL

"I was a scribe, princess. I knew no violence. All I did was in service to the king, walking from city to city, conveying messages. With the blessings of Enlil and Nanna, that was what my life would be, forever."

She listens to the fool speak. If he took the gag off her mouth, she would tell him that his lowly profession meant nothing to her. The son of whore dog daring to keep her, a *princess*, this way! Let me go back to Urim, you bastards!

He continues. "What bad did my wife do? She served you faithfully. She served all the royalty with dedication and respect. And even when she heard whatever she did, which was by chance, she sought to tell you first so you might walk away from the impure actions and return to the path of righteousness, to be by your husband and king, and to protect the people of the city that looked upon you with adoration."

Stupid bitch should have kept her mouth shut. Why sneak around the palace? And who did she think she is, telling me, a princess, a future queen, what I should do? Be happy I did not slice her breasts and throw her to the dogs.

Let him unburden himself, sentimental idiot. These sewer rats know nothing about what it takes for one to almost be queen, and have that cruelly taken away! What do these two want? Her as a ransom? King Kindattu would be willing to reward them handsomely, but these greedy fools want a lot more than a few shekels of gold. Or they wish to hold her in a neighboring governorate, using her as a pawn for safety.

She appraises the scribe. He is an almost good-looking man, she thinks distractedly, different from how she saw him almost a year ago. His muscles are tight and sinewy, his face is gaunt but rough, the eyes shine with a certain energy. Gone is the gentle demeanor of a writer, and instead it is replaced by an ever-present threat of violence. Exciting. Too bad he fell afoul of her.

Take off my muzzle, you cockroach, let me speak!

Nemur continues. "For her kind heart and her warning, you rewarded her with a lonely death. I have learned more about her last hours, and it fills me with grief every day. You took away my wife, my unborn child, and then you took away my home. You took away the king's domain, you took his son, and you condemned an honest high-priestess."

Such is the nature of conflict and victory, you idiot.

"We grew by the great river. The river Euphrates gave us life. You sailed on it to marry the prince. You brought great sadness to us all, a poison that coursed through the river."

Your poor and stupid people adored me. They had never seen anyone like me. I did what I had to because the prince was a weakling, impotent, useless. And he would never be king. Now let me go! I am the chosen one as queen, and I was always destined to be one!

"There is no remorse in your words, no kindness in your eyes, no softness in your thought. You have sucked evil from its abode and breathed it into our land."

Do not think of your king and his men as kind sheep. They have waged wars, killed people, raped helpless women, razed lands. Now shut up and let me go, and I will let you die quickly next time.

"It is because of my honor, and Enkidu's, that we have not done to you what you wanted to do to us. Or what Assyrians might to do their captive women. Or what the king would have done to a treasonous scum."

The only scum is low-borns like you. Ones with no sense of higher purpose, no taste for greater things, no drive or ambition, and not a drop of blood that has come down from the divine. Nothing but pig shit.

"I should bury you alive in a tomb, let you die slowly, over days—alone, afraid, and in darkness."

Your wife received poison to end her miserable life quickly. She did not suffer, you wretched lice.

She stares into his eyes and holds it until he looks away. Weakling.

Now take me where you plan to, and I will find my way. Once the new king realizes the story, he will butcher you like pigs, and I will watch you squeal.

They both leave her briefly and amble toward the river. The big brute, Enkidu, has said nothing at all. She hears shuffling sounds and them waddling in the water. When they return, Enkidu and the other guard pick her up by her arms and feet as she fights them again.

Don't put me on that stupid ass, let me walk!

But they carry her down a gentle embankment to the river and put her on a raft.

I know how to swim. Yes, let me float away.

The brute carries a flaming torch, and the two get on the raft with her. The sky is ablaze with a million stars, many long-dead queens, she is sure, and one day she will be one. Crossing the river is required to go to Isin, so it seems the two are going to Ishbi-Erra. She can find ways to entice that man, for he is not of royal blood and can be swayed.

She can convince Ishbi-Erra to become an ally of Kindattu and benefit from her being queen. The prospect of a new challenge excites her, assuming these idiots do not bungle the mission. If an Elamite garrison stopped these two, she would be able to convince them to take her back.

It is cold as the wind blows on the river's surface and grazes her skin, causing goosebumps. The two do not talk as the brute and a guard navigate the raft across the river. The scribe sits and looks at the sky. Pining for his wife. *Weakling.* The water flows gently—she can feel it from the sound of the paddles, the *slosh, slosh, slosh* that is both soothing and gentle.

Then they stop. Two of the men hold her firmly, and another puts the sack on her head, once again covering her. She struggles and kicks, but there is not much she can do. These imbeciles do not realize that it gets hot inside the sack and difficult to breathe. It is sacrilege that they treat a princess this way. *Stop it!* But then she calms down, because a sack concealing her presence is a method of safety. What are they waiting for? She senses them tying something to her foot.

Enough, you street dogs! I cannot run with my legs tied and while inside a bag!

Enraged, she tries to scream and kick, but the restraints offer no freedom. Someone reaches into the sack and roughly yanks the gag, but it is a struggle to breathe with the foul sack pressing on her mouth. They tie the opening again. The sack is a tight, smelly, suffocating cocoon around her.

"What are you doing, you vermin?" she screams. "You have no right to treat me this way! Let me out! I am your queen!"

But her shouting is muffled in the thick sack.

Suddenly she feels palms beneath her back, as if they are lifting–

NO!

The shock of the water is intense and frightening. She is seized with panic and terror and tries to kick without success. The weight on her feet drags her down rapidly, even as muddy water envelops her inside the sack, cold and dirty. The foul wetness enters her mouth, grainy, with disgusting detritus, choking her. She tries to spit, but more water gushes into her throat and nose, and when she opens her eyes, it is nothing but absolute darkness and terrible pain in the eyes as the mud fills the space.

Her mouth opens wide to breathe, and the soupy water rushes in and chokes her.

She thrashes and struggles as she hits the riverbed. It is soft. She rolls due to the current. Her entire being is in agony. *No! I do not want to become a demon of the netherworld without my queenly comforts! No! Please!*

There is no one to mourn her or hold her hands as her body finally stops thrashing.

CHAPTER 54

SOMEWHERE ON THE WAY TO ISIN

NEMUR

I watch as the sack sinks to the murky depths. The river that gave us life will now take that which sought to end ours. A gust of wind embraces me, and it is as if it is a message from the afterlife.

No remorse.

We return to the shore, and I get on my knees to pray. Enkidu joins me. We speak no words to each other and rest for the night. The next morning, the river is calm. We wash and begin our long journey north. The roads are deserted, and it will be months before a new system of garrisons is set up under a new king. Until then, the trade will remain muted, bandits will roam the roads, and people will suffer.

"Did you sleep?" Enkidu asks. His stubble is back. I limp along, and will sit on the ass when I can no longer bear the pain of walking. We have more of the salve and bandages left, and I hope it will last until we reach Isin, and that the governor will be kind to us.

"My body hurts from all the damage. I woke a few times, but I slept. Did you?"

He smiles. "My wife came in my dreams again."

"And?"

"She smiled this time. Gone was the frightening visage and the hair-raising howls of anguish. She is at peace, Nemur, and for you I am eternally grateful. She is walking the gardens of Enlil, away from the dreadful parts of the netherworld."

"It is you to whom I thank Enlil and Nanna for. You came as a guardian and teacher, helping me," I say. He nods, and there is no clever response or a tease. In an unexpected move, he turns and gives me a warm hug, causing me to wince in pain and enjoy the moment. He is my brother, father, teacher, one who has kept me alive. "And one day we will find out the killers of your wife."

He nods. But we both know that it is an unlikely scenario. Much time has passed, people have come and gone, many have died—and with the fall of Urim, a good portion of the city has dispersed, and many would be taken away as slaves. He then turns to me again. "Your hint that it was Ningal was based on Num-Assina's single sentence? It all came down to a cock?"

I laugh.

He slaps my back and causes me to howl. "You are a true leopard now, Nemur, worthy of his name. Your balls are bigger than a bull's!"

"Your writing has improved, Enkidu. Much better than a five-year-old's."

"I was kind to you, Nemur, but your arrogance has gone to your head. I was lying about your balls. They went down the river with Ningal."

"My wife was in my dreams last night. She said they were intact."

"Whatever was fondling you last night was not your wife. There are many feral pigs roaming here."

My ribs hurt as I laugh. But there is a sense of fulfilment. On this calm morning, under a rising sun and cool winds, I am finally at peace. I have righted a wrong, I have fought for my wife, and the gods have granted me my life. I have had the king's and chief priestess' blessings for worthy judgment for our wives, and I know that they will lead a more joyous existence in the netherworld.

"Burutur waits for you," I tell him.

"Once we finish this mission to Ishbi-Erra, using *my* handwritten tablet, all will be well, and we will return to Surimmu. Igigina will be waiting for you, ready to fondle your—"

The path ahead is desolate. The familiar *crunch* of the gravel beneath my feet and the dull shrubbery on the side bring comfort, for these are paths I have traveled many times. I look back at the direction of Urim with sadness— with King Ibbi-Sin dead or captured, this dynasty of our kings is over, with our land ruled by the new king of Elam. The Martu finally have a home for themselves. My mission is not over, and someday, with Enkidu by my side and Governor Ishbi-Erra in front of me, we will return to Urim.

We will win the land lost to us.

NOTES

Speak to my dear reader, they who have shown me benevolence, saying the words of Jay Penner, your author!

May the mercy of Enlil and the light of Nanna be upon you and may your farms (fridges) swell with bountiful fruit, beer, and barley!

Thank you for reading this fifth book of the Whispers of Atlantis anthology. I hope you enjoyed this as much as I enjoyed writing it. If you have a moment, I would greatly appreciate a few kind words on Amazon or a rating. Reviews are a lifeblood for authors like me!

Now, it's time for notes. You can go to this Google maps flyover of all the real (and fictional) locations of this book. It can be fun and informative. Go here: Whispers of Atlantis Maps

This book was set in the last year of the 3rd dynasty of Ur (called Urim) at the end of King Ibbi-Sin's reign, around 2000 B.C.

The Sumerians ruled southern Mesopotamia from around 5000 B.C. They were an amazing civilization that brought us the calendar, wheel, agricultural implements, and the first writing script with cuneiform. The civilization was disrupted from time to time, with the second dynasty upended by the Akkadians. King Sargon of Akkad ruled Sumer, and his daughter (and priestess) Enheduanna's poems still survive (she is the *oldest* known poet whose works have survived to date!). Sargon's successors could not hold the dynasty and lost it to the founder of the third dynasty of Ur, Ur-Nammu. He was an influential ruler who rebuilt not only Ur, but he also built the great Ziggurat of Ur, dedicated to the moon god Nanna. He was followed by four kings—Shulgi, Amar-Sin, Shu-Sin, and then Ibbi-

Sin, whose era was around 2020 B.C., ending around 2004 B.C. with the fall of Ur to the Elamite king Kindattu.

We do not know what the Sumerians called themselves as a "brand name," though they referred to themselves as the *black-headed people.* and their kingdom as "our land." We do not conclusively know what "black-headed" actually means either–color of their hair? skin? or some connection to the sheep they reared?

The word Sumer was used by Akkadians.

First, let's talk about the concept of the "death pit." This is not a made-up construct. Leonard Wooley's spectacular Ur excavations revealed royal tombs with resting skeletons, all of which seemed to have been sacrificed in a death ritual. One such tomb had harps, lyres, gold-leaf headdresses, and over seventy skeletons! The timeline was a few hundred years before the events of this book. It is possible that the ritual continued in some manner during Ibbi-Sin's reign.

King Ibbi-Sin's era was a tumultuous one. He seems to have ruled for about twenty years, but they were not all happy. He dealt with the continuous incursion of the Martu (called Amorites in the Bible) and then hostility from Elam, along with droughts and the drying of the Euphrates. Eventually, as this novel portrays, Kindattu, the king of Elam—possibly with the help of Amorites (Martu) and other tribes—overthrew Ibbi-Sin. There is a beautiful surviving work called "The Lament of Ur," which speaks of its destruction, and in that, it says that Ibbi-Sin was imprisoned and taken away, never to see Ur again.

We know little about Kindattu, except that he was the one who came from Susa and conquered Ur.

It is reasonable to assume that Kindattu took Ibbi-Sin to Susa, where the Sumerian king may have died in captivity. The Sumerian kingdom was a conglomeration of city-states ruled by influential governors. Ishbi-Erra, who seems to have grown under Ibbi-Sin and at some point was appointed as governor of Isin, eventually became powerful enough to declare himself ruler of Isin. He seems to have stayed away from trying to help Ibbi-Sin in his conflict, and we do not know why or what he thought he would accomplish by not helping Ibbi-Sin (or he may not have had the ability to help).

There were a couple of letters in this book between the king and the governors. These were modeled after real letters between Ibbi-Sin and others! Yes, there exists correspondence that has survived, thanks to Babylonian scribes and school students who used older Sumerian tablets to rewrite them. It is utterly fascinating to read these letters that are replicas of even older ones that are now nearly 4000 years old. And those letters are no different in their emotions from now. Grievances, complaints, requests—it's all the same. The situation between Ibbi-Sin and Ishbi-Erra was not concocted—there are letters between the two, with the king complaining that Ishbi-Erra was not holding up to his grain shipment promises and that he charged double the price.

You may have noticed references to the Epic of Gilgamesh in Nemur and Enkidu's conversation. The full surviving epic is in Akkadian, possibly compiled hundreds of years after the events of this book, and it is reasonable to assume that the story evolved from several older Sumerian poems. And therefore, maybe Enkidu of the novel inserted his name and created a part of the story, and some poet carried it forward! (In the Epic of Gilgamesh, the character Enkidu is his sidekick).

There were brief references to *Meluhha* from where Ishbi-Erra got his exotic spices, but there is lack of clarity of what Meluhha refers to. Some believe it is the Indus valley civilization that thrived at the same time period, or it could be western Afghanistan, or it might even be Bahrain. All references to *Meluhha* vanish a few centuries after the time period of this book, which also coincides to the gradual vanishing of Indus valley.

In the book, I portray the Martu (Amorites) as backwards nomads who are evolving. The Bible too suggests they were. But it's important to recognize that recent thinking makes the picture muddy—we do not have a good understanding of who they are, where they came from, and how they became powerful. Here's an interesting fact: about three hundred years after the events in this book, it was the famous Martu (Amorite) king Hammurabi who ruled Mesopotamia from Babylon. The Laws of Hammurabi are known even today, though it's important to recognize that the Sumerians had their own laws—called Laws of Ur-Nammu, that predate Hammurabi's, though they were not as extensive and documented/disseminated as Hammurabi's. In the span of a few hundred years, these so-called nomads gave birth to the powerful Amorite empire.

What was the role of women in ancient Sumer? We have very little information. They seem to have fulfilled traditional roles as in all ancient societies, focused on taking care of the house and husbands. Some may have even been scribes. Queens are shown prominently in ancient Sumerian artifacts, though it is unclear how much influence they wielded. Even literature that describes dialog between women was most likely written by men.

Many names in the book are derived from Sumerian words. I hope you'll enjoy these explanations.

Nemur - "leopard"

Dumumi-Ninshubur - Nemur's wife, "daughter of goddess Ninshubur."

Geshtinanna-Kalame - chief-priestess, "goddess Geshtinanna is for the whole land (of Sumer)"

Burutur - Enkidu's second wife, "little bird."

Igigina - Nemur's new love interest, "one with beautiful eyes."

Dumumi-Ningal - the villain princess, "daughter of the goddess Ningal."

Nigir-Kagina - the general, "herald who speaks the truth."

Enkidu - is an Akkadian name.

The king's names: Amar-Sin, Shu-Sin, Ibbi-Sin, are equivalent to Amar-Suen, Shu-Suen, and Ibbi-Suen, where the Sin/Suen is equivalent to the moon god Nanna. Nanna was the patron god of Ur, and therefore the city's rulers took the god's name as theirs.

THANK YOU

Please take a moment to leave a few kind words or rating if you can. It makes a huge difference to authors like me! You can also go to https://jaypenner.com/reviews for convenient links.

If you have read this book as a standalone, go and checkout the rest of the Whispers of Atlantis series!

What next? Go get The Last Pharaoh which takes you on an intrigue-filled journey with Cleopatra, the famous queen of Egypt!

THE LAST PHARAOH

WHISPERS OF ATLANTIS

May Enlil and Nanna bless you and your family!

Jay,

https://jaypenner.com

Printed in Great Britain
by Amazon